Echoes of Ancients

Book 2 of Lamentations and Magic

Russell Cowdrey

RPC Novels LLC

RPC Novels, LLC - Coppell, TX

The story in this production is fictitious. Some places, events, and people included in this book are based upon actual historical events, places, and people. All characters based on historical figures are deceased, and some details of their lives have been fictionalized. All events portrayed in this book, which include historical persons, have been fictionalized. For other characters, no identification with actual persons (living or deceased) is intended or should be inferred.

The lyrics of one public domain song is included in this text and is exempted from any copyright claims.

To find out more about this author, go to https://www.russellcowdrey.com.

e-book ISBN: ISBN: 978-1-960300-03-4

paperback book ISBN: 978-1-960300-04-1

hardback book ISBN: 978-1-960300-05-8

Library of Congress Control Number:

Without someone who believes in you, even when you are at your lowest, finishing a project like this would be impossible. That person in my life is my wife, Diana. Thank you for never giving up on me. Happy Birthday Gorgeous!

I would also like to thank my two editors, Brandon Purcell, and Patti Waldygo at Desert Sage Editorial Services, along with illustrator Alla Kholodilina for their invaluable contributions.

Compendium and Map

Series Compendium on RussellCowdrey.com.

https://www.RussellCowdrey.com/compendium

Partial Map of the continent of Khemet on Aaru.

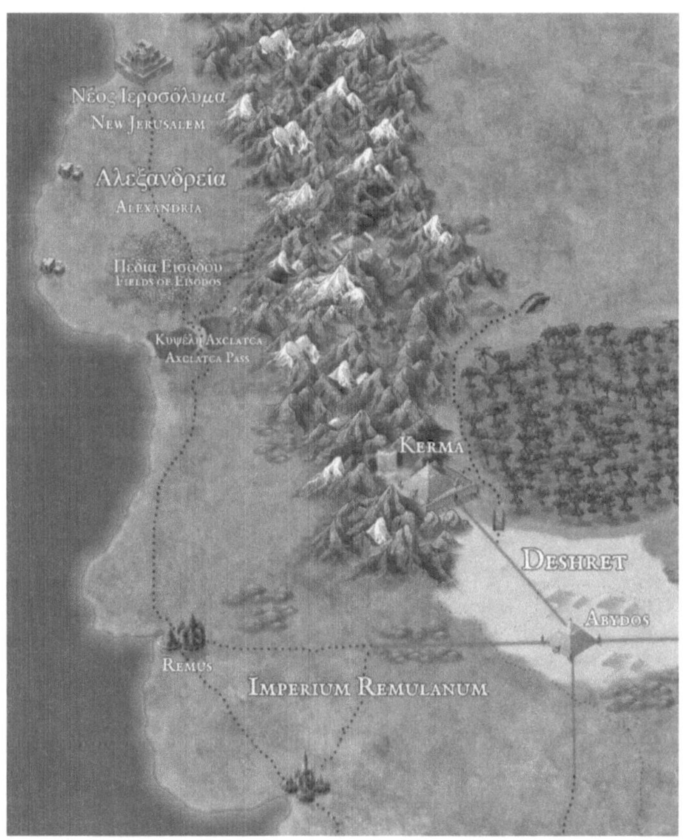

Chapter 1

Nippur, Welven City, Choru (current Aaruan month), An 5660 (current Aaruan year), Day 8 (since arriving on Aaru)(Earth Date – November 14, 1883)

The visions of her kidnapping and torture by that bastard elf were memories Louisa wanted to vanquish to the dark recesses of her mind, but they had already slithered into her idle moments and dreams. After her subsequent rescue—or was she captured?—by a group of welves, her fears didn't fade until she reunited with her friends. Yet within minutes of the reunion, seeing Ali's smirking face shattered her momentary peace.

Louisa smiled, remembering the gratifying smack of her fist connecting with Professor Ali Mousa's nose. Out of the blue, the man who called himself a Keeper of the Seba had the temerity to show up when Louisa had begun to feel safe again.

Louisa and Ben had met the stout professor a little over a month ago in Cairo. She and Ben had just begun their quest to find the tomb of Perdiccas. They had both hoped to discover a treasure map to a mysterious temple inside the Greek general's crypt. What they found was so much more than they had bargained for. During each step of the journey, Mousa and the villagers who served the temple had tried to stop them.

She glanced up at the tall, lean doctor walking beside her as they made their way up a mountain trail. A modicum of serenity returned to her as she tried to catalog every inch of Ben's face. She resisted the urge to reach up and run her finger along his prominent scar. It stretched from just in front of his left ear across his cheek and terminated at the end of his square chin.

What has gotten into me?

As if sensing her scrutiny, Ben's blue eyes caught hers. "You okay?"

Louisa cleared her throat. "I was just thinking how lucky the professor was that you were there to restrain me."

She got the exact reaction she had hoped for when Ben's scar tugged at his mouth to form an off-kilter grin. She stumbled over a fallen tree branch.

"Whoa." Ben grabbed her arm, pulling her upright.

"Thanks."

"Anytime. You sure you're okay?"

It depends on what happens next. Instead of vocalizing her thoughts, she nodded and stared at the forest floor, wary of more obstacles.

She had rejoined Ben and his adopted son, Abu, along with the Lancers. Then the welves, a ghost-white version of elves without the pointy ears, began guiding them up the mountain toward the welven city of Nippur. The steep hike had done an excellent job of cooling Louisa's anger toward their unwanted traveling companion.

The man had been behind the attempted robbery at the Shepheard's Hotel and again on the train to Pelusium. Both times, he and his cohorts had tried to steal the ancient Greek letter with its clues to the location of the temple. When being thwarted in the robberies didn't dissuade them, the professor and his ilk tried to murder the treasure hunters. They had hounded her and her companions every step of the way, until she and Abu, through an innocent mistake, had activated the Seba in her tent while Ben and the rest of the men were defending their camp against Ali and the temple villagers.

Created by a long-vanished race of immortal aliens, the Seba had transported Louisa and her group to the planet Aaru. To her dismay, Ali and the temple followers also traveled with them across the universe to wherever they were now.

What did the professor's appearance portend for them?

"Can we trust the professor?" Louisa asked.

Ben shrugged. "Trust has to be earned, but he did save my life after the ambush, so I'm willing to give him a chance."

Louisa gasped. This was the first time she had heard of an ambush or Ben being wounded.

Ben waved his hand in a circle. "We were tracking you and the kidnappers. We think they were working with the Remulans because some legionaries ambushed us." He grimaced. "I got stabbed."

"Did Khepri heal you?" Louisa whispered.

With a shake of his head, Ben said, "No, Ali was with the welves when they surrounded us. He's a life singer like Khepri. He healed me and several of the Lancers."

Louisa paused a beat. This information gave her a new perspective, but she needed to look Ali in the eye before she changed her thoughts about him. She would get the professor's side of the story, but it could wait. "I think I'm going to have a very serious conversation with Mr. Mousa when we get to where we are going."

Ben gave her a sideways glance. "Fair enough, but we have bigger problems than the professor."

"I know, but we don't have many choices right now." Louisa directed her gaze to the nearest welf on the trail.

Ben nodded. "I feel like we're trapped in a room with a locked box that may contain a bomb with a lit fuse. Do you fight to get away before the damn thing blows up, or do you ignore it and hope there's no bomb?"

"Huh?"

"According to Ali, the Lamentations could start at any moment," Ben said. "or they may never happen again. I don't want to be here when an army of alien demons shows up to kill everyone."

Her uncle's scratchy voice popped into Louisa's head. *Always plan two escape routes.*

The idea of a cataclysmic event like the Lamentations occurring had been so distant to her that she hadn't given it a second thought. Her motivation to power the Seba went as far as giving anyone who wanted to go home the option. For a woman like her, Aaru offered so many more opportunities than Earth.

"Do you believe we can learn what we need at the Tomb of Mortals?" Louisa asked.

Ben shrugged as he sidestepped a fallen branch. "Only one way to find out. We need to convince the welves to let us go. The faster they do, the quicker we learn what we need from the Ancients and go home."

"What if this could be home? What if we found a way back home for everyone who wants to go, but I stay?" Louisa asked.

Ben jerked to a stop, his eyes full of concern.

The thought of losing their fledgling relationship made Louisa's stomach churn. For a brief moment, she locked eyes with his and hoped he could hear her thoughts.

I don't want to come back alone.

Chapter 2

Nippur, Choru, An 5660, Day 8

Masako flattened herself against the storage room's chilly wall and squeezed behind the wine rack. She stretched her hand down, trying to reach the rare bottle of cherry spirits. It was shaped like a serpent wrapped around an arm while a hand restrained the viper's fanged head.

In a rush to get back to the mistress who had asked for the expensive vintage, Masako had been careless. Dust had flown into her face as she picked up the bottle. She sneezed, and it slipped from her grasp.

So stupid.

In desperation, Masako had thrust her sandaled foot out to keep the bottle from striking the brick floor. It bounced off the top of her foot and rolled under the shelf where it now sat a finger's width out of reach.

So lucky.

A cup of the cherry liqueur cost more than Masako's life. If the bottle had broken, she knew the welf who ran the kitchen would have sold her to pay for it, and slaves outside the palace did not live the protected life she knew.

Her fingernail scratched along the scaly glass, but Masako couldn't find a grip.

Next year, I'll be big enough to reach it.

With a shake of her head, Masako straightened and flexed her still throbbing foot. As the leather tip of her sandal hooked one of the viper's fangs, the door to the wine cellar creaked open. It had to be Bahram. If he had come all this way, the old man would punish her for sure.

Tilhar, the welf who ran the kitchen, stumbled through the light streaming from the doorway.

Masako released her toehold and tried to press herself into the wall. Between the shelves and the bottles, her eyes fixed on the tall, skinny man who followed Tilhar inside and gave him another shove. She clasped her hand over her mouth and held her breath.

The stranger moved with lethal fluidity as if the serpent from the bottle had slithered free and morphed into this creature. With pitch black-hair and red eyes glowing in his sneering, bleached-out face, he frightened her more than any welf she had ever known.

The broad-shouldered chief of the kitchen turned to face his assailant. "You are not supposed to be here, Enkara."

Before his words stopped echoing in the closed space, the tip of a dagger appeared under Tilhar's chin, and his eyes bulged.

"I'll do as I please," hissed the serpent come to life. "And you will do what I tell you, or I will visit your children next."

Tilhar's pale complexion lost more color, and he gulped. "What do you want?"

Blood oozed down the blade as the snake-man, known as Enkara, added pressure. "We may not be able to wait until the Summer Festival."

The master of the kitchen stretched his head back and asked, "When?"

"Tonight. At the banquet for the Earthlings."

Tilhar's voice became a whisper. "You can't kill the governess with only a few hours of planning."

The blade pulled away and flowed around Enkara's hand in a sinuous motion. In a trance, Masako's eyes followed the silver metal as it twisted and swirled.

When the steel blade stopped, Enkara stepped forward, his wicked smile only inches from Tilhar's face. "We will use the contingency. Do you remember your role?"

With a nod, Tilhar said, "The weapons will be where they're supposed to be." He straightened and pushed his chest out. "Now, leave my children out of this."

"Do your part, and they will be just fine." Enkara's red eyes sparkled as he smeared blood along Tilhar's sleeve to clean the blade. "There's also a chance we won't strike tonight. If that happens, we go back to the original plan. Understand?"

Tilhar glared. "Yes."

Enkara returned the dagger to its sheath, turned, and strolled out of the cellar.

The master of the kitchen pulled a dishrag from his pocket and wiped his chin. The bleeding had already stopped. He threw the cloth to the ground and stormed out.

Masako took a deep breath and shivered. She counted to one hundred before using her foot to pull the bottle closer. Soon she hugged it to her chest and moved toward the door. Her body still shaking, she poked her head out and looked down the hall toward the kitchen. With no one in sight, she sighed.

She felt a tug on her tunic. She yelped as she stumbled into the hallway.

"Where the hell have you been?" Bahram released the tunic and took hold of her by the back of her neck, just above her slave collar.

With the bottle clutched tight, Masako twisted her head around as far as she could, and her eyes darted toward the kitchen. Tilhar's broad shoulders filled the entrance to the hallway.

Masako looked up into Bahram's wrinkled face. "We have to hide," she pleaded.

"Bahram, come here. Now!" a voice roared like thunder down the passage.

The two of them looked in that direction. The master of the kitchen's face twisted into a murderous scowl. His hand clenched and unclenched the handle of a huge meat cleaver as he barreled toward them.

Bahram grabbed the bottle from her grasp and pushed her in the opposite direction. He shouted, "Run! You know where!"

Masako didn't dare look back as she took off. When she heard the glass shattering behind her, she churned her ten-An-old legs as fast as she could.

Chapter 3

Nefru Mountains and Nippur, Choru, An 5660, Day 8

Their *hosts*, the welves, soon directed everyone onto a horse-width-size path through a tangle of trees. After a few turns along the twisting trail, it became plain to Ben that someone had grown the trees and the underbrush to form a wilderness maze. A snarl of thorny vines and spike-leaved bushes created impenetrable walls between trunks whose canopy branches intertwined to make a latticed ceiling. Tiny threads of light pierced the pattern, casting hints of brightness just out of reach, like an early morning glow.

Several hours later, Ben's constant feeling of vulnerability had caused a knot to form between his shoulders. The single-file column still wound through the labyrinth, and Ben felt sure they had passed hundreds of ambush points, each engineered to annihilate anyone stupid enough to attack the welves' city through this mantrap of a forest.

Every new turn brought more of the same—a shaded tunnel of leaves and limbs.

Ben turned yet another corner of the maze, and his thoughts escaped him as he stared across a long valley. Like a view from the Austrian Alps, the Aaruan star, An, lit the scene with brilliant afternoon sunlight. Cloud shadows dappled the patchwork of crop fields, adding to the majesty.

A paved road led from the wooded maze, splitting the miles-long stretch of farmland in two. The top of the mountain they had hiked toward for the last few days loomed at the end of the highway. Two giant rocky arms stretched away from the peak as if embracing the beauty within.

Ben made a mental map of the terrain and hurried to catch up to Abu and Louisa. They marched through the pristine fields, spotted by the inhabitants of a few houses and barns. Hysakas and humans tended this lush garden.

Where are all the welves?

Taller-than-normal stalks bowed from the weight of their bounty in the wheat and bean fields they passed. Ben had never seen such abundant crops.

As they continued down the road, Abu pointed at a strange grove of trees next to the path. "Look at that!" His voice cracked as he said, "That's some pumpkins."

Within the orchard of maples, Ben marveled at the individual trees. Each had different kitchen necessities growing from the branches. There were bowls of various sizes hanging off one tree's limbs while hundreds of wooden spoons dangled from the canopy of another. The utensils came in many sizes, from sprouts of baby spoons to full-grown ladles.

Ben tore his eyes away from the magically enhanced crops to pay special attention to the welves guiding his party. All the albino-skinned welves, with their impossibly lustrous hair, wore goggles of dark glass. Made from different materials and a myriad of designs, the spectacles that protected them from the sun were as individual as their owners. Some frames used polished wood, with the embedded glass flowing like natural growths, while others used swirls of metal, wood, and crystal. The designs looked elegant yet practical.

Hidden under those smoky lenses were irises colored in vibrant hues of blue, gray, amber, and violet that no human eye had ever possessed.

These guys give me the chills. They remind me of those vampyre stories.

As they crossed the valley of wonders, Ben pondered how they would convince the welves to let them go. They didn't seem to be prisoners, per se, but it was clear they weren't free either. At least, the welves hadn't tried to disarm them.

A confrontation would have led to disaster. Ben had no illusions about it. They were well within the borders of the welves' home, and those strange eyes allowed them to see in the dark. If he and the Lancers fought the welves, no one from their expedition would leave the mountains alive.

For the moment, they and their remaining Alexandrian escorts were guests with one big restriction. They had to go where they were told. Ben didn't like it, but as with meeting the polemarchos following the battle, they once again had to put their future—if not their lives—in the hands of strangers.

He mulled over different scenarios that might arise when they met with the governess of the city of Nippur. The city name sparked Ben's archaeological memory. On Earth, there had been a Sumerian city-state of the same name. That town had worshiped the god Enil, known as the Lord Wind.

Should be interesting. But not important.

If they ever wanted to go home to Earth, they had to figure out how to power the Seba. Ben's plan to accomplish that meant exploring the Ancients' site, the Tomb of Mortals. He hoped he could find enough information there to decipher the long-vanished alien race's script. If he could read their language, he was certain he could unlock the secrets of their technology. To accomplish this, Ben had to convince the welves to let his group continue their journey.

The challenge would be their guns. The welves knew how powerful the Earthlings' weapons were, and Ben expected that topic to dominate any discussions. He glanced over his shoulder at the professor, who shuffled behind Ben's packhorse, his face full of resignation.

If the governess asked, he would stick to the strategy he had worked out with his group. As far as he knew, he was the only person on Aaru with the chemistry knowledge needed to create mercury fulminate, the critical component used to make primers for modern cartridges.

Whoever controlled the production of the substance had the literal power to conquer this world. Ben's only hope of getting the governess to allow them to visit the Ancients' site lay in the welves believing the lie that none of the Earthlings could reproduce the ammunition for their guns. Given enough time, the welves, the Alexandrians, or some other Aaruans might solve the primer problem on their own, but he hoped to stay in charge as long as possible.

These were variables Ben hoped to manage, but the potential threat of the Lamentations added an unsolvable equation to his calculations. From what he understood, the cycle had begun more than three thousand years ago. Every 551 Earth years or 688 An, an army of giant reptile aliens, known to the commoners as reapers, would come to Aaru using their own Seba device. The aliens' goal: wipe out all other intelligent life on the planet.

The eons-long sequence snapped during the last cycle when no invasion took place. This period became known as the Phantom Lamentations. Keeper Mousa had made it clear that if the pattern resumed, an invasion could begin at any moment, and Ben wanted no part of it. They had to get to the Tomb of Mortals, power the Seba, and do it fast.

The Nipponese got lucky. Good thing they didn't bring any muskets with them during the Phantom Lamentations. We dodged a literal bullet there.

Ben chuckled, but the laughter caught in his throat. Up ahead, he glimpsed the top of the familiar white postillion hat decorated with feathers and a ribbon of blue. The felt hat's once-pristine white had taken on an orange-red tinge from their days in the Egyptian Sinai.

Through some trick of his mind, Ben smelled the scent of Louisa's lavender-and-lemon perfume, and a weird mix of emotions overtook him. The bottomless desperation he'd felt when he thought he had lost Louisa warred with the joy that flooded his heart when she returned to him. He peered around the pack horse pulled by Abu, wanting another glimpse of the woman he loved. He took in her proud face as she studied the surrounding wonders.

Her revelation that she might not return to Earth didn't surprise him, but it was concerning. If he had to think only of himself, he wouldn't give it a second thought, but he needed to consider Abu's feelings as well. *Another bridge for another time.*

The more immediate obstacle in front of him seemed monumental. Like stepping over Colonel Travis's line in the sand, Ben had committed his everything to the cause, but getting Louisa to fall in love with him might be impossible. Thinking about the last battle his heart had lost, he wasn't sure he would ever have another chance if she were to reject him. He needed to call on his ace in the hole to help win Louisa's free-spirited heart.

I'm willing, but, God, this is all you. Tell me what to do.

With his worry now in God's hands, Ben refocused on the impossible wonders in the valley. They were passing a farm where the farmhouse and the barn appeared to have grown from two oak trees that had twisted themselves to become living embodiments of their intended use.

Instead of slatted boards, bark covered the outside walls, and where a chimney should be, a pipe made of fire-hardened wood poked at the sky. Like the welves' goggles, the windows melded into the tree, creating unique shapes like rain drops, birds, or animals. In an unreal display that shamed Earth's greatest stained-glass artists, colors transitioned within the crystalline surface, bringing each representation to life.

As they left the buildings behind, Ben looked over his shoulder. A golden-furred hysakas dressed in overalls approached the nearby barn. Double doors that looked like two enormous flat branches swung open for the seven-foot-tall tailless wolf. The hysakas had not touched the doors, yet the door-branches moved on their own to welcome the creature. As soon as the humanoid-like wolf crossed the threshold, the living building's doors completed their embrace.

Can Ali do that?

It took the group fewer than two Aaruan hours to cross the valley. At the foot of the mountain peak, the road broadened before disappearing into an ominous-looking tunnel. Enormous towers carved from the mountain's rock guarded the tunnel on both sides.

A portcullis stretched between the towers. The gate rose silently as they neared. Through the latticed steel, Ben saw a drawbridge lowering from across a wide chasm just beyond the tunnel entrance. The welves removed their shaded goggles as they passed under the sharpened points of the massive gate, now poised to drop fifty feet from the tunnel's ceiling back to the floor.

Ben sped up and crossed the threshold as his pulse raced.

How deep is that drop?

Chilled air flowed around them as they moved between the towers. The Lancers and the specialized Alexandrian soldiers known as the Lochem had to soothe the supply-laden horses while leading them across the long wooden span. As Abu followed Esther, the young officer in charge of the Lochem, he did an admirable job with the horse he led. Staying well away from the edge, Ben clenched the packhorse's reins as he peered over the side into depths that seemed endless. He gulped.

Don't look down.

Reaching the far side, they marched under a massive sheet of iron. If lowered, it stood at the very edge of the chasm, making it impossible for anyone to bridge the gap from the valley side. The farther they progressed, the more the light from the valley waned.

Beyond this door, thousands of murder holes had been built into the cavern ceiling. The sinister openings guarded the fifty yards of open ground the travelers had to traverse to reach the next wall that blocked their path. Ben's stomach grew queasy at their being so exposed, and goosebumps formed on his arms as the temperature dropped.

With only a sliver of light to guide their path, Ben assumed the wall spanned the entire tunnel. The visible parts of the wall had more archer slits and a few wider openings big enough for a ballista. A third metal door stood in the middle of this wall, blocking whatever attempted to go beyond. This portal also rose at their approach.

The light that filtered into the fortified tunnel from the valley behind could not penetrate this next tunnel. Luminescent lichens growing on the walls and the ceiling of the passage lit their way as they walked under more murder holes. A slight breeze of warm air with an earthy smell wafted through the dark, narrow, solid-granite walkway. Ben counted forty paces before the exit was visible. His spirits lifted at the site of gas-fed streetlamps illuminating their path ahead.

After exiting onto a landing, they came into a space so vast and so dark Ben could not estimate its size. Orange-, red-, and blue-flamed lamps appeared like stars, filling the night sky as thousands of flickering pinpoints hung in the darkness above. Floating among the stars were occasional ropes of light as if hundreds of lamps glowed next to one another.

Ben glanced down to ensure that he still stood on the stone surface. He followed the road toward a bridge stretching away from the landing into the inky blackness. He inched across to the beginning of the bridge and looked over the side. Thousands of sparkling lights reflected on the surface of a midnight lake.

It took him a moment to reorient himself to the fact that these were not reflections but more flames stretching away into the very depths of the mountain. Ben stopped beside Abu and Louisa for several minutes, amazed that the welves had created Nippur by hollowing out the mountain they had climbed for the last few days. Any worries about the upcoming meeting and what it meant for their future flew from his mind.

In silence, the three of them stared at the marvel in awe for several minutes before smiling. The rest of the parade had not paused, and Ben waved Abu and Louisa forward. They hurried to catch up to Ssherrss and Khepri, who now marched in front of them.

Ben clapped Abu on the shoulder. "What do you think?"

The teenager grinned. "I want to write it down as soon as I can." He fell silent.

The sounds of their boots, the clip-clop of horses' hooves, and the occasional conversations drifted like whispers into the void. The suspended expanse stretched into the darkness, and Ben leaned over to examine the supports. They appeared out of the depths as if the entire construction floated on a cloud of midnight black.

Ben's head spun with vertigo. *Stop thinking about it. You're not really that high up.*

Life-size sculptures made of blended glass, metal, and stone stood on top of the delicate-looking guardrail that ran along both sides of the bridge. These static yet lifelike imitations of people appeared at regular intervals.

The statues showed men and women in every occupation and activity. There were philosophers, merchants, soldiers, and even the occasional intertwined lovers. Simple gas-powered lamps stood halfway between each of the statues, holding the perpetual blackness at bay.

Louisa stopped in front of one stunning piece of art. The sculpture depicted a woman in the act of running. Her body was made of stone; her face, of steel; and her flowing locks, of hollow, lighted glass. Louisa moved her eyes in a chaotic rhythm, entranced by the woman's hair, its gas-fed flame of red dancing within the crystal tresses.

With a sigh, she turned away and caught Ben's eye. "It's like we're Alice, and the welves are our white rabbits. How are they able to create such beauty?"

Ben laughed. "You know the answer, Alice."

Louisa nodded. "Magic." She skipped down to the next lamp and stopped in the center of its brightness. Then she spun in a circle with arms outstretched, giggling.

Ben thrust the reins of his horse into Abu's hand and sped up to reach her. On her second spin, he grabbed her hand, halting her momentum. He straightened her arm and placed his other hand behind her opposite shoulder. Joy filled his heart as he looked into Louisa's sparkling eyes. She nodded and placed a soft hand on his shoulder while he pushed aside his discomfort from bending at an awkward angle.

With a crooked grin, Ben bounced two silent counts before stepping off into the Viennese Waltz. Louisa matched his rhythm, and they glided over the smooth stone path, spinning their way forward.

Catcalls, whistles, and clapping came from behind them. As they continued spinning, Ben spied the noisy audience. Jeevan, Abu, and several Lancers soon found their silent beat and clapped in unison. Ben's gaze returned to Louisa. She had grown quiet, her eyes searching deep within his own.

Ben's mind blanked, and he lost the beat, then stumbled forward several steps. Louisa took two quick steps backward to safety as he caught his balance. When he came to a stop, the yells from the cheap seats disparaged his lack of coordination.

Jeevan yelled the loudest, "What a gollumpus!" The duffadar followed his nickname for Ben's clumsiness with a big belly laugh.

Ben frowned. A little winded, he stammered to Louisa, "Sorry."

Louisa smiled and curtsied. "Thank you for the dance, Dr. McGehee. I didn't know you had it in you."

"I try. When we get home, would you . . . ?" Ben's face grew hot.

"I look forward to it." Louisa gestured toward the onlookers. "I think everyone's waiting for us."

The procession had stopped and turned to watch. Ben waved at the gawkers and started forward with Louisa by his side.

Abu pulled hard on the reins of both packhorses, falling into step with Louisa. "You were amazing. Do you think you can teach me to dance like that?"

Ben snapped, "What am I? A cow chip?"

Abu and Louisa looked back at Ben and said, "What?"

Ben said, "I can teach you."

"I'll go with the expert." Abu tilted his head at Louisa. "If you'll teach me."

"I will," she said. "And we'll do etiquette lessons as well."

Abu slumped, but his voice remained upbeat. "Great."

They kept walking three abreast, but the excitement of this incredible underworld had worn off, and they grew more subdued. Straight as an arrow, the road ran toward the center of the mountain. Ben could sense something waiting out there in the heavy night. The impenetrable darkness and the unknowable distance kept the complete picture out of reach. Much closer in their field of vision, the lit road-bridge branched to the left and the right. An occasional broad staircase materialized out of the oppressive fog.

The steps joined with a network of walkways crisscrossing the giant cavern. Dozens of welves and other types of humanoids moved along the spans closest to them, but the road they traveled remained empty of others.

Some strings of luminescence grew larger until they defined the outlines of buildings that morphed out of the gloom below the bridge and twisted like live vines growing skyward.

According to Ben's engineering mind, the towers carved from the mountain's stone heart had taken on structurally impossible shapes. Like stalks of granite, they bent and spiraled from the cavern floor on their way to the summit. The filigreed surface of each building showcased incredible displays of lighted designs made of glass and steel, interspersed by golden rays from hundreds of windows and balconies.

They hiked for several more hours before the mass at the center took form. A fairytale palace of quartz, pulsing with golden streaks of light, encased the massive rock column that held up this world's rock heavens.

Countless other buildings filled a circular plateau that stretched away from the palace. A pristine limestone colosseum on the scale of Rome's sat on the plateau's edge to the left of their road. If the plans for ancient cities ran to form, Ben surmised that many of the nearby buildings were for government or religious purposes.

As their bridge became a road on the plateau, more and more denizens appeared to stop and watch their group pass. Hundreds of welven soldiers lined the road, keeping the regular people from getting too close.

Bile rose in Ben's throat as he took in the people in the throng. Welves comprised only a third of the crowd. In smaller numbers still, there were the foxlike stirithy, some more of the giant wolf-like hysakas, and the occasional babiakhom with their strange double-lidded eyes that resembled a goat's with its horizontal pupils. The latter aliens' flaps of skin, which they used like wings, always made Ben think of them as a cross between a baboon and a flying squirrel. Humans made up most of the crowd. Almost all of them wore inch-thick collars of dull metal marked with silver cuneiform writing.

Unlike the slaves in Ben's past, these enslaved people came in every shade God had graced humanity with, except the ghost white of the welves. Similar to his previous experiences with this evil, their state of health and the look in their eyes shifted from desperate to defeated, to indifferent, to confident.

Ben knew this view into these poor bastards' souls depended entirely on their treatment by their masters. His gaze settled on a girl of about ten. Her ill-fitting collar hung loose around her neck and rested at an uncomfortable angle on her collarbone. Her large brown eyes held the look of one who had long ago lost hope, and she moved with the lackluster motions of the damned. Ben's pang of righteous indignation got smothered by self-recrimination that he had ever fought for such an evil practice.

Abu nudged him as Ben clenched and unclenched his jaws. He released the tension and looked at the teenager.

In a low voice, Abu said, "Dr. Ben, I have a bad feeling about this."

Ben forced himself to count to five and take several deep breaths before responding. "We have something they want. They won't try to do that to us. Besides, I would die killing a lot of these pasty bastards before they put a collar on any of us."

Abu frowned, and his voice grew solemn. "Dr. Ben, keep your head. There is nothing we can do for them, and we need you to get us out of this place."

Ben gave his son a rueful smile. "Yet. We can't do anything *yet*. But you're right. I'll keep my peace."

As they left the child behind, Ben knew the memory of her hopeless eyes would remain.

For another thirty minutes, they moved past temples and government offices. Like the organic monoliths along the road, each building had a unique personality. As the engineer in Ben studied them, he could see how the clever architects had worked structural soundness into each design. Not a seam, grout line, nail, or rivet marred these welven structures. Nearer to the palace, a work crew hung off a six- or seven-story building.

Suspended by a pulley system from the roof, four stirithy sat on dangling seats and concentrated their efforts on the third floor's outer wall. Ben stopped for several minutes to watch. Details appeared crisper to him than they had for decades. Grateful again for Khepri's life-singing ability to heal his eyes, Ben admired the fox crew's intricate teamwork. Somehow, they reshaped a straight piece of art made of silicon, metal, and rock. The distinct elements became semi-solid and moved like a layer of lava, then flowed into a spiral design before solidifying into merged elements.

Ben shook his head at the impossible sight and marched forward, focusing on their destination. Up close, the palace appeared ice-like, with golden flames licking at the transparent sheets from behind. An extensive park surrounded the ice castle. Massive toadstools in a rainbow of glowing colors set the boundary of this well-groomed yet surreal garden.

Flowers glowed in ordered beds, surrounded by manicured grass of shimmering green. Versailles-like hedges of some alien species partitioned the space. Waves of energy flowed along each shrub's wall of leaves. Other bushes grown into living sculptures came alive with the same biological electricity.

Dotted throughout were gas-lit lamps following abstract paths. Benches and children's playgrounds containing slides, seesaws, and swings stood just off the cobblestone walkways. Several hysakas dressed in white uniforms moved around the garden. Fresh growth sprouted at the wolf-creatures' touch or parts of a plant moved, reshaping itself to the life singer's will.

Ben shook his head again at the absurdity of everything as the enchanting palace drew near. The crystal spires rose so far up into the crushing darkness that their tops were not visible.

The road ended at huge double doors made of shiny brass. Engraved across them were prominent cuneiform symbols. When they came close enough, Ben translated to himself. It took him a good minute to work through the sentence.

Just as he finished, Abu said, "*Light lives only a moment, but the darkness*—Dr. Ben, what does the rest of it say?"

"*Rules forever. Light lives only a moment, but the darkness rules forever.*"
Abu shivered.

Ben stayed mum, his worry growing. The doors swung open like the other portals they had passed, with no sounds of cranking or movement, as if the process had happened by magic. Ben wondered whether they employed mechanical means similar to the pulley system used by the stirithy workers or if alien magic was the actual cause. They passed through the doors into an enormous courtyard formed by several outer buildings and many entrances to the palace.

The lead welven escort spoke for a while to Ssherrss, the grumpy stirithy who was a member of the Alexandrian army and had been their guide to the Tomb of Mortals. When the welf disengaged, he walked to the largest of several portals leading into the building. He turned and watched them as he placed his hands together, hanging in front of his waist.

Ben, Abu, and Louisa stepped next to the small stirithy and his giant spouse, Khepri. Ssherrss waited until Jeevan and Esther reached their group before speaking.

"The welf assked that only the leaderrss come with himm. The rresst of the mmen have quarrterrss in a guesst ssoldierrss' barrrrackss. Everryone can keep theirr weaponss. Leave the horrssess herre. Any quesstionss?"

None followed. Jeevan began giving orders to his lance duffadars while Esther instructed the remaining six Lochem. Before handing their horses to a Lancer, Ben and Abu grabbed their smaller pieces of luggage.

When everyone was ready, they followed the welven officer into the palace. The scent of unknown flowers prickled Ben's nose, and he sneezed. They passed through many extravagant rooms filled with sculptures, strange flowering plants, and intricate tapestries depicting scenes from welven history until they reached a long corridor with eight doors.

The welf said in Greek, "These are your quarters. Please remain in this area." He pointed to a silver cord hanging down from the wall near the entrance to the hallway. "If you need anything, pull on one of the silver cords. There is one inside each room." He wrinkled his nose. "I suggest you take advantage of the bathing facilities in the rooms. Tonight, you will have an audience with the governess."

The raven-haired, golden-eyed welf turned to leave.

Ben looked at Louisa, Esther, and Khepri. "Ladies, you get first choice."

Khepri jerked her snout down the hall toward an oversize door and said in Greek, "That one looks my size."

"Grreat. Jusst grreat," grumbled the diminutive Ssherrss. He marched toward the door, his head shaking and his bushy tail whipping back and forth.

Louisa bit her lip as she fought back laughter. "I'll take that one." She pointed toward the third door down. "I want a bath in the worst way. See you tonight."

Chapter 4

Plains of Nisaya, Choru, An 5660, Day 8

Djoser sighed, his weariness growing as he waited for an audience with the emperor. To catch up to the emperor's marching army, he had used every bit of singing he could muster. His lone surviving caracal, Bastet, raised his head from Djoser's boot and cried out. The anguished mewling forced Djoser's seething anger to the forefront, his weariness replaced by energy full of rage.

An irrational part of Djoser wanted revenge against the damn welves and the Earthlings for killing Kheket, his other caracal. That anger carried him here to report Iskur's failure. His rational side knew how lucky he'd been to escape the ambush with his life.

He shook his head, hearing his wise mother chiding him. *One should not spit upon Shai's favor.*[1]

I'll leave as soon as I report, Djoser thought as he repeated his father's wisdom to himself. *No profit, no job.*

"The emperor will see you." A centurion in a gold cloak held open the flap to the emperor's tent.

---

1. Egyptian God of Fate.

Wait here. Djoser sent the silent command to the caracal at his feet. The feline repositioned his head and closed his eyes.

The pleasant scent of hyacinths wafted through the opening as Djoser walked into the canvased pavilion. The emperor sat in the center, leaning forward in his folding chair with his hands clasped in his lap. An older man in his sixties stood on his right, and a babiakhom sat on a cushion behind him.

Djoser stopped before the most powerful man on the planet and bowed. As he straightened, the emperor said, "You are one of Iskur's men?"

"Yes, Emperor." Djoser didn't have enough singing reserves to translate his words to Latin, but he needn't have worried because the other babiakhom sang the song.

"And?"

"We caught up to the Earthlings in the Nefru Mountains and lost two men to their weapons when we captured a female Earthling. After we escaped their larger group, Iskur sent your gold cloaks to ambush anyone who followed. Welves attacked while we were questioning the woman. They took Iskur along with the woman. Only two of us survived."

The emperor leaned forward and put his elbows on his knees. "They would take them to Nippur. What of the other Earthlings? Why were they in the mountains?"

Djoser nodded. "I listened to them before we attacked. They were going to the Tomb of Mortals. I did not hear why. After escaping the welves' attack, I listened to the pasty demons as well. They were going to Nippur, but, on the way, they planned to meet a larger group of welves who had captured the rest of the Earthlings."

The emperor slapped his hand against an armrest, his eyes narrowing. "What of my men?"

"They attacked those who followed us. All of your men fell to their weapons except Primpilus Titus, and he lost part of his hand," said Djoser.

With a dismissive wave, the emperor asked, "Can you fly?"

Djoser shook his head. "I will need at least twelve hours."

The emperor turned to the older man beside him and said, "Aquila, send a messenger to Legate Saluvius. He will take all his men to the Tomb of Mortals and wait. I doubt the welves will ever let them leave, but if they do, we must be ready."

"I will see to it." The man gave a slight bow.

The emperor focused on Djoser. "As soon as you are able, return to Titus. Meet Saluvius and his men at the Tomb of Mortals. I want you to help locate the Earthlings if they show themselves."

Djoser did not answer. He chewed on his lower lip as he tried to think of a way to be free of this mess. An itch on the back of his right wing grew more intense with each passing second, but he didn't dare scratch it.

"Locate the Earthlings, and you will receive the same reward I promised Iskur." The emperor stared at him with a face that demanded his acceptance.

That sadistic bastard Shemush will want a cut.

Calculations flew through Djoser's head.

Half will have to do.

Djoser smiled. "Of course, Emperor. It is my honor to serve you."

Chapter 5

Nippur, Choru, An 5660, Day 8

Having enjoyed a good nap and his first hot soaking bath since leaving Cairo, Ben felt better than he had in days. He and Abu sat at a small table. His son leafed through a book he'd read several times with his eyes unfocused while Ben evaluated the bedroom's contents once more. Somehow equal parts plush and spartan, the room's furnishings held a lot of mystery. He wondered again at the craftsmanship of the two beds, the dresser, the table, and its two chairs.

Upon investigation, he found that the wooden bed frame was made with four pieces of solid wood that appeared to have been grown into the shape of a headboard, a footboard, and sideboards. It took Ben five minutes to find the minuscule seams connecting the boards. His instincts told him that the intricate designs on the exposed surfaces were organic.

The quality of the rest of the furniture pieces matched the bed's. With its strange flowing back, the chair had small cushions held in place by ingenious clips grown into the wood. It was, without doubt, the most comfortable chair Ben had ever sat in, in his life.

Lying on the plush feathered mattress, with its silky smooth linens, Ben had felt as if he were sleeping on a cloud. The construction of the ensuite bath and the accompanying water closets were marvels of Aaru's strange magical engineering. Ben made a mental note to ask Ssherrss how these mundane luxuries worked.

The palace bells chimed eight times just as a knock came at the door. Abu stood. "I guess it's time to go."

"I guess so." Ben got to his feet.

Abu opened the door to find Commander Shanesha waiting. The tall—at least, by welven standards—pale man with long platinum hair and startling amber eyes greeted them.

"I'm here to escort you to the governess," he said in perfect Greek. "Please follow me."

Shanesha stepped back into the hallway, allowing Abu and Ben to come out. Louisa, Jeevan, and Esther were waiting in the hall.

Louisa said, "You both look dashing." Then she snickered. "Sir McGehee, you look the cleanest I've seen since the mountain stream." Ben tried to think of a witty reply while she continued with an impish smile. "I'm unsure whether I prefer this outfit or the one you wore that day."

Heat rising in his cheeks, Ben remembered the freezing stream and the spectacle he'd made, but part of him stirred at her flirtation. Unable to think of anything better, he rolled his eyes. "Miss Louisa, you look lovely. Can I escort you?" He offered her the crook of his elbow.

She chuckled as she took hold of his arm.

A few moments later, Ssherrss, Khepri, and Ali joined them.

Ben nodded to Shanesha. Without waiting to see if they followed, the welf headed toward the main entrance at a brisk pace. When they reached the first grand hall, the welf led them toward a massive set of stairs before walking past the landing and taking a hallway that led deeper into the palace.

After several hundred paces, the corridor ended at a guarded double door. Two soldiers opened the portals, revealing a twenty- by twenty-foot space, with handrails attached at waist height to the room's three walls. Shanesha walked to the rear of the compartment and motioned them forward. When everyone had entered, the guards closed the doors.

Ben had never ridden in an elevator but assumed this must be an Aaruan version. Confirmation came when the floor trembled, and he felt a moment of added weight pressing on his knees. The almost imperceptible movement continued for a minute. As it had started, the room stopped with a slight lurch.

The doors opened, and the welf said in Greek, "I will be your liaison while you are in Nippur. Don't hesitate to ask questions."

The group moved with tentative steps into a room as large as St. Peter's Basilica. The voluminous space stretched forward for at least one hundred yards. Enormous glass columns encasing ice-blue flames lined the center of the room. Each stretched from the pitch-black marble floor up a hundred feet to the glass ceiling, which emanated a golden light, bathing the cavernous hall in a soft glow. A raised dais loomed at the far end while more people milled around tables set between the pillars.

Shanesha moved to stand next to the couple. "When we reach the governess, I will announce your group. Line up side by side. Is there one of you who will speak for the rest?"

After everyone looked at Ben, he said, "We will." He raised Louisa's linked arm. Her brow furrowed, and she tilted her head toward him with a quizzical expression.

"And how should I introduce you?" asked Shanesha.

"As Miss Louisa Sophia and Dr. Benjamin McGehee," Ben replied.

"Very well." Shanesha strode toward the raised table.

Jeevan and Abu came to stand on Ben's left, with Khepri, Ssherrss, and Ali forming the line to Louisa's right.

Esther edged between Abu and Ben, jostling both of them. "Excuse me," she said in Greek.

Abu grinned from ear to ear at the emotionless Alexandrian officer. Ben shook his head and stepped forward, arm in arm with Louisa. Every inhuman eye bore into them as they made their way between the poles of dancing blue flames.

They passed hundreds of welves sitting at the side tables. All of the immortals, with their ghost-like complexions, tried to outdo the other wraiths with extravagant tunics, dresses, and hairstyles. Scattered among the albino courtesans were many collared humans. In various stages of undress, the physical attributes of these slaves gave away their intended function. Ben pushed down his revulsion.

Focusing on one table, Ben spied a handsome twenty-year-old man sitting on the floor beneath a welven woman lounging in the seat above him. He stared in anticipation of his next command, like a dog with his master, while she rubbed her hand through his hair without thinking.

A whisper from Louisa tore Ben away from the disgusting spectacle. "Promise me you will do whatever it takes, so I never become one of those people." Her voice tightened. "Promise me."

Ben looked away. The thought of Louisa being a slave to these reprehensible people took his rage to another level, while being forced to do the unthinkable seared his very soul. Could he do it? Could he, like the defenders of Masada, kill his loved ones to keep them from living such miserable lives?

Anguished, Ben whispered, "I promise."

Louisa gave a grim nod. Ben scouted the head table. A beautiful welven woman with red hair the color of a dragon's fiery breath, , and golden eyes sat on a small throne at the center of the long table. She wore a pure white silk dress, and, like all welves Ben had seen, she appeared to be no older than her late twenties.

Behind the throne stood a babiakhom, and farther back along the wall were many servants, including more human slaves. To either side of the throne sat several welven men. Drawn to the strange group sitting to the left of the governess, Ben tried to make sense of the trio.

Abu said in a hushed tone, "It's a dwarf. Do you see the dwarf?"

Ben focused on the man sitting farthest left. The short mountain of a man had to be no more than five feet tall but weighed at least two hundred and fifty pounds. His long, braided blond beard and human complexion reminded Ben of a Viking warrior. The half-shaved head with a long ponytail tied to the top was similar to that of a seated Japanese warrior Ben had seen in a British gazette. The specific name of these fighters escaped him.

To the right of the miniature bull-man sat a tall woman—or did she merely seem tall in comparison?—whose face, hair, and eyes were the spitting image of the woman on the throne, except for her very pinkish human skin tone. A shorter but powder-pale woman with the same facial features as the two redheads at the table was next in line. No doubt related to the other two, her striking silver hair and muted brown eyes were incongruent by welven standards.

Ben came to a sudden stop when Louisa pulled him back. He had not noticed Shanesha come to a halt twenty feet from the main table. Their liaison raised his voice and spoke in the welven tongue, but Ben heard his words translated into English close to his ear while the actual Eblan echoed farther away.

"Lady Inanna, may I present our esteemed visitors? Miss Louisa Sophia and Dr. Benjamin McGehee will speak for them."

At the mention of their names, Louisa curtsied, and Ben gave a slight bow. Together, they took another step. Before he could speak, the governess smiled and leaned closer.

She placed her hands on the table and gazed down at them. "Miss Sophia and Dr. McGehee, the people of the city of Nippur welcome you. May Ereshkigal bless you. Please accept my friendship during your stay."

They worship the goddess of the underworld. Great.

Ben settled on being direct as their best strategy to free them from the clutches of the welves. For his pre-planned speech, Ben chose Greek and matched Shanesha's volume. "Governess Inanna, Lady of the Sky, thank you for receiving us. We appreciate the kindness you and the people of Nippur have shown." He smiled. "Please let us know how we can be of service to you while we are visiting your wondrous city. After our visit, we humbly ask for your permission to continue our expedition to the Tomb of Mortals, where we plan to study the Ancients' language."

The governess leaned back, but her smile never wavered. "Dr. McGehee, thank you for your kind offer. I'm sure we can deepen our friendship through the mutual sharing of information. I am curious, though, what exactly do you hope to gain from your study?"

Ben felt foolish continuing this conversation as presumed equals while under house arrest, but he played his part with, he hoped, sincerity. "We arrived recently from Earth and want to return to our home during our lifetimes. As of now, the hysakas can power the Seba device only once every five hundred An."

He raised his chin and waved his hand, palm up. He put as much confidence as he could into his next words. "We believe the Ancients would never have created a device like the Seba without a way to use it at will. Professor Ali Mousa here is a Keeper of the Seba." Ben pointed toward Ali at the end. The professor bowed his head. "He is working with us to find the Ancients' magic source to power the Seba again.

"The Keeper's goal was to bring us to help fight the ripvor because Earth possesses many new weapons not found on Aaru. Unfortunately, the most powerful weapons did not come with us because of a mishap. Of equal importance, the weapons we brought have limited projectiles, and we cannot make more. Our hope is if we can find some clue on how we can activate the Seba again, we can return to Earth and bring everything we would need for Aaru to withstand and even destroy the ripvor."

Ben glanced to his left as Esther's shoulder brushed against his arm. He leaned away from the young woman to stay focused on the governess.

With furrowed brow, the governess whispered to the man on her right. He nodded. She then looked toward Ali. "Keeper Mousa, you were not traveling with Dr. McGehee. Can you explain what your group was doing while they went to seek the Ancients' magic source?"

Ali stepped forward. "As Dr. McGehee stated, because of a mistake, we could not bring all the weapons we needed to defeat the ripvor."

He frowned. "While Dr. McGehee pursued the Ancients' power source, we were traveling to Memphis to see if any of the priests had the knowledge to reproduce bullets." He rubbed the stubble of his chin. "Bullets are what we call the projectiles shot from the weapons called guns."

The governess said, "I hope you do not mind if I confirm what you say is the truth."

Ali nodded. "Not at all."

The man to Innana's left said something to the babiakhom, and a few moments later, a large hysakas walked from the shadows up to Ali. He towered over the professor, who stood more than a foot shorter. The wolf-man enveloped Ali's hand in his.

Ben fought his increasing anxiety.

What the hell is happening? How can they tell if he's telling the truth?

Louisa squeezed his arm and whispered, "Life singers can do that."

Ben thought about the ramifications of this lie-detection magic while listening to Ali repeat what he had said. When he finished, the hysakas turned to the governess. "He speaks the truth."

Ben hoped they would not use this truth magic on the rest of them. He gave a prayer of thanks that he hadn't revealed any essential information to Ali.

As the hysakas walked away, the governess said, "This is a disappointing yet interesting development. We had hoped to learn all about you and your weapons. We must defend ourselves from others who might gain access to such things." She paused a beat, her eyes drifting to the table. Her radiant smile returned with her eyes full of certainty. "Dr. McGehee, I will grant your expedition safe passage upon four conditions."

Ben gave her a quick nod, knowing he had no bargaining power.

"Several of our representatives will go with you to observe your research. Second, you will share your findings with our representatives before returning to Alexandria. They will determine whether you may proceed. Third, before you leave Nippur, one of you must demonstrate how your weapons work and provide us with samples. Do you agree with these stipulations?" She raised her eyebrows.

Ben wished they could give the welves less information, but his group had no leverage.

Louisa whispered, "She said four but listed only three."

Damn, she's right. Ben patted Louisa's hand. *What is the governess up to?*

He painted on a smile. "These stipulations are agreeable to us, Governess. Professor Mousa will meet with your representatives. He can provide you with all our knowledge on the subject." He glanced at the professor.

Ali said, "I'm happy to share everything I know."

Ben asked, "And your fourth stipulation?"

"We will discuss it in private." The governess set her jaw.

Ben nodded.

Inanna spoke to the group. "I'm pleased we will work together *as friends*. Now, we've prepared a meal and entertainment for you." She gestured toward the large empty table on Ben's right.

Shanesha made eye contact with him and jerked his chin in that direction. They followed the welf to the table. Abu shoved his way between Ben and Esther while Ben assisted Louisa to her seat. As he took his chair, he sensed a change in the assembled guests' mood.

Heads swiveled toward the elevator with an audible "Ahh."

Surrounded by eight welven soldiers, a man with his arms and neck locked in a wooden stockade shuffled through the doors. Cuffed by leg irons connected with a short chain, the man waddled to keep pace with his captors.

Louisa shuddered. The fear on her face turned to a look of hatred. Ben squeezed her hand.

"That's the elf who kidnapped and tortured me," she said through clenched teeth. "I watched them stab him over and over. How is he alive?"

As the prisoner made his way forward, Ben noticed the pointy ears on the handsomest man he'd ever seen. He saw red and gripped Louisa's hand harder.

She pulled away and smiled, rubbing her hand.

"Sorry," Ben said. His gaze snapped back to the unfolding scene.

The guards and their prisoners stopped where Ben's group had stood. The room went as quiet as death. Ben looked for Shanesha and beckoned him over with a barely perceptible nod.

The liaison kneeled between their chairs, asking in Greek, "Can I help you?"

Ben said, "Please, explain this."

Before the liaison could utter a word, the governess stood and took a small piece of paper from the man on her right. She read, "Iskur, son of Sharum-Itur, first King of the Elves, we find you guilty of countless murders, including your father's. Above all, you are guilty of violating the sacred birthrights." She gave the elf a wicked smile. "For your heinous crimes, we sentence you to death. By what method do you choose?"

The handsome elf grinned. "Ah, Inanna, it has been too long. It would appear that this time will not be as pleasurable as the previous years we spent together."

"Answer the question, you piece of dung. How do you wish to die?" Hatred radiated from the governess's glare.

The elf laughed and said, "With a sword in my hand. I choose death by combat. I will slay as many of you abominations as possible."

With a vengeful smile, the governess said, "As the most aggrieved, I will grant your wish. You will die at the hands of—"

"No. *We* are the most aggrieved!" two voices rang out in unison. On the governess's right stood the two women Ben assumed to be related to her. The silver-haired welven woman put her hand on the shoulder of the taller redhead with the human complexion. "We have lived our entire lives in shame because of our father's violation of your birthrights. Mother, we demand the satisfaction of killing him ourselves."

A gasp came from the crowd. The governess said without emotion, "As you wish. If you fail, my champions will not."

The governess sank into her seat, deflated. The noise of the crowd rose in thrilled anticipation. Ben and Louisa turned to Shanesha.

The welf's smile had disappeared, and disgust dripped from his voice. "I will do my best to explain. The elven trash you see before you is one of our first elders. He was the oldest son of the ruler of Mari. After the awakening of our races, a three-way civil war raged for centuries. Eventually, we split into three nations. The regular humans, we first immortals, the Hum Ùri and the trash Ašte Asag—Pure Bloods and Pointy Demons in your language—each went our separate ways."

He shrugged, his voice normal again. "The humans multiplied as mortals do. They split into many countries or became part of the nations formed from Earthlings who fought in the Lamentations. Regardless of how the war ended, welves and elves continued to hate each other and, to this day, will kill each other on sight."

Louisa asked, "Why do elves and welves despise each other?"

Shanesha rolled his eyes and sighed. "After King Sharum-Itur found the Topek, he experimented on his political opponents. The purebloods were the result. Eventually, my ancestors escaped, but the experiments continued until the king turned his allies into those pointy-eared demons. The king tried to enslave the remaining humans now that he was immortal, but we upset his plans."

With a slight grin, he continued, "The king decided my people were an aberration and set out to exterminate us. At the end of the civil war, we went our separate ways, but Iskur, the king's son, wanted to continue the fight. He killed his father and claimed the throne.

"The elves, weary of fighting, instead banished Iskur. He has been a pariah ever since, but he is still a swordsman of unequaled skill. After forty mortal lifetimes of evil, he will finally face justice."

The crowd buzzed as the two women and the dwarf walked to the center of the great hall. They huddled with their backs to everyone. The women had donned banded armor of solid red and white, each suit gleaming from polished lacquer. The taller woman's red hair blazed from under her pearl-white helmet. The shorter sister's silver hair shone like a star as it flowed down her back against a breastplate of rose red. The bright colors worked to fill in the black-and-white picture of the Japanese warrior in Ben's mind.

Louisa asked, "So, what is a birthright? Why is violating it worse than murder?"

"Most of the human nations born of the first fathers have abandoned the old ways, but we have endured." Shanesha laughed. "Because immortal women only become pregnant every hundred An, we have strengthened our ancestor's rituals. When a Hum Ùri woman reaches maturity at age twenty-seven, she may auction her birthright."

With a wave toward the governess, Shanesha said, "Our women live independent lives while we men amass wealth to buy a birthright. When the woman turns one hundred and twenty-seven, she can become pregnant. The man who purchased her birthright will join her household. They stay together until any offspring reaches maturity. Then the cycle repeats. *Does this make sense?*"

He said the last part as if he were talking to a child, but Ben ignored it. "And what exactly is Iskur's birthright crime?"

Shanesha scoffed. "Isn't it plain?"

Ben shrugged.

The welf's golden eyes narrowed. "A little over eight hundred An ago, Iskur killed the welf who had Inanna's next birthright. He then kidnapped her, raped her, and kept her prisoner until the children were several years old. By then, she found herself too attached. She could not do the right thing and give them mercy." Shanesha shook his head. "The half-breed twins live in shame, as neither Hum Ùri nor Ašte Asag. They cannot give away their birthrights."

"That's horrific!" Louisa said. "Those children were innocent and shouldn't have to suffer. Besides, they are both stunning. How could they not find love?"

"Ah, you mortals and your love. Love rarely outlives the centuries, much less millennia." Shanesha laughed. "Very few welves—or even elves, for that matter—will marry, and only a handful of those marriages have survived. As for why the twins cannot find partners, why would anyone taint their bloodline with their defects?"

Before Louisa could reply, the welf held up a pale hand. "Immortals can only breed with each other. Given how we must constantly fight boredom, we indulge with our slaves unless we are raising children."

Ben's stomach lurched with disgust.

Louisa asked, "And why not just kill him?"

Shanesha stood up. "The trial by combat?"

Louisa nodded.

"It's another ancient tradition we have altered. It is how the aggrieved achieve true justice. In the end, it doesn't matter if Iskur kills his children. He will face challengers until he dies. Luckily for Lil and Ki, they were wronged in the same crime. A loophole in the law will allow them to face him together. I still only give them a slight chance of killing him."

"Why is he alive?" Louisa asked. "After I hit him with the rock—you're welcome, by the way—I saw your men stab him many times."

Ben had wanted to know the entire story, but he had refrained from asking to save her from reliving it.

Shanesha bowed, but his eyes were mocking. "Yes, well, thank you. And you're welcome for us saving you from torture and rape."

Louisa slumped, as if his comment had taken the wind out of her.

"Iskur is alive," he said, "because we immortals are difficult to kill. Our bodies never stop healing. Any injury begins to heal immediately but much slower than if a hysakas were to heal us. We could have killed him, but we only wounded him to bring him here. Killing him without giving the governess justice would have been unforgivable in her eyes."

Louisa turned away from the welf. "Thank you, Shanesha." To Ben, it sounded like a dismissal wrapped in appreciation.

"You're welcome. I'm at your service." Shanesha bowed again and went back to his seat behind their table.

The din in the chamber lessened as everyone's attention focused on the center of the room. The dwarf had returned to stand behind a nearby table, and the two sisters had turned toward their father.

Abu leaned in until his shoulder touched Ben's. "That was fascinating. Those Amazons are twins who want to kill their father. And he is the greatest swordsman on Aaru, trying to kill his children because he's the devil incarnate. Hafizna Allah [God, protect us]."

Too late, Ben realized that Abu shouldn't be watching this. It also dawned on him that he didn't want to see this gladiator display himself. How could Ben order his son back to his room when Abu had killed a man the previous day? No, an elf. The young teenager had seen and done too much for Ben to treat him like a child.

As he caught Abu's eye, Ben asked, "Wouldn't you rather return to the room?"

Abu steeled his gaze and replied, "I should, but this man kidnapped Miss Sophia and tried to kill my friends. I want to see him get justice."

With a feeling of resignation, Ben frowned but nodded.

In the arena, the guards unshackled Iskur from his chains and stockade. Ten men carrying crossbows ran forward and formed a loose ring around the elf and the twins. With a swing of his arms and a neck rotation, the elf grinned at the audience. A soldier stepped forward with two short swords. After laying them on the ground, the welf made a hasty retreat. The prisoner sneered with contempt at the man's fear.

Ten yards from the elf, his daughters stood out in their gleaming armor. They brandished several weapons Ben had never seen. Their father looked much less imposing in his tunic and sandals as he bent down to pick up the twin blades. His eyes never left his children as he rose.

The taller woman in the pearl armor held a giant, studded metal club with a large ring at the bottom of the handle. On her belt, she had a coil of chain and a sheathed knife about a foot long. Her sister looked menacing in her blood-colored helmet, breastplate, bracers, and greaves. She held a hand scythe with a chain connected to the bottom of the handle in her right hand and had the other end of the chain in her left. A long, curved sword in its sheath poked over her shoulder.

The last whispers of the crowd faded as the audience held its collective breath. At the silence, the governess stood. "My Daughters, may Ereshkigal, goddess of the underworld, grant you the revenge you seek. Begin." She sat, and all eyes latched onto the warriors.

Iskur yelled in an insolent tone, "I have admired the stories of my daughters' exploits. It's a shame that you choose to die."

The redhead sneered. "Lil and I have spent the last eight hundred An preparing for this reunion. You will find your confidence misplaced."

The silver-haired sister, Lil, remained silent. Then they moved as one, closing the space between them and their villainous father. White-clad Ki moved to the left while red-clad Lil moved to his right. The ball connected to the chain in Lil's left hand swung out. In that first salvo, Iskur almost made a fatal mistake as he stepped back and to his left.

Ki aimed for Iskur's waist with her giant club. She held the ring on the end with both hands, rotating her entire body. The club should have crippled the elf, but Iskur fell and kicked backward.

The head of the club had whipped over the elf so close that one stud tore his tunic. Iskur's fall turned into a roll. As he came to his feet, he parried a sweeping strike from Lil's scythe aimed at his knee. Then he danced away from an overhead strike by Ki's club.

She switched to a hand-over-hand grip and brought the heavy weapon down with astonishing speed.

Ben expected the lightning-quick elf to step around the club and strike at Ki. Instead, he jumped over Lil's spinning ball and chain, which came at him from behind.

The crowd oohed.

The twins' two-pronged attacks from different angles kept Iskur from going on the offense. The crowd repeatedly gasped, thinking the twins had dealt a death blow. Each time, the wily elf contorted himself out of harm's way.

Like everyone in the room, Ben fell into a rhythm of heart-pounding anticipation, followed by a stomach-lurching shock when the expected bloodbath did not happen.

The twins might have fallen into the same trance. They struck out again in tandem. Instead of going under the fast-moving club aimed at his stomach, Iskur surprised everyone by diving over the barbed cudgel. He landed headfirst and rolled up into a spinning crouch. The crowd shrieked, as Iskur's right-handed sword severed Ki's armored leg just below the knee.

"Holy shit!" Abu gasped.

Ki screamed and fell, her club skittering away. Screams echoed from the onlookers.

Iskur came out of the crouch. He used his left sword to block Lil's scythe as it tore toward his head. His right hand free, Iskur pushed his now-bloodied sword through the lacquered rose plating that protected Lil's stomach. The blade penetrated the tough armor by only an inch, but she recoiled in pain.

Iskur wore a cruel smile. "Lil, let us embrace one last time." He rammed his sword through his daughter until several inches of steel burst through her armored back. Lil's eyes bulged. Her scythe and chain clattered to the marble floor.

The father's and daughter's faces were inches apart when he brought his left-handed sword behind his head to strike her down with a killing blow.

A small metal ball trailing a chain flew from behind the elf and wrapped several times around his wrist.

The metal rope was held by Ki, half lying in a pool of blood. With her severed leg thrown several feet away, she had somehow still pulled on the chain with both hands.

A smile spread across Lil's face. She grabbed Iskur's wrist, locking him and the blade, while impaling her in place. She reached over her shoulder and said, "Goodbye, Father."

When her long sword came free, Iskur's eyes went wide. He then grew desperate, struggling to escape the twin restraints holding his wrists in place.

In one swift motion, Lil released her grip on Iskur's wrist, stepped backward, and brought her blade down with both hands. The sword impaling his daughter popped free with an ear-piercing screech as Lil's blade sliced through his collarbone. It cleaved through Iskur's torso and exited above his right hip.

With a stunned look, Iskur turned to stare at his freed sword.

In revolting slow motion, the top part of the dead elf slid toward the ground just moments before his legs buckled, and his lower half went to his knees. Lil staggered backward and crumpled to the floor while Ki loosened her grip.

The metal links ran through Ki's hands as her father's body half-squished, half-slammed onto the marble floor. She closed her eyes and lay back.

In shock, everyone watched in silence. Four hysakas rushed to the fallen twins. One hysakas grabbed Ki's severed leg and placed it back below her knee. Two other hysakas laid hands on the bloody nub, and the leg began to knit together. The fourth hysakas laid hands on the unconscious Lil. The trickle of blood seeping from her back slowed and stopped.

Several slaves ran forward with a small wheelbarrow and removed the two halves of Iskur. Other slaves cleaned the blood-spattered floor. The crowd grew noisy as the hysakas worked.

After twenty minutes, four slaves placed the twins on stretchers. They rose and brought the wounded twins to their mother's raised table. The governess stood, and silence reigned again.

One hysakas spoke, "Both shall live."

Inanna smiled, held her arms wide, and looked around the room. "Let messengers go throughout Kutha, carrying the news. The devil Iskur is dead, slain in combat by my daughters Ki and Lil. Let all Kutha celebrate these welven heroes. May their legacy be etched into the histories of our people. Let no one speak of their shame ever again."

The crowd went wild. Stomping and clapping, everyone cheered. A chant grew from a whisper in the din to a shout, "Hail, Ki! Hail, Lil!"

The chant went on for a good minute before the governess raised her hand. "Let my daughters rest." The stretchers and the attending hysakas moved toward the elevator. The governess looked at Ben and said, "Dr. McGehee, your party will stay in Nippur until my daughters fully recover. They will be my representatives."

Ben pushed his chair back and stood. "Of course, Governess. It will be our honor."

She smiled and turned back to the room. "Let the celebration begin."

Chapter 6

Nippur, Choru, An 5660, Day 8

Abu's heart raced. He had never seen anything like this. *Amazing.*

He sensed Dr. Ben pushing away from the table next to him. A firm tug at his shirt pulled Abu out of his seat and his state of rapture. Forced to look away from the naked and very provocative dance troupe, Abu frowned at his guardian.

Dr. Ben pointed toward the elevator at the far end of the great room. "Time to go."

The doors to the elevator closed, blocking out the carnival atmosphere of the great hall. On the ride down, Abu thought back to the troubling moments at the beginning of the night. Conflicted, he didn't pay much attention to their surroundings as the group went through the palace to their assigned rooms. Even seeing a tipsy Louisa clinging to Dr. Ben's arm couldn't distract him from his worry.

Abu didn't want to believe that Esther would threaten anyone he cared about, but he couldn't deny what he had seen. When Dr. Ben had spoken to the governess, Abu caught the glint of a blade in Esther's hand. During the exchange about guns, she had a look of determined dread, and her muscular body resembled a spring under tension.

Abu grasped his revolver, ready to defend the man who had come to be his family. Yet how could he use his gun against the woman who filled his every other thought with longing? A scant day earlier, he had used the same gun to save her life during the kidnapping attack.

What the hell is happening?

The entire surreal moment had ended when the veracity of Ali's story held up under the life singer's lie-detecting test. Afterward, Esther's shoulders slumped, and she closed her eyes. Abu had wiped his sweating palms against his pant legs. He tried to dismiss the threat as his overactive imagination.

With so much happening after those few weird moments, Abu concentrated on the strange events in the hall. First, there had been the gory, palpitation-inducing fight, followed by his having a front-row seat to the world's most extraordinary menagerie.

Overwhelmed by all the sights and sounds, Abu sat in awe as dozens of entertainers performed fantastic feats. His favorite—other than the last act—had been a giant puppet routine performed by a trio of babiakhom wind singers. While the creatures floated around the great hall with wings spread wide, confetti coalesced around their bodies, morphing them into giant frogs. Three to four times larger than the baboon-like creatures inside, these magic puppets acted out a play reminiscent of one of Aesop's fables: *The Frogs Who Wished for a King*.

The frogs' skin, made of countless strips of sparkling green paper, shimmered as they croaked to the heavens. They used no human language, but Abu assumed the once unfettered and frolicking frogs had begged the gods for a king out of boredom. Several times during their pleas, red-paper tongues shot from gaping mouths, snagging giant flying insects and yanking the confetti bugs into waiting maws to be gulped down.

For the play's finale, shards of sparkling green exploded away from one wind singer. The frog transformed into a giant crane as thousands of white and gray feathers floated over and around the puppeteer. The play ended with the frogs' new king, the feathered bird, gobbling up the remaining frogs to the explosive applause of the audience.

As they turned into their assigned corridor, Esther said something to Jeevan before she moved away from their quarters. Abu decided in that instant to keep an even closer eye on the dimaerites—if that were possible—hoping to dismiss his suspicious feelings.

Putting as much excitement into his voice as possible, Abu asked Dr. Ben, "May I go tell Umrao about the party? I want to tell him how much he missed. I'll catch up to Esther. She just headed that way." He grinned. "I'll feed and rub down the horses, too."

Louisa stumbled a step, and Dr. Ben grabbed her around the waist. Without looking at Abu, Dr. Ben said, "Okay, but go straight there and back. Are you sure you remember the way?"

Abu nodded. "Yes, sir. I'll be back in an hour."

Louisa had pulled Dr. Ben's arm and was whispering into his ear. With a wave, Abu took advantage of the distraction and headed in the direction Esther had gone. He sped up to a fast walk as soon as he turned the corner. He didn't want to run but needed to catch up to the Alexandrian soldier.

With the party still going on, every sound seemed eerie in the deserted palace halls. On reaching the intersection where he needed to take a right, Abu glimpsed Esther's blue chiton dress turning a corner down the corridor to his left. The sounds of more than one pair of sandals bounced down the hallway to where he stood. Confused, he hesitated.

What could possibly go wrong?

Abu shrugged and trotted down the hallway in pursuit. As he reached the next junction, he peeked. Esther and one of her soldiers turned to the right. After counting to five, Abu tip-toed to the next hallway as fast as he could. Greeted by the sounds of a subdued Greek conversation, he poked one eye around the corner. Esther and the accompanying Lochem soldier stood in the corridor while she spoke to an Alexandrian soldier in full armor. He had a short sword at his waist and held a polished silver shield.

The soldier said, "The consular general just returned from the party. Wait a moment. I will see if he is available." The man turned to the door before facing Esther again. "Who is your message for?"

Esther said, "Polemarchos Alexandria ben Zev i Hurasu. It's urgent I send her an update."

The Greek soldier nodded and disappeared.

Abu put his back to the wall until he heard the door open again. Risking another look, he saw Esther disappear into the room. He pulled back as the soldier with the silver shield and her Lochem escort set up guard on either side of the door.

It makes sense she would want to tell her mother about our detour.

With a shake of his head, Abu headed toward the stables. His mission tonight had gone as far as he could take it. As he rounded another corner, he realized he must have taken a wrong turn. So much of the palace looked the same.

As Abu made a slow circle in the middle of the intersection, he tried to remember where he had gone wrong. A silver rope hung down one wall to waist height and ended in a tasseled pull. He remembered Shanesha telling them to pull the cord if they needed anything, so he tugged it and waited.

Seconds later, Abu heard a commotion coming down the passage behind him. He glanced over his shoulder as a young girl of about eight ran toward him. An older man with gray fringe around his balding head was chasing after her.

That was fast. They don't have to run.

As the girl drew closer, her golden slave collar bounced from chin to shoulder. A sour knot formed in the pit of Abu's stomach. He glanced toward the man and saw a similar choker.

At the far end of the hallway, three welves raced around a corner and shouted at the escaping pair. The girl sped up into a full-out sprint as fear flashed across her face. She seemed to notice Abu for the first time and yelled at him and waved.

He didn't need to be fluent in the welven tongue to understand the universal gesture to run. Before Abu could react, a tall, thin welf with raven-black hair and red eyes hurled a knife at the older man. The blade struck the man in the back, and he screamed as he fell.

In shock, Abu couldn't move. His feet seemed stuck in place.

The girl reached Abu and grabbed his shirt, turning him around. She dragged him after her. He popped out of his trance as if pulled from a sucking mud.

Move. Ealayk allaena [Damn it].

Abu stumbled along with the girl.

In full panic, the servant girl let go and ran down the hall away from him. As Abu stepped after her, a war cry followed them. Heart pounding, he raced to catch up. She turned the next corner ten yards ahead of him. He sprinted round the turn and came to a faltering stop in the empty passageway.

"Psst."

One frightened eye stared at him from a crack in the wall. The sound of their pursuers followed him through the slim opening the girl had made. As soon as he stepped inside, she closed the hidden door and slid a bolt into place.

Enveloped by complete darkness, Abu strained to listen. The sounds of sandals and boots pounded past their bolt hole. As the footsteps grew farther away, he exhaled but couldn't calm down. In the oppressive blackness, he felt as if he were back in the unlit tunnels under the Tomb of Jonah.

While he tried to regain control of himself, Abu gripped the wooden handle of the revolver he didn't remember pulling from its holster. When a small hand touched his arm, he about jumped out of his skin.

Still trembling, Abu turned toward the touch that beckoned him farther into the darkness. He holstered his gun and held an arm out front to take small, shuffling steps forward.

It couldn't have been more than a few minutes, but to the newly blind teenager, it seemed like hours before he heard a door creaking. The girl pulled him forward a few more steps, and the door screeched to a close behind them.

Without sight, Abu sniffed the air, trying to understand his surroundings. The soapy smells of citrus and cypress filled the room. He winced as a spark flared, and a gas-fed wall sconce flickered to life. It took him a few seconds to shake the spots out of his vision and for the room to become clear.

Brooms and dusters hung from one wall while shelves covered the others. Different sizes of metal and pottery containers sat on the shelves. Next to the door, the young girl eyed him with caution. Her brown eyes watered, but she didn't let herself cry.

In the fright of the chase, Abu hadn't made the connection, but the girl appeared to be of mixed Asian descent. He held his hands open and kept his voice gentle. "I'm not going to hurt you." Then he switched to Greek. "Do you speak Greek?"

The girl cocked her head in confusion. A long braid of stringy brown hair hung to her shoulder.

"Do you speak Aaruan?" Abu asked in the planet's most common language. She shook her head.

That's good because I only know a few words.

Abu tried to think of a way to communicate with the frightened girl. His eyes landed on a large metal tin on a nearby shelf. He chuckled as he read the cuneiform words for olive oil.

The girl's forehead furrowed. Abu held his hand in front of her and drew invisible lines and dots on his palm, creating the word *read*. She nodded.

Great. Now we just need something to write with.

After he had put that word on his hand, the girl crossed to the far shelves. She returned with a piece of white chalk and a clipboard covered in Sumerian writing. Abu translated a few words out of curiosity before using his sleeve to erase the inventory list.

The two of them sat on the floor with the chalkboard between them. He wrote, *Why kill you?*

The young girl took the chalk and wrote, *We heard untranslatable Hum Ùri untranslatable kill untranslatable untranslatable.*

Abu understood. *The old man and the girl heard those welves plot to kill someone. What if they are planning to kill us?*

Abu took back the chalk. Not having mastered more of the Sumerians' written language frustrated him, and he promised to rectify that deficiency. Like a toddler, he wrote, *Hum Ùri kill my people?*

She shook her head and used her finger to underline the words for *Hum Ùri*.

To confirm, he wrote, *Hum Ùri kill Hum Ùri?*

She nodded.

He paused a second in thought, then asked, *Who you tell?*

Her brown eyes moved left and right several times, and she frowned while writing, *No one untranslatable untranslatable. Hum Ùri find me untranslatable kill me. Help.*

Trembling, she stared at him.

He scribbled, *You family?*

A glint of hope flashed in her eyes as she snatched the chalk and wrote, *Not here.* The girl pulled a small coin from her pocket and held it out to Abu on an open palm.

He picked up the tarnished coin and peered closely. On the first side was a triangle with an inverted triangle inside. It looked like three small triangles stacked to form the bigger one. He flipped it over and found three flowers over a stand of leaves.

Abu pointed at the coin and then at the cuneiform for *family.*

She gave two quick nods.

He scribbled, *Name.* He pointed at his chest. "Abu."

She pointed at him. "Abu." She turned her finger to herself and said, "Masako." Then her finger hovered over the word *Help.* She raised her eyebrows.

Abu thought, *What would Dr. Ben do?*

Dr. Ben would do the right thing. No matter the cost. But what would happen to them if Abu took the girl to Dr. Ben, and his guardian told the governess? Abu knew of two possibilities. They might get a reward or lose their heads.

Abu couldn't take that chance.

I'll need some help, but I can do it, Abu thought as the inkling of a plan formed.

With a big smile, he wrote, *I help you. Where my people horses?*

She jumped toward him and wrapped her arms around his neck, sobbing. With her face buried in his shoulder, the gold band around her neck dug into his collarbone. Enveloping her in a hug, Abu channeled the pain into white-hot anger.

———————————————

It took them an hour, going from one hidden servant's passage to another, to reach a tunnel that exited into a tool closet in the stables. Abu poked his head out and wrinkled his nose at the smell of animal manure and straw.

With the way clear, he looked back at the girl and held his hand up. "Wait here." He pointed at the ground.

"Heam," she affirmed with a nod.

Abu closed the door behind him. He walked down the path between stalls until he reached the wide wooden doors at the end. Set to the left was a human-size door, and he opened it into a courtyard.

"Abu? How did you get in there?" Sowar Singh asked.

Startled, Abu put on his most innocent smile. "Oh. Hi, Gian. I must have come in the back. Have you seen Umrao?"

"He's over there talking with the Alexandrian officer." The sowar pointed to the other side of the gas-lit courtyard.

As if he'd eaten a stone, Abu's stomach sank when he saw two shadows standing close together.

I don't have time for this.

"Thanks." Abu tried to appear nonchalant as he walked across the cobbled yard.

Umrao and Esther solidified from the shadows with their hands linked. Abu's jaws clenched. Even though he stomped his shoes against the stone, the pair didn't notice him at all.

Abu said, "Umrao. I need your help."

His friend sighed and broke eye contact with the much shorter Esther. "I'm a little busy."

Abu counted to three. "I hate to interrupt, but it's an emergency. Can you help me in the stables?"

Esther let go of his hand and patted Umrao's arm. She said in Greek, "It's okay. I will see you tomorrow."

Umrao's wide grin made Abu want to punch him in the face, but his jealousy withered at the thought of the big brown eyes of the little girl whose life now depended on him.

Chapter 7

Nippur, Choru, An 5660, Day 9

"You asked for me, Mother?" Lil scrutinized her mother's face, looking for some hint about the reason for the summons, but, as usual, she found nothing.

Her mother, the governess, sat in an oversize cushioned chair in front of a crackling fire. Like Lil's sister, her mother had flaming red hair, streaked with yellow. A pair of drinks sat on a small table between her mother's chair and an adjacent one. The governess waved toward the empty seat. "I need to speak with you regarding the Earthlings before you meet with them."

"And Ki?" Lil asked as she sat down.

"You should inform your sister of this meeting. I did not want to slow her recovery." Inanna's golden eyes twinkled. The infrequent event meant that whatever her mother was about to share would be of tremendous benefit to the governess. She leaned toward Lil and said, "Yesterday, I learned how the Lion's Pride has been countering all our recent moves. I plan to use this information to cripple them."

Lil raised her eyebrows with an unspoken question.

"They have been copying the messages we send by courier. Somehow, they also obtained our cipher."

Lil's mind reeled. She grabbed the crystal glass on the table and took two quick sips. A honeyed sweetness caressed her taste buds, easing the burn of the grape brandy as it hit the back of her throat.

How long had this been going on? Her mother's faction used thirty different couriers. To compromise one courier would be of limited value but workable. To have compromised them all seemed impossible. "How did they do it?" She put the drink down.

Inanna sighed. "My aide takes the letters directly to the couriers' office. She places them in a locked box until the manager can pass the letter to the next messenger in the rotation." She shook her head. "Damn metal singers dug a tunnel under the box and have been copying the letters."

That seemed plausible to Lil, except for the timing. It would take time to copy a coded letter. How would she do it? It dawned on her that the letters were always one courier behind. Since neither the aid nor the messengers dared read the notes, no one knew their contents. They would swap the most recent letter with the previous one. Because the office never closed, the worst that could happen was for a missive to leave the office eight hours later.

Ki would never have figured it out. Lil loved her sister, but clever she was not. Lil was sly and contemplative, like her mother, whereas Ki was brash and straightforward with little guile. In an instant, Lil understood how her mother would leverage this new knowledge.

Lil settled back in the chair. "You will use the Earthlings as bait for a trap using a false story."

"I knew you would understand." The words came without emotion or a hint of praise. Lil's mother shielded her daughters from an intolerant society. Still, the only emotion her mother ever expressed to her and her sister was resentment.

After several lifetimes of hating her mother, Lil had come to accept their relationship. Maybe a thousand An from now, her mother would see her and her sister in a different light. Until then, Lil would do her part to keep her mother and their faction in power.

She said, "I need more details."

With the slightest hint of a smile, Inanna picked up a folded piece of paper from the table and handed it to Lil. "The Lion's Pride is having a meeting of their leadership in two days. They are holding it in their stronghold outside the city. The letter says that I have told the Earthlings I will enslave them unless they attack the meeting. With surprise and their weapons, I promise the recipient that the Earthlings should be able to wipe out most of our opposition's leadership."

The underhandedness of the plan made Lil respect her mother even more as she said, "The Earthlings are not just bait, but also your scapegoat. Impressive."

Her mother nodded. "The Earthlings are of no real consequence to us now. If some survive the Lion's trap, continue to the Tomb of Mortals with them. They may still prove useful by uncovering some of the Ancients' knowledge for us to exploit."

"And their weapons?" Lil asked.

Inanna grimaced—another rarity. "I just met with our best academicians. They spent all morning with the Keeper, learning everything they could about the Earthlings' so-called guns. They said they now understand the principles behind the weapons but that it will take six months to a year to create a simpler version we can use. It may take years to equal the Earthlings' current weapons because of something the Keeper called chemistry."

Lil looked over the details of the letter one last time. She handed it to her mother and stood. "I understand. I'm already late."

Inanna grabbed her daughter's wrist. "Do not put yourselves in danger. Use that hideous fool who trails after your sister to spring the trap. Let him lead the way at the Tomb of Mortals as well."

And there it was. Her mother's concern.

Inanna let go. "Don't embarrass me now that you have won our family a little honor."

Lil rolled her eyes and sighed. "Of course, mother. We would never want to be an embarrassment to you."

Chapter 8

Nippur, Choru, An 5660, Day 9

Louisa's head threatened to explode, but the queasiness in her gut worried her the most. After consuming copious amounts of wine and food the previous night, she wondered whether ridding herself of her stomach's contents might not be a bad idea. Her hangover brought back memories of waking up on Aaru with this same feeling of spinning.

I don't need this to become a habit.

After the fight to the death, the banquet had become quite a spectacle. Acrobats, dancers, and singers provided entertainment while servers offered dishes familiar and exotic. Louisa couldn't remember her cup of delicious spiced wine ever running dry.

How much did I drink?

Louisa's memories of the evening grew more and more scattered until there was nothing. She could not recall when they left the party or how she made it home. She dug into the void, unearthing several hazy scenes of sexual debauchery. There were lewd and lascivious acts by two or more welves and others involving welves and their human slaves. She was not prudish, by any means, but just recalling what she'd witnessed made her flush with embarrassment.

Soon Louisa remembered less fuzzy scenes. She had confronted Ali and made it known she had her eye on him. Then the Good Doctor excused their group and hustled them all back to their rooms. Before she could search deeper, a loud knock on her door sent a cannonball bouncing around her skull, killing all other thoughts. Louisa lay still.

Go away.

Each rap felt like a giant BOOM as she struggled to her feet and made her way to the door. As she reached for the knob, a third wave of blasts began. Holding one hand to her aching head, she yanked the door open. A giant silk-clad and furred body filled the door frame.

"What do you want, Khepri?" Louisa whispered.

Her huge hysakas friend bent down until her head appeared inside the opening. Khepri placed a large, black-skinned paw on Louisa's shoulder. She chuckled deep in the back of her throat. "Did you drink too much, my friend?"

Louisa grabbed her head with both hands. "Stop shouting. Damn it. Are you trying to torture me?"

All of a sudden, between one throb and the next, the nausea in Louisa's midsection and the pain in her head eased. Louisa looked at her friend, whose eyes smiled back. A feeling of warmth flowed through Louisa's body until the pain she'd felt moments ago ceased.

With a sheepish grin, Louisa said, "Thanks. Sorry I yelled. If I knew you could do that, I would have knocked on your door as soon as I woke up."

Khepri patted her shoulder. "No need to apologize. Next time, though, you need to know that we hysakas make it a point not to cure hangovers unless paid a hefty fee. If we did it for free, even for our friends, the number of drunks would grow out of control."

"I'll remember that when I open that second bottle of wine. By the way, did I do anything embarrassing? My memory is a little spotty."

The big wolf-woman said, "Does telling Ben you thought he was handsome and asking him to kiss you count?" Khepri flashed a toothy canine grin, and laughter rumbled from deep inside her.

Dear Lord, Louisa thought.

A tunnel-vision view of her trying to kiss Ben when he brought her to her room popped into Louisa's head. Before she could feel her embarrassment, she remembered it. Ben smiled and turned down her advances while holding her shoulders to keep her at arm's length.

A flickering image of his smug expression turned Louisa's chagrin to anger. She knew she had no right to be mad. Ben had been the perfect gentleman, but even with her head pounding, she felt the sting of rejection.

With her cheeks growing hot, Louisa asked, "Did everyone see?"

The wolf shook her head. "Abu had gone to visit Umrao, and almost everyone else was in their rooms. Ssherrss and Ali were the only ones who saw the spectacle." She chuckled. "Despite being so stoic, that little stirithy gossip couldn't wait to tell me."

Louisa sighed. "I suppose it could've been worse. But his head will swell, and he'll never let me live it down."

"I doubt that," Khepri said. "Anyway, come to lunch. We are meeting our new traveling companions this morning."

Perked up by the news, Louisa let Khepri in and headed toward the bathroom. Then she turned to face her friend. "Do you mean we get to meet the twins? Last night, they were on their deathbeds. Is there anything life singers can't cure?"

"Death." Khepri shut the door.

Now dressed in her favorite floor-length, blue Grecian dress, Louisa followed Khepri and a servant through the palace maze. The ageless young woman with purple eyes led them to the twins' quarters. As Louisa entered the reception room, Ben and Jeevan were chatting on the far side of a table that took center stage.

Next to Ben, Ali spoke with Abu and Esther while Ssherrss sat at the table. The fox-like stirthy sat like a disgruntled child with his arms crossed and feet swinging back and forth.

Ki, the stunning redheaded half-elf, lay on a long, padded bench at the far end of the table. She rubbed at her leg while sipping from a chalice made of chocolate-colored crystal. Amazed, Louisa couldn't even see a scar on the once-severed leg. Along the wall and somewhat out of the way stood a babiakhom and several servants.

Louisa felt a presence behind her and turned. Lil, with her long, flowing silver hair, glided into the room, followed by the squat yet solid dwarf from the previous night. The shorter half-welf twin towered over Louisa and oozed danger like a panther on the hunt.

Ki said, "Where the hell have you been? I'm famished. Was about to get started without you. I've met everyone except for those two, which gives me the first selection." The song of the babiakhom wind singer translated Ki's speech in its usual seamless, continuous fashion.

Lil shrugged at her sister before turning to the room. "Hello, everyone. My sister and I are pleased to meet you. We look forward to joining you on the visit to the Tomb of Mortals. Our friend Thoresten will come with us as well." She stepped over to Louisa and stuck out her arm. "I am Lil of Nippur. Pleasure to meet you."

Louisa remembered how Esther had grasped Abu's forearm when they'd first met, and she did the same with Lil. "Louisa Sophia, a pleasure. I look forward to getting to know you better on this trip." Louisa's voice grew stern. "I'm grateful you and your sister brought that bastard to justice. I owed him a debt as well."

With a sly grin, Lil said, "Glad we could help. I hope we become better acquainted. I'm sure my sister will insist that you do. Excuse me." She then moved away to grasp arms with Khepri.

Taking her place, the dwarf stepped up to Louisa and grasped her forearm. A few inches taller than the dwarf, Louisa met his serious gaze and muscular yet not uncomfortable gesture of greeting. "It's a pleasure to meet you. I'm Louisa Sophia."

Thoresten gave a slight bow of his head. His deep bass voice sounded like distant thunder and almost drowned out the translation in the foreground. "It is very nice to meet you, Louisa Sophia. I am Thoresten Odachi. May you be healthy and happy."

He made to move away, but Louisa held firm. "Mr. Odachi, pardon me for being forthright. You are the first dwarf we have met on Aaru. When there is time on our journey, I hope you will share the story of your people with us."

With a sparkle in his eyes, he said, "It is an honor to tell the legend of the Sygnafylki. At the first campfire, until then."

Louisa let go of his arm. "Thank you."

Thoresten moved toward the rest of the group, and Louisa pivoted to see Lil stop at Ben. The silver-haired beauty leaned in and whispered into his ear. Ben's face turned a splotchy red.

Louisa clenched her jaws. When Lil walked away from Ben, the twin glanced back at Louisa and winked with a gleam of audacity. Louisa tossed her hair and turned her back on the vixen. She moved to meet the other sister, Ki.

With flaming red hair and wearing a white silk dress, the tall warrior welf lay on the padded bench. Firm muscles rippled under her long, supple form. Ki's smile said hello, but her eyes showed something Louisa could not pinpoint.

"Louisa. May I call you Louisa? My desire is that our acquaintance brings us great pleasure." Ki's sultry voice in the background dripped with unmistakable intent. Louisa considered herself a master of reading people, but she struggled to match the fierce warriors of last night with the wanton women of today.

Ki held out her hand to Louisa like a proper lady offering a dainty handshake. Seeing the ritual on Earth that was designed to force weakness upon females had always irritated Louisa. Finding it here on Aaru left her perplexed as well. Not taking the bait from this temptress twin, Louisa grabbed Ki's hand and turned it into a full-on handshake.

She said, "Yes, Ki. Louisa is fine. As I told your sister, thank you for bringing justice to that criminal last night. Most of all, I'm glad you'll recover from such a terrible injury."

Ki's smile became even more provocative as she squeezed to match but not exceed Louisa's hand pressure. "Thank you." She rubbed her leg. "By tomorrow, it will be perfect. I heard about my father's mistreatment of you. There's a way for you to show your appreciation." She tilted her head and raised an eyebrow. "You and your lover, Ben, is that his name? The two of you could join me tonight for a private dinner. I promise dessert will change your life."

Louisa had braced herself for something akin to Ki's bawdy invitation. Having worked her secret profession in the dark underbelly of some of Europe's biggest cities, she had been propositioned by many men and not a few women. Louisa figured that Ki's including Ben in the lewd suggestion was meant to elicit a jealous response from Louisa.

I'll play nice for now. Hussy.

Louisa put on her most gracious smile. "I'm unable to find that kind of pleasure in the company of a woman. Also, I do not share. I hope you understand." Her voice grew icy. "If you can respect my wishes, I'm sure we can work together. As for repayment, I struck the blow allowing your father's capture. So, consider my debt paid in full."

Ki threw her head back and laughed. "For such a little thing, you are full of fire. I like you. If you helped capture Iskur, then it's I who owe the debt. As for your man, I'll respect your wishes. I'm not sure my sister will do the same. Since I can't have fun with either of you, tell me about that dark, ruggedly handsome man." She jutted her chin at someone behind Louisa.

Louisa looked around to see Jeevan laughing with Abu and Thoresten. Louisa warred with herself for a moment. Should she protect her friend from this 650-year-old walking seductress, or should she get out of the way and let him enjoy a little attention?

While considering how best to respond, she noticed that Thoresten's eyes kept moving from his conversation back in her direction. No, he kept looking at Ki. The look of pain in the dwarf's blue eyes sent a bolt of understanding through Louisa. His longing and hurt paid testament to how much Jeevan might lose if he tangled with this welf.

Louisa said, "Jeevan's a wonderful man. He has no lover or wife and can make his own decisions." She locked eyes with Ki. "That said, I ask that you be completely honest with him. Tell him you are going to use him as your plaything and nothing more. If he knows it up front, he can guard his heart. I will be furious if he turns out like your current pet." Louisa's eyes flicked over to Thoresten before boring into Ki's golden irises.

Ki gazed at the dwarf and smiled. "Don't feel sorry for Thoresten. He and I were exclusive lovers for over fifty An. I'm sure he wouldn't trade the passionate love we shared and our current friendship to save his feelings now. Besides, he's had many lovers since. He is fine."

Louisa looked back at the dwarf and the pain hidden there. "Don't be so sure. I see a proud man reduced to being a lovelorn hanger-on." She shrugged. "He is not my concern, but Jeevan is. Treat him right. Do not let him fall in love with you."

Ki laughed. "I can't promise the impossible. Even If he doesn't fall in love with me, I will ruin him for future lovers."

"Oh?" Louisa's voice conveyed her doubt.

"Mortals don't understand. We welves have the bodies and desires of youthful humans combined with centuries of experience. I promise to tell him he is nothing but this moment's distraction, but that is as far as I can go."

Louisa glanced toward Ben, who sat on the other side of the table. With Abu on his left, the chair on the right was still open. Louisa smiled at Ki. "Let's enjoy lunch."

She turned and made her way to the open seat. Out of the corner of her eye, she glimpsed a flash of silver moving around the table. When she reached the empty chair, Louisa came face-to-face with Lil, who asked, "Do you mind if I sit here?"

Louisa felt danger oozing from the welven warrior. She straightened her shoulders and said, "This seat's taken. And so we don't have any future misunderstandings, this *seat* will *always* be *mine*."

The room grew still. All discussions died out as everyone's attention shifted to the pair.

With a predatory expression, Lil looked Louisa up and down, then replied in a dismissive tone, "So you say. We'll see." Her sly smile flashed in Ben's direction.

Louisa resisted the urge to look at Ben. She stepped closer to the welf until her chest bumped into Lil's. The smile evaporated from the welf's face as Louisa growled in a low whisper, "No, we will *not* see. You do not want me as your enemy, or you will make enemies of my tribe. You may be immortal and an incredible warrior, but if we ever come to blows, you'll find out about a new Earth saying: 'You shouldn't bring a knife to a gunfight.'"

Lil laughed. "You're a refreshing surprise. It's been a long time since anyone caught me off-guard." The welf grew serious and pressed her ample bosom against Louisa, pushing her back an inch. "Be careful, little topper, or you may grab a dragon by its tail." She spun and made her way around the table to sit in front of Abu.

Louisa mumbled, "Skýla."

Ben appeared concerned as she took her chair. His eyes darted to the revolver she half-concealed in her right hand. With a sheepish smile, she made the gun disappear.

Ben whispered, "What the hell was that?"

Louisa gave him a sympathetic smile, as she would any child who could not comprehend a grown-up topic. "Establishing a few ground rules with our new traveling companions."

Ben grunted. "It looked like you were about to fight over *me*."

With a pat on his hand, Louisa said, "Don't get a big ego. I'm protecting you from getting in over your head."

The servants brought food to the table as Ben continued in a low voice, "I can look out for myself. Besides, I didn't know you cared."

Louisa stared into his deep blue eyes. "I do. So that we are on the same page, this is me reserving my right to explore that possibility. It's not like you've been subtle with your looks. Don't tell me, Dr. McGehee, that you haven't thought of courting me."

Ben covered his mouth and coughed.

Louisa continued the lecture. "Let me be as clear with you as I was with the twins. I expect you and I to figure out our feelings before considering other offers.

Especially a lewd offer like I received from Ki or the one I'm sure you received from that tart, Lil."

Ben's face turned bright red. He cleared his throat and took a drink from a blue crystal chalice. "I see."

Louisa turned to regard the rest of the table's occupants and said, "I'm sure you do."

Chapter 9

Nippur, Choru, An 5660, Day 10

The door closed with a soft click, and Abu padded down the hall a ways before picking up his pace. During the previous two days, he and Umrao had taken turns bringing food to Masako while she hid in the tunnel connected to the stables. Today, he would make good on his promise to help her.

He and Umrao were supposed to meet an hour before sunrise at the stables. If it were not for the bells that rang every hour on the hour, he would never know the correct time in this strange underworld. The lighting inside the palace never changed, and when he stepped outside, it was always midnight.

Umrao waited in the gas-lit courtyard, pacing and fidgeting. The youngest Lancer kept rubbing his hands together with nervous energy until he saw Abu wave. Umrao paused then started wringing his hands again.

"Stop that," Abu demanded, grabbing his friend's arm.

Umrao hissed, "Where the hell have you been?"

Before Abu could reply, the palace bell rang out the hour. "I'm exactly on time," he said. "Why are you so jumpy?"

The tall Lancer whispered, "The welves were searching the tunnels, and I had to hide her with the horses."

Abu kept his voice low. "She okay?"

With a nod, Umrao turned and opened the door. "Yes. In the stall, under some straw."

Abu walked into the stable with Umrao on his heels. The space bustled with activity because at least half of the Lancers had arrived early to prep the horses for travel. Abu had thought they would have an hour's head start, but the fastidious Lancers had once again exceeded his expectations.

Abu went down to where his pack horses hung their necks over the stall doors. With heads swaying back and forth, they watched all the activity in anticipation. Stacked in the walkway, out of reach of the nosy horses, were several pieces of luggage on top of Dr. Ben's large travel trunk.

When they saw Abu, the dun-colored mare whinnied while the bay nuzzled at his pants. Abu laughed and pulled two apple slices from his pocket. He held one on each palm as the mares used gentle lips and teeth to gobble them down. He tried to locate Masako's hiding spot, but all he could see were piles of straw in the back corners.

Abu put his hand on the gate and said to Umrao, "Let's get started. We'll secure the other bags first."

Before Abu could pull open the door, they turned to the sound of Jeevan's drill sergeant voice. Next to the duffadar stood Commander Shanesha, the platinum-haired, purple-eyed welf. Beside him was a female babiakhom wearing cropped pants and a sleeveless shirt that covered her torso but left her wings free.

"Let me have your attention. Please provide Commander Shanesha and his men with any assistance they need."

Not good.

Shanesha took a step forward and said, "I am sorry to interrupt, but two of the palace staff have gone missing. We want to make sure they have not stowed themselves away."

Abu's face grew hot hearing the commander's speech in his native Arabic. He shared a look with Umrao. The Lancer started rubbing his hands together until Abu elbowed him in the side.

Shanesha gestured over his shoulder, and ten welven soldiers moved past him and Jeevan. Pale welves began rifling through baggage big enough to hide a small child. The teenagers stepped aside as a welf with golden hair and purple eyes went through their luggage.

Queasy nervousness settled into the pit of Abu's stomach. After the welf dropped a handful of loose clothes back into the trunk, he nodded toward the stall.

Think. Think.

As the welf opened the stall door, inspiration struck, and Abu shooed both horses back. He stepped between the mares as the welf started toward the rear of the pen. With a quick pinch, Abu twisted the dun's ear. The horse whinnied, kicked a leg, and lurched forward, trying to bite Abu's hand. With a jerk, he pulled away as the horse's teeth snapped shut.

The welf jumped back and glared at the horse.

Abu shrugged. "Sorry, she doesn't like strangers."

Frowning, the man gave a dismissive wave and walked out of the stall. Abu sighed in relief and flicked his hand, trying to dislodge all of the horse spit covering it. When the welves were gone, Umrao and Abu moved the luggage and the trunk into the stall.

Umrao slapped Abu on the back and grinned. "I was about to pee myself."

Abu put a finger to his lips. Umrao tilted his head, and Abu poked at his ear. The Lancer's mouth opened into a silent "Ah."

Abu laughed. *My heart almost exploded.*

A sneeze from the closest pile of straw was a somber reminder of how close Masako had come to being found. Abu bent down to the pile and whispered, "Soon."

Umrao and Abu put on the horses' harnesses and loaded the bay mare with the regular luggage. The bigger dun would hold the chest on one side and the medicine bag on the other to counterbalance the load. When they finished with everything except the crate, Abu retrieved the chalkboard and the stick of white limestone from the toolshed where he had left it.

As Abu put chalk to slate, he realized he didn't know the words for the first instructions. He shook the mound of hay and said in a whisper, "Psst."

The top of the pile rose, exposing Masako's eyes.

Abu pointed at Masako and then to a mound of horse manure on the ground. After he repeated the motion twice more, the puzzled girl blinked with understanding, and she nodded.

The boys stepped outside to give her privacy, and Umrao went to retrieve some supplies. A few minutes later, a wooden knock came from the stall. Abu stepped back into the enclosure. He scribbled in cuneiform, *Go box*, before pointing at the bigger chest.

Masako nodded.

Go. Sleep. Knock when need. With a glance toward the dung, the girl understood.

Umrao returned with a loaf of bread and a canteen. Abu opened the chest, and Masako climbed inside. The Lancer handed the girl the food and water. As she settled into the bed of clothes, she gave Abu a tight-lipped smile. Abu reached down and plucked a long piece of straw from her hair. He tried to put as much reassurance as possible into his expression as he closed the lid.

Chapter 10

Nippur, Choru, An 5660, Day 10

A mere khonsu after entering Nippur, Ben's group left the city. He thought the multinational, multi-species traveling companions made quite the motley crew. He also found it interesting that he had been so quick to adopt the two-day counting used on Aaru. As they marched out of the dark mountain into a life-affirming sunrise, one moon stood high in the sky, the other sank below the horizon in the east, and An rose in the west.

Breathing in the clean mountain air, Ben contemplated time. The welves had to put their clocks to good use inside the city built within a mountain, but everyone who had access to Aaru's sky needn't worry. Except for a few hours of each khonsu, An, Aaru's sun, and the planet's two moons, Mata and Shu, ensured that there were always two heavenly bodies in the sky. He would have wagered that even young Aaruans could tell the time within a few minutes, based on the star and the two satellites' locations.

So much had happened since Ben had witnessed the twins killing their father, Iskur. He looked forward to the hike to the Ancients' site. Lil, who had replaced Ssherrss as their guide, said it would take another khonsu to reach the complex. This gave Ben plenty of time to contemplate their explorations and his other concerns. He and Abu pulled their pack horses back through the forest maze and up the mountain path, which ran along the side of Nippur's mountain.

As he marched, Ben considered the incredible feats of magic combined with engineering that hollowed out the mountain and created the wonders inside. What he had seen so far on Aaru rivaled and, in most cases, surpassed the innovations taking place on Earth. Yet the very thing that made these wonders possible—magic—also retarded the Aaruans' innovations in mathematics, the sciences, and engineering.

This dichotomy was stark and fascinating. Ben couldn't help but feel excitement and trepidation in equal parts. People there could accomplish so much if they managed to marry his knowledge of the sciences with their mastery of magic.

A hint of lavender brought his mind back to the previous day's lunch. He tried to pinpoint what had shocked him more: Louisa's admission that she would be open to him courting her or the obscene proposition from Lil, the silver-haired fox.

When Lil had approached him, his survival instincts screamed beware, as they recognized a predator putting him in her crosshairs. He remembered the welf's suggestions. In just a few words, she had described acts that no East End, three-penny-upright had ever mentioned to him.[1]

Part of him wanted to tell Louisa she had nothing to worry about. Even before the confrontation between her and the welf, he'd dismissed any thought of a dalliance with the ancient seductress.

Glancing back to check on Abu, he asked, "Where's Jeevan?"

"Over there." The teen pointed toward a couple down the path.

The duffadar's jovial chuckle joined a hearty laugh from the redheaded Ki. Ben watched the taller welf sister touching Jeevan in a not-so-subtle way.

---

1. Victorian nickname for a prostitute.

Ben realized what had happened. Before their early morning departure, Jeevan had been nowhere to be found during the group's breakfast. Instead, he had met them at the stables when they joined the rest of the Lancers. Ben had not spoken to or seen Duffadar Nahal since lunch yesterday. Two plus two were four, or in this case, one and one became two.

Good for you, Jeevan.

With a jolt of trepidation, Ben thought about the secrets they all needed to guard.

Be very careful there, buddy.

The sharp, dusty smell of aspen trees caused Ben to take stock of his surroundings. Several tree-mammal hybrids grew among the slender white trunks decorated with golden-yellow leaves. The melabu's strange red fur added to its alien nature. As they moved higher, the pine and the hardwoods of the lower elevations had become scarce.

Ben took another deep breath, and the smell of lemons turned his thoughts to Louisa. She had laid claim to him without a single thought about what he wanted. How should he feel? Flattered? Angry? Why did this woman confuse him so?

Louisa had caught Ben flat-footed when she called him to the mat about his interest in her. He thought he had been successful in hiding his desires. That assumption had been as wrong as his assuming she had no interest in him.

Her drunken advances after the banquet should have spelled it out loud and clear, but he still needed her sober confirmation to see the truth.

Ben tried the logical approach and devised a list of positives and negatives he might encounter if he set out to woo Louisa. On the negative side was the age difference. Thirteen years seemed like a lot to Ben. Since no woman near his age had yet to penetrate his heart's defenses as Louisa had, he rationalized away this negative. Instead, he placed her youth, energy, and beauty in the positive column.

At least, it is for me, Ben thought. *Where would she put the age difference on her list?*

The differences in their personalities first went into the negative list. Yet after a short deliberation, that, too, went into the positive column. Louisa's spontaneous, outspoken personality countered Ben's serious nature. She pushed him to go on adventures he would otherwise avoid.

Ben's thoughts turned to the current adventure. Adding romance to their predicament might be like throwing wet mesquite on hot embers. Instead of the desired flames and heat, the two of them might make a smelly, smoky mess of things.

As he dodged a section of scree on the path, Ben refused to let fear keep him from pursuing Louisa. Not only did he desire her, but he could visualize loving the fierce, proud woman and making a home with her and Abu.

Ben sensed she had guarded her heart in the past, even more than he did his own. What hurts had caused her to form such defenses so young? There had to be more there than her father's sins. His concern for her wellbeing urged him to protect her, but he knew she would say she didn't need his protection.

How do I get her to let her guard down?

Traditional, formal courting would allow Louisa to keep Ben at arm's length. As Ben reviewed the times they had connected on an emotional and physical level, each had been a spontaneous confluence of events. Could that be his answer?

We don't have to rush or force anything. I have to go for it when the time is right.

———————————

Lil stepped next to Ben, matching his stride. He hadn't sensed her presence until it was too late. His eyes darted to Louisa, ten yards up the path where she and Khepri carried on like best friends.

"Ben, tell me about Earth," Lil said in Greek.

Ben glanced over to detect any sign of guile on the woman's face. Lil smiled, her brown eyes hidden behind her glasses' dark lenses.

"What do you want to know?" Ben asked in the same language.

"Start with what's happened in the last six hundred An."

Be very careful, Ben thought.

"Not much and a lot." Ben looked down and shook his head. "Men continue to figure out new and more diabolical ways of killing one another, but in some meaningful ways, we have risen above our baser instincts."

"How so?"

Thoughts of the little girl with hopeless eyes sparked Ben's anger, and he stopped walking. "For one, slavery is now being outlawed in most places."

Lil halted to look at him. "How noble, but since you don't have magic, how do you feed so many people without slaves?"

"We've created advancements in agriculture equipment and fertilizers. You have magic. Despite that, you have slaves. Why?" He glared at her.

Lil shrugged. "Kutha is not unique. Almost every nation condones it. Yuhi is the exception. Even your friends, the Alexandrians, use slavery to pay off debts or as a punishment for crimes. Ki and I have spent the last several hundred An away from home. We were with the Nipponese in Yuhi and with Thoresten's clan of dwarves. We never acquired slaves or a taste for the practice."

As Ben considered her words, the steam of his anger released.

Can't hold her to a higher standard than myself.

Ben started forward again. "What were you doing there?"

Lil stepped off with him. "Training. The Nipponese are the best fighters on Aaru. Ki and I learned as much as they could teach us."

"It paid off."

Lil's infectious laughter led Ben to laugh with her. She slapped his back but appeared to be staring straight ahead. He followed her gaze to Louisa, looking over her shoulder. Lil's cunning smile made Ben choke off the humor.

Should have known.

"Well, I better go check on my son," Ben said. "I'll see you around."
He turned to look for Abu, who had dropped back to hang out with the Lancers.

"Yes, you will." Lil's chuckles followed him down the hill.

In the afternoon, the trail turned toward a long, wide valley between Nippur's mountain and its neighbor. Ssherrss told them the Ancients' site lay over a small pass in yet another valley on the other side of the new peak. Other than a small climb up a section of that mountain, the rest of the way would be more straightforward.

As they entered the valley and their path widened, Ben chose to walk with Louisa. He hoped this would keep Lil away so he could avoid any potential issues between the two fiery women. Untenable as a long-range strategy, he still sought to avoid conflict as long as possible.

His efforts appeared unnecessary because Louisa showed no evidence that she'd even noticed Lil's attempts to stir her jealousy. As in his discussions with Lil, Ben ensured that the conversation never approached specific topics. To his relief, Louisa seemed content to discuss everything except romance or Lil. More at ease, Ben felt as if the rest of the day flew by.

A few hours before Triplets, or 6 p.m. back on Earth, Ssherrss called a halt to set up camp near a small grove of trees next to a rushing river. The stirithy said they would reach the Ancients' site well before sunset the next day.

With a few extra hours before sundown, Ben thought it might be a good time to speak with Jeevan. He feared the jolly soldier had jumped feet first into a rattlesnake nest. Ben instructed Abu to put up the tents and tend to the horses. He told the teenager and Louisa that he would be back for dinner and grabbed his Winchester.

Ben found the head of the Lancers discussing guard rotations with two of his lance duffadars. "Jeevan, do you have a moment?" Ben asked.

"Captain Ben! It is good to see you. Yes, I have time." To his men, he said, "Make sure everyone keeps a good watch. Esther said that the welves following us disappeared when we entered the valley. We are once again on our own."

One after the other, they saluted. "Yes, Duffadar." Then the two went in separate directions.

Jeevan gave Ben a big smile. "What can I do for you?"

Ben couldn't help but smile back. "Are you up for a short hunt? I thought we could chat while rustling up dinner."

Jeevan appeared ready to agree but paused. His gaze roved around the campsite, searching for someone.

Ben put his hand on the duffadar's shoulder. "I'm pretty sure Ki is with her sister and the dwarf, scouting ahead."

Sheepish, Jeevan whispered, "Why would I be looking for her?"

Ben slapped him on the back. "Jeevan, my friend, you are one of the worst liars I have ever met. And I mean that as a sincere compliment. Grab your rifle, and let's go."

Jeevan trotted to where a sowar rubbed down a reluctant Chetak. The magnificent war horse seemed upset they had reduced him to being an ordinary pack horse. The duffadar rubbed the stallion's nose and spoke into his ear before picking up his carbine.

Without talking, Ben and Jeevan made their way out of the grove. They hiked up the left slope of the valley into a large section of aspens. Entering the tree line, Jeevan broke the silence. "I'm surprised you want to go into the woods after tangling with that giant rat."

Ben laughed. "Why do you think I asked you to come along? You are here to provide a distraction."

Jeevan grinned. "At least, you brought Agnes this time. Let's find something to eat. The lamb jerky will get old fast."

The friends crept along the faint animal path for thirty minutes, looking for signs of prey. They found no scat or other indications of a giant roly-poly, much less anything that looked like a deer.

Ben stopped and pointed at Jeevan's canteen. "Can I have a drink? I left mine at camp."

The Lancer unslung the container and passed it to Ben. As Jeevan started to turn back to the trail, Ben grabbed his arm. "Before we go, let's talk about that person you weren't looking for back at camp." Ben took a couple of gulps of water.

Jeevan got a distant look before his gaze dropped. "Just having a bit of fun, Captain Ben." Then he looked up. "No. That's not true. It's the most fun I have ever had with a woman."

Ben punched his arm. "What, were you a virgin?"

Jeevan's dark complexion grew reddish. "I'm no innocent. This woman is amazing. In my misspent youth, I studied the *Kamasutra* and all the *Kamasastra*. I learned all the alinganas, all the chumbanas, mardanas, everything. Then I spent all my free time, for years, perfecting the life and love skills I had learned. But Ki. Well, she could write all new pachivedes to add to the *Kamasastra*. Don't worry. She told me I was just a distraction. I know where my loyalty lies and what I can and cannot say."

Ben nodded. "So long as you keep it straight. As I said, you are a terrible liar." He looked around the woods. "We're not going to find anything. Let's head back."

As they neared the campsite, Ben asked, "What exactly is this *Kamasutra* thing you studied, and if it's a book, do you have a copy?"

Chapter 11

Nefru Mountains, Choru, An 5660, Day 10

With eyes darting at every sound in the overgrown forest, Abu unbuckled the strap and raised the trunk's lid for the fourth time that day. Masako held her hand over her eyes and grimaced. Even under the shaded canopy, it was the most light she had seen in hours. After a few more blinks, she climbed out of the trunk still attached to the dun-colored horse. Abu grabbed her under her arms and lowered her to the ground.

Masako stretched toward the sky, then rubbed her calves. A twig snapped behind them, and her head shot up. Abu stepped toward the sound, putting his body between her and any possible danger. His hand went to his revolver.

"It's me," Umrao said. "I brought the spare tent."

Abu said, "Good. We'll put it in those brambles over there."

Shuffling leaves behind him made them glance back. Masako was hustling away from the horses.

"Hey," Abu said.

As she turned, Masako pursed her lips and did a backhanded wave to shoo him away. Abu nodded, and she disappeared into the bushes. While she was gone, Abu and Umrao unstrapped the trunk from the mare and pitched a two-person tent inside a tangle of vines covered in thorns.

As Abu stepped back to inspect their camouflage and ensure that it hid the tent, Masako joined him with a sheepish smile.

"Hungry? Udsua?" Abu asked.

With several vigorous nods, Masako rubbed her belly. The boys laughed, and Abu dug into the horse's saddlebags. He handed her a sack with some lamb jerky and then another with several scone-like biscuits.

Umrao passed her a big canteen. "I've got to get back. Ram has been giving me sideways looks already." He took a few steps and stopped. "How long are we going to keep this up?"

Abu shrugged. "As long as we need to. The welves would take her back if they found out."

"Captain Ben and the duffadar would not allow that."

"Remember, the welves own these mountains. I'm not sure the Lancers could stop them." Abu shook his head. "The longer, the better."

Abu felt a tug on his shirt. Masako thrust the slate board in front of him. The cuneiform on it read, *When you come back?*

Abu said, "Breakfast. Kignim."

Masako looked around the darkening woods with trepidation but soon steeled herself and nodded. After pulling a blanket from the trunk, she crawled through the small opening in the vines and into her tent.

Louisa sat cross-legged well away from the heat of the central campfire. She sipped her evening tea as Ben and Jeevan walked into the camp empty-handed. A smile touched her lips. Less than ten minutes after the pair had gone hunting, Ki and Thoresten had caused a stir as they strolled into camp.

With no signs of strain, the dwarf held a gutted doe's hind legs above eye level with one massive hand. Louisa assumed Ki had killed the animal using the unusual curved longbow strapped across her white-armored back.

As Jeevan and Ben worked their way around the fire, they dodged this evening's designated cooks, who were busy roasting venison over the open flame. They laughed at a joke and appeared in good spirits, despite their lack of success.

"No luck?" Louisa asked.

"No, Miss Louisa, we didn't see a thing." Jeevan grinned. "It looks like someone had good luck, though. It smells wonderful."

Louisa smirked. "Thank your girlfriend and her special friend. They returned with a deer just a few minutes after you two disappeared."

Without flinching, Jeevan said, "Oh? Ki mentioned she was quite the archer. I wish she had let me know she was going hunting. I would have loved to see her in action."

Louisa couldn't resist the opening. "I'm pretty sure you've seen her in plenty of action by now."

Nonplussed, Jeevan struggled with his retort when Louisa heard Ki speaking Greek behind her.

"I suspect you are expressing your regrets. Don't fret. You have a standing invitation."

Now it was Louisa's turn to blush. Jeevan, learning to speak Greek, couldn't follow, but Ben's eyes widened at Ki's insinuations.

Ki's hair tickled Louisa's neck as the welf continued in a sultry whisper, "I owe you a big thank you. My handsome Kuru warrior is the single most talented human I have ever met in the arts of pleasure. It would appear his ancestors learned many new skills since Kuru's first elders came to Aaru."

The breathy voice disappeared, and an armor-less Ki brushed past Louisa. She sashayed to Jeevan's side while giving him the most lascivious look Louisa had ever seen. The amazon warrior ran her finger around the duffadar's ear, appearing as if she would gobble him up. She asked Louisa in Greek, "Can you translate?"

Louisa gulped before nodding.

The welf said in Greek. "I was thoughtless, lover. Next time, I will take you hunting."

When Louisa repeated in English what Ki had said, she replaced *lover* with *sweetheart*.

Ki touched Jeevan's palm, tracing her finger in a slow, provocative manner. She completed some sort of symbol before circling the soldier, moving her hand over his chest and shoulders. The duffadar stood at attention as she circled around him.

Using his drill sergeant voice, Jeevan said, "I'd appreciate that, Miss Ki. Excuse me. I need to check on the lads." With a slight bow to everyone, he marched off.

Louisa repeated his words in Greek for Ki, who shrugged. A few seconds later, Thoresten appeared as if by magic. He took Jeevan's place and sat cross-legged with Ki near the fire.

From out of the gloom Abu appeared and stepped next to Ben, who sat on a small log.

Abu asked in Greek, "Miss Ki, can I ask you a question?"

The redhead looked up from where she'd been staring into the fire. "Abu, correct? What is on your mind?"

"What is that device around your neck?"

For the first time, Louisa noticed the strange goggles hanging by a silk string from Ki's neck. Made of metal and glass, they were about the size of Louisa's hand. They differed a great deal from the colored glasses the other welves wore to protect them from sunlight.

Ki smiled, brought the necklace over her head, and placed the glass part of the goggles in front of her eyes. "This magical device was created by the Ancients. Lil and I discovered the goggles on one of our journeys. With these, I can see in the dark like any full-blood welf."

Excited, Abu asked, "Would you mind if I examined them?"

Ki paused a moment before saying, "You can, but only with me. They're my most prized possession." She patted the bare ground to her right.

Abu made his way over, and the two began discussing the goggles.

Ben opened his mouth but shut it when Lil appeared next to Louisa. Without asking, the welf sat in the spot Abu had vacated. She held a wooden cup and took a sip before saying in Greek to no one in particular, "This is remarkable tea. It's better than any Kuru tea I've had. As hard as it is to admit, it's better than any tea from Yuhi. I pray one of your soldiers has some seeds."

Louisa smiled. "It is fantastic. I'll ask around. Maybe Sowar Jadav has some."

Lil nodded. "If you find any, have one of the life singers that specializes in agriculture grow the first crop. Perhaps they can sing even more flavor into the leaves."

Across the fire, Abu exclaimed, "That's amazing!" He held Ki's goggles to his face and pointed into the darkness, away from the fire. "Dr. Ben, the trees over there are sharp and clear. It's like I'm looking through a yellow windowpane during the middle of the day."

The pair of glasses were a tad small for Abu's slender face. Louisa looked in the direction he'd pointed but saw only a hint of the forest's shadowy outline.

Abu spun to face the group and jerked the goggles away from his face. "Woah. Don't look at the fire. It's like staring at the sun." He rotated the goggles and appeared to fiddle with something before placing them in front of his eyes again. He repeated the process a couple more times.

On the fourth try, Abu became animated again as he stared into the shadows. He grabbed Ki's wrist. "Miss Ki, did you know they could do this?" He handed the warrior woman the goggles.

Ki held them up to her face and gasped at whatever she saw. "How did you do this? Show me." She gave him the goggles again, and the two put their heads together.

"I pressed these three symbols simultaneously, and it changed from seeing the trees to being able to see where all the people and animals are in the woods." He started laughing. "Someone is squatting over there."

Everyone looked in that direction but saw nothing but blackness.

After following his instructions, Ki put the lenses over her eyes. She brought them down, pressed again, and stared through the glasses into the woods. She repeated the process one last time for the rapt audience. "It's incredible. I would have never found this myself. Thank you." She handed the goggles back to the teenager.

Abu looked through the lenses and said, "There are three kinds of vision. One that is normal. Like looking through a clear lens. The original ability to see in the dark and a new type. The trees are just shadows, but I can see every warm-blooded creature like they are on fire. I saw two birds chasing each other."

Bent at the waist, Abu stared at the ground. "I found something else. It's like looking through a telescope or microscope. Using these two symbols, one at a time, I can get closer or farther away from whatever I see. Try it."

She took the goggles and grinned while looking around the campfire. "Lil, I can see the specks of gray in your brown eyes." She pumped her fist into the air. "Fantastic! Thank you, Abu." She handed the goggles back.

During Abu's discoveries, Khepri and Ssherrss had joined the ring of campers. Ssherrss raised his voice. "Therre'ss a legend about mmagic glassssess crreated to help sstirrthy worrk in mminess."

Ki tilted her head. "I had always thought they were for a child. They are the perfect size for a stirithy, though. We found them in an abandoned diamond mine." She nodded at her sister. "Lil, I can see in the dark better than you."

The albino sister smiled without replying. As Abu continued his experiments, the rest of the group stared into the flames, each lost in contemplation.

Jeevan returned and squeezed between Ki and Abu. He sent a searing glance at the dwarf who occupied his previous position. Esther and Ali took the last empty spots around the fire as the cooks handed out wooden plates filled with beans and roasted venison.

Between bites, Louisa continued small talk with Lil and Ben while monitoring Thoresten. She wanted to hold him to his promise. When she was sure he had finished his meal, she asked him in Greek, "Thoresten, would you mind sharing the story of your people?"

Thoresten replied in Greek, "It would be my pleasure." He stood and looked around the fire to catch the eyes of everyone in attendance. With a rapt audience, he spread his arms wide. "What follows is the tale of the Sygnafylki people and our first ancestor, Ragnhild Gullskjegg, brother to the king of Sygnafylki on Earth."

The dwarf dropped his hands. "Ragnhild heard the call from Harold Hiltertooth, king of the Danes and East Götaland. The king meant to meet Sigurd Ring, king of Sweden and West Götaland, in battle upon the Moors of Brávellir.[1] You need to understand that Sigurd Ring was a vassal of King Harold. There were no reasons for them to fight, but King Harold was getting old. He prayed for death in battle so he could feast in Valhalla."

---

1. Legendary Norse battle that took place sometime around 770 A.D. and is mentioned in the accounts found in the Gesta Danorum and the Sǫgubrot saga. Earth archaeologists still debate whether the battle is fictional or historical. In the Aaruan timeline, the battle takes place in 781 A.D.

Behind those in attendance, Thoresten strolled around the circle. "For seven years, the two sides gathered their armies. All free-born warriors who wished to make a name for themselves heeded the call. Legend holds that fifty thousand men were in each army as they met upon the moors. During the battle, Ragnhild was leading the men of Sygnafylki. They came to blows with the men of Keklu, Karl of Svealand, and the men of Rørek, the son of King Harold himself."

The dwarf paused, letting his words settle over the fire. "As the fighting began, the Seba took these three groups to Aaru. When they awoke in the Fields of Eisodos, an army of men and demons greeted them. The first ancestors believed the gods had sent them to Helheim."

With a shake of his head, Thoresten began his stroll once more. "They prepared to fight the strange people who had summoned them. Thank Oden, the Aaruans convinced the three leaders that real-life dragons were coming and that the Norse gods brought them here to fight the ripvor. For their help, each leader would receive a kingdom of his own."

Thoresten stopped behind Ben. "The onetime foes joined forces to fulfill their individual ambitions. They marched across these very mountains, across the plains of Hurra, and into the jungles of Pastruus." He locked eyes with each in the circle before continuing. "While in the jungle, Odin, through the voice of a seer, led the war band to a cave. They found hundreds, if not thousands, of the Ancients' artifacts.

"The three leaders each took an artifact from the cave and left the jungle with a map that would lead them back to the treasure. Rørek ended up with the Topek. When the war band reached the walls of Kerma, they found the city besieged by an army of the bedeviled dragons."

Thoresten's tone became more assertive and his cadence faster. "They joined the battle, and the demons bloodied our people. By the small hairs of Njǫrd, they made it inside the great walls of Kerma before the reapers slaughtered them.[2] As they licked their wounds, Rørek brought forth the song of the Topek. To his surprise, he found his strength more than doubled."

The dwarf laughed. "Always the smart one, Rørek challenged Ragnhild and Karl Keklu to a wrestling match. The winner would become the unchallenged leader of the army until the Lamentations were over. Also, the winner would own all three of the relics. With his added strength, Rørek defeated my ancestor, Ragnhild, along with Karl Keklu, with ease."

Thoresten curled an arm and winked as he showed off his giant biceps. "Rørek knew the army was no match for the ripvor without the magical strength that now flowed through his veins. He activated the Topek, giving the gift of strength to every Norseman. Thus, the dwarven race was born."

The dwarf's arm fell to his side. "By that time, the armies of every kingdom of Aaru had converged at Kerma to destroy the ripvor threat. The third battle of Kerma took place during the Seventh Lamentations. Half a million ripvor fought three hundred thousand Aaruans, made up of humans, hysaksas, elves, welves, stirithy, and babiakhom."

Thoresten glanced up and ran two fingers down a blond braid of his beard. When he looked back at his audience, his eyes narrowed. "In the end, the ten thousand Norsemen from Earth, filled with dwarven strength, turned the tide. Rørek held our army out of the battle. He waited for the perfect moment when dwarven power would make the biggest impact. With the battle going against the Aaruans, Rørek led the Norsemen against the ripvor's right flank and their most elite warriors."

The dwarf's eyes sparkled with glee in the firelight. "The fighting was fierce. Even with the added strength, the outcome hung in the balance until my ancestor,

---

2. Njord is the Norse god of wind, sea, and wealth.

Ragnhild, went berserk." Thoresten's voice boomed on. "He killed dozens of ripvor in his frenzy. His men, inspired by their leader, became crazed with the same rage. The Sygnafylki decimated the ripvor's elite fighters. The ones possessed with the same magical strength."

His voice slowed, returning to his normal bass. "When the enemy's elite fell under the might of the Sygnafylki, the reaper's flank collapsed. Normal ripvor are no match for dwarves. To this day, the bards sing about Rørek the Wise, Father of Dwarves. These same bards sing of Ragnhild, the Berserker, whose bravery and prowess in battle saved Aaru."

The dwarf stopped. He had made a full circle and reached down to take a drink from his wooden mug. No one dared to speak as the audience waited in anticipation. He smiled. "The leaders were each granted a kingdom. Ragnhild wanted to strike out on his own. He established his kingdom on the continent of Maan Alu. My people reigned supreme until the Phantom Lamentations brought us the Nipponese."

Thoresten shook his head. "These strange warriors came to Maan Alu and took over one of our vassal states. Despite our strength, we lost almost every battle against these upstarts. Their warriors, called samurai, were so skilled in the arts of war that they neutralized our muscles. We settled into a stalemate with the Nipponese."

With a nod, Thoresten said, "Over the last six hundred An, we have adopted many of their ways. Now, Sygnafylki warriors follow the Bushido while seeking Valhalla through battle. Because of Odin's blessings, we are now the most feared warriors of Aaru."

The stocky man sat on the ground next to Ki. Jeevan, with Abu's translation, gave an enthusiastic, almost breathless response in English. "Brilliant! What a fantastic story!"

Louisa added in Greek, "Thank you, Thoresten. Your people's story is fascinating. What happened to the Topek and the other Ancients' devices?"

"After the battle, the Aaruans, fearing the power of the Topek, stole the devices and maps. No one knows where they went." The dwarf shrugged.

Louisa frowned. "What a pity. One of those maps might have led us to what we need to power the Seba."

Ali spoke, drawing everyone's attention. "I don't know about the devices, but one of the dwarven maps is in our Temple library. The Keepers in Memphis know where the other maps are. Of course, they will allow no one to see them."

"How did a map end up at the temple on Earth?" Louisa asked.

A piece of bread in hand, Ali waved it in circles as he spoke. "During the Phantom Lamentations, a dwarven Keeper named Ubbi came to Earth. Our records say his fellow priests caught him with the map. He tried to steer the retrieval party back toward the Norsemen's homeland."

Ali took a bite and placed the bread back on his plate. "Instead, the group traveled the silk road, crossed China, and went to Japan. They heard of the elite warriors in that country and that there was an ongoing civil war. Easier to capture an army that way. Surrounded and contemplating suicide, the losers of the civil war were convinced by the Keepers to come to Aaru. Two members of every retrieval party always stay behind and provide details. That's how we also knew that Ubbi had escaped when the party passed through Antioch."

Ben interjected in Greek, "I have a question for Thoresten."

The dwarf raised his eyebrows.

Ben said, "Your first ancestors were stronger than humans but normal. How did you populate your countries? You couldn't have had many women in that first army."

Thoresten nodded. "You're correct. After the Lamentations, only four thousand dwarves remained. A mere three hundred of them were shield maidens.

Dwarves, unlike elves and welves, can breed with regular humans. During those first generations, our people mixed with the human women we received as a tribute and later took during our raids. After several generations, our people became shorter and more muscular. By the fourth generation, the bodies of human females could no longer accommodate dwarven babies."

The dwarf's eyes narrowed. "Now it is against the law for Sygnafylki men to breed with humans. In most cases, the mother and child die before childbirth. The other dwarven nations have not outlawed the practice, but only the most vile dwarf would do so."

Louisa shuddered, thinking about Khepri's story and the dwarven barbarians who killed their families. There was no telling what other evils they must have committed.

"You mentioned Bushido. What is it, and how does it work with your Viking—I mean, Norse—heritage?" Ben asked.

Thoresten's forehead furrowed. "That is the second time one of you used the word *Viking*. What does it mean?"

Ben smiled. "Ah, yes. That is a term given to Norsemen later in Earth's history."

Thoresten's fingers switched to a new braid. "Interesting. As for your question, Bushido is a code of conduct for warriors. Unlike the Nipponese samurai, which are hereditary, any Sygnafylki free man or woman may become a warrior. If they desire to become the best warrior possible, they choose to follow Bushido's eight virtues.

"For the first seven hundred An after our first ancestors arrived, we acted like our cousins. We raided, killed, and stole from anyone too weak to defend themselves. A warrior's only thoughts were living for today's pleasures, building his legend, and dying in battle so that he could feast in Valhalla.

"After the Nipponese defeated our raids, Sygnafylki warriors set out to learn our neighbors' secrets. The discipline gained from following the warriors' way helps us to hone mind, body, and spirit."

Louisa asked, "How does this make you different from your cousins?"

The dwarf stretched his arms above his head before dropping them into his lap. "We have combined Bushido with our god's desires for us to seek battle. In that, we have changed not at all. Through Bushido, we learned better ways to seek what our gods desire. The primary difference between the Sygnafylki of today and our ancestors is that we no longer kill the weak or enslave anyone."

Louisa thought she understood. She would never steal from the poor but had no qualms about doing so from anyone else. "That's a slight improvement. Besides making you not hurt the weak, how does this code make you better warriors?"

Thoresten rubbed his chin. "Explaining the Bushido should be done with deliberation and thoughtfulness. I would only teach the code to those mature enough to accept a life of discipline in all aspects of one's actions."

Louisa sensed the dwarf had reached the end of what he cared to share. She stood up. "Thank you for entertaining and educating us tonight. Before I take my leave, I invite everyone here to join us at sunrise tomorrow. Lance Duffadar Ram has agreed to continue our training in Kalari. His classes teach you how to fight, but, as you said, they also build an individual's mind, body, and spirit. Good night."

As she headed toward her tent, Louisa's mind was a tangle of thoughts. Earlier, she'd debated not extending the invitation but decided otherwise. It would be an excellent way to build group cohesiveness. As for why she wanted the classes to start up again, she needed to do something. Since her ordeal with Iskur, Louisa had been having trouble sleeping and was a little paranoid. Getting back to learning Kalari would distract her from her capture and make her feel more in control.

She pondered how much more Ben must have endured during the war for his symptoms to be so significant. She knew the best remedy was to take control of any future situations. To prepare for the next Iskur in her life, Louisa would throw herself into the training.

Chapter 12

Nefru Mountains, Choru, An 5660, Day 11

As Lance Duffadar Ram called the class to a close, Ben rubbed his right hamstring with one hand and his jaw with another. When he'd woken up that morning, he had been unenthusiastic about attending the Kalari training. Yet his pride again won over his good sense.

At sunrise, Ben joined his dinner companions, minus Ali, Ssherrss, and Khepri, in an open field near the river. Ram took them through the normal Prana Vayu poses before any martial instruction. Ben's nonexistent flexibility had regressed, if possible, since they'd paused their training.

As the class began, Ben had hoped Thoresten would have similar trouble with the poses. Instead, Ben flopped to the ground several times while the stocky warrior kept pace with everyone else.

Ben waited until the rest of the students left the clearing before he allowed himself to rub his inner thigh. Louisa had landed a rather vicious kick. The petite woman was responsible for delivering all his aches and pains. It didn't take a medical degree for Ben to understand what had inspired Louisa's aggressiveness.

Despite her insistence that the kidnapping no longer bothered her, Ben knew that some of her deepest scars were invisible. It was his rotten luck that Ram had asked him to play the role of Louisa's attacker while the soldier taught them how to break various holds.

Knowing what drove her ferocity, Ben took the lumps without complaint. He shook his head at his close call. If he hadn't twisted at the last second, Louisa's kick would have ended their courtship and his hope of biological fatherhood.

As he hobbled back to his tent, Ben pitied the next fool to lay hands on Louisa without her consent. Nearing the tent, he sensed something amiss.

Huddled together, Abu and his friend Umrao looked like they were up to no good. The young Lancer tugged on Abu's shirt, pulling him away from camp. Each teenager carried a sack as they hurried off toward the river.

Ben set aside his thought of asking Khepri for a bit of relief from his aches and took off after the teenagers. He followed their trail alongside the river until it reached the valley's righthand slope. The distinct rumble of a waterfall added to the sounds of the rushing river.

Using as much stealth as possible, Ben walked along the path of disturbed leaves through the dense undergrowth. The noise grew more intense until he saw water falling through gaps in the treetops. No longer needing to be silent, Ben rounded a stand of trees and found Abu and Umrao leaning head-first into a large holly bush, their sacks on the ground behind them.

Both boys ignored the pricks of the thorny leaves as they pushed through the foliage. Abu excitedly grabbed Umrao's right shoulder and shook it. Ben walked up behind them. With two hands, he cuffed the boys upside the backs of their heads.

The waterfall's roar drowned out their yelps as they scrambled out of the bush. Both teenagers tripped on their bags and fell in a heap at Ben's feet. The boys gave each other an "uh oh" look.

As they struggled to stand up, Ben scowled and said, "Go." He pointed back toward the camp.

Umrao and Abu snatched up their bags and fled as fast as they could. Ben turned to follow them but then felt the cold, sharp tip of a blade at his throat.

He raised his hands in surrender and froze.

Lil was staring at him with laughing eyes. She wore a wicked smile and not a stitch more. Ben tried not to look, but he could not control his male instincts as he glanced down at the dripping wet, pale nakedness of the voluptuous welf.

Damn.

Ben forced his gaze up to Lil's face. She sneered. He flashed his eyes toward the camp, but Lil shook her head. The blade of her sword sparkled like polished silver as she rotated it and placed the flat side against his cheek. Slight pressure directed him to turn around. With the flat steel against his back, she coaxed him around the bushes the boys had used as a blind.

His hands still held high, Ben shuffled as if marching toward the gallows. The plunging water filled a large pool at the base of the mountain. Standing under the rushing water, soaping their bodies, were the two redheads, Ki and Esther. Ben tried to turn away, but the blade touched his cheek, forcing him to keep the entire scene in view.

Ben's face grew hot as he saw the sight he had imagined for several months.

Dear God.

Oblivious to his presence, Louisa strode out of the pool of water, both hands squeezing her jet-black hair. Her olive skin glistened as she walked toward a towel and her clothes. Ben's brain screamed, "Close your eyes and turn away, even if the welf kills you!" but his eyes and feet refused to obey.

He would never forget the seconds before this scene or those that followed. Everything he'd envisioned was but an inadequate fantasy when he faced the reality of Louisa's beauty on full display.

Ben's baser instincts took over. Like an eagle spotting its prey, he desired only to hurl himself forward, to wrap his arms around her and make her his.

Those thoughts slammed to a halt when Louisa picked up her towel, and her eyes met Ben's. She screamed and used the towel to cover her nakedness. In that instant, her accusing glare pierced his very soul.

Shaking his head, he mouthed, "Sorry."

Louisa pointed toward the camp, saying the same thing he had just told the two teenagers, "Go!"

No longer feeling a blade on his body, Ben turned to make a strategic retreat. Lil still had the same wicked smile. He gave her a death stare. As he rushed past, she winked and slapped his butt with the flat of her sword.

Entering camp, Louisa felt refreshed, embarrassed, and furious. That incorrigible skýla, Lil, would not let up. The trollop had admitted to seeing Abu and his friend spying on them and then watching as Ben sent them packing. The welf thought it hilarious to force Ben not only to see her own stunning body but to make him watch the rest of the women in such a compromising scenario.

Ben lumbered toward her with bowed shoulders, his head hung in shame.

Now what to do with him?

Should she let him off the hook or hold his feet to the fire? Thinking back to when she'd first seen Ben by the pool, Louisa remembered his face. His look of unbridled lust had shocked her as much as seeing a man where he shouldn't be.

Ben stopped in front of her, shuffling back and forth and refusing to look up. At last, he raised his head but avoided her eyes. "I didn't mean to see you like that. I was looking to wash up. And Lil . . ."

His white lie, combined with her memory of his lust, sealed his fate. Louisa poked him in the chest. "Don't blame this on Lil. You looked guilty as hell." She jutted her chin up. "Did you like what you saw?"

Ben stood taller and peered into her eyes with an intensity she had never seen in the man. Louisa began to pull away from the heat radiating from his eyes, but Ben clasped her hands, including the one still poking him in the chest. With a gentle motion, he kept her in place. "More than I could have ever imagined."

Louisa forgot the words poised on her tongue. She uttered, "Ah, well."

She returned his embrace as Ben leaned forward. Her breath caught in her throat as his lips drew closer. At the last moment, he moved to the side. His lips brushed her cheek, then her ear. She felt his warm breath.

Louisa closed her eyes. A tremor flowed through her body. Ben said in a low voice, "Louisa Sophia, you are the most beautiful woman I have ever seen. I will count each minute as privation until I can look upon your loveliness again. I promise to . . ."

Louisa's mind reeled. The flattery of countless men had shattered upon encountering the iron encasing her heart, but his words sliced through her armor like molten steel. Still feeling his hot breath and a tickle of stubble on her cheek, Louisa leaned into him.

Promise to what?

Another heated breeze. "Be the man you trust to catch you when you fall."

Ben's words sank into her soul. Since she was a child, Louisa had to be the strong one, the one who protected, the one who consoled, always in control. He promised the one thing she hadn't known she wanted and never knew she needed until that moment.

Her mind spinning, Louisa tried to reconcile her new feelings. When everything clicked, she knew that for the first time in her life, she embraced—no, she exalted in—a new facet of being a woman that his promise had set free. Louisa trembled, her face flushed. She ached for his words to be true, for Ben to be the partner she could lean on, someone she could trust with her life. She was thankful that he held her hands.

She felt a profound sense of loss when Ben pulled away and let go of her hands.

As Louisa opened her eyes, she found that the stoic Good Doctor had returned. His change triggered the memory of what had started the conversation. She blushed, cleared her throat, and added authority to her tone. "I don't want to see a repeat of what happened today. Do we understand each other?"

Ben looked serious. "Yes, ma'am." Then he gave her that mischievous, crooked grin. "From now on, you will be the only woman I watch bathing."

Louisa's jaw dropped at the audacious comment.

Ben chuckled as he walked away.

Chapter 13

Nefru Mountains, Choru, An 5660, Day 11

"This path will save us several hours." Lil pointed at the narrow trail that wound uphill into an older, denser section of mountain forest.

"You're sure the pack horses will fit?" Jeevan asked.

Lil nodded. "Shanesha said he has traveled this way many times. I trust him."

The duffadar looked at Ben and shrugged. Ben understood Jeevan's reluctance. The tight space would make it hard to see anyone sneaking up on them, and the dense woods would neutralize the Lancers' rifles. Then again, the trees would also limit the usefulness of Aaru's preferred ranged weapon, the bow.

Ben returned his shrug.

With a wave, Jeevan said, "Lead the way."

As the column moved farther up the trail, an unknown species of tree grew taller and thicker. The trunks of this new type of conifer reminded Ben of the small copse of redwoods he'd seen at the Royal Botanical Garden in Kew. The primary difference was this tree's thick, rubbery leaves, were similar to some succulents. Aspens filled the space between the enormous trunks, somehow surviving under a canopy so thick and shadowy that Lil had removed her sun goggles.

Just wide enough for the horses and their loads, the path made it difficult to walk side by side. Ben looked over his shoulder, past the bay. Abu gave him a thumbs-up as he tugged on the reins of the dun packhorse. Ahead of Ben, Khepri chatted over her shoulder with Louisa while Ssherrss led the couple's horse in front of the big wolf-woman. Lancers were scattered throughout the long parade, with the duffadar somewhere up front, along with the twins and Thoresten.

During the next hour, Ben floated up the path. He still felt the softness of Louisa's cheek, luxuriated in the delicious scent of her clean body mixed with lavender and lemon, and heard the raggedness of her breathing when she responded to his touch. Someday, he promised to thank Lil for her little stunt.

Ben's embarrassment at the waterfall had been a small price to admit his full intentions to Louisa. He laughed at how the pale vixen's prank brought him and Louisa closer.

Every so often, Louisa would steal a look behind her. Each time Ben felt Louisa's gaze, it evoked his smile, but a hint of doubt lingered in his mind. Had she at that moment expressed her true heart, or had it been nothing but a physical response? She vexed him on so many levels.

Hieroglyphics are easier to read. God, send me Louisa's Rosetta Stone.

With no tablet forthcoming, her body's response would be Ben's compass. He hummed the "Yellow Rose of Texas" as they moved into deeper shadows on the trail.

Ben jerked his head around at the high-pitched squeal of a horse in pain. Abu's mare reared up, a black arrow protruding from her shoulder. Abu tried to hold onto the reins while dodging the dun's kicking hoofs. As Ben pulled his revolver, rifles and pistols popped up and down the trail, the thick foliage muffling the blasts.

A man with a blackened face, his body covered in yellow aspen leaves, ran toward Abu's unprotected back with a raised sword. Ben stepped down the slope toward the teenager. He twisted his horse's reins and turned the horse to protect his side while aiming his Pocket Army. With his sight pointed at the twigs poking up around the head of the camouflaged man, Ben squeezed the trigger. The attacker's head snapped to the side, and his body spun around as he fell.

The legs of Abu's horse buckled a second after the man struck the ground. The mare collapsed with Ben's trunk tied to her side, crushing the downed attacker. A shriek came from the box as it crumpled.

"No!" Abu screamed and scrambled toward the mare.

Ben yelled, "Abu, defend yourself!"

The teenager looked toward Ben in panic.

Ben's instincts took command. He dove down the hill and turned over. A curved blade that might have been a khopesh flew a foot above his face. His back struck the ground, and he skidded head-first down the mountain with rocks scraping his back.

The pain woke the monster within Ben, and it roared in rage from the back of his throat. He pulled the trigger three times in quick succession. The ambusher's brown-trousered leg exploded, and he toppled. The second round whistled through empty space while the last lead slug tore away the falling man's windpipe.

Ben rolled to his stomach and used his free arm to halt his slide. He scrambled to his feet and heard a revolver go off right next to him. He turned away from the report to see another leaf-covered man drop his sword and clutch at his chest. The wounded man's head snapped back at the sound of another blast.

As Ben turned in a circle, he sought another target while Abu spun from his victim toward the far side.

When Ben glanced uphill, the bay blocked his view.

Louisa.

Ben ran up the trail. The horse moved, and his sight line cleared. Louisa was crouched on the ground, pressing her free hand against Khepri's back as fire erupted from her revolver.

A camouflaged man stood a few feet from her. He ignored the sticks that flew away from his chest and raised his axe.

"No!" Ben screamed. He yanked his gun toward the man but knew he would be too slow.

A snarling, furry brown streak struck the attacker under his arm before the axe fell. The pair hit the ground and rolled twice. They stopped with Ssherrss sitting on the man's stomach. Steam rose from the ambusher's chest as the stirithy yanked two super-heated daggers from the man's body.

The stirithy plunged the red-hot steel into the attacker's flesh again. Blood popped and hissed as it quenched the blades. The man screamed for a second before going silent. The smell of burned flesh filled the air.

Her face twisted with fear, Louisa ignored all the action and used both hands to press the bottom of her tunic into the gash on Khepri's back.

Ben scanned for another attacker near Louisa before he checked on Abu. Sowar Betigeri and a Lochem soldier were guarding the woods while Abu worked feverishly at the buckle of the cracked trunk.

"Help her," Louisa sobbed.

Ben yelled for Abu to bring some bandages, but his son's arms were full. A young girl clung to his neck, crying. Blood trickled down her face and cheek.

Focus on the now.

"Betigeri! Get Professor Ali!" Ben yelled at the sowar.

The Lancer acknowledged with a nod and headed toward the back of the column.

Ben ignored Abu as he jogged to the other side of the still-whimpering dun and untied his medicine case.

Abu stepped around the horse. "I can explain."

As he gathered his sutures and some bandages, Ben growled, "Later." Full of anger, he stared at his son. "Remember what I told you. Focus."

As Ben turned his back on the teenager, a panting Ali stepped beside him.

Ben grabbed the professor's arm and jerked him up the hill. He commanded, "Khepri's wounded. Help her."

Ali stumbled a step, gave Ben a sideways glance, and said, "Okay." Before he scrambled around the bay, Ben dropped the armful of supplies back into the case and followed the professor.

"Why can't she heal herself?" Louisa asked, her voice cracking.

Kneeling next to his spouse, Ssherrss shook his masked face and whined.

Ali kneeled beside Louisa and replaced her hands with his on the bloody wound. "Life singers can't heal themselves."

Louisa fell back onto her bottom. She rubbed at the sides of her tunic, leaving a bloody mess.

"Don't shoot! The welves are on our side!" Jeevan's voice boomed.

The duffadar hopped over the dead man and jogged past them. He took in the scene before bellowing the command again, "Don't shoot! The welves are on our side!" He kept going down the column.

With the toe of his boot, Ben nudged the dead ambusher lying a foot away. Dead eyes of piercing cobalt blue stared at nothing.

Welves.

As Ben turned to warn Jeevan, Commander Shanesha poked his head around an enormous tree on the uphill side of the path and waved at Ben.

"She'll be fine in no time." Ali stood. "I need to see to the other wounded." He trotted toward the cries of an injured man up ahead. Ssherrss let out a howl and rubbed his face against Khepri's head as she moved and tried to roll over.

"Shanesha, what the hell happened?" Ben asked in Greek.

"Yesterday," Shanesha said, "after we stopped escorting you, one of my men caught sight of two scouts. They led us to a group of about fifty welves laying this trap." He pointed to the body of a dead attacker. "We started taking them from behind when we saw you coming. We had probably killed or captured two-thirds of them before the ambush."

"Get back! I will shoot you!" Abu yelled. The pop of a revolver followed a second later. Ben raced toward his son.

Masako had a death hold on Abu's waist, but he ignored the distraction. He moved the barrel of the Schofield revolver from the ground near the welf's foot to line up with the man's nose. The welven soldier and his partner had stopped in their tracks when he fired the gun. Abu cocked the hammer as Sowar Betigeri stepped beside him. The sowar's pistol pointed at the second welf. The Lochem soldier, armed with a spear and shield, stepped to Abu's other side. Their presence gave him some hope.

Abu dared a glance at the movement coming from uphill. Dr. Ben came around the rump of the bay, followed by Shanesha. The pair squeezed into the cramped space.

Dr. Ben thrust his hand forward, palm out. "Don't shoot, Abu. They're on our side."

Abu said, "They're trying to take Masako." He locked eyes with his guardian. "I won't let them."

"She's the missing slave girl from the palace," Shanesha said in Greek as he tried to step around Ben toward Abu.

Abu aimed at the commander. "Don't move."

Dr. Ben put his hand on Shanesha's chest to stop him and said in Greek, "Everyone, stop. I'm sure this is all a misunderstanding."

"This should be interesting," Ki said from a few feet up the trail behind Shanesha.

Dr. Ben spoke to Abu in a calm voice. "Lower the gun."

Abu looked for a long second into his guardian's eyes. His gun barrel drifted from Shanesha's chest toward the other welves. With as much strength as he could muster, he said in Greek, "I had to help her escape. They were trying to kill her." The girl had buried her face in his back and was still crying. Abu reached behind with his free hand and patted her shoulder. "They would have killed me if it wasn't for Masako."

"Okay. I believe you. Who was trying to kill her?" Dr. Ben's voice remained steady.

"Some skinny welf with black hair and red eyes." Abu shook his head.

"Enkara," hissed Ki.

Dr. Ben looked at the red-haired welf. The broken shaft of an arrow stuck out of her armored shoulder, and streaks of blood crisscrossed her stark-white breastplate. "Who is that?"

Ki nodded. "He's an assassin who works for one of the competing factions in Nippur." She looked at Abu but spoke in Eblan for several seconds.

A trembling Masako peered around Abu's waist.

The girl replied to Ki in Eblan. They continued their conversation for over a minute. The name Enkara was the only word Abu understood.

Abu's revolver felt heavy, his hand twitched, and sweat stung his eye, but he didn't dare look away. As Ki and Masako spoke, his eyes darted among the three welven soldiers.

Masako finished and buried her face in his back again.

"The girl heard the head cook plotting with Enkara to kill my mother," Ki said. "The assassination is supposed to occur at the Summer Festival."

Shanesha turned to Ki and spoke in Eblan.

With a nod, Ki replied in Greek, "We will have to run to get there in time. I'll get Lil." She disappeared.

Shanesha looked back at Abu and said, "About the girl. She belongs to the governess."

Abu blurted out, "I'll pay for her."

Shanesha laughed. "Those that wear the gold band are very expensive. How can you afford the cost, boy?"

Abu looked at Dr. Ben and took a deep breath, trying to think.

What do they value the most?

His eyes settled on the camouflaged body lying on the side of the path. Abu pointed his revolver at the dead man. "I killed him with this." He shook the gun in his hand.

Shanesha looked at the leaf-covered body and Abu's gun.

The gun flipped in Abu's hand, and he held the Schofield out, handle first. "I will trade my weapon and thirty bullets for the girl."

Shanesha's amber eyes twinkled at the gun, but they narrowed when he looked at Abu. "Fifty. What did you call them? Bullets?"

Dr. Ben said, "Deal."

With a huge smile, the commander took the revolver from Abu.

It took some effort, but Abu broke Masako's desperate hold on him. He turned and scooped her up to hold her on his hip. "It's okay. You're free." With a look of horror, she hid her face in his shoulder. "Commander Shanesha, tell her she's free."

The welf said a few words, and Masako popped her head up. She looked at the welf, who seemed to confirm Abu's words. A laugh burst out for a second before she started bawling. Tears ran down her cheeks, and snot bubbled out of her nose. She used her free arm to wipe her face.

Abu laughed and said, "I'll get the bullets."

"Good. We must hurry," came Shanesha's reply.

Chapter 14

The Tomb of Mortals, Choru, An 5660, Day 11

Louisa watched Khepri mending the leg of Abu's injured packhorse. The giant wolfwoman moved as if she hadn't had one toe in the River Styx just an hour earlier. The desperation that had overwhelmed Louisa when she thought she'd lost her new friend still rattled her. She grappled with how much Khepri's selfless act had challenged her.

Sacrifice.

A hard word. Louisa's mother had been the one person who'd loved her enough to sacrifice everything for her. Everyone else—her father, uncle, partners in crime, suitors—was out for himself. Even most of the nuns at St. Denis bartered the education they offered for her unflinching obedience. In the theoretical sense, Louisa understood the sacrifice Jesus Christ had made for her. It took an alien she'd known for fewer than two weeks to display the word in action.

The pack horse tucked her legs under her chest, raised her head, and pushed off with her forelegs before standing. Khepri patted the mare's nose. "Better than ever."

Louisa stepped to the hysakas and craned her neck to look Khepri in the eyes. "Thank you," she whispered, sniffling and throwing her arms around the enormous wolf's waist as far as they would go.

Two big hairy arms swallowed Louisa as Khepri returned the hug. Her big hand patted Louisa's back as she whispered, "There. There." After another couple of pats, Khepri pulled back and bent down to Louisa's level. She leaned in and nuzzled Louisa's cheek with her own. "Anytime, my friend." The giant wolf rose.

Tears moistened the fur under Khepri's gold and brown eyes.

"I'll see if anyone else needs help." Khepri moved down the trail.

In the past, Louisa had put her life on the line for others, but it had always been out of a sense of justice. Before she stepped off the train in Cairo, there was only one person Louisa cared about. Since that day, the number she would consider making a sacrifice for had exploded.

There were the Lancers who became the brothers Louisa had never known. Khepri and Esther were the girlfriends she hadn't had since boarding school. Abu brought to life maternal instincts she didn't know existed, and, of course, there was Ben. She respected him for the good man he was. With no prior experience, she didn't know how to classify the swirling feelings she felt when he was around. Even now, she struggled to process the words he had spoken just this morning.

If we live long enough, we'll figure it out.

By the time Khepri disappeared around a bend in the path, Louisa had regained control of her emotions. She turned her attention to the luggage stowaway. The girl kept a vice-like grip on Abu's hand as Louisa bent on a knee to meet her.

"Hello. I'm Miss Louisa." Louisa pointed to the middle of the clean tunic she wore. She had swapped it for the blood-drenched one after the fight. "Miss Louisa."

The girl blinked at her for several seconds. "Miss Wusa."

Louisa chuckled. "Miss Loo eee sa."

"Miss Loo isa." The girl giggled. "Miss Louisa." She patted her chest with her free hand. "Masako."

Louisa gave her a big smile. "Nice to meet you, Masako." She pulled a hand-kerchief from her pocket, uncorked her canteen, and wet the cloth. Taking hold of Masako's chin with one hand, she said, "Let's clean you up." She scrubbed the blood and dirt away from the girl's face, then inspected her work by moving the girl's chin left and right. "That's better."

Masako bowed at the waist. "Haisha moushiagemasu." (A humble way to say thank you very much to someone above your station in Japanese.)

Louisa stood. "You are welcome." She patted Abu on the arm. "You did a wonderful thing. I'm proud of you."

The teenager's double-cheek dimples appeared along with his grin. "Thank you." Abu waved over her shoulder and said in Greek, "Ssherrss, we need your help."

The four-foot-tall fox-like stirithy trotted over. "Yess?"

Abu brought Masako in front of him. "She's free. Can you take it off?"

"With pleassurre." The stirithy approached the young girl, who was only a few inches shorter than him. Masako drew back until Ssherrss said some words in Eblan.

Masako's shoulders relaxed, and the metal singer put his hand-paws on either side of the collar. Where Ssherrss touched it, the metal became soft until one side separated and the other bent. The metal singer pulled the collar apart.

Growling, Ssherrss pulled his arm back to toss it into the woods, but the girl grabbed his black wrist. She whispered into one furry, pointed ear, and Ssherrss purr-chuckled.

The metal singer refocused on the symbol of the girl's bondage. Gold plating and silver lettering dissolved into two floating streams of liquid. The non-precious part of the collar formed a large liquid blob that solidified into a useless lump of gray metal that thudded to the ground. A strand of gold and one of silver began weaving through and around themselves. The levitating weave curved in on itself.

Tiny leaves grew on thin liquid strands that became branches. Ssherrss nodded, and the liquid froze solid.

A golden laurel, its leaves veined with silver, levitated away from his hands toward Masako. The girl straightened her shoulders as the crown settled onto her head. She beamed with pride.

"Done," Ssherrss said.

With a shriek of delight, Masako threw her arms around Ssherrss's neck. The taciturn stirithy recoiled for a second before allowing the full embrace. "Well. That'ss good. You arre welcomme." He said something in Eblan and patted her on the head. Masako broke the hug, a single tear running down her cheek.

As they turned onto the original trail, Abu hoisted Masako up to the mare's back to sit between the luggage. The life singer–healed packhorse had more energy than before being injured and didn't seem to mind the passenger.

Maybe Khepri healed something we didn't know about, Abu thought.

With the entire morning lost, Ssherrss pushed them hard. They would reach their destination close to sunset. Abu looked at the young girl and wondered what to do now. He suspected that Dr. Ben would soon want to have a discussion, but his guardian appeared deep in thought.

Abu wanted to know more about Masako but didn't want to use the unwieldy chalkboard while they were on the move.

I wish she could speak English or Greek.

Abu patted Masako's leg, and she looked down at him. He pointed to the horse. "English, Horse. Elliniká, álogo."

The young girl repeated the words several times with a few corrections from Abu, then pointed and said, "Eblan, Sisi. Nipponese, Uma."

Abu laughed. Masako had decided to teach him as well. For Abu, new languages were simply puzzles to be solved. The prospect of learning several more excited him. Besides his native Arabic, he was fluent in Turkish, Farsi, English, and Greek. He could also fluently read Latin. Since the Lancers had begun escorting their expedition in Egypt, he had become more than a novice in their native Dogri. After coming to Aaru, he soaked up Aaruan words whenever possible. With Aaruan being a close cousin to Ancient Egyptian and the most common language in this strange world, it made sense to prioritize the language.

Why not learn two more?

As the pair rotated roles from tutor to student, the column traveled toward the opposite end of the valley from where they had spent the previous night. When the group stopped for a late lunch, Abu and Masako sat on the ground with a small cloth between them. As they ate small strips of charred venison with some pita bread, a shadow fell over them.

Abu flinched. When he recognized the guest, he nodded as Thoresten squatted beside them. The dwarf picked up a piece of meat and ripped it in half with his teeth. As he chewed, he glanced from the girl to Abu and back again.

With a raised eyebrow, Masako looked at Abu. He shrugged. After another uncomfortable minute, Abu asked in Greek, "Can I help you?"

"Maybe," Thoresten rumbled like crashing waves. He poked the half-bitten piece of venison at Masako and spoke in Nipponese.

Masako's eyes lit up as she replied. The exchange went back and forth, with Abu's head swiveling between them. He didn't understand a word they were saying. The conversation stopped as Masako reached into her pocket and dug around. With a triumphant smile, she withdrew her hand and opened it. Lying in her palm sat the coin she had once shown Abu.

Thoresten picked up the small token between a thick finger and a thicker thumb. He swallowed the last bite of meat and turned the coin over to inspect the other side. With a deep harrumph, he looked at Abu. "She does not know how special she is." He held his palm toward Abu and pointed at the coin. "This is the shogun's symbol." He flipped it over again. "This is the Hojo clan crest. Do you understand?"

At the mention of the word *Hojo*, Masako grinned and said, "Me, Hojo. Hojo Masako."

Abu looked at the dwarf and shook his head. "No. What does it mean?"

"She is Yuhi royalty."

Abu glanced at her slave collar-turned-tiara. *Royalty? Woah. A real princess.*

Thoresten returned the coin to Masako, saying, "There can only be one half-Nipponese child who is royalty. The shogun's third daughter married Alexandria's second prince."

Abu whispered, "Does this mean she is also an Alexandrian princess as well? I need to tell Esther." He started to stand.

A meaty hand pulled him back to the ground. "No," Thoresten commanded. "Like Nippur, the Alexandrians play politics. Some might use her in their games."

Abu didn't want Masako to become a political weapon. He remembered his suspicions about Esther during the banquet. He warned himself not to forget how little he knew about the people of Aaru, what they wanted, and who each nation's rivals were.

"I understand." Abu lowered his voice. "What happened to her parents?"

"My cousins attacked their ship. They killed her parents and sold her and an older woman, the girl's nanny, into slavery." Thoresten frowned. "Masako was three. The caretaker never told her about her birthright. Just gave her the coin. The old woman died last year."

His heart aching, Abu tried to regain control of his emotions. His parents' murder flashed through his mind, replaced by an imagined scene of the toddler Masako torn from her mother's arms. "What should I do?" he whispered.

"When you get back to Alexandria, give the girl to the king," Thoresten's whisper rattled like distant thunder.

Abu needed time to think through everything he'd been told. His concern for Masako had caused a question to slip his mind. "Who were the ambushers? Why were they after us?"

"The attackers were part of a faction that opposes Inanna. The people trying to assassinate her are yet another faction. It is all part of a thousand-An feud."

Abu shook his head. "Is there anywhere on Aaru where people are not fighting for more power?"

"Does such a place exist on Earth?"

Abu chuckled. "Touché." He added in Greek, "No, it doesn't."

The dwarf stood, and Abu jumped to his feet. He stuck out his hand. "Thank you. I'll keep her safe until I can return her to her family."

Thoresten clasped Abu's forearm.

"One more thing. Why didn't you go back with Ki and Lil?"

Laughter rumbled. "Strong, I am. Swift, I am not." The dwarf walked away.

Abu returned to his seat on the ground and picked up a piece of bread. A distant crash turned his eyes to the sky. Darkening clouds stretched between the peaks of the two mountains that formed the valley. He sniffed the air, filling his lungs with the pleasant earthy scent that signaled impending rain.

Need to get the ponchos.

Dr. Ben arrived at their little picnic and kneeled next to Masako. He held his hand out to the girl. "I'm Dr. Ben."

As she looked between Abu and Dr. Ben, she shrugged. Abu reached across the cloth and shook Dr. Ben's hand. "Like this."

Dr. Ben nodded and held his hand out again.

The girl gave him a tight-lipped smile and shook his hand. "Hojo Masako."

"Nice to meet you." Dr. Ben looked at Abu, his eyes uncertain.

"Masako."

"Nice to meet you, Masako."

She kept shaking Ben's hand and said, "Nice meet you."

Abu laughed as they broke their grip.

Dr. Ben said, "Didn't you tell *me* not to do anything *stupid*?"

With a sigh, Abu said, "I'm sorry I didn't tell you, but I didn't know whether her story would get us killed. I just did what you would have done."

Dr. Ben picked up a stick and began poking at the ground. "You know we can't keep her. As soon as we return to civilization, we will find someone to keep her safe."

"It might not be that simple." Abu told Ben what Thoresten had said.

With a distant expression, Dr. Ben lapsed into silence until the grumble of the approaching storm brought him back. He said, "Grab the ponchos, and get Masako my umbrella." He rose.

Masako wrapped the remaining food in the cloth and stood up.

Dr. Ben gripped Abu's shoulder. "For now, use my extra Pocket Army." He put his other hand on the girl's shoulder and looked between them. "We *will* figure this out."

An occasional shilling-size drop of rain pelted Ben as the group broke from lunch. The wind and the rain picked up when the path's incline rose on their way out of the valley. In rolling waves, chilled sheets of water smacked him in the face. Underfoot, tiny white-water rivulets raced down the rocky path, turning sure footing into a muddy scramble.

The frigid, high-altitude rain had saturated every bit of Ben's clothing despite his waterproof poncho. With chattering teeth, he kept his head bowed, using the brim of his pork pie hat to deflect each slap of rain. Louisa gripped the parasol shaft to use as a shield against the onslaught. The sure-footed young woman slipped several times in the worsening conditions. Both times, Ben caught her before she slid down the hill.

As the clouds moved over the ridge at the top of the valley, the torrent came to an abrupt stop. Visible for the first time in hours, Aaru's twin rings stretched across an orange-and-mulberry sky whose beauty preceded the coming sunset.

Ben removed his hat and shook like a wet dog. The droplets scattered in every direction.

"Do you mind?" Louisa pointed her parasol toward him, opening and closing it several times.

Ben chuckled as a small shower flew in his direction, replacing all the water he had removed.

An eye for an eye, this woman.

Increased chatter from the people ahead got their attention. Together, Ben and Louisa crested the valley's rim and stepped onto a small plateau. The storm hid the view of what lay below until a web of lightning flashed within a small vale, followed by a thunderous boom. At the center of the depression, light bounced off a colossal pyramid of solid glass. Ben and Louisa ground to a halt.

Rain from dark, angry clouds distorted the details of the buildings that flanked the monument on three sides. The storm couldn't hide the hundred yards of mirrored glass that extended away from the base of the pyramid's fourth side. As the Tomb of Mortals blinked in and out of view to the chaotic rhythm of the storm's light show, Ben retrieved his binoculars.

Magnified and visible one second at a time, the glass field appeared to be the same width as the pyramid. Scattered along the flat, shiny surface were hundreds of bleached skeletons. Some bones poked out from corroded armor that had proved useless to its owners. After several flickers, Ben identified a strange object in the center of the field.

At first glance, it appeared as if two giant gleaming white eggs were standing twenty yards apart. Each egg seemed to be floating. Another burst of illumination lit up a thin line connecting the objects. Thinking it was a trick of the eyes, Ben watched the shadows cast by each flash of light, both with and without the binoculars. No matter how he studied them, he came to the same conclusion. The eggs were floating above the ground.

Ssherrss yelled over the rolling thunder, "We cammp herre tonight!"

Ben handed the binoculars to Louisa.

"Thank you." Louisa scrutinized the scene.

Jeevan made his way to them and asked in a serious tone, "Thoughts?"

"We need to stay away from the front of the pyramid." Ben pointed at the mirrored boneyard that lit up for half a second. "We should investigate the three buildings first. We'll get a better view in the morning and make our plan."

Another crash of thunder echoed up the hill. The pyramid pulsed like a beacon over dark seas, warning everyone away from its rocky shores. No matter how much Ben tried, he couldn't shake the feeling that they were again diving into the fire.

Chapter 15

The Tomb of Mortals, Choru, An 5660, Day 12

Louisa crept on her fingers and toes, backing out of the small tent she shared with Masako. She tried not to disturb the young girl, whose quiet snores revealed just how exhausting and stressful the previous day had been for the former slave. Louisa pulled herself into a cross-legged position to sit outside. She rolled her long braid into a bun and pinned it to the back of her head.

There were at least two hours left until An showed his face and the camp would be in full motion. Last night, as a water-logged Louisa took in the storm-lit Tomb of Mortals, she had an almost uncontrollable urge to explore. To be the first to glimpse the Ancients' legacy. Her plan was to get to the edge of the sandy field that surrounded the buildings. If the first rays of the morning An did not expose any visible perils, she would approach the closest rectangular building and do what she did best.

With the familiar jolt of energy that came at the start of every job, Louisa popped to her feet and trotted into the woods. She stayed well away from the guards' campfires, which gave off more smoke than light because of the still-damp kindling. It took her a few extra minutes to get to the path leading down.

For this job, Louisa had eschewed her soft burglar shoes for sturdy boots and was grateful she had as soon as she began her descent into the valley. The rain had turned the mountain path into a sluice of loose rocks and slippery clay. Louisa stepped off the path and used the trees as handholds as she made her way down the steepest part of the trail.

Her senses were alive as she moved her fingers from the tender bark of an aspen tree to the rough, sappy skin of a big pine. The occasional small animal skittered through the underbrush, avoiding her. An owl hooted a warning to the nighttime interloper navigating its hunting grounds. She forced herself to slow down and pay attention to each step. To turn an ankle or to fall would be most embarrassing.

The angle of the path leveled off as Louisa neared the bottom. She crossed over the track and stepped into the woods on the opposite side, then made a beeline for her first close view of the Tomb of Mortals. At the boundary of the field and the forest, she could just discern the outline of the pyramid and two rectangular buildings. The trio of outer buildings resembled handmaids attending to their monarch. She waited several minutes for An to light her way.

To fill the time, Louisa examined the delineation between the wild underbrush of the woods and the straight line of sand that marked the field. Above, branches extended over the sand, but not one grain had blown into the mossy ground on her side of the partition. Curious, Louisa buried her toe in the sand and shoveled a toe's worth of the grains onto the dirt in front of her.

Oh, my, Louisa thought as the grains flew back across the border like metal shavings tugged by a powerful magnet.

Light broke across the jagged ridge above, forming chevrons of golden rays across the field and the facility. Where light touched the pyramid, its glass sparkled like a thousand diamonds. A tingle of excitement flowed down her spine, and she had to fight the urge to rush forward. With light illuminating more of the field, she noticed several small dunes that had not been visible from the campsite.

Louisa moved down the line of trees to get close to a small mound of sand lying ten yards from the forest. Out of the pile poked several bleached bones and the unmistakable grin of a human skull.

Not good.

The killing field extended to the sands as well. At ten, Louisa stopped counting the little graves on this side of the complex.

By her calculations, the reward did not equal the risk, but Louisa knew she was to blame for getting them into this mess. She felt compelled to be the first one to put herself in danger. Even if she didn't want to leave Aaru, her tribe deserved to have the option.

I've come this far. Why not?

Prayers were never part of Louisa's burglar routine. The gambles she took were never greater than her skill and her confidence, but this was so foreign to her normal experience that she needed to lean on her limited faith.

Louisa shook her head. *Not foreign. Alien.*

With a deep breath, she crossed herself and stepped onto the sand.

"What the hell are you doing?" Ben demanded.

Louisa's head snapped toward the sound. Farther down the tree line, Ben glared at her.

How did he get here before me?

Louisa put both hands on her hips and glared back. "Exactly what it looks like." She jerked her head toward the complex. "I'm going to explore."

Ben stomped toward her. "Are you out of your mind?"

For the first time, she saw the puffy bags under his eyes.

He didn't sleep again. I need to remind Abu to get me when he's like this.

Ben pointed to the nearby bones. "Are you blind?"

No excuse to be rude. Louisa growled, and her back grew stiff with ire. "I am neither." She took another backward step onto the sand. "Someone has to be first."

Ben's jaw softened, and deep pain saddened his blue eyes. "It doesn't have to be you."

The depth of Ben's concern washed away Louisa's indignation but not her guilt. "I'm responsible for us being here. If anyone should risk their lives to get us home, it should be me."

Ben held his hands out the way he would to a spooked horse. "It doesn't matter how we got here. We will get home together." His eyes flicked to the pyramid and then back to hers. "Help me scout out the entire valley." He held out his hand.

Louisa hated that he was trying to placate her. To keep her safe. It grated at her sense of independence. Lifting her chin, she said, "We'll do it your way. For now. But don't think to stand in my way the next time I decide to help the group."

Ben gave her the lopsided grin that usually made her forget herself, but this time it irritated her.

"Yes, ma'am," he said.

Louisa stepped off the sand and brushed past his outstretched hand. "Let's go."

He suppressed a chuckle and said, "Please, lead the way."

As he and Louisa reached the site of last night's camp, Ben found Jeevan pacing in front of the group. Everyone had lined up in a single-file column, loaded horses included.

Jeevan grinned. "Good, good, good. You did not tell the guards that Miss Louisa went with you."

"It was impromptu." Ben pointed across the valley. "We skirted the edge of the site. There is a little stream with a clearing just off the path on the far side."

Jeevan nodded and gestured down the line as he said in Greek, "Esther. Join us, please."

The young Alexandrian officer jogged forward and stopped in front of them. "Yes?"

Jeevan stroked his silky black beard. "I'm going to place two men here and two more on the ridge on the other side of the valley. Can two of your men stay with each group?"

"Yes. I'll see to it." Esther turned and jogged back to her men.

"What's the plan, Captain Ben?" Jeevan asked.

As Ben and Louisa had made their way back to camp, he had been working on that very answer. "Move camp near the stream, and then," Ben drew a crude map on the ground with the toe of his boot, "establish watch posts on all four sides of the complex." He carved four x's into the dirt. "We observe the rest of today. If there is no activity from the buildings, tomorrow I'll take a small group to scout."

Jeevan nodded and turned to the column. "We're moving to the far side of the valley." The duffadar raised his voice. "Watch your footing going down. As Captain Ben would say," he added a twang to his voice, "the trail is slicker than a slop jar."

"Here he comes," Ben said. "Act normal."

Louisa chuckled. "Maybe you should take your own advice."

With a bucket of water in each hand sloshing back and forth, Abu and Masako took short, steady steps as they trudged out of the woods toward the cooks.

Everyone in camp stared at the pair, and Abu gave the group a corkscrew eye. "What's going on?"

Ben sang off-key, "For he's a jolly good fellow which no one can deny."

The crowd picked up the song, and, like a nightingale, Louisa's voice cut through the din of tone-deaf men and clapping Aaruans who didn't know the song. Abu's face turned brownish red, and a bewildered Masako gawked at the crowd.

All of a sudden, Thoresten's thunderous voice drowned out the rest of the singers. He tried to repeat the part of the song that he had heard. "Wit no booty da nie."

Louisa gave him a disapproving shake of her head, and the boulder of a man lowered his gaze and fell silent. The crowd parted to allow Sowar Ram to step in front of Abu. The Lancer carried a plate stacked high with flapjacks and a single lit candle.

Ben waved his arms like a choir director. "For he's a jolly good fellow. Which no one can deny."

When the singers echoed the last line, Ben said, "If my calculations are correct, it's November thirteenth back home." He slapped Abu on the back. "Happy Fourteenth Birthday."

"Blow out the candle!" Jeevan yelled.

With puffed cheeks, Abu blew the flame out.

"We made you a present." Ben held out his hand. "Can I have my revolver back?"

Abu pulled out the pistol and presented it handle first. Khepri and Ssherrss stepped forward and presented Abu with a shiny replica of a Pocket Army. Silvered filigree swirled in the dark gray metal that composed most of the revolver.

Made of a dark Aaruan hardwood, the handles were pieces of art. One side contained a life singer–grown pyramid and the other a roaring ninkilim.[1]

Louisa gifted Abu the necklace Ben had once confiscated from her. It had a Horus pendant carved from a strange yellow gem hanging from an ancient chain of gold. If they weren't a world away from home, Ben might have objected to the stolen relic being a gift. As she placed it over his head, Abu's face lit up, and Ben forgot his concerns.

Adding to his gifts, Jeevan gave Abu a notebook of poems written in Sanskrit while the Lancers gave the young man his first sip of whiskey. Abu whispered, "Allah yaghfir li [God forgive me]," then gulped down the spicy surah. As he coughed and sputtered, Esther approached the teenager. He cleared his throat.

A full hand shorter than the birthday boy, the stout redhead stared up as she came to a stop. In Greek, Esther said, "Don't get the wrong idea." She grabbed Abu's cheeks, pulled his face to hers, and gave him a long kiss. Catcalls, whistles, and applause filled the campsite.

Ben coughed as the two kissed and thought to himself, *The kid's kissed more girls in the last few months than I have in years.* His eyes flicked to Louisa, who was laughing and clapping. A deep, aching desire slammed into Ben at the sight of her smile.

The cheering stopped. Esther pulled away and held Abu at arm's length. "That's for saving my life." She shoved his chest, and he stumbled backward.

Abu blinked multiple times, and a smile of wonder spread across his face.

---

1. On Earth, Ninkilim is known as the Lord of Rodents, a Sumerian god. On Aaru, it is a cougar-size mammalian predator with giant pincer-like teeth that are used to pierce and latch onto its prey.

Chapter 16

The Tomb of Mortals, Choru, An 5660, Day 13

Jeevan frowned in distress. "Are you sure about this, Captain Ben? I should take some of the lads to scout the way forward."

Ben shook his head. "No, I'll take Chib and Lama with me. You and your best marksmen will cover us from the woods. Whatever happened to the other explorers, the danger seems limited to the sand and glass. When we reach the grass courtyard, bring the group."

With a tip of his cap, Ben caught Louisa's attention. He didn't like her putting herself in danger, but he could control her about as much as he could domesticate a tiger. He jerked his head toward Abu, and she gave a slight nod.

They'll be okay.

As he faced the complex, Ben noted the construction of each building around the center point. Midnight black, the building closest to them soaked up the light. Its hard granite walls were the color of unpolished coal. Behind the pyramid stood a building of red stone speckled with black spots. A dull gray metal alloy composed the building on the far side.

Ben waved the two Lancers toward the sand, and Thoresten stepped with them.

Thoresten said in Greek, "I will join you."

Ben eyed the massive block of a man who called himself a dwarf. He had a better chance of holding Louisa back. He replied in the same language, "Fine."

Ben nodded, and the group stepped onto the sand.

Here we go.

Ben held his Winchester at the ready. The Lancers walked with the butts of their carbines on their shoulders, barrels pointing toward the complex. The desert-like dirt shifted underfoot, making Ben's progress slow. Beside him, Thoresten pumped his legs with less caution, an ax in each hand. The ten gun barrels at his back gave Ben a little more confidence that they wouldn't end up inside one of the small grave-like berms.

Ben's fear at being so exposed brought back memories from previous decades. He slowed down as he relived the nightmare. He was charging on foot across a muddy Mississippi field toward a line of trees that some union soldiers had entered moments earlier.

A puff of smoke had risen out of the woods. A whining sizzle accompanied a meaty whack. The man next to him screamed, grabbed his gut, and fell to the ground. Several other gray-clad men threw themselves down, but Ben knew from crossing other blood-soaked fields that the desire to hide led to death.

As he ground to a halt, Ben pulled his Merrill carbine to his shoulder. Heart racing, he aimed several feet to the right of the smoke and fired. The fear of imminent death made him feel more alive than ever as he ran. From his mouth, the demon's scream pushed him on as he scrambled across the mud. The beast's hunger to kill drove him faster.

From another world, Abu shouted, "Something's coming out of the pyramid!"

Ben blinked, and his nightmare disappeared. Halfway to the corner where the black and red buildings were closest, his eyes darted to the top of the glass building. It took him a moment to find the reflections of two small triangular shapes and their shadows as they floated down one side of the glass. He tracked the silhouettes until two hatbox-size pyramids swooped down and flew over the black building. Composed of the same material as the giant pyramid, these children had to be the aforementioned Ghosts of the Ancients.

One ghost took up a position in the gap between the red and the black building. The other levitated over the field to bracket his scouting party from two fronts.

Jeevan bellowed commands. "To the left of me, you have the thing at the corner! To the right of me, aim for the one in the field!"

As if a wind singer sang, a loud English-speaking voice boomed in Ben's ears, "You are trespassing. Leave immediately, or you will be terminated."

Ben pointed Agnes at the object near the corner, and the two Lancers aimed at the object floating above the field to their right.

Before Ben could pull the trigger, a high-pitched sound emanated from the flying object near the corner. Pain seared Ben's eardrums and threatened to churn his brain to mush. He dropped his Winchester, grabbed his ears, and screamed as he fell to his knees.

The whispers of guns sounded, and the ghost near the corner shattered. Reflective shards fell to the ground. Relief washed over Ben as the pain ceased faster than his fading scream. He grabbed his rifle and struggled to stand.

More carbines fired, and a green light pulsed away from the second flying object. Like flies stuck in jade molasses, the bullets slowed and froze before dropping to the ground.

First to his feet, Sowar Lama aimed at the remaining ghost. A flash of lightning shot out from its apex, striking him in the chest. The Lancer exploded with the horrific sound of wet mud being squashed underfoot. Bits of flesh and bone shot up like a geyser.

———

Next to Louisa, Abu sobbed, "Eazizi Allah, la [Dear God, no]."

Another volley thundered.

Louisa had a death grip on Abu's arm. Her eyes slammed shut at the gruesome sight, And her heart stopped at the thought of Ben dying like Sowar Ganju Lama. The sowar's laughing face replaced her imagined scene of Ben's death. In her memory, she, Jeevan, Ben, and Ganju raced up the hill in their search for the temple. Anger welled up inside her.

Gunfire cracked and popped, spreading the acrid smell of burned black powder.

Louisa forced her eyes open.

More carbine blasts echoed in the small vale, but the last ghost appeared invulnerable. At each black powder explosion, a green light pulsed outward from the front face of the little glass pyramid.

Then, in a blink, the pulses stopped. An ax clipped one of the little pyramid's glass corners, and the pyramid spun away.

Thoresten flung his second ax. Before it was halfway to the target, there was a distant shot followed by the tinkling of shattered glass. The spinning specter plummeted toward the ground, and the ax passed through empty air. Ben fired twice more in quick succession. Both bullets struck the wounded ghost. Splinters blasted away as the fractured pyramid plunged into the grass.

Thank God.

"Hold your fire!" Jeevan called out.

Louisa fought back anguish while everyone waited and watched. All eyes stared at the giant pyramid, anticipating more of the glass tomb's devilish flying children. After several minutes, Ben started back to the woods, and Jeevan went as if to meet him. Without a word, Jeevan marched around Ben, straight to the crumpled pyramid.

With his rifle in his left hand, the duffadar pulled his revolver and fired all six shots. Only tiny fragments remained of Sowar Lama's killer. With one last act of defiance, Jeevan spat on the pile of glass before standing near the scattered remains of his soldier. Ben stepped next to the duffadar and put his hand on the Lancer's shoulder.

After another minute, the two spoke, and Ben dropped his arm. His face a thundercloud of rage, Jeevan said something to Sowar Chib as he stormed back to the woods. He yelled, "Ram and Judge, take six men! Two men to a side of the pyramid behind each building. Stay in the woods. Watch for more of those bastards coming out of the pyramid. Shoot anything out of the ordinary. Signal when ready."

Two men shouted back in unison, "Yes, Duffadar!" More instructions drifted through the woods, and several men moved off.

Jeevan said, "We will wait for thirty minutes. If nothing comes out, the second group can move to the corner. From there, we will cover Captain Ben and the scouts as they look for a way into a building. Acting Lance Duffadar, pick a man and go help the sowar retrieve the body of our brother." Two of the Lancers ran from the tree line toward the sowar, who knelt among the bits of remains. The men laid out a rectangle of cloth and began the disturbing yet necessary task.

Ben and Thoresten had reached the far corner of the black building and had put their backs to the buildings.

Two rifles poked out from the tree line, aimed at the top of the glass structure.

The top of a pyramid is called a pyramidion, Louisa thought as her geometry lessons came rushing back. *That's not important now.*

"Ready," echoed around the complex as the snipers reached their designated locations.

Time seemed to slow down as they watched and waited.

Abu's face had an ashen color.

"Are you okay?" Louisa received a silent nod and a gulp from the young man. She said, "I know."

With his pocket watch open, a frowning Jeevan gestured toward the trees. He turned and started forward.

Her hand on Abu's elbow, Louisa walked out of the trees between him and Esther. They angled around the remains. Ali, Ssherrss, and Khepri trailed a few yards behind Louisa with several Lancers following them. Louisa avoided looking at the last place she'd seen Sowar Lama and where his friends now worked in grim silence.

She blinked away tears that threatened to become a torrent. She stepped closer to Abu, seeking a safe harbor from despair. The sand slipped with each footstep, forcing her to watch the way forward while keeping a wary eye on the glass tomb.

As they passed the broken remains of the first flying pyramid, Abu detached from Louisa and veered toward it. He kicked through the debris. After wiping his foot in the sand, he hurried to rejoin her and the dimaerites.

Louisa stepped behind Jeevan as they reached the corner of the coal-colored building. A sowar had positioned himself at the corner of the red building. Ben and Thoresten jogged toward the middle of the black building.

The red building had a large entrance set in the center. The duo disappeared into a similar cutout in the black building.

After three or four minutes, the lanky human and the short, muscle-bound dwarf jogged back to them. Disappointed, Ben said, "There's a set of sliding doors, but no matter what we tried, we couldn't pry them open. We're going to check out the red building and then the gray one." He slapped his thigh. "There must be a way inside."

Jeevan said, "We'll follow and provide cover from the other corner."

Khepri said in a saddened voice, "We have angered the spirits of the Ancients. I don't think we should stay here."

Ben shook his head. "I know you're scared. Those who don't feel safe can return to camp. I'm staying until I get inside a building. Otherwise, Sowar Lama's death will have been for nothing."

Ssherrss put his four-thumbed paw on Khepri's arm. "We will sstay. I mmay be able to open the doorr. If anyone iss injurred, Kheprri will help." Then he whispered to his spouse, "It will be alrright, mmy love."

Khepri leaned down and nuzzled Ssherrss's ear before standing tall.

Ben tapped Thoresten on his armored arm, and the pair jogged toward the entrance to the red building. He and Thoresten again stepped out of sight.

Close enough to almost touch it, Louisa took full measure of the pyramid. A fifty-foot-wide strip of short turf separated the rectangular buildings from the shiny tomb. A single piece of mirror shot up at a sharp angle from the lawn, meeting the other sides of the monument at the apex. The corner where each edge of the mirror touched showed no sign of a seam, only a single sharp edge.

As Ben came into view, he waved them forward.

Jeevan admonished the non-soldiers to spread out to make themselves difficult targets. Louisa's anxiety grew as she walked fifteen feet behind Esther. Instinct told her to avoid the glass building, so she hugged the red stone wall. Everyone else did the same, staying as far from the mirrored surface as possible.

At the entrance, Jeevan sent two Lancers to the far corner.

Louisa peered around Esther and Jeevan, trying to see into the covered entrance. The same strange red stone covered the large inset area from the floor to the ceiling. Thoresten and Ben stood on either side of a gap between two enormous steel doors in what amounted to a graveyard.

The gap existed because some previous explorers had opened the doors at the cost of many lives. Countless bones, bits of armor, and other debris filled the landing. Shorter and twice as thick as human skeletons, a group of dwarfs had died here.

Wedged open, the doors held a dead explorer's rusting breastplate and sword like a vice. As a testament to the man's determination, a single arm and skeletal hand stretched out of the breastplate, stabbing upward. The point of the rusted blade held back the left door while the pommel pressed against the door on the right. Tarnished and pitted, the armor and sword looked as if they could give way at any moment.

Thoresten kicked a bone on the floor. "These are dwarven. From the number of remains, there must have been at least ten of them. They forced the door. Maybe some got inside."

With his foot, Jeevan raked the bones and rusted pieces of metal toward the grass. Louisa and the others stepped back to let him sweep.

When the way was clear of bones, Louisa said, "I'll go in and check it out." She shuffled toward the gap, but Ben grabbed her arm. She glared at him.

I thought we settled this.

Ben shook his head and let go. "You can go first, but let's make sure we can keep this open. The sword and armor look like they're about to crumble."

Ssherrss, the foxlike creature with a raccoon's bandit face, sauntered up to the gap. He moved his splayed hand in slow circles over the metal doors, close to where the rusted sword held the gap open. His hand lingered for several moments before moving over to the red stone. There, his hand hovered for a long second.

The metal singer shook his head. "I amm unable to mmanipulate the mmetal in thesse doorrss orr the sstone. It iss sstrrange, I have neverr sseen mmaterrialss like thesse. Sstarr ssteel iss mmalleable, even if I cannot crreate it."

With a wave of his hand, Ssherrss said, "Doess anyone have sommething to wedge in placce at the top and bottomm of the doorrss?"

Thoresten pulled a strange short sword from its scabbard. "I have this."

"And this." Esther held her khopesh. "Any chance we can get these back?" She flipped the blade from her right hand and caught it in her left like a practiced juggler.

Ben shrugged. "Ssherrss, what do you think?"

The stirithy held out a hand to Esther and curled his thumbs twice. She placed the hilt of the khopesh into Ssherrss's black hand. "I will usse thesse until I can rretrrieve other mmetal. Then I will rresshape thesse betterr than new."

Ssherrss stooped low and placed the hilt against the right door. He rotated the question mark–shaped blade until it touched the left-hand door. Two inches longer than the dead dwarf's sword, Esther's khopesh warped.

As Ssherrss purred, the metal softened. The door seemed to push into the steel at the tip and the brass on the pommel, and the metal parted down the middle at both ends. Ssherrss lowered the weapon until it reached the bottom of the threshold, and the metal hardened. Instead of a precarious wedge created by the hilt and the tip of the rusted blade, a two-pronged fork hugged the door.

With a silent curl of his thumbs, Ssherrss asked for the second sword. He motioned his spouse forward. "I need to sstand on yourr sshoulderss."

Like a mother lifting her toddler, Khepri grabbed Ssherrss around the waist and lifted. The two worked together until the fox-like stirithy stood on the giant wolf-woman's shoulders. She kept him steady, holding the backs of his calves as his bushy tail waved over her head.

Ssherrss ducked his head to stay under the ceiling while he worked. He purred as he repeated his sword transformations. In less than a minute, he had created another double-forked wedge, this one bracing the tops of the doors.

"I'mm done," Ssherrss said as he bent down.

The big she-wolf grabbed the fox-raccoon by the waist once more and lowered him to the floor.

Ssherrss pried the bony hand free from the hilt of the rusted sword. Its age-old vigil finished, the hand and arm bones thumped against the breastplate and broke apart.

Ssherrss clasped the rusted sword in one hand and the once-gilded armor in the other. In seconds, he pulled them free.

"It iss all yourrss." Ssherrss and his spouse moved out of the entrance, and he dropped the relics in the grass next to the pile of bones.

Louisa said, "Abu, light some torches. I'll go in first."

"Yes, ma'am."

Abu untied the bag he carried over his shoulder and retrieved two torches. He held one out to Ssherrss, who pulled out a dagger. The tip of the blade turned red hot, and he touched it to an oil-dipped cloth wrapped around a tree branch. The cloth caught fire. Abu lit the other torch and handed it to Louisa.

Stomach flip-flopping, Louisa had gory visions of Sowar Lama and the bleached bones of the dwarves. She gripped the handle of her revolver and took a deep breath.

Ben touched her elbow. "Be careful."

"When necessary." Louisa winked at him.

With the flames of her torch leading the way, she inched up to the opening. After examining the floor inside, she thrust the torch into the darkness. There were no obvious signs of triggers or pressure plates. She skipped sideways over the brace and landed on the other side. Her flame's aura spread into the darkness.

Where's a welf when you need one?

Louisa held the torch low, scanning every inch for signs of a trap. After taking several steps, she turned to the door and called out in Greek. "There's a large foyer immediately behind the doors. A hallway branches to the left and right. That is all I could see from here. I heard nothing."

Ben asked, "Did you see any writing or decorations?"

"No."

Ben looked over his shoulder. "Jeevan, can you and Ali run over to check out the gray building? If it's open, come back and tell us. If it's closed, we'll dismiss it. We'll start with this one, regardless. While you're gone, we'll go in and secure the foyer. We won't explore any more until you rejoin us."

Jeevan's voice carried inside. "Ready, Professor?"

"Jolly good." The sound of footsteps faded away.

"Abu, light a couple more torches," Ben said. "Esther and Thoresten, follow me."

With a powerful urge to explore, Louisa started forward. The glow from her torch illuminated the shadows, lighting up an enormous staircase. She glanced up at the landings above. Behind her, the light from the doorway flickered as others moved inside.

After she took another step, the entire room lit up like a spring morning in an instant.

"Whoa. How did you do that?" Ben stood in the foyer.

His words reverberated around the high ceilings. Louisa turned in a circle, seeking the source of the illumination without success. She hypothesized that the light emanated from the walls themselves. "No idea."

Torchless, Esther wormed her way inside. She had to do a few contortions to bring her shield through the gap.

The squatty samurai turned sideways and wedged into the gap. After a moment, he stepped back and removed his weapons. Holding his axes and another sheathed short sword above his head, Thoresten went for attempt number two. Halfway through, his shiny black armor scraped against the doors, and he came to a stop. With a grunt, the dwarf popped through the gap, leaving a long scratch along his armor's lacquered surface. Scowling, he moved to allow Abu inside.

Louisa felt drawn toward the giant stone staircase. Deep and tall, each step would be a challenge for someone of her stature. Each five-foot-wide step sat two feet higher than the last. The stairs might be comfortable for Khepri, but no one else. The path branched at the landing set along the back wall.

A red stone railing led up to the bright banister that ringed the oval opening above. Unlike large foyers back home, it had no domes or impressive murals. The entire room had an emotionless, utilitarian quality.

Silence reigned while everyone absorbed the strangeness of the Ancients' building. Ben turned in a slow circle as Louisa said, "Where to, o' intrepid leader?" Her words echoed back in a whisper.

Abu gasped. Everyone turned toward the hallway on the left. Tall and wide, the corridor now glowed with the same bright energy as the foyer. The passage stretched to the end of the building with inset doors, two to a side.

Ben jerked his chin toward the light. "That way looks good."

"Isn't this some nanty narking?"[1] Jeevan poked his head inside the door. "Captain Ben, no luck with the other building. I'll tell the lads to pull back and guard the entrance."

Louisa caught Jeevan's attention with a wave. "Can you ask them to put the torches out and give them back to Abu? We might need them if the lights go dark."

Jeevan stepped inside and made a quick circuit, then took Ben's and Louisa's lit torches to the opening. He handed them off to a Lancer on the other side. A minute later, Ali entered, followed by Khepri and Ssherrss.

Ben and Louisa led the group down the left passageway. The group's level of apprehension rose.

---

1. Nanty narking is a tavern term, popular from the early 1800s, meaning great fun.

About a fourth of the way down the hall, Louisa and Ben came to two doors set across from each other. Made of opaque glass, the portals were six feet wide and ten feet tall, with nothing visible beyond.

Thoresten brushed past Louisa, moving her aside like a child's toy. He said in Greek, "Stand back. I will shatter the glass."

Ben yelled in Greek, "No!" He stuck out his arm to bar the dwarf's progress. "We don't know what could happen. The Ancients might blow up the building or send more of those ghosts. We need to unlock the door. Everyone back up, except for Louisa, Abu, and Ali."

Frowning, the dwarf retreated into the hallway. Ben stepped to one side as Abu and Ali moved beside Louisa. Ben pointed toward a series of symbols on the door.

Four and a half feet off the ground and embedded in the surface of the glass were pale white glyphs in the Ancients' script. Below them was the outline of a triangle. Smaller Ancient text appeared next to each line that made up the triangle.

"Any idea what this says or does?" Ben asked.

Nothing came to anyone's mind.

Abu stepped forward and touched the triangle. All the letters and the lines brightened. He used his index finger to touch the script above one line. The letters jumped from inside the glass to Abu's finger, similar to the magnetized sand surrounding the complex.

Several exclamations broke the silence. Abu jerked his hand away. The characters moved back to their original position and grew dim.

With eyes narrowing in concentration, Abu placed his finger against the surface above the alien letter again. "I think it's the Pythagorean theorem."

He moved his finger along the glass, and the character tracked with his digit along the surface. The onlookers gasped. He drew a circle around the diagram and the other text until a rectangular area to the right of the diagram lit up.

Back and forth, Abu moved his hand. The glyph appeared to wiggle away from his finger when it moved over a certain spot. Abu pulled his finger off the glass, and the letter dropped into place.

"Hmm, which do you think is the symbol for squared?" Abu whispered to himself.

Ali bonked his forehead with the palm of his hand. "Of course, Abu. That is exactly what this is. Why would the Ancients create a locking mechanism that uses math?"

Ben nodded. "If it is a lock. And why did they even need locks? They were in complete control. What did they have to fear?"

Ali's brow furrowed. "All the slave races would have known this theorem. It's not a particularly good combination."

As they spoke, Abu continued building the algorithm. His challenge became finding which glyphs represented the addition and equal signs. The first time, Abu guessed and dropped a letter where the addition sign should go.

The area of the equation flashed, and the door reverted to its original state. Undeterred, Abu tried again. This time, his guess worked. As he dropped the third of the squared symbols over the line representing the hypotenuse, there was a brief double flash.

The door slid open, and the room beyond lit up with the same springlike radiance. Abu moved to the side with a proud smile and held his hand open in invitation.

As he passed, Ben patted Abu on the shoulder. "Great job."

Louisa mouthed, "You are outstanding," as she passed by. She heard the others' congratulations behind her.

Once again, Louisa sensed the room's utter strangeness while feeling that she had been in similar rooms. That significance evaded her like a terrible itch. The long rectangular room held eight counters, four to a side, separated by a wide aisle.

As if one end were levitating, the glass counters extended from the stone walls and stretched to the aisle but had no legs. The tabletops were around four feet high and three feet wide. Louisa made her way between the first and second counters closest to the door while Ben walked down the aisle to the back of the room. The rest of the crew spread out.

With a whoosh, the door closed. A moment of panic hit Louisa as she realized they had forgotten something important. She spun, saying, "How do we open the door from this side?"

To her relief, Abu, holding a pencil and a notebook, waved from the corridor. The opaque glass had become clear. Thoresten walked toward Abu, and the door slid open well before he reached it.

Relieved, Louisa smiled and looked for Ben. With the counters reaching up to her chest, she stretched to see over the tops. She estimated that anyone using these as counters would need to be at least Ben's height.

Don't assume.

Louisa asked the room, "Do you think these are counters or benches? Either way, the Ancients were tall."

Thoresten exclaimed, "Faen! ['Damn,' in Norwegian]."

The dwarf stood across from Louisa between the second and third counters. Ancient text glowed inside the glass between them. Everyone else rushed to the blocky, black-armored warrior.

"What did you do?" Ali asked.

Thoresten shrugged. "I laid my ax on the table."

Louisa placed her hand on the glass. Bluish-white script appeared inside. She recognized one letter from the Seba, though it was inverted from what she was familiar with. She removed her hand and turned to face the door and the other counter. She put her hand on the surface again, and the same alien runes glowed around it, but this time in the correct direction.

"Amazing," Louisa whispered.

Ben sidled next to Louisa. "What is this?"

She pointed.

Ben said, "If I have to guess, it's some sort of technology like the scroll. It must be harnessing electricity or even light in ways we can't comprehend." He stepped farther down the same counter, putting some space between them. He placed his palm on the surface, and the same text became visible in front of him.

"It is the Ancients' magic. They have sung their magic into these tables," said Khepri.

Ben and Louisa shared a smile and nodded at Khepri. Louisa didn't want to explain their hypothesis about the types of technology it would require to make these incredible creations. Technology that most people on Earth had yet to even imagine.

With a finger, Louisa touched the groups of characters that she thought of as words and sentences. Each one brought forth more indecipherable text.

"I touched the glass with my finger, and the writing disappeared," said Thoresten.

Khepri placed a big, sharp-clawed hand on the glass. Nothing happened.

In the same row but across the aisle, Esther shrugged. "It works for me."

Louisa pointed to Ssherrss. "You try it."

The stirithy harrumphed, his eyes and ears the only visible part above the counter he stood beside. He reached over the edge of the counter and slapped his hand on the glass. Again, nothing.

Ali frowned. "It doesn't work for me either."

"It has to be something to do with their magic," Ben said.

Louisa poked at another group of letters. "That's what I thought."

Soon, all the regular humans in the group were experimenting with the tables. Ali stayed with Abu, providing suggestions. No one could do any more than Louisa.

After about ten minutes, Ben said, "We can come back and try more things later. Let's explore the rest of this building."

With a shared sense of frustration, the group moved across the hallway to the next door. This one sat on the left and had a similar locking mechanism. Ben made quick work of the door's math problem. Identical to the first room, it had eight counters, and the same glyphs appeared when a non-magic user touched the glass. The group gave up after a few minutes and moved down to the third room.

The lock wasn't a challenge, and once inside, they found much of the same. Thoresten pointed out something everyone else had missed. "The tables are getting shorter. This one is at least half a foot shorter than in the first room we entered."

Everyone agreed. Otherwise, the room's mysteries remained elusive. They continued to the next door, and, as Ben neared the entrance, the glass slid open with no need to unlock it.

As he walked inside, Ben looked over his shoulder. Louisa followed him and noticed the pronounced difference in the height of the counters. At only three feet tall, these tables were a perfect height for her. She touched the closest tabletop, activating more Ancient characters. They differed from those in the other rooms.

As Louisa touched the first symbol, the script formed into nine rows of five letters and a last row containing only two. She poked the first emblem in the first row. A squawking sound came from the table, and the crowd jumped. Louisa pressed the second glyph, and it made a very different bird-like tweet.

Ali positioned himself beside Louisa and smiled. "There's no doubt now. We are in the kindergarten room of a school for Ancients. I'm ninety-nine percent certain this will allow us to learn the Ancients' alphabet. Also, did anyone else notice that the math problems were getting progressively easier?"

Abu responded, "I noticed. If the pattern repeats, the math problems should get harder as we go down the other hallway. Of course, the easiest room may be at the other end. Either way, we can quickly test that theory."

Ssherrss purred, "I have evaluated the glassss in each rroomm. It iss immposssssible for mme to duplicate. Therre arre mmaterrialss I do not know. I amm not even able to sseparrate themm."

On the other side of the counter from Louisa, Ben rubbed his chin. "Maybe every building created by the Ancients is the same."

Ssherrss shook his head. "No. Sstarr ssteel is mmalleable, and mmost of it commess fromm an Ancientss' building."

As Louisa pressed more script, Ali said, "This is so amazing. I would assume the children progress through the rooms at their own pace. It will take a while, but I'm sure we can learn everything this room can teach."

Ben asked, "How long do you think it will take you to learn to read Ancient? Also, Ssherrss, maybe later you can explain this star steel. I've heard you mention it a couple of times."

The stirithy nodded. "Lil's ssworrd that killed Isskurr is sstarr ssteel."

Ali looked up, his face lit by the glowing script. "This bird-like language will make it difficult. If it's a phonetic alphabet, then probably a few days to a week to learn the basics. That's if I have someone to help me."

Abu had made his way to Louisa's other side and touched the tabletop. After a few pokes, a flower popped up from the surface as if by magic. It floated a foot above the table.

Startled, Louisa took a step back while Abu stayed still. Made up of a long stem and yellow spiky petals, the flower had non-Earthlike qualities. The plant appeared as real as the flowers in the grassy field where they had first arrived on Aaru.

The onlookers held their breath as Abu moved his finger forward. He pressed against one petal, and they heard a series of squawks and tweets. Four characters appeared, floating below the flower. Abu had retracted his finger at the noise but now tried to grasp the stem. His hand passed through it as if it were an apparition.

Oohs and *ahs* came from the watchers. Abu's hand moved up and down, and his palm passed through the vision of the flower. He punched at the symbols on the table. The flower disappeared, replaced by a miniature tree.

Fingers drumming on the glass top, Ben said, "As incredible as all this is, we need to explore the rest of the building before we start kindergarten classes. Let's stick together. If you're right, Ali, the math problems will progress, and we will need everyone to work them out."

Ben led the way to the last door on that end of the corridor. The glass portal slid open at his approach. As Louisa entered the room, its familiarity brought back a few fond memories, but most of those reflections made her want to leave as fast as possible.

Similar to the dormitories at the Maison d'éducation de Saint-Denis, beds were spaced equally around the room. Unlike the narrow, uncomfortable beds of her teen years, these were large oval *nests*. That was the only word Louisa could think of to describe them.

Set into the ground, each bowl contained a cushioned interior made of a shiny material Louisa had never seen before. The stark white cushions matched the oversize white metal dressers beside each bed. Melded into the wall, a large mirror sat above each chest of drawers. Big by human standards, the furniture's scale matched the kindergarten size of an Ancient.

Ben used both hands to yank on two metal handles, which opened the middle drawer of the closest dresser. He pulled out a big vest made of a material similar to that covering the cushions. The vest had several pockets and some hooks, which Louisa imagined holding different types of tools.

Ben said, "Each of you take one or two dressers and search them. If you find anything interesting, show the group, then place it in the middle." After closing the open drawer, he reached for the top one.

Louisa moved to a dresser and pulled the top drawer open. She went up on her toes to peer inside.

Good thing this is child-size.

Slow and steady, Louisa removed a miniature suitcase and placed the box on the ground. After inspecting every inch of the outside, she opened the lid an inch at a time, ready to jump away. Inside, brushes lay in a small divider while jars of what appeared to be dried paint filled most of the larger compartment.

Abu yelled, "My bottom drawer has a baton and some curved glass thing."

Louisa looked over at the teen holding up the two objects.

"Same here," Ali said.

Squatting, Louisa pulled open the bottom drawer and found the same things. She laid them next to the small case before moving to the last set of handles. The middle drawer held several vests, colored in the same speckled red as the building.

As she ran her hand along the surface, she tried to gauge its origin. As smooth as silk, the cloth amazed her. When she pulled it, the material stretched before snapping back to its original size and shape. Determined to make an outfit from the wondrous material, Louisa emptied the suitcase before placing all the folded vests inside.

She held a paint jar above her head. "Ben, what do you think the paints are for?"

He popped his head up from digging inside a second dresser. "No idea. They did not seem to care about art. Makeup? Maybe that's how they personalized themselves." He shrugged. "I just don't know."

Louisa placed all the dried containers in a drawer before picking up the baton and the glass artifacts. She placed them in a growing pile in the middle of the room before searching the last dresser. It contained the same items as the first. The vests went into her suitcase while the stick and the shallow translucent bowl joined the combined cache.

Abu sat cross-legged next to the pile of objects, turning a squarish stick around in his hands. Louisa sat beside him. She picked up two of the curved objects, comparing them. It took a moment, but she realized there were slight differences. Grabbing another one, she determined it to be about an inch longer and half an inch wider than either of the previous two.

"These are all slightly different." She held up two of the crystal objects.

"Maybe they are custom-designed for each student," Ali conjectured.

"Could be," added Ben.

"Incredible," Abu said.

The teenager had half of the stick in each hand. A thin piece of bendable glass stretched between the two parts.

"How did you do that?" Esther asked.

"Pull it apart." Abu demonstrated by pushing the two pieces of metal together. The glass disappeared somewhere inside, and the pieces met with a click. He pulled the metal from each edge, and it separated without a sound. His arms stretched apart until there were twenty inches of the thin material between the two-foot-long sticks. Laying the glass on the ground, he touched it. Nothing happened.

Ssherrss yipped and threw one of the curved objects into the pile. He bared sharp teeth with a growl.

Khepri asked, "What happened?"

The stirithy grumbled, "Put it on mmy head, and it sstung mme."

Ben asked, "Why did you do that?"

"I thought it mmight fit."

Khepri picked up the same curved object and moved it cautiously to her head. As soon as it touched her head, she yelped. "That hurts."

"Let me try." Louisa held out her hand.

The hysakas handed it to her. After removing her hat, Louisa placed the curved glass on her head. Nothing happened.

Ben grabbed a different bowl and placed it on his head with no ill effects.

Everyone watched as, one by one, the group tried on the curved artifacts. Thoresten's face scrunched as if he'd bitten something sour. He removed the object and said, "It stung me."

The dwarf held it out to Ali, who shook his head.

Nothing happened when Esther or Abu put it on their heads.

Ali said, "Like the counters, these things sting those of us with magic because they're built to keep the Ancients' slaves from using them."

Ben gave a crooked grin. "Most humans don't have magic. The Ancients must not have built a defense against regular humans." He picked up one of the long sticks. "Maybe the artifacts that aren't working need power. We'll expose the Ancients' hats and these sticks to the sun and test them later. Let's pack these in the cases and go check out the other end of the hall."

Ben and Louisa led the pack toward the other end of the building. As they crossed the foyer, lights flashed on, illuminating the corridor ahead.

The pings of multiple rifle shots sounded through the gap. Jeevan rushed to the door. As he poked his head outside, the muffled bangs fell silent.

A sowar said, "Duffadar, we destroyed two more of the flying things."

Scowling, Jeevan turned to the group. "We need to hurry. I don't like the lads exposed like this."

Shaking his head, Ben said, "We will move as fast as we can, but we need to be thorough." He waved toward the hall, and Louisa led the way.

At the next door, Louisa found a geometric problem waiting, but, unlike the other static diagrams, this one moved. She observed the problem cycle through several iterations. It showed a circle rolling across a straight line and a semi-circle appearing as it rotated.

"Ali, what do you think?" Ben asked.

The professor scrunched up his forehead while Ben tried to will the answer to come forth. He mumbled, "I know I've seen this one."

With an air of superiority, Louisa said, "Really?" She touched the letter she guessed to be the number four. Holding her finger on the glass, she moved over the line representing the circle's diameter and let go.

The door slid silently open. Slack-jawed, Ben and Ali looked at Louisa in surprise.

"The length of a cycloid is four times the diameter of its generating circle." Louisa shook her head and sighed. "What exactly do they teach at those American and Egyptian universities?"

"I knew I had seen this before," Ben said with fake chagrin. "I would have gotten it eventually, Miss Know-It-All."

Louisa shared a smile with him. As she stared into his blue eyes, she forgot where they were until Ali added, "I believe Christopher Wren created this proof in the sixteen hundreds. That means, if the locks keep getting harder, we'll only be able to open one or two more doors."

Ben blinked several times, then shook his head as if waking from a dream. "We'll find out soon enough. Let's investigate this one, shall we?"

Ben and Louisa walked through the threshold, shoulder to shoulder. She so wanted him to grab her hand. Greeted by more of the strange counters, Louisa saw something different out of the corner of her eye. She let out an involuntary scream. "Mítir Theoú!"

Before Louisa's call to Mary left her throat, Ben pulled the trigger of his revolver. The bullet struck the back wall and ricocheted. Louisa ducked below the closest countertop.

An ax flew over their heads toward the giant lizard in the leftmost corner. Like the bullet before it, the ax flew through the beast and bounced off the back wall. The dwarf yelled a war cry and charged.

"Stop! It's not real!" Ben yelled in Greek.

Like a boulder, Thoresten rolled to a stop in front of the lifelike brownish lizard.

Or is it a bird? Louisa thought.

The creature stood on its hind legs and had long arms that ended in hands with five clawed fingers and a thumb. A long, curled tail poked over the thing's head, making Louisa think lizard, but the creature's head screamed bird. With an eagle-shaped head and body covered in small reptile scales, the creature had traces of feather follicles on its long arms.

After picking up his ax, Thoresten poked the creature with the sharp end. An ax blade appeared behind the scaly, lizard-like skin as if the animal were partially transparent.

Ali's voice filled with awe. "By Allah, it's a reaper."

Esther said, "I think you are correct. I have seen old sketches and the bones of a dead one."

"At the temple, we had an extensive library documenting the previous Lamentations. Several books had very detailed drawings." Ali rubbed the thick stubble on his chin. "There is no doubt."

Louisa's heart rate moved closer to normal. She took out a handkerchief and dabbed beads of sweat on her forehead. "That was frightening. I would hate to run into a real one."

As Ben moved toward the ripvor, he kept shaking his head. Louisa followed while the rest of the group filtered into the room. The creature's huge clawed feet were a strange hybrid between an ostrich and a regular garden lizard. A chill ran down Louisa's spine when she saw the sharp point of the ripvor's beak, poised to strike.

"Interesting," Ben said. "Why would the Ancients be studying a ripvor?"

With a shrug, Louisa said, "It's probably like dissecting an animal for them."

Ben removed his hat and wiped off the sweat beneath the brim. "It is rather hot. Do you think the building is being heated?"

"It has gotten considerably warmer since we entered," Louisa said.

"No! They are the Ancients," Thoresten's voice thundered in Greek.

"What did you say?" Ben asked.

The dwarf ran his hand down a braid on his long beard. "Think about it. The creature's size fits with these tables, and it might sleep in a nest, similar to the sleeping quarters."

Louisa held up her finger and placed her Ancient case on the nearest counter. She pulled out one of the glass objects and walked over to the giant lizard. She reached for the creature's head but it remained an inch beyond her fingers.

"Allow me." Ben held out his hand. Louisa gave it to him. Ben positioned the bowl over the creature's cranium. The curvature of the bowl wasn't an exact match, but it was the correct shape, only scaled for a smaller skull.

Her head craned back, Louisa said, "From what we've been told about the ripvor, they could never have built this place. They're not smart enough."

"A mystery, for sure." Abu grinned.

"One we won't solve right now. We need to keep going. These countertops are just as undecipherable as the other ones. I want to clear the building before we start our studies in earnest." Ben stepped away from the lighted glass to move toward the exit.

The next door contained a math theorem that the group's collective mathematical knowledge could not puzzle out. The rest of the doors in the hallway were the same until they reached the end. At the first of the last two doors, Louisa found a nonmathematical lock with Ancient text. There seemed to be some sort of question with no obvious answers.

As Louisa touched the text in the glass, the door let out several squawks. She jumped back, bumping into Ben's chest. He grabbed her shoulders to catch her. She was already hot, but the temperature in her cheeks rose several degrees. She inhaled his virile scent. "Any ideas?"

"None," he said in a husky voice as time seemed to stop.

"Let me try." Abu rolled his eyes as he scooted by.

Ben let go of her shoulders.

As Abu poked at the glyphs on the door, Louisa tried to grab his wrist. "Don't!" she warned.

Squawks, much louder than before, blared at them and bounced down the passage. The warm light inside the building flashed green, then blue. The colors cycled as a loud, almost debilitating whistle blew, and the building trembled.

Merde.

Abu mouthed, "Sorry." He put his head in his hands.

Ben yelled at the top of his lungs, "Get out of the building! Run!"

The Good Doctor grabbed Louisa's wrist and spun her around. She managed to grab hold of Abu's shirt collar and tug him along with her. Together, they stumbled after Ben. In front of them, the rest of the crew barreled down the hallway toward the foyer. Louisa fought the instinct to panic and pushed Abu ahead of her.

Khepri and Ssherrss were already outside when the rest of the group reached the gap in the entrance doors. The reports of more rifles rose above the screaming squawks and intense whistling. The big doors drew back. The top brace fell to the floor outside the entrance, and the bottom brace bent when the two doors sprang back toward the center, keeping the others inside. At the bottom, the double-forked khopesh held the gap open.

Ssherrss scrambled for the fallen brace. As he rose, the metal of the transformed sword seemed to stretch wider. He tossed it over his head to his spouse, who caught it with one hand. She jammed one forked end onto the edge of a door. She tried to line up the other end as the doors once more parted. When they slammed together again, the top brace held but with a sound of wrenching metal.

Ssherrss stood to one side, holding the bottom brace. Clutching the other forked brace, Khepri stood to the other side with one hand extended high. Esther tossed her shield through the gap and side-hopped through. Jeevan followed, carrying one of the Ancients' suitcases mere moments before the doors slammed together a third time. The broad-shouldered dwarf waited several seconds for the doors to open wide again and hopped with light feet across the threshold. When the doors came together again, the metal braces screamed and crackled.

Louisa shoved Abu toward Ben. He yanked the teenager through the doors as they swung wide. Hanging onto the Ancients' case, Louisa took two quick steps and dove toward where the gap should be.

As several tons of steel came together like two great hammers, she spun the case with her hand and twisted her shoulders to fly sideways. Khepri and Ssherrss pulled their hands away a moment before the two halves slammed into the braces. The khopesh and the sword snapped on impact but provided a hiccupped pause to the doors' inevitable reunion.

Louisa's feet cleared the portal by several inches as the two ends shut with a thunderous bang. She brought the case to her chest and curled into a rolling landing until a giant hand grabbed her ankle.

For several seconds, Louisa swung back and forth like a pendulum before coming to a stop. With a death grip on the Ancients' case, she stared at Khepri's knees while dangling upside-down. The big hysakas lowered Louisa to the ground before releasing her ankle.

The deafening whistle still echoed around the courtyard. Louisa hopped to her feet and dusted dwarf bone particles off her hands. Another small flying glass pyramid shattered nearby. Mirrored shards bounced and skidded down the large pyramid's glass side.

Jeevan waved them toward the field of sand. "Keep moving." The duffadar turned his carbine skyward and backed toward the corner between the two buildings. Louisa ran behind Khepri through the grass and onto the sand. More shots rang out, and Louisa glanced back. Ben had stopped at the corner and was shooting. Jeevan and the Lancers raced toward him.

Heading for the trees that represented the finish line, Louisa slid and stumbled through the shifting dirt. It seemed to take her forever to reach the safety of the shaded canopy. Exhausted, she hugged a tree and tried to catch her breath. The whistle still blew, but her ears no longer hurt at the sound. Using the trunk as support, she turned to make sure everyone had made it.

Ben and Jeevan were the last to step out of the sand. Their bodies still heaving, they turned and aimed their rifles across the field. Louisa tried to shift the sand in her boots.

From his knees a few feet away, Abu gasped a ragged, "I'm sorry."

Louisa started laughing. Abu's shocked face made her double over, her guffaws coming between wheezing breaths.

For the second day since leaving Nippur, Louisa had cheated death. Joy filled her heart until her gaze fell on a patch of pinkish-red sand. With an abrupt choking cough, her laughter died, and she collapsed against the tree. For the first time in years, Louisa wept.

Chapter 17

The Tomb of Mortals, Choru, An 5660, Day 14

In the first hour after dawn, Masako held Abu's hand and stared up at his bloodshot, sleepless eyes. Her heart ached to see him in so much pain. She wished she could do more to stop the tears running down the cheeks of the young man who had become her protector.

Most of the people in Abu's group stood around a fire, watching the remains of the soldier who had died the previous day become ash. The soldiers who wore the strange hats that Abu had called turbans were chanting in yet another foreign language. With their limited ability to communicate, Abu had told Masako that she had to stay at the camp when he went to the glass pyramid the previous day.

Not long after Abu left with his family, two distraught soldiers returned with a large sack that dripped blood. Masako couldn't speak with the men, but she knew that something awful had happened.

After years of degradation, Masako didn't know whether the gods existed, but she was sure that if they did, they hated her. Then came Abu.

While she watched the men stack wood for a big fire, Masako had reached out to whatever power existed beyond what she could see and touch. She prayed that Abu and his family would be safe. To her relief, they returned three hours before sunset. With slumped shoulders, Abu had shuffled into camp. He became inconsolable when he saw the bloody sack sitting on a platform built over a large woodpile.

Unable to calm him and frustrated at her lack of words, Masako had sought information from the grumpy stirithy who spoke the welven tongue. He tried to explain why Abu and his people had gone to the strange buildings. She couldn't grasp most of what he said, except for three things. The Ghosts of the Ancients had killed a soldier, and Abu's people were from a place called Earth. They needed something from inside the buildings to find their way home.

The chants came to a sudden stop, and Masako squeezed Abu's hand tighter, trying to find a little comfort of her own.

Will I ever have a home?

After a somber evening spent remembering the life of the happy-go-lucky Ganju and his sunrise funeral, Ben searched for the proper words. He stood in front of everyone except the guards on the ridges. They had formed a semicircle, waiting for direction from Jeevan and him. He looked past the eyes full of heartache and latched onto the cause for which they fought.

"Home. Today, that word seems so very distant because a piece of our home," Ben patted his left breast with his hand, "the part we carry in our hearts, will remain here forever." He added strength to his voice. "We don't know whether we are any closer today to fulfilling our quest to return to our families, but I am asking you not to lose your resolve."

Ben pointed toward the now placid complex. The whistling alarm had stopped a few minutes after the harried explorers had moved into the trees. "We will watch the buildings today. If everything remains calm, tomorrow we will attempt to enter the pyramid. We don't know whether we will have an opportunity like this again." He lowered his voice. "We must fight on."

Several heads nodded when Jeevan stepped forward. "We've paid a heavy price, but, lads, I expect you to soldier on. To do your best. Not for Queen and Country but for one another, for Sowar Lama." The duffadar straightened to attention and saluted his men. The Lancers returned his salute. "Back to your posts. Dismissed."

With the crowd dispersed, Jeevan asked, "Do we have to go back?"

"Are you asking whether I think we will get what we need?" Ben said. "I doubt we will even be able to get inside. But, as I said, we have to try. We may never have another chance to get this close to ruins like these. At least, we know how to beat those flying murdering bastards."

Jeevan frowned. "For now." The duffadar's proud smile raised Ben's spirits. "If we shoot them from multiple sides, the ghosts appear to be vulnerable. But what if they send out something new, or they alter their tactics? What if our sharp shooters miss? We are playing a very dangerous game."

"If we don't get inside on the first try, I promise we'll go back to Alexandria as fast as possible. In the meantime, let's see if the devices we found will work any better after some time in the sun." He walked toward a patch of grass in the clearing where all the artifacts lay. It was the one spot that had avoided shade from the surrounding trees all day.

Masako, Louisa, and Abu had beaten them to the spot. They sat around the artifacts, each holding a device. Soon Esther and Thoresten joined the circle while Ali stood over Abu's shoulder.

"Look at this!" Abu's excited voice captured everyone's attention. He held an expanded stick, and its connecting bendable glass lay on the ground in front of him. He touched the thin flat surface, and the familiar squawk of the Ancients' third letter in their alphabet bounced off the buildings.

Ben stepped behind his son. From this new angle, he could see the same characters they had worked with on the tables in the kindergarten room.

"This one works," Esther said in Greek.

"This is fantastic!" Ali said with a grin.

Ben couldn't remember the man ever looking that happy.

He sat beside Louisa and grabbed a stick. It split as if he'd pulled apart two magnets. Inside, bendable glass unspooled as he moved the metal ends farther apart. He placed the glass on his lap and poked the surface.

The now-familiar glowing blue glyphs appeared inside the thin glass. By pressing his finger a few times, Ben accessed the Ancients' alphabet and then the picture word game. Unlike the lifelike pictures that floated over the countertops in the classroom, this time the image of a fish appeared inside the glass itself. Pressing on the fish brought forth the Ancients' squawking word for fish.

After a few more minutes, the group had confirmed that all the metal batons had soaked up enough energy from An to function.

Hope they work when we leave the valley.

Ben collapsed the pieces together and placed the long stick in his belt, intending to test the device when they left the Tomb of Mortals. He reached for one of the shallow bowls and balanced it on his head. Louisa mirrored him.

She laughed. "Maybe it's a crystal ball. Tell me what you're thinking."

The crystal on his head slipped, and he had to hold it in place.

Crystal ball. Why not?

Ben concentrated on sending her the words he didn't dare speak out loud.

I'm in love with you.

Louisa's eyes grew distant for several seconds. Then her mouth fell open.

Uh oh. "Did you hear me?" Ben asked.

Louisa shook her head in slow motion as she smiled. "No, but I got it to work. Instead of trying to read thoughts, ask it a question."

"What do you mean?"

"Just what I said. Think of a question, but use images," Louisa urged with a nod.

By now, Abu and Esther were staring at the pair.

Here goes. Ben thought. *What is this place?*

Ben pictured the giant pyramid and then visualized the Ancients' character in their grammar that represented a question. Images and Ancient text flooded his mind. A picture of two ripvor popped up. Faces painted yellow, one ripvor wore a gray vest, and the other, a black vest. An image of several large, blue-speckled eggs replaced that of the ripvor before a new scene flickered by, of the eggs hatching. Several ripvor sat at the counters in the classroom before Ben's mind went blank.

Ben whispered, "The pyramid's a hatchery." Then louder, "I just asked 'What is this place?' meaning the pyramid, and the answer popped into my mind as images and text. I saw some sort of mating selection ritual between two ripvor, then giant eggs, the eggs hatching, and then scenes of ripvor in a classroom." His words came fast. "Louisa, what did you ask?"

"I asked, 'How do these glass things work?' and more text and moving pictures than I could comprehend flashed through my mind. Didn't understand any of it, but it showed me everything." Louisa shook her head. "Then I asked how to power the Seba, but I guess I don't know the right way to ask the question."

"You'll get it, eventually." Ben put the glass bowl down and plucked the stick from his belt. "I'm going to start learning Ancient."

Chapter 18

The Tomb of Mortals, Choru, An 5660, Day 15

Several wisps of smoke marked the location of the Earthlings' campfires on the far side of the valley. The white tendrils signaled they had recently doused the flames, and Djoser wondered if it meant that his quarry was on the move.

Should I have the Remulans lay a trap on the path back to Alexandria?

Bastet, Djoser's caracal familiar, shifted in the harness strapped to Djoser's chest. The wind singer sent the thirty-pound feline instructions to be still. Designed for two, the harness was unbalanced since Kheket, the caracal's partner, had died. Djoser refocused on the land below. From a thousand yards above the Tomb of Mortals Valley, he could not see many details of what the Earthlings were doing.

Two days earlier, Djoser had flown over the Ancients' pyramid. He confirmed that the Earthlings and their Alexandrian allies were exploring the ruins. After locating the guard post set on the ridge between the two valleys, he reported back to Legate Saluvius. The leader of the Remulan's Pretorian Guard had pushed his men hard. Now they were within striking distance.

Fifty legionary scouts were waiting for Djoser's command to begin the assault on the ridge. The wind singer did not doubt they could take the high ground, but the attack required the scouts to move uphill, over open ground, for over a quarter of a mile. The primary force of more than a thousand men would reach that last cluster of woods within the hour and follow the initial attack.

As Djoser made a wide turn, his martial eagle, floating hundreds of yards above him, sent a message: *Prey in the open.* Djoser caught movement on the crystal field in front of the glass pyramid. Several humans were making their way across the glass.

They're not leaving.

Pointed in the direction of the Remulan scouts, Djoser flew over the ridge and began losing altitude. He needed to be within a quarter of a mile to send the attack signal. With the Earthlings distracted, there would be no better time.

Djoser's thoughts became words in the ears of the two centurions hidden in the forest below. He received one legionary's acknowledgment, followed by: *All glory to Ahura Jupiter.*

In a ragged line, the Remulan scouts jogged out of the trees, their gold cloaks fluttering behind them. Individual legionaries went from one large boulder or felled tree to another, looking for anything that might provide cover. As Djoser watched the soldiers, he leaned into a turn and heard the first loud bangs from the Earthlings' weapons.

One legionary fell to the ground. As the wind singer shook his head, a searing pain tore through his right patagium. He pulled his arm inward. His mind reeled from the injury, and all his singing stopped. Body flipping and twisting in midair, he plummeted toward the rocky slope of the ridge.

Fly, Djoser's mind screamed as he tried to regain control.

With an angry snarl, he forced his arms wide. The excruciating stinging made his head throb, but he kept his wings extended. Upside-down and doing an off-kilter circular motion, he sang the flight song. Fear of death strengthened his every action. With a slight twitch of his wrist and hand, he flipped over. The ground rushed at him, and on instinct, he tucked his arms a little and leaned into the fall, gaining speed. Yards from the red, rocky ground, he spread his wings and arched his back.

The skin ripped around the hole in Djoser's wing, slamming him with fresh waves of pain. As he flew level for several seconds, the weightlessness of his fall lessened until he climbed, and gravity once again tried to pull him back to the ground. His wing couldn't take much more, but he had to climb. The copse of trees that once hid the Remulans grew larger as he hurtled down the slope.

Another projectile accompanied by a whistling sound whizzed close by. Djoser added a slight turn to his climb. With the shapes of the leaves now visible in pristine detail, he cried out to his eagle. The bird acknowledged his message to bring Shemush, a heartbeat before Djoser smashed into the yellow-leafed canopy. His feet flipped over his head, and his body tumbled. Countless branches slapped and cut at him. His entire body seemed to rip apart as everything went black.

Ben's scalp itched, and he adjusted the strange contraption on his head. As part of the plan to get inside the pyramid, Louisa had insisted they bring the crystal bowls they had taken from the Ancients' nursery school. The ability to query the device for helpful information might prove useful, but Ben had warned them to be careful when using the device. For several seconds after the answers came, each receiver had appeared paralyzed.

After supper, Louisa and Khepri had sewn special scarves made with material from the Ancients' vests to keep each bowl on the wearer's head. They sewed a little pocket for the curved glass, along with a hole in the middle. The device would not work without direct contact with skin or hair. Finally, they sewed two long strips to the holder, completing the weird bonnet.

Feeling like an idiot, Ben pressed his hat harder onto his head. One tiny solace, his pork pie hid everything but the ties.

Only Ben, Jeevan, Esther, and Louisa would make their way across the glass piazza to the covered entrance into the pyramid. Ben reasoned that Ali, Ssherrss, Khepri, and Thoresten carried the Ancients' slave-magic. It might set off alarms just by their presence. Everyone but the guards on the two ridges watched from the trees, with snipers surrounding the pyramid.

Ben couldn't see inside the walkway, but he had used the device to show him a locked door at the end. There were no visions of ghosts or other traps. If they opened the door, Ben would figure out Plan B.

The ultimate pessimist, Ssherrss, had revised Ben's Plan A. He insisted that when (not if) they failed, the group should immediately begin the trek back to the Alexandrian border. His exact words were, "When yourr explorrationss go to sshit."

At first light, the fox-raccoon ordered camp broken and the luggage packed. They only needed to load the baggage onto the horses to hike out of the Nefru Mountains.

Staring across the field of glass, Ben wondered whether they had taken enough precautions. Snipers were relocated to have a clear view of the front of the pyramid and could hit any object from three directions at once.

Ben looked left and right. Esther stared at the pyramid with determined intensity. Louisa tilted up her chin. And Jeevan gave him a wink, which Ben took as a sign that the duffadar's melancholy had broken.

Ben looked toward the enclosed hall that extended away from the center of the slanted glass. He picked a path through the remains and the debris leading to his destination. He closed his eyes and spent another moment in silent prayer. *I am willing.* He had to trust that God was able.

Ben crossed the small barrier of sand and stepped onto the platform of glass. Boots clicking with each step, he kept Agnes at the ready. The teams' footsteps followed him.

Nearing the first of the uncovered mass graves, Ben thought, *So far, so good*. He rapped his knuckles twice on the wooden stock of his rifle. Their path took them halfway to the floating eggs.

Ben told himself he would investigate them after the pyramid. He sent a simple mental question to his magical headgear. He used the ancient tongue and pictured the eggs. *What does that do?*

As before, visions filled Ben's thoughts. In the scene, ripvor creatures entered open doors in the two eggs. Squawking narration accompanied his lifelike dream.

The doors closed, and both eggs levitated higher. Tethered together, the oblong spheres flew over a landscape very different from the Nefru Mountains. The scene changed with the eggs rotating around the tether. They flew higher and higher until the eggs spun through the darkness of space. The machine headed toward a yellow-red moon or planet backlit by more stars than Ben had ever seen.

A vigorous shake on his shoulder stopped the vision. As if waking, Ben blinked. He realized he'd come to a stop amid the scattered remains of previous explorers.

"What's wrong?" Jeevan.

"I'm okay. I made the mistake of asking what those eggs did." He stepped toward the entrance.

Jeevan followed. "And?"

"I'll tell you when we're done. It's amazing."

"I can wait." Nervousness crept into the duffadar's voice. "I'm getting that creepers feeling again. The sooner we're done, the better."

Ben gave the white eggs one last look and could have sworn he saw a glowing aura encasing the white objects. After he closed and opened his eyes, the strange light disappeared. He dismissed it as an illusion created by the weird mind-answers.

It took them several nerve-wracking minutes to reach the walkway. Ben crept into the shade within, and, as with the school building, the walls lit the path. At the end of another thirty-yard walk, they reached a giant opaque glass door set inside a cutout built into the base of the pyramid.

It had a lock different from any Ben had yet seen. "Stay alert," he said. "I'm going to ask the bowl how to unlock this."

The information came in a flood, showing Ben how to access the lock but not how to answer the question that kept the door closed. In the wall next to the door was a square hole five feet off the ground. Above it was a large, glowing blue circle.

Ben said in Greek, "We're out of luck. To open the lock, a ripvor looks into the blue light, and then a puzzle pops up in the square."

Esther pointed at the cutout with her new khopesh—the one Ben had found in the tunnel near the Temple of the Crescent Valley back on Earth. "We suspected these doors would have an actual lock."

Their heads snapped back at the crack of a rifle. They looked down the covered walkway leading to the field of glass.

Ben started running and soon passed Esther, who had been closest to the exit. The groups' footsteps reverberated through the glass hallway. As they emerged into the mid-morning light, a half-dozen shots rang out.

Ben never slowed as he took in the chaos unfolding. Ali ran across the platform, yelling and waving. "Remulans! Run!"

Out of the woods closest to the path burst the two Lancers and two Lochem guards from the valley entrance. The men stopped and formed a line across the path, with several more Lancers joining them.

With Masako wrapped around his neck, Abu sprinted away from the shooting toward the campsite.

Racing to the action, Thoresten crossed paths with Abu. Several Lancers and the remaining Lochem were close on his heels.

As if on cue, the woods spit forth dozens of Remulan legionaries running in a disorganized mass. They screamed an incomprehensible battle cry at the sight of their quarry. The gold-cloaked soldiers picked up their pace as they split into two groups. The majority headed toward the Lancers and the Lochem on the path. With shields and swords leading the way, at least another dozen Roman legionaries ran onto the glass platform toward Ben and his scouting party.

How the hell? Ben shuddered as fear-fueled adrenaline filled his veins.

He yelled, "Louisa, go to Abu!"

Louisa slowed and looked for the teenager. She changed direction and ran to meet the two youngsters near the far corner of the glass field.

Ben stopped and aimed.

Esther raced past him toward the battle line forming on the path.

A Remulan turned to cut her off. Ben led him by a few feet and pulled the trigger. The man's left arm went slack, and the weight of his shield made him stumble. When the large wooden rectangle struck the glass, he tripped and fell.

Ejecting a spent cartridge from the breach of his carbine, Jeevan stepped beside him.

Agnes spit fire, and another legionary grabbed at his chest. As the soldier's face smacked the mirrored surface, his helmet came free and skidded across the glass. His two comrades raced around his body. Ben dropped the one on the left, while Jeevan killed the one on the right.

"We have to keep moving." Jeevan tugged on his sleeve and headed toward the path, trying to outrun the gold cloaks.

After chambering another Winchester round, Ben sprinted after him.

The Alexandrian soldiers had built a line across the dirt path. The Lancers formed wings to the sides and a little behind the Lochem. Twenty gold cloaks slowed enough to form a straight line, their shields touching. In lock step, the Remulans on the path jogged toward the Alexandrians who waited to meet them.

Well ahead of Ben, Esther reached the end of the platform and leaped into the air. She slammed her shield into the side of the legionary at the end of Remulans' line. Her khopesh took the first man's leg off below the knee, and he stumbled into the gold cloak beside him. Thoresten raced around the Lancers and threw himself into the off-balance legionary next in line. His axes flashed, and a helmeted head popped several feet into the air. The black-armored ball of death pushed forward, bowling down the line.

More shots rang out. Ben saw several charging Remulans collapse. His quick assessment concluded that the legionaries on the glass boneyard had the angle on them. Ben and Jeevan both raced toward the grassy mountain path, but the legionaries were about to cut them off. Ben skidded to a stop, determined to make sure Jeevan survived. While he took aim at the legionary closest to Jeevan, Ben blocked out any thoughts of his own mortality and allowed his rage to rise. The hyper-awareness of battle lust possessed him.

The first of several dozen legionaries were fewer than twenty yards away, and Ben relished the thought of killing the enemy. He drew in a breath, then exhaled and pulled the trigger. The bullet punched through the first Remulan's shield, striking the man in the throat. The legionary twisted to the ground.

Ben growled, cocked his Winchester, found his next target, and pulled. A second soldier and then a third dropped. Jeevan had come back to stand next to him. The duffadar fired his Enfield revolver again at the closest gold cloak.

Two more. Then revolver. Like a whisper, rational thoughts echoed inside Ben's animalistic mind.

"Ghosts!" rang out in English as Ben took his next shot.

The warning was repeated in Greek. The beast inside Ben ignored the words, refusing to loosen its grip on his mind. This unforgiving demon had first visited him in Arkansas and countless times since. An unseen struggle raged inside his soul. His fear for Abu's and Louisa's safety won the skirmish, and he swung back toward the pyramid. Four of the small glass ghosts floated away from their mother, straight toward the glassy boneyard where Ben stood.

Jeevan raised his revolver to aim at the ghosts. Ben lurched forward, jerking the duffadar's arm down. Jeevan glared at him as Ben said, "We can't win." He pointed to the battle on the grassy mountain path. "If we end this threat, everyone else will be safe. The ghosts can finish the Remulans on the glass. You and I can't."

With a grimace, Jeevan nodded. The two of them spun back to the Remulans charging across the glass boneyard. Ben expected to be vaporized at any moment but kept shooting the Winchester from his hip, cocking and firing until the trigger clicked empty. Next to him, Jeevan fired his revolver at the enemy until he needed to reload.

Close enough for Ben to see their fanatical, fearless faces, the rest of the attackers continued, undeterred by their losses. At least another twenty legionaries followed the handful who were almost on top of him and Jeevan. He dropped Agnes and pulled his revolver.

Ben started to squeeze the trigger but hesitated. As if choreographed, the closest ten Remulan legionaries on the glass field lost all semblance of balance. After a few stumbling steps, they collapsed to the ground, clasping their hands to their ears.

One of the ghosts levitated closer to Ben and Jeevan. A light shone from the top of the small pyramid, bathing Jeevan and Ben in blue. A small jolt of electricity ran through Ben's body, and then the light stopped. The ghost rose to line up with its three brothers.

Three streams of lightning shot from the pyramids floating above Ben's head, and three of the gold-cloaked soldiers who were not writhing in pain on the ground exploded.

Dear God.

The grotesque scene added another bleak dream to Ben's catalog of nightmares.

Why did it ignore us?

Ben scooped up his rifle and ran for the path while shouting to Jeevan, "Get to the woods!" A strange physical vibration penetrated his back and shook his bones as he fought to run.

Pop, pop, pop followed Ben. He tried not to look back, but the hum rattling his teeth made him glance over his shoulder. Surrounded by a pulsing glow that matched the frequency of the hum, the two eggs exploded skyward. A solid wave of sound and air picked him up off his feet and flung him forward.

Tumbling feet over head, Ben held tight to Agnes. His shoulder slammed hard into the crystalized ground, and he yelled in pain. He rolled a few more times before coming to a stop on his back.

Like small peas rotating around a string, the eggs kept going higher. Their revolutions came faster until a flashing white saucer hung in the sky between Aaru's two planetary rings. Poof. Like a streak of light, the white shrank to nothing. Ben struggled to get up when Jeevan pulled him to his feet.

With a mirthful grin, Jeevan said, "I told you that I had that creeper's feeling." He loped toward their group's battle line.

Ben hobbled after him, checking on their Remulan pursuers. The men who had collapsed from the sinister sound lay still, while the rest of their comrades struggled to regain their feet after the shockwave.

On the mountain path, the Lancers' rifles had decimated the attackers whom Thoresten and the Lochem had not killed. Another series of pops came from behind Ben, and the last few gold cloaks on the glass field fled to the woods.

Ben was only seconds from reaching the end of the glass platform when an arrow slammed into the crystalline surface and snapped in two. Ben instinctively changed direction and heard the whoosh of an arrow missing him by inches. Jeevan gave a garbled cry and fell a few yards away.

The duffadar grasped behind him, trying to reach the green-feathered shaft sticking out of his shoulder blade. Another arrow jutted out of his calf.

Ben zigzagged to his friend. As he grabbed Jeevan's uninjured arm, Esther ran two steps past them. An arrow thunked into her shield as she stood between them and the archers hiding in the woods. Ben swung Jeevan's arm over his shoulder and pulled the duffadar to his feet.

Jeevan let loose with an agonized scream. "Argh! That hurts like hell! Gada! ["shit" in Punjabi]."

A block of black armor appeared and hoisted Jeevan over his shoulder like a sack of potatoes. Thoresten turned and jogged toward the Lochem shield wall with no hint he carried a two-hundred-pound human. The dwarf's every other stride brought forth invectives from Jeevan in his native Dogri.

Another arrow plunked into the shield. "Move," Esther admonished Ben.

The Lancers continued to shoot until no more arrows came from the woods. A near silence fell over the vale as they reached the path. The only sounds came from Jeevan and the other wounded men.

Khepri helped the dwarf lower the duffadar to the ground.

With his friend receiving the best available medical attention, Ben said in Greek, "Esther, take your men and some Lancers up the path. Take care of any Remulans you find."

Lance Duffadar Ram said, "Captain Ben, these are just the advance scouts. At least a thousand men are coming up the valley on the other side."

One of the Lochem told Esther the same in Greek. "How long do we have?"

"Half an hour, maybe less," Ram answered.

Esther gave Ben an expectant look. "What do you want us to do? We can't go back the way we came."

Ben paused a beat to consider their options. "Take care of any stragglers and, in ten minutes, run back to meet up with us."

The young Alexandrian officer nodded and began giving orders.

To Lance Duffadar Ram, Ben said, "Take your four best shots to the ridge. Slow them down, but no heroics. Stay well ahead of them."

The Kalari expert and the shortest of the Lancers gave Ben the same grin he used when he was about to kick someone's butt. "Yes, sir." He trotted away, bellowing orders.

Ben grabbed Sowar Chib's arm. "Get everyone else back to camp. Load the horses."

"Yes, sir." The sowar took off down the trail.

Ssherrss stepped beside Ben and poked him in the side. "Therre iss only one placce to go. We will go to Grrommerrk."

Ben's brows knit together. "What's that?"

"It iss the sstirrithy capital. I think they will allow uss to enter ssincce you arre Earrthlingss," Ssherrss said.

Ben shrugged. "Doesn't look like we have a choice."

Chapter 19

Grrommerrk, Capital of the Stirithy Nation, Choru, An 5660, Day 16

Louisa's foot snagged on a rock hidden in the shadows, and she grabbed Ben's elbow to steady herself. Surprised, it took him a moment to find his balance.

"Sorry," she whispered.

"Not a problem," Ben mumbled.

"Ben, what are your thoughts on the space vessel?" Louisa said as she kicked an unseen loose rock and sent it skittering off the path.

"What does it portend? I wish I knew. It scares me. Now, more than ever, I feel like we are running out of time." He paused for a long beat before continuing "It's like the bells of Big Ben are ringing, and when they stop, something awful will happen."

Louisa rubbed the back of her neck to work out the tension. "We should look on the bright side."

Ben laughed. "And that is?"

"We're alive. Focus on that."

"Are you forgetting the thousand angry Italians trying to kill us?"

Louisa had not forgotten. Her aching legs would not let her. They had been running from the Remulans for the last thirteen hours with just enough rest stops to keep her legs from going rigid with cramps. "See, it's already working." Louisa chuckled. "You're worrying about the things you can control."

With a grunt of acknowledgment, Ben went silent. Louisa's thoughts turned inward while she scanned for obstacles in the blackness. Not for the first time, she longed for a pair of goggles like Ki's.

Not only would the glasses allow her to see tonight, but they would make Louisa's primary trade that much easier. Of course, she might never need to go back to that life, but it didn't hurt to be prepared. Even the light of Aaru's two moons, Mata and Shu, did not make up for the shadows of the forest on the mountain trail.

She meant to ask Ali what he thought about the orbits of the planet's moons, which perfectly matched the times of the Khonsu. Louisa had never studied astronomy with any genuine interest. Yet even as a novice, she thought it improbable that two heavenly bodies could line up like that without some sort of divine or maybe magical intervention.

At that moment, two crescent moons hung in the sky, stacked upon each other in a near-vertical line. The natives called the approaching midnight hour Twins. It heralded the beginning of the second day of the Khonsu.

To keep her mind clear at this late hour, Louisa reviewed the moons' improbable interactions. The larger moon, Mata, meaning "Mother" in Aaruan, traveled the equator from east to west. Unlike Earth's Luna, the speedy Mata circled Aaru twice a day. Shu, the smaller of the two, meant "Son." He traveled an eternal path along Aaru's equivalent to the prime meridian, moving from south to north, but his circuit took two full days. Of course, during the daylight hours, An, the Father became part of the three-way dance. Louisa gave them one last glance. The two moons were in a perfect line, and the new day had begun.

For five seconds, she stopped and closed her eyes to regain a bit of night vision. She focused on the shadowy ground in front of her and started forward but turned at the sound of running. Like a ghost, Ssherrss padded out of the darkness up to Ben. The stirithy's eyes glowed within his black face.

Ben kept his voice low and asked in Greek, "What news?"

Ssherrss said in a normal tone, "The Rremmulanss arre two hourrss behind. The ssniperrss sslowed themm down. They ssent sscoutss to flank the mmen, but I took carre of themm. The garrlic eaterrss go verry sslow now. We arre increasing the gap." Fox-like ears twitched back and forth in the moonlight. "We will rreach the rriverr in thrree hourrs and rresst forr an hourr until firrsst light. Then trravel the Grrommerrk rroad."

"Will the gap be enough?" Louisa asked.

Ssherrss nodded. "Plenty. Let'ss keep mmoving."

Several twisted ankles and three hours later, the exhausted group threw themselves down on the grass near a shallow, slow-moving river. His black armor a hole in the night, the big dwarf sat with a *thud* next to Louisa.

Jeevan sat next to Thoresten and said in his best Greek, "Thank you for helping me."

Thoresten turned to Louisa and his bass voice rumbled, "Please translate my words to him so that he understands."

"Okay," Louisa agreed.

The dwarf's dark helmet turned back to Jeevan. "You mean nothing to me. I only saved your stupid, always smiling face for Ki."

Louisa gulped and began to translate to English when Jeevan said, "No need, Miss Louisa. I understood enough." Grinning, Jeevan slapped the dwarf on his back. "Still, I owe you one."

"Leave, or I will give you one that requires a life singer to reattach your teeth."

The duffadar jumped to his feet and laughed. "Good, good, good." He shuffled into the gloom.

The enormous block of black armor lay down and in a few moments was snoring. Exhausted, Louisa used her knapsack as a pillow and joined him in slumber.

She felt as if she'd just closed her eyes when Abu shook her awake.

"Miss Louisa, we're leaving in five minutes. I have some breakfast." Abu handed her a hard biscuit and a slice of cheese that reminded her of Manchego.

She rubbed her eyes and bit into the biscuit. It was so hard, she had to use her back teeth to tear off a piece. With a little cheese, it tasted quite good, even if it made her jaws sore from chewing.

"Where's Masako?" Louisa asked between bites.

"Asleep. It's been a long two days for her."

"For all of us. Let me know if you need help."

Abu shook his head. "She's a good kid. Besides, I'm responsible for her being here."

"I know, but don't be afraid to ask for help. We will find her someplace safe because God knows being chased by Remulans and wandering around alien ruins is not a good situation for her."

A sigh was Abu's only answer.

When the pre-dawn allowed them to see more than five feet ahead, Ssherrss had them moving again. Louisa chuckled at the sight of Ssherrss riding on Khepri's shoulders as the pair stepped into the water. The river came up to the giant wolf-woman's calves as the caravan followed the couple down river.

Louisa refused Ben's suggestion to ride a packhorse, not wanting to further burden the poor animal. She waded into the stream, teeth chattering, which was much colder than the bath at the waterfall. She wondered whether the storm from a few days prior had helped thaw some of the snow still lingering at the higher altitudes.

To her amazement, Louisa found sure footing on the riverbed stones, despite the tug of the current. She sloshed along in front of Abu and Ben, who pulled their reluctant steeds. Masako sat between the luggage on the dun mare.

Ben commented, "I think the stirithy shaped the riverbed. They must have made it less slippery."

Too tired and cold to make conversation, Louisa mumbled, "Uh, huh." She trudged along following the men in front of her. Behind her, Abu and Masako continued their language lessons, even as Abu's teeth chattered.

As the column came to the incline on the side of the valley, they waded into a narrow, winding canyon. The walls climbed higher and higher until Louisa had to look straight up to see the sky.

Several toes had lost feeling, and she regretted not riding. Then Khepri stepped out of the river and disappeared. One by one, they walked onto a flat landing at an almost invisible switchback cut into the canyon wall. Louisa climbed onto the stone surface, and painful tingles shot up from her feet.

The horses' packs scraped the walls of the narrow path as they progressed through many twists and turns. Louisa stomped her feet, trying to restore blood flow while following the Lochem soldier in front of her. When the path opened, the dripping caravan emptied into a long, wide area that ran beside the river.

Ten elongated boats with shallow bottoms were tied to a wooden dock running the length of the shoreline. Along the wall next to the clearing sat a barracks-like structure. Scattered throughout the clearing were giant gas-fed fire pits.

At least ten welves and ten stirithy directed the group to the fires to warm themselves. Grateful, Louisa went to an uncrowded firepit in the center and warmed her legs. The men unloaded the horses and transferred the baggage into two of the longboats.

Ali, Esther, Ben, Abu, Masako, and Thoresten soon joined her around the fire.

"Once we're dry, we'll all load into the boats. The stirithy will blindfold everyone for the rest of the journey," Thoresten said.

"Even you?" Ali asked.

The dwarf nodded. "Even me. The welves are allies, but the stirithy take every precaution. They are fierce warriors, but because of their stature, they can never go toe-to-toe with the other races. Thus, they make the path to Grrommerrk impossible to find, and it's as well defended as Nippur."

"How will they keep the Remulans from finding this place?" Louisa asked.

Thoresten rubbed his fingers up and down the two braids of his beard. "There is a guardhouse near where we stepped out of the river. The stirithy can open and close the wall so you can't see the entrance from the water."

Balanced on one foot, Ben held the sole of his other boot toward the fire. "I know it's easy for us to ride in the boats, but how will they get the horses to cooperate? I can't see Jeevan leaving Chetak behind."

The dwarf shook his head. "You Earthlings have much to learn. Your men will need to get the animals onto the boat and have them lie down. Then Khepri will make them sleep. They should not waken until we are at our destination."

"That's amazing," Abu exclaimed. "I'm going to go watch." He moved toward the horses tied up closest to the docks.

Masako watched him go and shuddered.

"You can ride with me." Louisa put an arm around the girl's shoulders.

Masako seemed to relax a bit. "Thank you, Miss Louisa."

After giving her hand a reassuring squeeze, Louisa turned to the dwarf and asked in Greek, "Is this where we part?"

"I will send word to Ki that I am here. I will stay until I hear back, but, yes, I will go to the welven embassy once we reach the city." Thoresten paused and added, "We should rename the Tomb of Mortals as 'School of the Ancients.' I will tell

Lil to add that to the report. I'm taking some of the devices as part of the report to the governess." Thoresten saw Jeevan at another fire, and his eyes narrowed. "I hope that this is goodbye."

Louisa ignored the poor man's feelings and asked Ben, "What's our plan? Where do we go from here?"

Ben pushed his hat up and scratched around the special bonnet. "I'm not sure where we can go from Grrommerrk. The goal is still the same: we need to find a way to power the Seba. I'm thinking when we're safe, we can query the bowls for the answers we need."

"If we can't go back the way we came, are we closer to Hurra or Alexandria?" Ali asked.

"You are closer to Hurra but very far from a major city in either nation. The closest city is Kerma," Thoresten answered.

"We will figure it out," Ben said. "Let's get to Grrommerrk first. I'm ready to get some sleep."

––––––––––––––––

Abu watched Khepri put the horses to sleep. It was *magical*. Once a Lancer had coaxed a horse into lying down in a boat, the life singer had the Lancer hold the animal's head. A long touch from the hysakas caused the horse's head to loll as the animal became drowsy and in a few seconds fell into a deep sleep. During the current ride, Abu wished Khepri would have done the same for him.

Being blindfolded for hours as they sped down the river gave Abu plenty of time to think. He kept turning over the improbability of some mystical source powering the incredible feats of the wind, metal, and life singers like Khepri.

Abu thought of experiments he might try to see whether there were differences between the human magicians and the other races that did the same singing.

Ali is also a life singer. Maybe he and Khepri would help me.

When his mind wandered, a myriad of visions dominated, and all of them starred Esther. His pulse raced at the memory of her wet, naked body. He remembered how she used her finger to twirl her red hair when concentrating. Anytime his memories showed her laughing with that twinkle in her eye, he smiled. No matter what he remembered, his vision ended with his lips touching hers.

Each time, Abu allowed himself to indulge in these thoughts for a few seconds before forcing himself back to more serious subjects. Like where were they going? The welf and stirithy guards had blindfolded their entire party. Then the smaller stirithy took charge of the longboats, navigating them into the slow-moving river.

A few minutes after leaving the docks, Abu's darkened sight went pitch black. The smell of the air became dank and oppressive while echoes of rushing water reverberated at a different cadence. They had entered a tunnel. After the first twenty minutes, he lost count of the number of turns and twists, so he spent the rest of the trip pondering those other matters.

Without warning, the blackness turned to dark red, and the air freshened. The muffled lapping of water against the prow of the boat was drowned out by birds chirping. It gave Abu hope they were close to their destination. The purrings and mumblings of a stirithy came closer, and then small hands touched his shoulder. Deft fingers lifted his blindfold, and Abu blinked, turning his head away from the bright afternoon light of An. When his sight adjusted, he gawked at his surroundings.

The river had widened to six boat lengths, and its crystal-clear water deepened until the light no longer reached the bottom. On either bank, groves of enormous trees grew as far as the eye could see. Through the occasional gap in the canopy, he made out mountain peaks in the distance.

Unlike any wild forest Abu had experienced in the past—not that he had encountered many—this one had an unnatural order. Unnatural did not mean unpleasant. It was perhaps the most calming place Abu had ever been.

The nearest tree soared a hundred feet in the air, but most amazing were the other natural elements intertwined around the base and the lower branches. So incredible were these additions to the tree, it took Abu a moment to find where an element of wood, stone, metal, or glass ended, and another began. The designs were like the welven homes of stone. Both integrated all the elements controlled by the metal-singing stirithy, but where Nippur was a beautiful tomb, this city overflowed with life.

While he drifted by, Abu might have believed that he looked upon a tree that grew inside a giant sculpture. His fantasy burst when a hidden door opened. A female stirithy, wearing a bright yellow shirt and a matching skirt, walked out from the treehouse. Her puffy brown-furred tail swished back and forth. Seeing the visitors, she waved to the boats. Without thinking, Abu raised his hand and returned her welcome.

He intuitively knew that the grassy areas between trees were the streets and the roads of this city made of forest. There were no free-standing buildings. Every enormous tree acted as the foundation of a home, a store, a pub, or a warehouse. Everywhere, there were stirithy moving about their daily business wearing bright-colored outfits. A dock with one or two small boats was built near every building-tree next to the river.

Abu's boat floated by vessels going in both directions, captained by diminutive fox-sailors in bright outfits. Laughter and cheerful conversation drifted across the water, bringing an undercurrent of joy to the harmonious forest city.

To add to the merriment in their lives, each of Grrommerrkss' citizens wore ensembles of cotton shirts, dresses, pants, or skirts in various hues of flamboyant reds, yellows, blues, greens, and oranges. Some wore matching attire, but just as many wore tops and bottoms of complementary colors.

River traffic traveled in both directions until the river split at a large junction. Branching out like the spokes of a wheel, straight canals went off in eight different directions. On a center island, a single larger tree stood, at least two times the height and girth of the other trees Abu had seen in the city so far. An open piazza filled the space between the river and the massive trunk of the tree.

All river traffic rotated counterclockwise around the center tree before turning down its chosen path. The oarsmen for Abu's group of boats made their way around before choosing the center canal and continuing in the same direction they had been going. They traveled at a steady but slow pace, passing three more spoke-and-wheel roundabouts in the river, before the river emptied into a vast lake.

At the center of the lake, on a large island, stood a gigantic tree taller and wider than Abu could have ever imagined. From his studies, he knew some trees reached three hundred feet in height, but this tree had to be at least twice that. Its diameter had to be hundreds of feet wide. In every way, the tree dwarfed the great pyramids he had seen in Cairo. Near the edge of the island and surrounding the giant tree stood a forest of *smaller* tree-buildings. They appeared as sprouts in comparison.

It took them twenty minutes to cross the lake and pull up to a series of long docks that stretched into the water. They unloaded, and once again Abu watched Khepri at work. Each Lancer in charge of a horse would hold the animal as she woke it. She took much longer to bring the horses out of their slumber to make sure the animals did not startle while in the boats. An army of stirithy longshoremen, dressed in bright coveralls, unloaded the boats and the baggage while everyone gathered on the shore.

Abu caught up with Umrao, walking shoulder to shoulder with Esther. It irritated Abu that they appeared to be having a private discussion. A sheepish Umrao said in passable Greek, "Uh, hi, Abu, doesn't this place take the egg?"

Umrao gave Abu another awkward glance. Umrao had not been learning Greek until he met Esther, and the speed with which he'd picked it up spoke to his newfound passion.

The whole mess brought a sour taste to Abu's mouth. "I guess so," he replied. "What were you guys talking about?"

Umrao shrugged without commenting, but Esther didn't hesitate. She smiled that smile he'd thought of so much as she said, "We were talking about spending some time together," before emphasizing, "alone." The look she gave Abu dared him to say something. A little more softly, she said, "You don't mind, do you? Umrao and I have a lot to discuss."

As if squeezed in a vice, Abu's heart constricted. He fought to hold back his resentment and stammered, "Uh, no, no problem." Then, with a little more sternness, "You don't have to tell me twice."

Abu rushed away from the couple without knowing where to go. Behind him, he heard Umrao say, "You didn't have to be so harsh with him. He's just a kid."

To which Esther replied, "It's better this way." The rest of her sentence drifted away as Abu pushed through the Lancers, the Lochem, and the stirithy working the docks.

Abu needed to get as far away as he could. The tears he'd fought so hard broke through in a rush. Desperate, he looked for anyplace he could be alone. He left the long dock and found rows of crates stacked up next to a tree-warehouse. He squeezed down several rows of boxes until he felt no one could see him. As he leaned back against a crate, he sank down sobbing.

———————————

It had been a long day, but Ben had to push his weariness aside to meet the city's seven governing counselors, known as Haty-a. For the third time in as many weeks, he prepared to meet people whose decisions would determine his group's fate.

This is getting old.

He did not feel the same sense of helplessness as when entering the welven city. Still, he chafed at the lack of control that he and his friends had over their future.

As they made their way toward the gigantic tree in the center of the island, Ben realized Abu had disappeared. Louisa handed Masako over to Khepri and joined him to search for the teen. They headed toward the docks, yelling Abu's name. As Ben's concern turned to worry, an embarrassed Abu stepped out from behind a stack of crates. His eyes were puffy, and his face, flushed.

"What's wrong?" Ben put a hand on the teen's shoulder.

"Nothing. I just fell asleep," Abu mumbled and wiped his face. "I'm sorry."

Louisa touched Ben's elbow with a slight shake of her head. Confused, Ben cut off his next question. He left it alone, planning on asking her later. Instead, he said, "Try to stay with the group or at least tell someone where you are."

"Yes, sir."

Ben needed to sort out this new parenting conundrum, but they had some place to be. "We need to hurry." He started back toward the gigantic tree. Louisa put her arm around Abu's shoulder as they followed.

Find out tonight.

The inner circle of Jeevan, Ali, Esther, Ssherrss, and Khepri, holding a sleeping Masako over her shoulder, waited for them at the entrance. They stood before a monstrous complex, built around, in, and up the giant tree. At the sight of the trio, Ssherrss said something to the small detachment of stirithy soldiers. The soldiers heaved opened huge, thick doors made of translucent amber.

Frozen in time within the yellow substance swam a multitude of feathered fish, each a different color of the rainbow. Ben's group proceeded down a hallway for a long time. He thought they must have reached the trunk of the tree but could not tell because the smooth white marble of the walls and the floor never changed.

An itch made him adjust the strap under his chin, and he became self-conscious. He untied the bonnet and handed it to Abu. "Put this in the luggage when we get settled."

Abu took it and nodded, his eyes vacant.

At its end, the hallway opened into a large amphitheater-like chamber. Spread around the curve of the room and raised twenty feet high were seven pulpits. The oval chamber continued behind Ben and his friends. Stands were filled with stirithy wearing every color imaginable. The large, vibrant crowd was silent as his group formed a line facing the pulpits.

Ben tapped Ssherrss on the shoulder and bent down. "Why the public meeting?"

The whiskers on Ssherrss long, narrow snout twitched. He purred, "Sstirrithy have ssuperriorr goverrnmment. All deccissionss musst be trranssparrent. Do backrroomm deal, loosse powerr, and go to jail." The stirithy lifted his snout, taking on a smug countenance.

Wow. We would need more prisons, Ben thought.

A stirithy in a bobby-blue uniform stepped forward and purr-grumbled in Aaruan. Ben heard the words in English. "Please stand for the honorable Haty-a Mmarrssheltokssimm." The foxlike creature's dark brown fur was brindled with strands of white, and he wore a drab gray smock as he stepped to the front of the middle pulpit.

Ben lost track of the list of stirithy names as each man and woman of the council stepped forward to look down at them. Ben never saw a babiakhom but knew there must be one somewhere in the room.

When the introductions ended, the constable said, "Please present yourselves to the Council."

Ssherrss did the introductions for himself and the others. During the drawn-out process, Ben considered what to say when it became his turn to represent their group.

The first stirithy pointed at Ssherrss. "Outlander Ssherrsslatigausss, you have brought many strangers to our home. As interesting as they are, we hope you have a good reason." He looked down his snout at Esther. "Daughter of ben Zev i Hurasu i Enoch, we welcome you to Grrommerrk. Many An have passed since your mother's last visit, and we remember her fondly. She helped our people in a time of need. Her prowess in battle and grace in diplomacy are the stuff of legends. You are always welcome here."

The leader paused for a moment and looked at Ben and the Earthlings clumped together. "People of Earth, welcome to Grrommerrk. We hope your stay will be pleasant. May I ask what your plans are?"

Hope I get this name right. Don't say marshmallow.

Ben bit back a laugh, cleared his throat, and stepped forward. "Haty-a Mmarrssheltokssimm, thank you for your hospitality. We had planned to return to Alexandria after visiting the Tomb of Mortals, but Remulans attacked us and forced us to flee. We have had no time to consider our next steps."

"What was your business at the Tomb of Mortals?" asked, the Haty-a.

Give them only a little.

As he held up two fingers, Ben said, "We visited the Tomb of Ancients for two reasons. First, we wished to learn the Ancients' language." Ben dropped a finger. "We hoped that understanding their language would help us grasp how the Ancients powered objects like the Seba and enable us to find a power source."

The leader's whisker-like eyebrows rose higher. "Were you successful?"

Ben nodded. "Partly. We found a codex to the Ancients' language but have yet to learn how to power the Seba."

The Haty-a said, "Interesting. I—"

Ali broke in. "Your Honor, may I speak?" Ben gave Ali a baleful look as the professor continued. "I am a representative of the Keepers of the Seba from Earth. The Keepers tasked me with bringing warriors to help fight in the Lamentations."

The Haty-a held up his hand-paw, cutting Ali off. "You mean the Lamentations that may or may not occur."

Ali nodded. "Yes, Your Honor. On Earth, we had no way to know about the Phantom Lamentations. Now that I do, it does not negate the need to prepare. I could not bring a large fighting force to Aaru, but we brought weapons, which should give us an edge against the reapers if they return." He rubbed his pant leg with nervous energy and smiled. "I would ask that your council consider helping us create some of these weapons as a precaution. If the weapons are needed, time will be of the essence."

What the hell, Ben thought. *He doesn't know we can make bullets.*

The seven council members stepped away from their pulpits and appeared to be having a spirited debate. Somehow, the hidden babiakhom allowed them to have a private conversation, even spread around the room.

After a moment, the leader returned to the platform. "We have considered your request. Ssherrsslatigausss informed us of the power of these guns. He said they would not work without the help of someone from Earth. There is some unknown magic needed to make the black powder arrows it shoots."

Ali waved toward Ben. "This man can perform the magic needed to create bullets."

Who told him?

Ben glared at the group. Louisa shrugged. Abu had his back to Ben and his hand locked onto Esther's wrist. Her eyes went wide as Abu shook his head.

What is this?

Ssherrss's chin dropped to his chest as he mumbled, "He ssaw the planss for the deviccess."

Damn.

Esther shook free of Abu and glared at Ssherrss.

The primary counselor's foxlike ears pivoted, and his jaws moved like a hand puppet, but Ben heard nothing. After several seconds, the counselor said, "We will help you create two thousand guns of each type. You need to create a thousand special arrows for each weapon, but know this: We will make an equal number of guns for ourselves. And you will help us design them for stirithy to use and provide arrows for our guns."

How do I salvage this?

Ben gave Ali another scowl before saying, "Haty-a Mmarrssheltokssimm, that is wonderful news, but we, the Earthlings, will build the cartridges, what you called the special arrows, in secret. Please understand, we fear what might happen if the ability to make guns and bullets falls into the hands of a nation such as Remus. They could conquer all of Aaru if they monopolized the weapon."

"Then why not tell everyone how to make them?" the leader asked.

His voice firm, Ben said, "In the end, we may do that. Disseminate the knowledge to everyone at the same time. If you cannot respect our condition, then we ask permission to leave as soon as possible."

The council had another private discussion. Esther made emphatic hand gestures as she whispered to Ssherrss. Ali wore a smug smile, and Louisa gave Ben a conciliatory pat on his arm.

Ben had to hold firm on control of the mercury fulminate and primer production.

When the chairperson spoke, his voice sounded upbeat. "We accept the limitation so long as you provide us with five thousand bullets for each of our guns." He raised his snout.

"We agree."

"You have made a strenuous journey, and we will let you retire to your quarters. We ask you to enjoy the hospitality of our great city for as long as it takes to create the weapons. Our representatives will work with Ssherrsslatigausss to organize the effort. If you have any needs, please convey them to him. Enjoy your evening." The chairperson of the council bowed.

"Thank you, Your Honor." Ben painted on a grudging smile and bowed.

As different as a thunderstorm and its life-giving aftermath were Ssherrss and Sekhrey Rrummblinss, the stirithy escort assigned to Ben's party. He was a soldier in the small Grrommerrk army, whose title meant Captain of the Troop in Aaruan. Blondish fur added to the captain's sunshiny personality.

With stirithy-accented Greek, Rrummblinss said, "I'mm verry exccited to be yourr hosst. Pleasse, assk mme anything. We don't get mmany guesstss sso pleasse forrgive uss. Mosst of yourr mmen have been quarrterred in the barrrrackss. We rresshaped themm ssomme human-ssize bedss ussing two mmatrressssess. Luckily, ccity hall hass sseverral quarrterrss for welvess and hyssakass. We have given the thrree welf-ssize rroommss to the ladiess and the thrree hyssakass-ssize rroomms forr the gentlemen. What do you ssay, sshould you wrresstle forr firrsst pick?" He chuckled.

Ben deadpanned his reply. "No need. Abu, and I will share one of the hysakas-size rooms. I would think that Ssherrss and Khepri get another one. That leaves Jeevan and Ali to share the last one."

"Esther, Masako, and I can share a room." Louisa waved to the girls.

The teenage Lochem said, "I need a room for myself. I plan on having a private guest."

Louisa's eyebrows shot up, and Khepri chuckled.

What am I missing? Ben thought.

Ali raised his hand. "If there's an extra room, I will take it for myself."

Jeevan shrugged.

Ben caught Abu's downcast look, which reminded him to inquire later about what had upset the boy. He said, "Abu, can you go with Rrummblinss and bring our baggage?"

The teenager shuffled after Rrummblinss as the rest of the group made themselves at home. Ben found it difficult not to compare these quarters to those of their welven counterparts. Just as before, each suite contained a water closet and a bathroom with hot and cold indoor plumbing. The quality and comfort of the furniture were similar, but here metals and stone dominated instead of wood. The biggest difference, the hysakas-size bed and chairs, made him feel like a child.

When Abu returned, Ben asked, "Abu, do you mind sharing what's wrong?"

The teenager plopped himself into a large plush chair. His hands fidgeted with nervous energy. He sighed and said, "I'm an idiot."

"I don't understand," Ben said. "Why would you say that?"

"It's not important. There is nothing I can do about it," came Abu's dejected reply.

Wishing he had conferred with Louisa, Ben pressed on, "Maybe. But I can't help if you don't tell me what happened."

In a resigned tone, the teenager said, "There's a girl I like, but she likes Umrao. So now I feel like a fool, and I'm mad at them both."

Ben rubbed his chin. "I get it. I know how you feel."

Abu asked, "What do you mean? How would you know?"

Ben chuckled. "Abu, I wasn't always this old. I courted more than a few women in my days. One of them hurt me so bad, I didn't think I would ever recover."

Abu pulled himself up from his slouch to give Ben his full attention. "What happened?"

Ben settled into the other chair to recount a part of his life that, for once, no longer made his heart ache. "Do you remember when I told you about having to leave Georgia?"

Abu nodded.

"Well, I moved to North Carolina to attend college at Chapel Hill. I already had my engineering degree, but I wanted to learn more about, well, everything else. I took classes to get a Bachelor of Arts degree. To live and pay for my studies, I found work as a civil engineer. Soon, I befriended and became partners with Armistead Wilkes. We were like you and Umrao. He became like a brother to me."

With Abu's eyes wandering, Ben jumped to the heart of the matter. "About six months after I arrived, I met Nannie Stuart. She was the daughter of a general who'd died in the war. We met at a school social. She was so beautiful, so smart, and so charming. I was smitten. We courted for a year before becoming engaged."

The lovesick teenager now hung on Ben's every word.

"Right after graduation, I started plans for the house I wanted to build for Nannie. I had so many dreams about the family we would raise there. I was as happy as I had ever been." Ben sighed. "It was a month before the wedding when I walked in on her and Armistead in bed together."

Abu gasped.

"To say I felt betrayed is an understatement. The two people I trusted most in the world hurt me worse than any bullet ever had. Until recently, I thought I could never love again."

The boy grinned. "You mean Miss Louisa."

Ben smiled. "Maybe a little, but the first person who allowed me to love again was you."

Abu blinked in surprise. "Me?"

"Yes, Abu. I know it hasn't been long, but to me, you are my son, and I love you." Ben's eyes watered. "You see, what you feel right now is just a little of what I felt back then."

Nodding, Abu said, "Thanks, Dr. Ben. I know I should feel lucky. The only person I can blame for the way I feel is me. Umrao didn't really betray me because Esther never liked me that way. I'm also lucky that I have you, Dr. Ben."

Knowing it would take more time, if ever, before Abu said he loved him, Ben took what he could get. "One way to get over the way you feel is to be a good friend. You could try to be supportive of their relationship. Help your friend find happiness. Having a loyal friend is more important than a relationship that never was."

Abu grimaced. "I like that plan, but it may take some time before I can be happy for them."

Chapter 20

Grrommerrk, Choru, An 5660, Day 17

"Are you sure we can be here?" Abu asked in Greek as he looked to Rrummblinss. If a fox or a raccoon could smirk, the stirithy did just that before winking at him.

"Mmy frriend Abu, you sspoke to mme of unrrequited love. Did you not? Ass I have told you, I amm an experrt in love. Everryday, I fall in love a hundrred timmess. And each day mmy hearrt brreakss ninety-nine. But each night, I love one lucky one until the mmorning commess."

The blond stirithy shook his head, and his voice filled with melancholy. "Alass, I mmusst brreak herr hearrt beforre I rrun. Sso I have brrought you to mmy temmple forr brroken hearrtss. If you pay trribute to the goddessss of losst love, sshe will help you forrget yourr trroubless. Afterrwarrd, I will take you to the only placce in Grrommerrk wherre a young humman can sseek new love."

Abu's instincts screamed a warning about the coming trouble, and he hoped he could blame it on his mischievous host. But he needed to stay away from his quarters to avoid seeing the new couple together, so he dismissed the sinking feeling in his gut.

He ducked through the five-and-a-half-foot-tall doorway, following the stirithy into a pub made of multicolored glass. The crescent-shaped interior of the establishment was built into a smaller tree on the island of Government Circle.

A large semi-circular bar made of blue glass followed the curve of the trunk. Swinging doors led into the tree itself, out of which moved staff members holding serving trays of food. To the left and right, French doors stood open, leading to parts unknown. Rrummblinss didn't wait. He walked a wavery line toward the bar as he dodged other patrons in the crowded tavern.

"Excuse me," Abu said in Aaruan, as he maneuvered between occupied tables and chairs to catch up.

Abu stepped next to the stirithy, and Rrummblinss popped onto a barstool. The bartender evaluated the strange pair while rubbing the inside of a light blue glass with a cloth. Unlike most of the fox-people, he wore a dark brown shirt. The barkeep said something in Aaruan to Abu's partner in crime.

From the tone, the conversation did not start on a friendly note. Rrummblinss's long response came with his normal aplomb, followed by hissing, purring laughter from the bartender.

Abu's only previous experience with stirithy came from his interactions with Ssherrss. The foxlike laughter had caught him off guard the first time he heard it. Not anymore, though. He found the stirithy people to be a pleasant race filled with passion for life. Every other fox-raccoon he'd met except for his grumpy traveling companion had been quick with a joke and even quicker to laugh.

Abu sat on the way-too-short barstool and spread his legs, trying to find enough room not to be cramped. He felt as if he'd been invited to a little girl's tea party. He wondered whether Masako ever played like that.

The bartender poured red liquid into two blue glasses. Inside the blue, the liquid took on a purple hue. Words from the Quran popped into Abu's head. Its prohibition on drinking and gambling gave Abu pause, but his stomach soured, and his heart ached as the vision of smiling, tanned, freckled-faced Esther reminded him why he was here. With a shake of his head, Abu reached for his glass and turned to Rrummblinss.

The Captain of the Troop clinked his glass with Abu's and said, "Brrummlax!"

"Brrummlax." Abu raised the glass, pausing a moment to sniff the fruity scent before taking a large sip. A spicy pepper taste soon overwhelmed the initial flavors of strawberries mixed with figs, making his eyes water. Then the strong burn of alcohol made him choke.

Abu coughed for several seconds. His drinking partner slapped him on the back twice while shaking with hissing laughter. Abu's sinuses opened as the pepper finished the experience.

As he wiped his runny nose, Abu choked out, "That's interesting."

"Don't worrrry, by the ssecond glassss it will go down eassy."

Abu coughed again. "I'll take your word for it." He worked up his courage to take a bigger swig. He choked much less this time. By the third sip, he enjoyed the multilayered experience.

Over two glasses of the fiery liquor, he watched Rrummblinss flirt with every female in the room. Even the ones with dates. Two of the men took offense and stood up before their dates led them away. Abu wondered why they seemed so wary of his drinking companion.

As Abu finished his second glass, he felt like he did the night of his birthday party. He laughed along with the waitresses who flirted with Rrummblinss, even if he didn't understand a word. He called for a third round when Rrummblinss waved off the barkeeper.

"The goddessss hass given you herr blessssing. I hope you have been watching how it'ss done, young apprrenticce. It'ss timme forr you to commplete yourr worrsship."

A little befuddled, the teen commanded, "Lead on, Casanova."

Ben took a long gulp of cool water and swished it around before spitting it out. He repeated the process several times, trying to get the chemical taste out of his mouth. The fumes from the various distilling processes had got to him so he had stepped outside for a break.

Leaning against the building, he wondered where Rrummblinss had taken Abu. He had asked their escort to distract the moping teenager, as much to let Ben focus on the task at hand as to help his son.

After breakfast, everyone in the entire group went in different directions. Louisa and Abu were to continue studying Ancient. Jeevan had taken the Lancers out to put them through their paces. Ali and Ssherrss joined Ben to work with the group of stirithy, hysakas, and babiakhom assigned to manufacture the guns and the ammunition.

It took them a while to locate a well-ventilated facility far enough away from other buildings not to pose a danger. The pace picked up when Ssherrss presented the distilling equipment. The stirithy had magically manufactured everything needed to produce the chemical ingredients for mercury fulminate.

On its face, the process needed only mercury, nitric acid, and ethanol, but creating nitric acid required a lot of work. First, Ben had to make sulfuric acid, which took several steps. Then he needed silver nitrate to mix with copper to make the copper nitrate necessary to produce nitric acid. Creating ethanol, by contrast, would be child's play. Every one of these chemical steps had to be done with the utmost care to avoid a catastrophe.

Ben estimated it would take him three days to perfect all these critical processes and make the first small batches of primers. Then it would require more experimentation to refine the black powder in combination with the primers and the new bullets to get the right mix.

The only people Ben could use in the process were Earthlings. He didn't trust Ali, especially after the professor volunteered their group to manufacture weapons in the way he did. Ben doubted he could keep Ali from learning the entire process, but he would delay that day for as long as possible. He recruited the steadiest Lancers to help. Once he perfected one chemical's process, he moved on to the next ingredient he needed while leaving a Lancer in charge to create the necessary quantities.

At lunch, Abu had looked miserable. Umrao and Esther had held hands and giggled together the entire meal. Afterward, Ben had spoken with Louisa about it, and, taking her advice, he had asked Rrummblinss to see whether the stirithy could distract his son.

Not seeing Abu at dinner, Ben wondered whether he'd made a mistake. He knew he was being silly. Abu could take care of himself, and he even had a native host.

No, I don't have anything to worry about.

Ben took one more drink and headed back inside. He needed to test the newest Ssherrss-wrought device. The two-chambered furnace was connected to a boiler. In the first furnace, sulfur burned to create sulfuric dioxide. The gas flowed over heated lead in the second chamber, oxidizing into sulfur trioxide. That was mixed with water in the boiler to create sulfuric acid.

Louisa ducked under Esther's latest strike, a spinning backhand. She dropped almost to the floor, then twisted at the waist to put more power into a kick. It landed on the Alexandrian's left thigh. Louisa used the point of her boot to drive the force deep into the stocky girl's muscle. Esther gave a small grunt. Then Louisa hopped backward, dodging the return kick she had anticipated.

Louisa shot her right foot out, keeping it low and turning the side of her foot. She connected with Esther's left shin as the soldier stepped forward to close the distance. No sounds came from her opponent, but Esther staggered for just a moment.

Louisa placed her kicking foot on the ground to act as a pivot. She spun her left foot up, angling her pointed toe toward Esther's midriff. The teen stepped into the kick with a grunt. She used her left arm to wrap around Louisa's leg, pinning it to her side.

Having been on the opposite side of the leg grab while sparring with Lance Duffadar Ram, Louisa knew what to do. She continued the momentum of her kick and twisted her body to her right. She brought her right leg up in a heel kick that connected with Esther's chin. The teenager staggered under the blow, loosening her grip. Louisa, suspended in mid-air, used this moment to twist her leg free and fall to the ground, graceful as a cat.

Louisa pushed herself up into a defensive stance. Esther was still wobbling. Louisa charged and jumped at the last moment, raising her knee for a front kick. The young soldier lowered her hands to block, but Louisa brought her right fist down to smash the Alexandrian soldier in the nose. A loud crack led to blood flowing from Esther's nose as she staggered backward.

Sitting next to Khepri, Masako gasped.

"Halt," the Lance Duffadar commanded a second before Louisa began her next attack.

Esther gave Louisa a bloody smile with her nose bent to the side. Then she said in Greek, "Great job. You're becoming dangerous. I'll remember that last move."

Esther held out her hand, and Louisa gave it a quick shake. Khepri stepped up to the sparring partners and took Esther's face into her hands. Within moments, the stocky red-headed soldier's nose righted itself until the blood on her face was the only sign of injury.

Ram said, "That's enough for today. Louisa, do you remember the second counter to the leg grab?"

"Yes, Guru. I remember. Next time, can you show me a third counter?"

"Remind me tomorrow. There are two variations to the second move. Have a good evening, ladies." Their slender instructor headed toward the barracks.

Louisa waved Masako over to where she and her two companions stood in the small grassy park. Their stirithy hosts had allowed them to use the area for Lance Duffadar's yoga and Kalari lesson while the Lancers trained on the parade grounds used by the city guard. The girl jogged over to them with a big smile and grabbed Louisa's hand.

Since Louisa had reinstated the martial arts lessons, Khepri never took part but came to lend her healing hands to the inevitable injuries. This let the trainees be more physical during their sparring. Louisa had never gotten to appreciate a victory because Khepri usually needed to heal her at the end of their classes.

As for Masako, the eight-year-old had followed Louisa around like a lost puppy. Louisa hadn't noticed at first, but the girl did everything for her, fetching her towel after the bath and laying out her workout clothes. After a half-day of this, it dawned on Louisa that Masako reminded her of the girls who had enrolled at St. Denis at a very young age. The rulebook had beaten any sort of individuality out of them, making them compliant and subservient.

Not on my watch, Louisa had thought. She made it clear to the ex-slave in the few words they shared that Masako was not Louisa's servant but her student. She insisted the young girl participate in the Kalari training except for the actual sparring. When Esther gave Masako a small knife, Louisa took it as a sign and instructed Lance Duffadar Ram to train the girl on how to use it.

Louisa smiled at her adult friends while thinking out loud, "I wish we could find someplace to have a drink."

Khepri raised her snout and let out a low howl. "Now you're talking my language. I'll ask Rrummblinss tomorrow. Until then, I have a bottle in the room."

"Won't Ssherrss be there? And what about?" Esther side-nodded toward Masako.

"No, he's working with Ben. I think they'll be at it deep into the night," Khepri replied.

"I'll drop her at the room and have her study the Ancients' scroll. She is picking it up faster than any of us." Louisa smiled at the girl who grinned back with eyes blank.

That won't last long. Need to watch what I say.

"Okay, I can have one drink. I don't want to keep Umrao waiting too long." The seventeen-year-old laughed.

Louisa forced herself to push down her judgmental thoughts. She asked the question she'd most wanted to ask since she'd found out the young woman and the young Lancer were having sex.

"I'm sorry to be nosy." Louisa chuckled at her pun. "But don't you worry about getting pregnant?"

The other two shared a look as Khepri replied for them, "No, life singers can postpone a women's menstrual cycle. We can do this in any race except elves and welves, who are only fertile once every hundred An." Khepri pointed her snout to Esther. "She came to me last week for help, and it lasts a month." Her tongue fell out of the side of her mouth before she licked her chops. "I can do the same for you if you want to sample Ben's abilities."

At the thought, Louisa turned red and stammered, "No, uh, no. I'm not ready for that."

Surprised, Esther asked, "Is this some religious requirement on your part? I know what I am doing is sinful in HaShem's eyes. But as a soldier, I know any day could be the end for me. Umrao is not my first, and, unless one of us gives up our profession, I doubt he will be my last."

"No, my faith is not holding me back."

The young woman tilted her head. "Are you a virgin?"

Louisa frowned, her voice a mix of sadness and disgust. "I am, but I almost wasn't. Not by choice." She shuddered at the memory.

Khepri and Esther reacted in unison, with one giant hand going to Louisa's shoulder and a smaller hand clasping hers. "I'm sorry," said Khepri.

Masako gave Louisa's hand a comforting squeeze.

Louisa shrugged, but her sadness remained. "It was a long time ago. I want to forget it, but I know that's one reason I keep every man at arm's length. Ben's the first man since who made my heart race at all. I'm afraid I'll mess up our relationship if it becomes physical."

"Take it as slow as you need," Esther said.

Patting Louisa's back, the hysaksas said, "I think Ben is the kind of man who will go at your speed. I love Ssherrss because of the trust I have in him and how safe he makes me feel. Louisa, you deserve the same."

Louisa smiled at her friends, and her tone lifted. "You're right. I want the kind of love you and Ssherrss share. I need to trust him completely before I can be vulnerable enough to become intimate."

Esther said in an angry tone, "I hope the man who hurt you experiences all of HaShem's wrath."

With a grim smile, Louisa said, "I made sure he'll regret what he did for the rest of his life."

Khepri's eyebrows lifted. "How so?"

"I ensured that he can't hurt anyone like that ever again."

A few shades lighter than some of the Nubian tribesmen Abu had seen in Egypt, the Kerman servant asked him in Aaruan, then Latin, then Greek, "What language do you speak? What is your name?"

"Greek is preferable. Abu Saqr."

"What does your name mean?"

"Father of the Falcon."

"That won't do." The man banged his staff on the marble floor twice. In perfect Greek, he said, "Presenting Lord Abu Saqr, Noble Falcon of Earth!"

Abu's face turned red, first from the title, then redder as all conversation ceased in the large, lavish parlor. Every head in the room swiveled to inspect the guest of honor. Abu gave a simple nod before being pushed forward. He took two involuntary steps into the room.

From behind he heard, "Have fun, mmy young apprrenticce. Fall in love and brreak ssomme hearrtss. You can thank mme tommorrrrow. I will wait outsside the embassssy, but take ass mmuch timme ass you need to refrressh yourr hearrt."

Abu closed his eyes and took a deep breath to steady himself, as Lance Duffadar Ram had taught him during their yoga lessons. He opened his eyes. Seeing the other guests of this hastily called soiree made him doubt he'd be thanking Don Juan Rrummblinss on the morrow.

On the way over, his love tutor had told Abu how he'd asked the ambassador from Kerma whether he would host a party for Abu. The ambassador invited all the teenage human children of diplomats from the various embassies. At least, Rrummblinss hadn't exaggerated about the guest list. In a city of seventy thousand stirithy, present were most of the community's human teenagers. At the sight of a young female welf, Abu thought, *Well, maybe not one hundred percent human.*

A young man, a few years older than him and dressed in a short white Egyptian tunic, approached and gave a slight bow. "Welcome, Noble Falcon. I am Gorte, and my father is the Kerman ambassador."

Doing his best to emulate the bow, Abu said, "Thank you for the invitation. I'm honored."

With a gleaming white smile, Gorte said in a deadpan voice, "Don't thank me yet. Besides, you honor us with your presence." The young man opened both hands as if presenting something to Abu. "To meet a real Earthling is something I never thought possible. You must have many wondrous tales to share about your world." He leaned forward and lowered his voice. "As my guest of honor, I need to give you one small warning. The other guests are the offspring of diplomats, and you will find our nations' interests are as much at play here as in any official diplomatic gathering."

Abu whispered, "Thanks for the warning. Sounds like dealing with neighborhood bullies." He smiled and switched to his normal voice. "Are there events like this often?"

With a laugh, Gorte said, "Oh, much, much worse than bullies, and yes, we have monthly gatherings like this. It's good diplomatic training and gives us something to look forward to." He shrugged. "Bored teenagers are the worst. Just let me know if there is anything I can get you."

Gorte waved to a servant, who brought a tray holding two crystal flutes with what appeared to be white wine. Gorte took the two glasses off the tray and handed one to Abu.

Abu looked past Gorte. It appeared that an anxious crowd was allowing the host to have his time. The young man put his hand on Abu's shoulder as he raised his voice. "To Noble Falcon, long life, true love, many successes, and many children! Nefer!"

Everyone lifted their glasses and repeated, "Nefer!"

Abu raised his glass to the room and took a sip. The crisp white wine was much easier to drink than the liquor Rrummblinss had ordered.

His host leaned close. "Good luck, Abu. I will take my leave as you have double the trouble heading your way." Gorte grimaced at the sight of two approaching blonde girls and made a hasty retreat.

Abu turned his attention to the women. They shared the same almond-shaped faces, petite noses, thin lips, and big blue eyes. The sisters were pretty if Abu ignored their pretentious aura.

The taller and less curvaceous of the two acted as spokesperson. She held out her hand, palm down. In Greek, she said, "I'm Livia, and this is my sister, Lucille. Our father, Titus Selendius, is the ambassador of Remus to Grrommerrk. It is a pleasure to meet you."

Visions of the flirtatious Rrummblinss popped into Abu's head. Still feeling the effects of the drinks at the bar, he thought he shouldn't follow the flamboyant gal sneaker's lead.[1] Then, when Esther's face popped up, he pushed all cares away.

Why the hell not?

With as much debonair flair as possible, Abu took Livia's hand and bent to give it a gentle kiss before looking into her eyes.

---

1. A gal sneaker is Victorian slang for a playboy.

As she smiled, Livia's eyes narrowed as if she were reevaluating her previous opinion of him. Abu's head spun, trying to recall some romantic lines he'd once read. Still holding her hand, he rose and smiled to show his dimples. He took a risk and used his Latin to say, "I never thought I'd be lucky enough to meet such a beautiful girl. But now I've met two."

Lucille giggled, drawing Abu to the shorter, curvier younger sister. He released Livia's hand and reached for Lucille's. With a boldness he didn't know he possessed, he repeated the kiss.

After another giggle, the younger sister gave Abu a big smile and said in Latin, "I'm Lucille." She blushed as she stumbled over her words. "But you already know that. Silly me. Oh, you are quite handsome. I did not expect—" She stopped herself and looked down.

Abu caught Livia frowning at her sister. Then her lips turned up in a charming smile, and she touched his arm. "Do you go by Lord Saqr, or is it okay that I call you Abu?"

Abu chuckled. The sister's Latin came too fast for him, and he switched to his more dependable Greek with a snarky reply, "Oh, no, please call me Lord Noble Falcon."

The two girls laughed.

"Abu is fine."

"I'm not sure you are aware of the political situation here on Aaru, but Remus is the most powerful nation on the planet," the older sister said, switching back to flawless Greek.

In a sullen tone, Abu said, "I've had a little experience with Remulans." As muddled as his mind might be, he remembered every run-in with the Roman imposters. His memories started with Remulan soldiers attacking the Alexandrian defensive wall. Then he remembered the Remulans' hired henchman almost killing Umrao and Esther when they kidnapped Miss Louisa. His mental inventory finished with the attack at the pyramid. His jaws clenched in anger.

Livia frowned. "From your reaction, it would seem your experiences with our countrymen did not go well."

Abu said, "You could say that."

"I want to apologize for any slights you've suffered." Livia squeezed his arm. "I can assure you we just want to be friends."

Abu wanted to stay jovial, but his words came out as pure sarcasm. "So far, you two haven't tried to kill me or anyone I care about. That's an improvement on the Remulans I know."

Lucille touched his other arm. "Oh, Abu, I promise we're not like that. If Ahura Jupiter wills it, we will become great friends. We can help you in all kinds of ways."

With a cough, her sister interrupted. "What my sister is trying to say is that we can make your wildest dreams come true."

"How's that?"

"If you come to meet our father," Livia said, "he has the power to make you very rich. Gold, slaves, land, you could even have your pick of one of us to be your wife."

Disgusted at the mention of slaves and startled at the mention of marriage, Abu fought to keep his emotions from showing. "And what do I have to do to gain all these wonders?"

"Just share what you know about your weapons and everything else you know about Earth. Then you'll get anything you ask for."

Abu's voice lost all pleasantness as he hurled his words at the pair. "All I have to do is betray my friends and help the Remulans and this Ahura Jupiter conquer all of Aaru."

Livia released his arm and took a step back while Lucille said, "It is Ahura Jupiter's will for the Remulan Empire to rule all of Aaru. Why shouldn't you take advantage of it?"

Abu laughed. "If it was his will, the Remulans would have overcome the Alexandrians in the Axclatca Pass, but they didn't because my friends stopped them. That was Allah's will."

Lucille responded, "Just a temporary setback. Even now, Gorte's precious Kerma is close to falling to the empire. Soon his father will be out of a job and is probably already looking at how he can attach himself to our empire." She tilted her head at him. "What would it take for you to meet my father?"

All thoughts of flirting gone, Abu let his anger seep into his reply. "More than you or your precious empire could ever offer. Ladies, I would say it's been a pleasure, but I think I've stepped on less dangerous vipers." He touched two fingers to his forehead and gave them a dismissive salute. "Goodbye."

With that, he spun around and marched toward Gorte, hoping to free himself from these treacherous sirens.

Before Abu could reach the Kerman teenager, another young man stepped into his path. Closer to Umrao's age and height than Abu's, the tanned, blue-eyed young man spoke in Greek. "Hello, I'm Jason. I apologize for being late. I would have protected you from those snakes." Jason focused over Abu's shoulder and held out his arm in a forearm greeting.

Abu grabbed the older teen's arm and shook. "Thanks, but I handled them just fine." He rolled his eyes and said, "I'm Abu, by the way." He scarfed the rest of his white wine. "Do you know how I can get another drink?"

Jason got the attention of a servant standing at the edge of the room. "I won't keep you, but I'll give you some advice. Everyone here has an agenda, so be careful what you say and more careful with who you trust. You are predator or prey, and today you are on everyone's menu."

"Gorte said something similar. What's your agenda?"

"Whatever is in the best interest of Alexandria."

Thoughts of a tarnished coin and the little girl in his trust somehow pierced his fuzzy brain. *Jason might know some of King Phillip's people. Let's see what his agenda is.*

"Aren't you going to try to get as much out of me as possible?"

Jason said, "No."

Abu traded his empty wineglass for a full one the servant offered, then asked. "Why not?"

As if speaking for his entire nation, Jason said, "We believe your group of Earthlings already trust Alexandria. Dimaerites ben Zev i Hurasu i Enoch gave the embassy staff a full report. Many of you have befriended her, the stirithy, and the hysakas, who are all Alexandrian soldiers."

"We haven't given Esther or any Alexandrians our secrets. Besides, I'm not so sure about all Alexandrians' intentions."

"As you shouldn't. But Esther explained to my mother, the ambassador, why you are protecting those secrets, and we agree with your reasons. My agenda is to help you keep them. If you need any assistance tonight, just catch my eye."

"One question before you leave. Are you related to Basilius Phillip?" Abu took a sip.

"A very distant relative. My mother comes from a long line of diplomats. Why do you ask?"

As Abu rubbed his chin, he could have sworn he felt a few small hairs. "I'm looking for someone whom your king trusts completely. I have come into possession of something that is for the king or his family alone."

Tilting his glass toward Abu, Jason said, "You are full of surprises. My family stays neutral in our nation's internal power struggles. Our concern is her place amongst all the nations of Aaru. There is no one like whom you seek in Grrommerrk. The closest person would be the ambassador to Kerma. He is the king's brother-in-law."

That doesn't help.

Abu took a big gulp of wine. He had begun to regret being there. "Okay, Jason. I doubt I'll stay long. Thanks for the advice, but I've kind of lost interest in all this."

Jason laughed. "Too late. Now that you are here, protocol dictates that you meet all the guests. And you need to share something interesting about Earth. I'll leave you to meet the rest." Jason pulled his fingers through his dark brown hair. "The faster you get to it, the faster you can excuse yourself. Good luck. Remember, I'm here to help." He bowed his head and wandered off.

As Abu turned to look around the interior of the room, he almost ran into a petite young woman. She had skin two shades darker than his own and coal-black hair, but he couldn't see her lowered eyes. She wore a long blue skirt and a red wrap around her breasts, leaving her midriff exposed. A large gold medallion belt accentuated her slender stomach and curvaceous hips, while several gold necklaces drew his eye to her ample bosom. Another gold chain stretched from her nose to her ear.

All thoughts of leaving vanished in an instant, and Abu gulped. "Excuse me. I did not see you."

The shy young lady raised her dark brown eyes in a slow, seductive manner, capturing more than just his gaze. She smiled, and her pearl-white teeth lit up her slender face. She replied in Greek, "Do not worry, Lord Saqr. I should have been more careful."

"Uh, call me Abu." He found himself at a loss for words.

She waited several seconds, while Abu berated himself. Finally, the girl took hold of the discussion. "I'm Madri. My father is the Kuru ambassador. How old are you, Abu?"

"Uh, I'm fourteen. How old are you?" The words spilled out, slow and awkward, as if Abu needed great effort to speak.

The girl's tone turned dismissive. "I'm sixteen." She appeared to be about to say more but clamped her mouth shut.

"Oh." Abu took another drink, then brought up mental images of Rrummblinss on the prowl. He thought to himself, *What would Rrummblinss do? He would go for it, that's what.*

"Well, Madri. It appears your beauty has left me speechless."

She rolled her eyes.

No half measures. Abu flashed her his dimples. "Maybe we could get together again. Would you like to go on a walk with me tomorrow? I haven't seen much of the city."

The young woman thought about his invitation for a few seconds before saying, "No, I can't." Then she rushed out the next words. "I'm not trying to offend you, but you're just too young."

Abu flinched. "Oh, okay. Well, um, nice to meet you. Have a good evening." He gave an insincere smile, which she returned.

Walking away, Abu thought, *How can Rrummblinss take this much punishment? Every day.* The stirithy had gotten rejected at least ten times in their short time at the pub. *You would need to develop a thick skin to do this over and over, but would you want to?*

Abu finished his second glass of wine and thought maybe he should slow down on the drinks. Dejected, he sat on a long, cushioned couch. As he stared into his empty glass, trying to quell the sinking feeling in his stomach, someone sat so close to him that their arms touched. A hand went to his knee.

The pale, refined fingers squeezed with some force, bringing Abu out of his reverie. He followed the slender wrist up to the stunning face of a teenage female welf who gave him a shy smile.

If the Kuru girl's hair had been black, then this young lady's hair was the pitch in the phrase. Abu became lost in her amber eyes, more hypnotizing than a cobra's stare. She licked her full pink lips seductively. Her skin was flawless and powder-white.

Her lips moved. "Abu Falcon. My name is Ningal."

Her bright smile lifted Abu's heart with the same stirrings he'd felt when he first saw Esther. He smiled back. "Hi, Ningal. You can call me Abu. Let me guess: you are the daughter of the ambassador from Kutha."

She chuckled. "And to think the Bacchus twins said you were a dolt."

Not knowing whether he should be offended, it took a moment for Abu to put two and two together. "Ah, you mean the Roman god Bacchus, the fool. A very fitting name for those two." He glanced at his empty glass. "I'm not sure I've done anything to prove them wrong. Yet." He gave her a shy smile. "But thank you for the benefit of the doubt. Would you like another glass of wine?"

Ningal shook her head. "No, I'd like to spend some time with you. Would that be okay?"

Speechless, Abu nodded.

"Good. Tell me about yourself, Abu."

Abu's intoxicated mind sobered a bit as his personal story brought up memories he did not want to remember. *Stick to recent history.* "Well, I'm Dr. Ben McGehee's assistant. He's an archaeologist."

"Archaeologist?"

Abu's face reddened. "An archaeologist is a scholar back on Earth who studies ancient civilizations."

Ningal nodded, so he continued. "We were studying some Ancient Egyptian ruins when we found a temple with these strange priests, which turned out to be hysakas. We also found the Seba device and accidentally came to Aaru. Now here we are."

The young woman's brow furrowed. "But what about you, Abu? Where are you from? What about your parents? Do you have any siblings? What do you like to do?"

Abu's heart ached, and it must have shown on his face because she patted his leg and said, "I'm sorry if I said something wrong."

With a shake of his head, Abu said, "No. It's not your fault. My parents died last year, and Dr. Ben took me in. I don't have any other family." Trying to lighten the mood, he switched gears. "As for what I like, well, I love to learn." The cadence of his speech picked up. "Math, languages, history, science. Anything. I also love to ride horses and practice shooting."

His tactics changed again as Abu tried to emulate his furry Casanova friend. "But most of all, right now, I love talking to you." He showed her the dimples. "You are incredibly beautiful." Then, thinking about his most recent rejection, Abu thought he'd better get clarity before going forward. "How old are you, Ningal?"

She blushed. "Thank you for the compliment. You are very handsome as well." Ningal flashed that smile. "I just turned fifteen. How old are you?"

Abu sat straight and puffed up his chest. "Fourteen. Is that a problem for you?"

Ningal tilted her head. "Not at all. Why should it be?"

"No reason." Abu smiled.

With a frown, Ningal looked away. Abu followed her glance. A young elf girl approached their couch.

Ningal turned back to him. "Abu, I need to go, but I will wait for you after the party is over. Would you walk me home? I want to get to know you better." As she said this, her hand moved up from his knee to his upper thigh.

Abu squeaked, "Uh, yes. I'd like that very much." He made his voice as deep as possible. "I hope you don't mind, but I have an escort. We won't have much time alone."

The welven beauty used Abu's thigh to push herself to stand up. He almost jumped to his feet. Ningal offered him her hand. He took it and bent to kiss it, never looking away from her eyes.

Electricity shot through him as his lips touched her skin. He inhaled her intoxicating scent mixed with hints of rose water. "I look forward to the end of the party."

Ningal removed her hand from his and said, "Until then."

The young elf had stopped a few feet away, and Abu watched the two glare at each other.

Ningal deadpanned, "Hello, Zanna. A pleasure, as always."

With a touch of venom, the girl said, "It's too bad you *must* leave."

The welven girl brushed by the tall elf, bumping her. Abu wasn't a hundred percent sure, but he thought he heard one of them whisper, "Zae shah." While the other whispered, "Zae nig."

Abu's mind raced to the Sumerian cuneiform and its language syntax. He knew *Zae* meant "you." Then the other two words popped into his mind at the same time: "pig" and "bitch."

These girls do not like each other.

Abu watched Ningal walk away in her black Greek-inspired dress.

"Why don't you close your mouth before a fly gets in?"

The sarcastic words were like a verbal slap. He focused on the young woman glaring at him. "Uh, um. Sorry. Nice to meet you. Um, Zanna is it? I'm Abu."

Her fierce green eyes sent barbs his way. "At least, you remembered my name. It is yet to be seen whether it will be a pleasure or not." The brown-haired teenager took a deep breath. "I really shouldn't be mad at you. It's not like you should understand how things are here on Aaru." She took another deep breath. "How about we start over? Do you think we can do that?"

As she held out her hand, she gave a hint of a smile. Abu nodded and went to repeat the kiss. Instead, she grabbed his hand and squeezed it in a vigorous shake. "Good. My father is the sub-ambassador of Ur."

Abu said, "Like the city of Ur in ancient Sumer?"

Zanna let go, her smile widening. "Yes. Our first elders were from Mari, but legend goes that Ur was the greatest city in the world when our ancestors lived on Earth."

All wariness flew from Abu's mind as his scholar's brain took over. "It's incredible that some of your first elders are still living. People who actually lived in Mari. Have you met any of the elves from Earth?" Now that her temper had subsided, he did not dislike speaking with the pretty young lady at all. Despite her being tall enough for him to look her in the eye, he guessed from her youthful appearance that she might be his age or a year younger.

"No. There are fewer than ten still alive, and most of them have withdrawn from public life. They say that after five thousand An, most people lose interest in going forward, but I think they just want to be left alone."

While Zanna spoke, the points of her ears poked out of her long, straight hair. Abu forced himself not to stare and said, "I didn't get to speak with him, but I saw one of your first elders when I was in Nippur. His name was Iskur."

Zanna's eyes grew wide. "Did you see him fight Ki and Lil? His daughters."

Abu nodded.

"Oh, my. When you share a story, Abu, share that one."

Abu asked, "Wouldn't they want to hear something about Earth instead?"

Zanna's smile grew, and Abu found it to be infectious. Unlike her welven counterpart, she had a golden complexion and a diamond-shaped face with ruddy-red lips. The more he looked, the more he realized that Zanna's youthful appearance kept her from having the same mature feminine qualities as Ningal.

He also realized that in a few years, Zanna would be Ningal's physical opposite but very much her equal in beauty.

"Yes and no. We have all heard about the duel, but no one has heard a first-hand account. Iskur was the most reviled elf in the world. That his own children killed him has already become a legend." Zanna touched his elbow. "Tell us something incredible about Earth. Something we won't believe, then tell us everything about the fight."

"I think I can do that. How old are you?"

"I turn fourteen next week."

"Brilliant! My birthday was a few days ago. I'm fourteen. What do you like to do?"

Zanna chewed on her lower lip. "I don't want to be forward, but if you are still in the city next week, would you come to my birthday party?"

Abu's answer tumbled out. "I would like that very much." He found himself smiling more and wondered whether he should feel guilty for liking this girl as much as Ningal when the two hated each other.

"Great," Zanna said. "I will give you an invitation tomorrow when I see you."

Abu tilted his head. "Tomorrow?"

Zanna laughed. "Madri turned you down to tour the city. I will take her place."

"How?"

With one finger, Zanna tapped the tip of her ear.

Abu swallowed. That meant she'd heard everything he'd said to Ningal as well.

As if reading his mind, Zanna said, "Yes, I know you're walking her home tonight. I won't hold that against you. I mean, she's not an idiot like some other girls I know." She made a point of looking around at everyone else at the party. "If she wasn't a welf, she and I might be friends. But given our heritage, that's impossible."

Abu remembered the history of the two immortal races and said, "Like the Montagues and the Capulets."

"Huh?"

"It's a famous play from Earth." Abu shook his head. "It's not important."

"Ah. Maybe you can tell me about the play tomorrow. I love to learn anything new."

Something tingled in the back of Abu's mind, but it worked more slowly after his fourth drink of the night. He blinked a few times before it came to him. "There you go again. Using my other conversations against me. How can I trust that you love to learn? You need a test."

Zanna laughed, and he laughed along. "Do your best, Earth man."

Abu liked how she called him a man. He ran a hand through his hair. "What is your favorite and least-favorite subject?"

"I love history and art, but I have a love-hate relationship with one of them. You guess," came Zanna's sassy reply.

Abu wagged a finger at her. "You didn't answer my question, but I'll play your game." He looked her up and down, trying to get a better read on the teenage girl. Zanna's floor-length green dress matched her eyes but did little to enhance her tall, slender, girlish physique. She wore very little in the way of adornments. A silver silk rope acted as a belt while small emerald stud earrings with a matching emerald pendant hung from a thin silver chain. The necklace drew his eye to her long neck. As he came back to her face, she smirked.

Fifty, fifty. Just guess. "You love art and have a love-hate relationship with history."

Zanna pouted. "Oh, brilliant detective, how did you conclude that?"

With a triumphant grin, Abu said, "Hah! I think you've met your match. My powers of deduction are as good as Aguste Dupin's. I figured out it was a trick question."

"How so? And it has yet to be seen if we are a match, Mr. Falcon."

The last innuendo made Abu falter for a few heartbeats, unable to remember what she'd asked. Zanna tilted her head, and he remembered. "How did I see through your tricks? Most artists wear too much jewelry, but you think that is pretentious. That is why I chose art as your true love. You're intrigued with history but struggle with it."

With a shake of her head, Zanna said, "I don't know who that Augie person is, but you are so wrong." Abu frowned as she continued. "History is easy for me, and I can tell you anything about Aaru. I also love art and music but cannot draw, sing, or play an instrument to save my life."

In a sarcastic tone, Abu said, "I guess that's it then. I was dead set on a girl who could play an instrument, sing, or dance."

Zanna giggled and lowered her eyes. She glanced up with a sultry look. "Who said I couldn't dance?"

Abu shook his head at the pretty girl who'd given him a mature look well beyond her age.

Zanna mimicked his shaking head and whispered, "No, you don't want me to dance for you?"

"I would very much like to see you dance."

"We'll see. Gorte is trying to get your attention."

The Kerman teenager was waving him over. Abu held up a finger. To Zanna, he asked, "When and where do you want to meet?"

"How about nine in the morning in front of the amber doors?"

"Great, I'll see you then. Just one last question."

She tilted her head toward him.

"What does Zanna mean?"

With a wry smile, she said, "I think a skilled detective like you can figure that out yourself. Pass that test, and I'll dance for you, Mr. Noble Falcon."

"Challenge accepted. I'll know it before tomorrow."

"I'd expect nothing less."

The tightness in Zanna's stomach and the giddiness she felt were so foreign to her. The analytical side of the young elf knew this must be how infatuation feels, but she found the actual experience to be almost overwhelming. It was stupid to even think about falling for a human. Their brief lives made it a losing proposition. She knew loving a mortal meant watching them grow old and die while she retained her eternal youth.

Along with Zanna's infatuation came intense jealousy, irritating the always level-headed young woman. Watching Abu escort Ningal out of the party made her feel raging anger she didn't know she possessed. No, anger did not describe how she felt. She loathed the welf and wanted to punch the young man from Earth. When she pictured it, though, she made sure not to hit his handsome face.

When the attendees had gathered on the couches to listen to Abu, it took all of Zanna's concentration to listen to the story instead of just staring at him. That cleft chin and those dimples were so, so mesmerizing. And his smile. She thought he had great teeth for a human. Oh, and the way he moved.

Abu was graceful and sure of himself while so many boys she knew were in that awkward stage. Thank the gods, he didn't exude the dangerous faux confidence of so many young men who couldn't control their newfound strength. No, the wisps of hair on Abu's face testified he was growing into the man he would become. Zanna imagined that man, and it made her swoon.

His story about steam-driven trains and ships left the audience with so many questions. Though a little drunk, Abu handled every question with intellect and aplomb that belied his age. His confidence was sexy.

Zanna had never used that word to describe anyone. Ever.

In the end, Abu had the partygoers on the edge of their seats when he recounted the duel between Ki and Lil and their evil father, Iskur. He went so far as to act out some parts. Toward the end of his soliloquy, Zanna felt that first twinge of jealousy when she saw Ningal catch his eyes by showing her leg. She was glad Abu had the decency to blush when Zanna caught him. She hoped he didn't see the obvious flames of jealousy in her eyes.

As Zanna gathered her cloak, she decided to ignore Abu and Ningal. She would go straight home. But it didn't help that she could hear everything the two of them said. Sometimes, she wished she could turn off her sense of hearing.

Then Ningal said something with so much innuendo baked in that both Zanna and Abu missed a step. Her thoughts of ignoring them evaporated. She began following the two teens as they met up with their escorts and made their way toward the Kuthan embassy.

By the time they reached Ningal's home, Zanna was ready to storm up and slap that welven trollop. She had to hold herself in check and stay far enough away that even if the welf saw her, she wouldn't be able to identify her. Zanna watched the pair walk up the steps of the embassy and disappear under its large, covered landing.

Even with her enhanced hearing, their words came to her as whispers. When the words stopped, so did her heart. She heard the unmistakable sounds of kissing and heavy breathing. Tears of anger and heartache flowed down her cheeks as she turned and fled.

Chapter 21

Grrommerrk, Choru, An 5660 Day 18

"Zanna, it's so good to see you again." Abu moved to take her hand, but she flinched and drew away. Thrown off by her narrowed eyes and pursed lips, he wondered what might have upset her.

Girls are so confusing sometimes.

Zanna deadpanned in Greek, "Hello, Abu. I take it you had a good night."

Visions of the beautiful Ningal flashed into Abu's thoughts. He remembered the softness of her lips, the hungry passion of her tongue, and how her desperate hands sought to touch him. Finally, he felt the shadow of the emotions that had burst forth when he'd returned her hunger, touching soft curves through the thin fabric of her dress.

Abu flushed. He saw green fireballs erupt from Zanna's irises. He imagined she was attempting to burn him to ashes.

Abu's panicked first thoughts were, *Does she know?* Followed by, *Lie!*

"It was okay. Nothing special." Abu cringed. He felt a vast sense of disappointment with himself for lying to her.

Say something, you idiot! he screamed inside.

For the first time that morning, Abu looked at the young elf. Really looked. He noticed slight puffiness under her eyes as if she hadn't slept enough. Her short, dark blue chiton highlighted her intelligent green eyes while showing off her long, athletic legs. As he soaked in every aspect of her, his panic melted away.

At that moment, Abu allowed himself to luxuriate in the contentment her presence brought him. But what he sensed was so much more than congenial familiarity. He experienced the same wonder he felt when given the privilege of seeing something new, beautiful, and rare. Zanna was winter's first snow and a rosebud beginning to bloom, all at the same time.

"You're so beautiful," Abu whispered under his breath.

Only an elf could have heard the words he spoke to himself, but he saw the instant effect his words had on her. Emerald flames turned to jade smoke. Zanna averted her eyes, and a slight uptick of a smile touched the corners of her mouth. Similar to last night, his spirit lifted at the slightest sign of happiness on her face.

Abu needed to make this young woman smile. At that very moment, he could think of nothing he wanted to see more. Ignoring Rrummblinss and her armed escort, Abu said, "Thank you for doing this, Zanna. I'm excited to see the city with you." He shifted from foot to foot. "Would you mind if I held your hand?"

As she met his gaze, Zanna's face brightened with a grin. "I would like that."

Abu took hold of her hand and smiled at her. "Where are we going first?"

"Have you been to the Pools of Dancing Lights?"

Abu shook his head.

Zanna let go of Abu's hand and grabbed the crook of his elbow with both hands. "Good, we'll save that for last. It's so much better after dark." She moved her body closer. "Let's start at the docks, then go to the workshops. You won't believe what the metal singers can do until you see them sing their creations to life."

Tugging his arm, she guided him forward. They strolled away from the amber doors and the giant tree housing the city's government. They walked toward a copse of *smaller* tree-buildings closer to the big island's shoreline. All around them, stirithy went about their business in bright clothes.

With a hearty *Good Morning* in Aaruan and a wave, a nod, or a tip of a cap, the foxlike people greeted them like honored guests. Any unease Abu had felt at exploring the alien city melted away. The route took them into a large open area between several trees. Four young stirithy children in matching orange outfits raced past them and swarmed over an area at the heart of the park to play.

Two of the three-foot-tall boy foxes jumped onto the ends of a seesaw. They bounced up and down while their younger sister hopped into a swing that hung from the limbs of rather normal-size trees growing nearby. At the top of each arc, a loud trill sounded as the girl kicked and pulled, seeking ever greater heights. As a young boy growing up in Aleppo, Abu had played with similar equipment.

No matter how different, children all seem to be the same.

Yet there was one strange contraption in the middle of the park that Abu could not fathom.

The oldest of the raccoon-faced children headed for what appeared to be a dead tree. Large hollows in the tree, acting as balconies, were all around the trunk. Arrayed at irregular intervals and various heights, pairs of branches stretched away from the supporting column. Tied between the V-shaped arms were triangles of material forming horizontal sails.

With a powerful two-legged hop, the tallest of the stirithy boys launched himself toward the first sail. Zanna's laugh tinkled. The fox struck the sail with both feet, and the material stretched down with his motion. He bunched himself into a ball and threw his arms above his head as the sail swung upward, catapulting the young fox toward another sail. With his bushy tail swaying and twisting for balance, he took two more big jumps before landing in the tallest tree hollow.

As he peered down at his siblings, the youngster thrust a fist into the air and let out two loud, raspy bark-cries.

"Amazing," Abu said.

Zanna stopped giggling and squeezed his arm. "Do you not have fot fots back on Earth?"

Abu shook his head.

"You should try it." She tugged Abu in that direction.

"I'll tell Miss Louisa about it. I'm sure she would enjoy it." Abu steered them back onto the path. "I would break my neck."

"Let's hurry." Zanna picked up her pace. "I want to show you the fishmongers before they close their shops."

"What's so special about a fish market?" Abu asked.

As Zanna returned a wave to another passing stirithy, she pointed her chin toward the stirithy woman in a yellow blouse and a blue skirt. "Did you notice how nice the stirithy are?"

"They are the nicest, most welcoming people I've ever met."

As a strong breeze brought the first hint of fishy smells, the low rumble of scattered voices reached them.

"Wait until you see them haggle over fish." Zanna chuckled. "These sweet creatures transform into demon-possessed fiends." She pulled on his shirt and jogged toward the growing din.

———————————————

Ben took a sip of tea, sitting around a small table with Jeevan, Louisa, and Ali. He wanted to laugh at their appearance, but he knew he must look equally silly. With straps tied under their chins, each of them except Ali wore the special bonnet that held an Ancients' crystal bowl.

Ben smiled. "I know we haven't had much free time since we got to the city."

"Speak for yourself," said a dour Ali. "I've had a little too much time on my hands. I'm free to help with the chemical processes whenever you need me."

Louisa answered for the majority. "We've been over this. Just a few short weeks ago, we were on different sides. We're not ready to give you access to anything."

"I haven't forgotten." Ali sighed.

Louisa shook her head. "Be glad we are letting you learn Ancient and take part in this effort."

Ali scowled. "Even when I have someone to help me, each scroll only works for a couple of hours before it needs to be placed back in the sun. Maybe you can ask those," he pointed to Louisa's head, "how to keep track of where we are in the lessons. I have to start over with each device."

Louisa shrugged. "I've tried asking that exact question a hundred different ways, with no answers. Rotate the same four or five scrolls, so you are not too far behind each time."

The professor slumped. "I'll try that."

Ben tried to get them back on track. "That's not why we're here. We need to find an Ancient source to power the Seba. I know we have all tried asking that question on our own, with no luck. Maybe we can work together to get the answers."

"I've never been able to get it to work at all, so I'm not sure I can help." Jeevan shrugged.

Louisa patted his hand. "I'm sure it'll work for you, too. You just need to visualize your questions."

Ben asked, "Since we're all here, are there any other questions we need to answer?"

When no one else offered a suggestion, Ben closed his eyes. "Then let's get started. If you get something, tell us exactly how you visualized it so we can all try to see the answers."

The four of them went silent. Ben forgot about everything except the ghosts at the Tomb of Mortals. He visualized the flying glass pyramids, then pictured electricity as lightning. When that did nothing, he tried to see the ghosts flying, a steam engine, and then electricity. Still nothing.

Groans and sighs filtered into Ben's hearing as he tried solving the problem for several more minutes.

"I've got it," Louisa exclaimed.

Ben's eyes popped open.

"Picture the big pyramid, then sunlight hitting the glass. After that, think about one of the flying pyramids lying still. Show the sunlight touching it, and, finally, make the Ancients' *question* symbol sound. Try it."

Ben closed his eyes and tried her formula. It took him three tries before his version of those images worked. A white ball of light as bright as the sun popped into his mind. The rays radiating from the ball pulsed with energy, which moved down wires and flowed into black blocks. Ben thought these must be batteries because the energy moved away from the blocks and went into a platform on which a smaller pyramid sat. The ball of light dimmed and disappeared as if snuffed out like a candle, after which a second set of images started. Sunlight struck the glass and became energy, which raced into the batteries and then to the platform and the flying pyramid.

As Ben opened his eyes, he glanced around the table. "Did everyone see it?"

Jeevan shook his head. "Still nothing."

"Did the ball of light go out for you, too?" Ben asked.

Louisa replied, "Yes."

"It would appear the ball you saw was the primary power source for the pyramid. When it stopped, it used sunlight instead. At least, for the ghosts." Ben scratched the stubble on his face.

"If sunlight is the backup power source, how do we figure out how things like the headgear and the Seba get power? I wish we knew the symbol for power or electricity," Louisa added.

Ben had an idea and closed his eyes. He pictured the Seba and sunlight and then the white power source and then pictured the energy going to the batteries and then to the Seba. He finished by adding the sound for *all* and the one for *question*.

The first vision repeated, followed by a similar sequence, but instead of the ball of light, Ben saw steam rising from a lake of boiling water. The steam caused bright silver turbines to spin, its energy went to the battery, and so on. A third series of moving images showed rushing water turning sparkling turbines. This created electricity that went to the batteries. The last vision was of the Seba absorbing energy from the sun.

Ben opened his eyes and grinned. "I saw most of it." He described how he did his question and what he'd seen.

Louisa and Jeevan tried it. This time Jeevan yelled. He jerked the headgear bonnet off his head and tossed it onto the table. "Damn. It takes over your thoughts."

Everyone chuckled except Louisa. Her eyes were closed and moving back and forth under her lids. A few seconds later, she looked at them. "I used the symbol for *where* with the steam and then the water."

"And?" Ali urged her.

"There were several places with boiling lakes, but it showed me a picture of Aaru, and it looked like a globe, but it was real. Like a photo of the planet from the surface of one of the moons. I think those power sources were on different

continents." Louisa looked around the table, ensuring she had everyone's attention. "Last, I asked about the water, and there were three locations. Two of them
are very far away, but I think one is on this continent. There was a giant waterfall
turning gigantic turbines. At the bottom of the waterfall there appeared to be
more Ancient buildings. Like a city. From the globe view, it zoomed in, and I
think it's close to these mountains."

"Fantastic." Ali stood up. "I'll go ask Ssherrss or Khepri where we can find a
giant waterfall near a city with Ancient ruins." He left to find a native.

Ben tried her question formula, and on the second try, he saw the same images.
This success gave him hope. A few minutes later, Ali returned with Esther in tow.

Excited, Ali said, "Esther, tell them what you told me."

The Lochem officer appeared confused by his excitement. "Tefnut Falls is the
largest waterfall on the continent of Kemet. The Tefnut River runs through the
capital of Kerma, which was once a city of the Ancients." She pulled at a loose red
curl. "It's not far. The river we traveled to Grrommerrk feeds into the river itself."

Ben perked up. "Great. We will leave for the falls as soon as we finish the rifles
and bullets."

"It might not be that easy," Esther declared. "The Remulans have surrounded
the city, and it is under siege. We would need to break through enemy lines to
reach the waterfall."

Chapter 22

Grrommerrk, Choru, An 5660, Day 19

Louisa walked into the common area. She had left Masako in their room, working on a puzzle she had created for the girl.

"Where is Khepri?" Louisa asked in Greek.

Esther grinned. "She didn't tell you?"

Louisa shrugged, trying not to show her irritation. How could Khepri tell Esther something and not tell her? It occurred to her that for the first time in her adult life, she had girlfriends. The idea of having a friend who could make her jealous about not getting all of her affection shocked Louisa enough that she didn't hear what Esther said.

"Uh, sorry. What did you say she was doing?"

"What were you thinking about? You seemed a mile away." Esther giggled. "Were you thinking about Ben?"

"No, silly. I was thinking about friends."

Esther's face became stone cold. "You may be my elder, but say that again, and I'll have to kick your butt." She punched Louisa in the arm before grinning.

Louisa rubbed what would be a bruise unless she found her giant furry friend. "Like the last time? What exactly does a broken nose feel like?"

Esther laughed. "You win. She is out trying to find another mate for Ssherrss."

"What? I knew she had mentioned it. I didn't think she was serious."

"Very. She had Rrummblinss put out feelers to his network."

"How could that silly raccoon help?" Rrummblinss had rubbed Louisa the wrong way from day one. Despite his non-human appearance, she knew his type. Males like the gold-furred fox were why males of all species had such poor reputations.

Rrummblinss used his cockiness, charisma, and witty sense of humor to blind foolish, desperate women who couldn't see his real identity. Even if he was an alien, he was just another boisterous, self-indulgent, petty womanizer. She didn't know whether she had a mother's instinct, but something told her Abu shouldn't spend so much time with the stirithy version of Lord Byron.

Esther tucked a red curl behind her ear. "Not sure what a raccoon is, but why don't you tell me how you really feel about him?" In a lower voice, she said, "And don't let a stirithy hear you use that word. They don't seem to mind being described as foxes, but they might take the other word as an insult."

"Fine." Louisa gritted her teeth.

"Everything you dislike about the irascible fox makes him the perfect agent for Khepri. He has been with hundreds of loose stirithy females. If anyone can find a female desperate enough to join a family that includes Khepri, it's him."

That made sense. Birds of a feather and all that. Louisa hadn't put much thought into how difficult it would be to accomplish Khepri's dream, but the promiscuous Captain of the Troop was just the scumbag for this specific job.

"Louisa, can I ask you for a favor?"

"Sure, Esther. Anything, you know that."

"It's a little embarrassing."

Louisa tilted her head. "For you?"

"No. Umrao." Esther's face turned the same color as her hair. "He's inexperienced. I've tried to speak with him, but he's shy."

Louisa's head tilted further.

The teenage girl lowered her voice. "As a lover."

"Oh." Heat bloomed on Louisa's neck and cheeks.

Esther sighed. "I heard Ki brag about Jeevan. I wanted to ask whether you could speak with the duffadar. Ask him to give Umrao some pointers?"

Louisa sighed. "I'll chat with him for you and make sure he keeps it private."

"Thank you."

"Sure. I told Ben I'd help him with one of his experiments. See you at dinner."

Ben double-checked the test rifle one more time. He made a note, denoting the rifle being used, the black powder batch, the primer identifier, and what number this test would be for this combination.

In the correct column, Ben finished his notes by writing *12*.

The last configuration made it past twenty before Ben identified significant issues. The experiment required fifty successful bullets from a single batch before being declared good enough to go to human test-firing. For the tests, he used stirithy-made replicas of the Lancers' Martini-Henry carbines, which made the testing that much more stressful.

Before reaching this part of the testing, the metal singer–created rifles had to cycle through several Earth-manufactured rounds with success. Most of the replicas were solid until matched with the Aaruan-made cartridges. The native black powder, combined with Ben's homemade primers, made for a volatile mixture. The growing pile of destroyed test carbines testified to the challenge.

Ben grabbed the string attached to the test carbine's trigger and scooted behind the blast shield, where Louisa and Jeevan waited. The two-inch-thick wall of steel had protected them many times from flying shrapnel.

"You can count on me. If the lad's willing to learn, I'll help as much as I can."

Ben was curious about who they were discussing and filed that question away. He needed to be single-minded during this process.

Ben asked, "You two ready?"

They nodded, and Ben put his back to the shield, placing his free hand over one ear as he tugged hard on the string.

Bam!

That sounded right.

He moved to the carbine and inspected the outside of the rifle before pulling the lever to eject the empty shell. He let it fall to the ground and picked up the hot casing with a gloved hand.

"One more thing, Jeevan," he heard Louisa say.

"What's that?"

Ben made a note that the rifle and bullet casing looked normal.

"Don't tell Ki about this."

Jeevan's jolly laugh echoed around the firing range. "That assumes I'll see her again, but no problem. I'm already keeping plenty of secrets from her. Besides, I wouldn't embarrass one of mine."

Ben felt relieved they weren't discussing Abu but broke his self-imposed promise. "What are you guys talking about?"

Louisa shared a look with Jeevan as she said, "Nothing important. How did the test go?'

Ben must have revealed his doubt because Jeevan added, "Just addressing something about one of my lads."

"Okay." Ben held up the empty shell. "The test went well. I'll get ready for the next one. You both don't need to stay. We only need one partner to help in case something goes wrong."

Jeevan smiled. "If you don't need me, I'll get ready for today's drills."

The duffadar made his way toward the exit to the long barn-like structure. Louisa joined Ben as he walked toward the target board set up at fifty yards.

"I'll show you how to check the target against the Earth bullet benchmark." Ben pointed. "As soon as we fire the rifle, you head this way and determine the result. I'll check the gun and the casing."

"Okay. Once we have this worked out, how long before we can leave?" Louisa asked.

"To create enough black powder and then finish the cartridges, five days," he answered.

"It's a good thing they have so many metal singers making the parts. The quality is equal to what we brought with us from Earth."

"True." But as amazing as metal singers were, they couldn't keep pace with machine manufacturing on Earth. Ben hoped he would never need to automate the process, but he had no delusions. The nature of man ensured that the Pandora of guns would haunt Aaru forever more.

As they reached the target, he picked up a foot-long wooden rod with a red mark a couple of inches from one end and marks like a ruler on the other. Using the rod, he slid it into a bullet hole circled in red. The mark on the rod matched the depth of the hole.

"We shot one of the Earth cartridges to set the benchmark. It penetrated about two inches."

After he found the one hole without a blue circle, Ben stuck the rod into the newest hole. The bullet had gone in about a quarter of an inch deeper.

"Make a note about the difference in depth, then note where it landed on the target. When finished, circle it in blue."

As Ben handed Louisa the blue chalk, their hands touched. She smiled, and he remembered some promises he had yet to do anything about. Louisa marked the bullet hole. Using the other side of the rod, she laid the rod between the new blue and the red circles.

Two green lines created an axis with the Earth bullet's indention at its center. Ben used the rod to point to the graph. "In this case, it landed in quadrant two, six inches from the center."

"Makes sense, but why is that important for it to gauge the accuracy?" Louisa pointed to the red circle.

"It's a way for me to measure the consistency of each batch of black powder." He indicated a discarded target board in a pile a few feet away. A few holes were scattered all around the edges of the board, nowhere near the Earth-marked hole. "The cartridges didn't destroy the rifle, but most of the bullets missed the target entirely. Both high and low." He shook his head. "A terrible batch."

"Show me how to inspect the rifle and cartridge. We can trade off, or do you plan on running me ragged today?"

With a chuckle, Ben said, "Right." They made their way to the rifle. "Louisa, I meant to get your opinion about Abu. Am I wrong to let him go out so much?"

They stopped beside a rifle strapped to two supports, shaped like Y's.

Louisa asked, "Have you met the girl he went out with today?"

Ben let the clipboard hang at his side to give Louisa his full attention. "No, I haven't had time. And that's part of what worries me. When he got home last night, he mentioned not just one girl, but two."

Louisa frowned. "You need to speak with him about how to show a woman proper respect." She shook her head. "As in Cairo, we are about to move on so it might not matter, but he shouldn't be playing with these girls' emotions. Do you know anything about them?"

Ben said, "Rrummblinss told me that one is an elf, and the other is a welf. They are both about his age."

"There's your problem," Louisa snarled.

"What do you mean?"

"The captain is a bad influence."

"How so?"

She sighed. "Men." She shook her head. "McGehee, you need to pay more attention. That golden fur ball chases every female stirithy in sight. I'm sure he's been encouraging Abu to do the same."

Comprehension dawned, igniting Ben's concern. First, for Abu, who might pick up bad habits, and second, for his failures as a father. He'd follow her advice. "Thanks. I'll talk to him tonight. One other thing: how are we supposed to go about this?"

"This?"

Ben moved his hand back and forth between the two of them. "You and me."

She chuckled. "I'm not sure. I've never done *this* before. Besides, we are running out of time and must get to the waterfall. Maybe after that, we can work on *this*." She waved her hand between them.

"I appreciate this side of you." Ben gave her a wry grin. "Much better than the Louisa with her special surprises that I've come to expect."

"Don't get complacent, Dr. McGehee. Those surprises make life worth living."

"I won't." Ben shook his head. "I won't."

As they walked back to the rifle, Ben's giant mental checklist filled his thoughts. He hoped he had time to work on his side project before they left. He had completed the designs, and these tests would help move that project along as well.

Louisa nudged Ben with her elbow and raised a quizzical eye. He cleared those other concerns from his mind and said, "I was just thinking about what you said. The clock is ticking. Let's do the next test."

Abu raced through the grove of tall, slender trees, trying to catch Zanna before their escorts caught up and ruined the game. His fleet-of-foot quarry stayed well ahead, weaving through the trees. Her long brown hair floated in and out of sight. It provided the carrot needed for Abu to add a burst of speed as he tried to guess her path.

Abu cut to his right and sprinted down an animal path toward an open grove. He would beat her there and wait. As he neared the opening, his foot snagged, and he went sprawling. Swinging his arms in rapid circles, he tried to stay upright, but his head was too far over his feet. Leaves flew into the air as he landed. A small pile of withered foliage helped to break his fall.

Zanna's laughter reached him despite the pain shooting through his scuffed palms. He pushed himself to a sitting position. Doubled over, the elf maiden tried to catch her breath between guffaws. She had one hand on the tree where he had "snagged" his foot. His pain and anger were fleeting, and he joined her infectious laughter.

"You got me," Abu mumbled in Aaruan. He had worked hard to pick up as much of the language as possible from the two young women he'd been spending the bulk of his time with.

With her hands on her hips, Zanna puffed up. "Again, you mean."

"Yes, again. I think you take joy in causing me pain."

Zanna held up her thumb touching a forefinger to gesture *a little bit*.

Abu stood and brushed off the leaves and grass.

"Look out!" Zanna flashed by him with a dagger in hand.

What? Unable to comprehend what was happening, Abu turned.

Two fist-size balls streaked toward him. Zanna's dagger sliced through a cord connecting the two spheres. Momentum sent the rounded stones streaking past Abu, inches from each side of his head. Time seemed to slow. Abu followed the missiles out of the corner of his eye.

As he sought a target, he pulled his revolver. Time sped up.

Zanna cried out and fell forward, an arrow shaft protruding from her back. Fear shot through him, and he froze.

Dr. Ben's words were his only thoughts. *Get mad. Get plum mean.*

Adrenaline washed away Abu's fear, and hate-filled rage took hold of him. Intent on revenge, he flashed on his fallen friend.

Two men with covered faces and wearing all black raced across the grove toward him. One swung another set of balls over his head, while the other held a gladiator net overhead.

Abu ignored the itch that warned about the archer behind him and set his feet. In his two-handed grip, the Pocket Army lined up on a target.

Abu exhaled and pulled the trigger twice in quick succession. Without looking at the results, he moved his sights to the lone man who threw his arms out. The net, with small weights around the edge, spun toward him as Abu squeezed his finger again and again.

The web landed over Abu, and the momentum from the weights pulled the strands tight around his upper body. The same helplessness he'd felt while watching his parents die made Abu channel his anger into intense focus.

Yells and the ringing of steel on steel entered his consciousness.

There was another threat, and Abu forced himself to stop his useless struggle. The netting limited his visibility, but he was determined not to go down as a helpless victim. With careful steps, he turned in a circle, seeking the archer.

A duel raged near the edge of the woods. Zanna's bodyguard, one arm flopping by his side and dripping blood, stabbed a black-clad attacker in the thigh. As the assassin fell screaming, Rrummblinss danced between two more men in black.

A blur of steel hit each man twice before they could locate their attacker. Both men yelped in pain and stumbled back. One fell to his knees, his hamstring severed. The other attacker tried to hold his intestines in place with one hand while attempting a weak swing of his sword with the other.

Zanna's bodyguard parried a strike from his original foe and then blocked a slice from a second attacker who had joined the fray. Still wrapped up in the net, Abu gained a minor victory as he worked the barrel of his Pocket Army through the strands. With the revolver still trapped against his waist, he aimed at one of the bodyguard's attackers.

Abu pulled the trigger, and the bullet struck the man in his butt. The assassin screamed and reached for the wound. The rangy elf turned aside the second attacker's strike and spun, sending the wounded man's head flying from his shoulders. Blood shot across the short distance, splashing onto Abu.

Abu looked for another target. He hopped from side to side, trying to line up on the man fighting the whirling stirithy dervish from his knees.

Rrummblinss dispatched Abu's target with a lightning thrust to the throat and spun around. With a flick of his wrist, the swashbuckling fox-raccoon sent his rapier flying toward the man engaged with the bodyguard. The blade struck the last assassin in the back, penetrating his heart. The attacker collapsed, dead, before hitting the ground.

Seeing no more danger, Abu yelled, "Check Zanna, and get me out of this!"

The bodyguard kneeled next to the young woman. Rrummblinss, his fur matted with blood and gore, glided over to Abu. Eyes glowing with excitement, the stirithy held another long thin blade.

"Hold sstill." The knife sliced through strands of netting faster than Abu might have liked, given how close those strands were to his skin.

Abu made a silent plea to Allah as he threw off the tattered netting. "Is she alive?"

The elf said, "Barely. Need to get her to a life singer."

"We need to find Khepri."

As Abu went to his knees next to Zanna, she took a ragged breath. He evaluated the situation and made a quick decision. The bodyguard couldn't use one of his arms, and Rrummblinss was too short. It would be up to Abu.

Abu said, "Help me get her on my back."

He grabbed one of Zanna's arms and shifted her to a sitting position, her chin against her chest. Together, the three of them lifted her onto Abu's back. With her head lolling and arms hanging loosely over his shoulders, he stood. Leaning forward, he took off.

"Merciful Allah, please keep Zanna alive," Abu whispered over and over in Arabic. When his legs grew tired, he gritted his teeth and sought the anger. He thought about the times he had lost people he loved and the times he had almost lost more of them.

When his memories reached the pyramid and the attack by the legionaries, the Remulan sisters from the party flashed into his mind. He had no proof, but his gut told him who was responsible. With his hatred fixated on a target, he dug deeper. The burning in his legs drove him forward. So lost in his anger, he almost didn't notice the amber doors opening ahead as Rrummblinss ran past him.

"Kheprri!" Rrummblinss jogged past Louisa in the hallway. "Wherre iss Kheprri?" he added in Greek.

The sight of the stirithy's blood-soaked clothes and fur registered, and Louisa followed him, her concern growing.

The giant wolf's head filled the top of the doorway leading into their private dining room. "I'm in here," Khepri said in Greek.

Louisa heard shuffling and looked over her shoulder. Covered in blood, Abu staggered down the hallway with the limp form of a girl draped over him.

The sight frightened and relieved Louisa at the same time. Abu was alive, but was he hurt? Ben appeared behind the teenager. Louisa was grateful to see him.

Khepri yelled in Greek, "Bring her here! Put her on the table."

"I've got her, Abu." Ben tried to lift the girl.

The young man resisted at first, still fighting to place one foot in front of another. Ben took the girl under her arms and lifted her off his son's shoulders. Abu fell to his knees, gasping for breath.

As Ben started to cradle the girl in his arms, the feathered shaft got in the way. Instead, he faced the injured girl and backed down the hallway. Louisa leaned against the wall as Ben disappeared into the dining room.

Louisa put a hand on Abu's shoulder. "Are you hurt? Is any of this blood yours?"

Unable to catch his breath, Abu shook his head. With his chest heaving and tears mixing with the blood on his cheeks, he used Louisa to pull himself up. They both turned at the sound of dishes crashing to the floor. She guided the shocked teenager forward. More feet scraped the marble floor behind her, and Louisa looked over her shoulder. Jeevan had the arm of a wounded elf over his shoulder.

Entering the room, Louisa heard Abu repeating the same Arabic words, which she took to be a prayer. Khepri sat on the table's long bench with both hands on the girl's bare back, encircling the shaft.

As they neared the table, Abu stumbled forward and gripped the wooden edge. Louisa went to grab a jar of water and a towel.

Slumped in a chair, the wounded elf looked as pale as a welf. Ben pressed a fragment of a sliced tablecloth into the elf's almost severed arm, trying to stanch the flow of blood. Only a few tendons kept the arm attached to the shoulder. The elf's head dropped.

Ben shook him and yelled, "Stay awake! Look at me!"

Louisa poured a little water on the elf's face. He sputtered, and his eyes came into focus.

Ben yelled again, "Khepri, how's it going over there? This guy needs help soon!" He scanned the room. "Where's Ali?"

The hysakas, her focus on the wounded girl, ignored him. An unusual stirithy stood at the other end of the table, wiping dirt and grime from the injured girl's face. With nondescript brown fur, the stirithy woman wore a blue skirt and blouse. Her striking eyes, one blue and one brown, filled with concern for her patient. Those eyes reminded Louisa of the portrait of Alexander the Great they'd found in Perdiccas's tomb.

Hearing the girl's ragged breathing, the stirithy woman reached up with her other arm—a handless arm—to stroke the girl's hair. Louisa caught herself staring and forced herself to refocus on Khepri's treatments.

Louisa found it so wondrous each time the life singer healed someone whose life hung in the balance. Khepri kept one hand on the girl's back while she pulled up on the shaft in one steady motion. The arrow came free with a sucking sound.

The big hysakas must have sensed Abu's distress because she said, "Don't worry, I dissolved the arrowhead. She'll live. The arrow nicked the heart, and she lost a lot of blood." Khepri looked toward Ben. "I'll be there soon. I need to fix a lung and close the wound."

The bloody hole shrank until the skin grew together. Louisa wet the towel and wiped away all the crimson from around the wound. She stared in amazement at the miracle of the young woman's flawless pale skin. Khepri pushed herself up and hurried to the wounded man.

Abu shuffled around the table to take Khepri's place. He lifted the young elf's hand and held it with a look of desperation mixed with relief. He seemed to recognize the stirithy with the heterochromia eyes, and he whispered, "Thanks for helping, Hemmetrre."

Taken aback, Louisa wanted to talk to Khepri when things calmed down because it seemed like everyone knew about the big changes in Khepri's life but her. Seeing Rrummblinss waiting in silence behind Abu, Louisa grew agitated. She marched straight over to the roguish stirithy and said in Greek, "What the hell happened?"

"The childrren rran off playing ssome gamme. Enli and I chassed afterr themm. When we got therre, they werre underr attack, and Zanna wass wounded." Rrummblinss lowered his gaze and scratched his foot back and forth against the stone floor. "I think they trried to kidnap Abu. Therre werre sseven hummanss, and we killed themm all."

Stomach lurching, Louisa was struck by the reality of how close they had come to losing Abu. Once again, the power of her feelings caught her unprepared, and she staggered backward. The backs of her knees touched the cushion of a dining room chair, and she fell into the seat.

She choked back a sob as a wave of dread washed over her. She sensed Ben behind her.

Ben asked, "Who was it?"

Rrummblinss shrugged. "It sshouldn't take long to find out. We know everry-one who commess and goess in Grrommerrk."

A soft voice cracked, "It was Remulans."

As Abu stared at Zanna's face, he said in a louder voice, "Who else would do this? They tried to bribe me at the party, but I told them to go to hell."

Rrummblinss leaned closer, his voice racked with concern. "Abu killed two mmen. Watch himm."

Louisa reconsidered everything she'd thought of Rrummblinss. Whatever his failings, he cared about the teenager. She jumped from the chair and hugged the stirithy. "Thank you for bringing him back."

The small fox-man hugged her back. "You'rre welcomme. I'll do betterr next timme."

"I'm sure you will." Louisa backed away and looked down. She would have to discard yet another bloodstained chiton.

"Yes, thank both of you for saving them." Ben's voice cracked.

Louisa grabbed his hand. "What now?"

Ben's expression grew fierce. "We make them pay on the way to the falls."

As long as I don't lose any of you, Louisa thought, her heart pounding with the strength of emotions she had never known.

Chapter 23

Grrommerrk, Choru, An 5660, Day 20–23

Louisa stopped at the bookcase and reached for a red-bound book on the highest shelf. Even though she stood on her toes, her fingers were a few inches short.

"I'll help, Miss Louisa," said the ever-present Masako. The girl hustled across the small library to a stepstool and struggled to pick it up.

Louisa sighed. *This subservient nature must go.*

Carrying the stepstool an inch off the ground, Masako waddled toward her.

"Stop. Put it down," Louisa commanded.

Masako's almond-shaped eyes grew wide. She lowered the steps and shuffled toward Louisa, her head bowed.

"Look at me." Louisa tried to think of the best way to communicate what she needed from the eight-year-old with their limited shared vocabulary.

The young girl raised her head, and Louisa pinned her in place with a look. "You are not my servant. Do you understand?"

After a slight nod, the girl stood still, her body stiff.

Louisa pointed at her. "You are free. Not a slave. Not a helper. Not a servant. Understand?"

"Yes. I am free. Not a slave. Not helper." Masako shook her head. "I want to stay. I help."

"Ah." Louisa squatted down to Masako's level. "You can stay until we find your family. Until then, you will learn how to take care of yourself. You will not help. Learn."

Masako relaxed and smiled. "I learn."

"I *will* learn."

"I *will* learn." Masako gave her a thumbs-up.

"Good, let's have some fun." Louisa put her hand on Masako's shoulder and guided her out of the library.

"Where are we going?"

"For a climb."

———————————

With one boot wedged into the crack between two large pieces of bark, Masako reached up. Sweat dripped from every inch of her skin as she dug her gloved fingers into another piece of wood. With a hard tug, Masako made sure the flaky wood would not shear away. After several frightening experiences and Louisa's admonishments, she had learned to always check.

Masako let go of the iron grip she had on the tree with her other hand. After wiping her eyes and forehead with her leather glove, she reached for her next target. She pushed up with one leg and jammed her free toe into place. Her eyes darted to the next handhold. A rope tied to her waist led up to the rung some fifty feet above her head.

Miss Louisa had tied the safety line to the metal ring after hammering the spike on the other end into the solid part of the tree. She hung from the bark several feet higher than the ring and smiled down at Masako.

Just a little more. Then back down, the young girl thought.

Abu had promised to meet her in two hours to continue her swimming lessons. He said she would learn more than floating and treading water. The thought of jumping into the Tefnut River's cooling waters made Masako want to speed up the climb, but Miss Louisa's instructions echoed back to her. "Go too fast, and you die. Think, then move. Plan every foot and handhold first. Go faster than you think, and you die."

Peeking down the rough wood trunk to the ground, Masako shook her head. They were hundreds of feet above the surface but only two-thirds of the way to the tree's giant branches. The first day they'd started practicing, Masako thought she would never get over her fear of heights.

The more she watched Miss Louisa, the more Masako wanted to feel the same joy that her instructor felt the higher they climbed. Even after several falls in which she was saved by the safety line, Masako began to lose her fear by the end of that first day.

It was good that Masako had lost her fear because tomorrow Miss Louisa said they would sit on the first branch. But that was tomorrow.

Focus.

Chapter 24

Grrommerrk, Choru, An 5660, Day 24

Ben looked over the feast laid out on the dining room table. Abu placed a tray of the Lancers' sweetbreads on the table. The aroma of roasted zehorg was different from the roasted chicken, quail, or turkey his mother had served, but the scene still brought forth a flood of childhood memories for Ben. He never wanted to lose the ties to where he came from or to the people who helped make him who he was.

Today was Ben's attempt to bring a bit of home to his rag-tag group. And maybe, just maybe, this day would be the start of many traditions for the family he longed for.

"Abu, can you go get Louisa and Masako? I'll tell everyone else to come to dinner."

"Yes, sir. Are they climbing again?" Abu asked.

Ben placed a plate on the table and side-stepped to the next seat. "I think so. Go ask a guard to bring a wind singer."

"Why?"

"Yesterday, I saw them reach the crown of the city hall tree. They will never hear you if they are that high."

The teenager asked, "You're not worried?"

Ben tried to muster up a reassuring smile. "Louisa uses ropes to make sure Masako can't fall. You'd have to blindfold me and tie me to the tree itself, but the two of them are fearless."

"I'll go get them." Abu headed for the door.

____

At the end of the long table, Ben stood and raised his metal chalice. He said in Greek, "I'd like to say a few words." He waited until the conversations around the table died out and he had everyone's attention. If he had told himself just six months ago that he would celebrate this holiday with such an eclectic group, he would have laughed.

Around the table was an Egyptian professor who had tried to kill him a few weeks ago, a giant talking wolf, her much smaller grumpy fox of a spouse, another young stirithy woman Ben had just met, his friend the jovial duffadar from the British Indian Army, a Greek general's daughter with her young Lancer boyfriend, an eight-year-old ex-slave girl, his adopted son, and the woman who had captured his imagination, along with his heart.

Ben smiled, thinking about the last time he had celebrated this day with his family. At just sixteen years old, he knew nothing but hope for the future and gratitude for his blessings. How fast things had changed.

As he choked back his feelings, he forced his voice to be steady. "Back home where I'm from, we used to celebrate every year on this day. The last time I was with my family we celebrated Evacuation Day." He chuckled. "I know. Not a good holiday name. A few years ago, they changed the name to *Thanksgiving*

Day." His scar tugged at the corner of his mouth as he grinned. "We spend this holiday with friends and family, giving thanks to God for all the good things in our lives." He raised the chalice higher. "Today, I am grateful for all of my new friends."

"I hope you consider us friends as well," said Lil.

All heads turned toward Ki, Lil, and Thoresten, standing just inside the doorway.

Great.

Ben glanced at Louisa, who was frowning. Jeevan stood and rushed around the table to hug the red-headed twin, Ki. Before Ben could say anything, the two began kissing with unrestrained passion.

Not knowing what else to say, Ben waved toward the table. "Please come in and find a seat." He coughed until Jeevan gave him a one-eyed glance. Ben raised his eyebrows, and the kissing couple stepped apart.

With his beard split into a broad smile, Jeevan said, "Well, yes. Come with me." He grabbed Ki's hand and led her to his seat. Ali had stood to let them sit together and went to retrieve another chair. Lil and Thoresten squeezed between Abu and Khepri's family of three.

When everyone had settled, Ben asked Lil, "What news?"

Lil's brown eyes sparkled with mischief. "I should ask you the same. You are making the weapons you told my mother you couldn't make."

Nothing they can do to us here.

Ben laughed. "I lied. But we have not given the secrets to anyone. We control how many bullets get created. What about your mother?"

Lil pressed her lips into a grim line. "We stopped the assassins, but she is no longer in charge of Nippur. No one is. My mother fled the city and is fighting to regain control. You might not know, but my sister and I are not popular in Nippur. There is not much we can do to help the situation." She waved toward

Ki. "When we received Thoresten's message from the embassy, we came to see what trouble the crazy Earthlings were getting into."

Ben raised his drink again. "If you want some adventure, then you came just in time. We are about to leave for Kerma. You're welcome to join us."

Lil's eyebrows rose.

"We'll speak later." One last time, Ben raised the chalice. "Happy Thanksgiving, everyone."

Louisa stood up. "I hope you don't mind, but I would like to sing a song to show my thanks."

Ben nodded and sat. He remembered his first experience of Louisa singing. The echoes of the tragic Greek love song, with its haunting melody, still filled him with sadness.

For this occasion, Louisa chose a song full of wonder and hope. To share with their new friends, she sang an American song in Greek. Ben did not need to translate it back to English because he knew the words by heart. A sense of joy overcame him, and, with a soft voice, he sang along to "All Things Bright and Beautiful."

All things bright and beautiful, all crea-
tures great and small,

All things wise and wonderful, 'twas God
that made them all.

Each little flower that opens, each little bird
that sings,

He made their glowing colors, and made
their tiny wings.

All things bright and beautiful, all crea-
tures great and small,

All things wise and wonderful, 'twas God
that made them all.

The purple-headed mountains, the rivers
running by,

The sunset and the morning, that brightens
up the sky.

All things bright and beautiful, all crea-
tures great and small,

All things wise and wonderful, 'twas God
that made them all.

When Louisa's voice trailed off, Ben stood with the others to applaud. With her song acting as the celebration's prayer, he gestured toward the table. "Let's eat."

Chapter 25

Grrommerrk, Choru, An 5660, Day 25

Abu hadn't seen Zanna since the day of the attack. He hated that he'd missed her birthday. He never wanted to leave her side, but Dr. Ben forced him to stay at city hall. Part of him understood the need for safety, but he also resented Dr. Ben for keeping him away from her. Ningal became his only visitor during those five long days. He let her visit just one time so he could say goodbye. He felt so guilty about seeing her while he couldn't see Zanna.

At some point, Dr. Ben asked Abu about both girls and attempted to give him one of those parental talks about how he should respect women and not lead them on or lie to them. Abu had done none of those things, so he didn't feel guilty for that. Both girls knew about the other, just not the details. Besides, they were both very honest with him. As much as they liked him, relationships between mortals and immortals always led to heartbreak.

One thing Abu's adopted father said during his lecture struck a nerve. It made him look deep into his feelings as they related to each girl. Dr. Ben said there should be a physical attraction between a man and a woman. But more important was having a foundation of mutual respect and trust that could grow into a genuine friendship.

When he thought about Ningal, their physical relationship was always the first thing on his mind. Nothing but kissing and touching had happened, but whenever he saw the welf, his blood boiled. He enjoyed spending time with her and liked their conversations. When they were away from each other, though, he missed her kisses the most.

When Abu had last seen Ningal, she was disappointed about him going, but, true to her word, she kept her emotions in check. She told him she hoped their paths would cross again and he would always hold a special place in her heart. If they met again, he wondered what he would feel.

Abu's thoughts about Zanna were so different. He admired her natural beauty, how pure and innocent she seemed to be. Of course, when they kissed, he came alive with desire, but when he missed her, he pictured her smile, her eyes, and her laughter.

Hours with her flew by in the easy manner of best friends. No, their relationship felt much deeper than what he shared with Umrao. Was that the way of friendships between lovers? Abu now knew his crush on Nashwa had been but a shadow of the relationship he shared with Zanna.

The sadness he felt while waiting for her to arrive weighed him down. In a few hours, he would leave. Chances were that he would never see either girl again. Hearing knocks on the door, he put on a brave face. His mind settled; he would tell her what she meant to him. A silent prayer went to Allah. He prayed that her immortal heart felt the same as his mortal one. Even though he would try to move on, his heart now belonged to her.

Tears streaming down her face, Zanna watched Abu's boat disappear around the bend. When she had gone to see him for the last time, Zanna had promised not to cry until he left. Her promise broken, she wept when Abu told her he thought he was in love with her. They hugged, and their kisses were salty from tears. Together, they mourned for a love that could never be.

Abu told Zanna to forget him and to move on with her life while she implored him not to look back and to keep his heart open to love another. With only the ripples of his boat's wake still visible, Zanna knew for certain that no matter how long she lived, she would never forget the young man from another world.

———————————

As they had on the way into Grrommerrk, the non-stirithy spent half a day blindfolded. Their boats rocked with each twist and turn on their way out. About four hours after the boats pushed away from the docks, they reached the stirithy fortress at the head of the Tefnut River.

When the blindfold came off, it took Ben almost a minute for his eyes to adjust. They disembarked inside a castle made completely of steel. Built over rushing water that emerged from the mountain, the structure sparkled as the light of An bounced off the shiny surface.

Ben marveled at how much metal had gone into the fortress and how, even against modern artillery, the structure would have been indestructible. He also found the scale of the corridors, the doors, and the rooms to be a little odd, built for the smallest of the Aaruan races. He thought of the number of times he'd bang his head should he try to navigate the redoubt's short doorways.

Rrummblinss stepped beside him and said in Greek, "Verry imprressssive, issn't it? Therre iss also enough ssteel insside the tunnel to commpletely seal the entrrancce. No one iss going to rreach Grrommerrk without perrmmisssssion, unlessss they arre flying."

"Incredible. By the way, I'm glad the council allowed you and your men to join us."

"I'mm looking forrwarrd to it. We sshould have ssome fun getting passt the Rremmulan sseige. I bet you can usse ssomme mmetal ssingerrss when you get to Kerrmma."

Ben nodded, thinking about his side project, as Thoresten joined them. With a hint of anticipation, the dwarf asked in Greek, "Do you think we will have to fight?"

"Mmosst ccerrtainly. The Rremmulanss have a Legion guarrding the rriverr apprroach to Kerrmma." Rrummblinss curled his hands into fists and held them about a foot apart "They've put a forrt on each bank of the Tefnut and built a temmporrarry brridge between the two. They contrrol all trraffic ussing the rriverr. They have ssiege enginess bommbarrding the Kerrmman wall that prro-tectss the fallss."

Ben asked, "Is there no way to sneak past the forts?"

"No, the valley is narrrrow at that point in the rriverr, but don't worrrry, I have a plan."

"Remulans are assholes, but they are worthy warriors." Thoresten smiled and patted the ax on his hip. "My axes are thirsty."

Taken aback at the blood lust from the quiet, contemplative dwarf, Ben said, "Good, I guess. How long will it take us to reach the forts?"

"Tommorrrrow afterrnoon, we will put asshorre and wait until darrk." Rrummblinss's voice purred with excitement. "Arround Twinss, mmy trroopss will mmove into possition and causse a diverrssion. Ben, you can lead the attack on the brridge. At fourr in the mmorrning we will sstrrike, and our boatss will be passt the Rremmulanss beforre they can rrecoverr. I jusst hope the Kerrmmanss will let uss in when we get to the gate."

Chapter 26

Tefnut River, Choru, An 5660, Day 26

Ben swirled his left hand and kicked his feet against the current, working with Esther, her Yoke, and two Lancers. His team was attempting to keep their log from floating within sight of the guards on the Remulan bridge blocking the river.

He tried to ignore the cold seeping into his bones and glanced again at the tree limb. He confirmed that his Winchester and holster were secured on top of the tree trunk and well away from the water. His eyes darted to the medium-size barrel of black powder tied to the middle of the rudimentary raft. He shivered, but it wasn't from the cold.

Ben wondered how much longer they would need to hold their position. When would Rrummblinss and his two strike teams launch their attack?

Let's start already.

After hearing the full plan, Ben had doubted the Captain of the Troop could pull it off. Then the twenty-five stirithy soldiers put on their camouflage. Around midnight, with both moons casting enough light for people to see ten feet, Ben and the rest of the observers watched the metal-singing soldiers use their magic.

Everyone stood mesmerized as the ground beneath the stirithy came to life. The soil inched up the backs of each warrior's legs, up to his waist, up his back, and over the top of his head and much of his face. The diminutive warriors' backs were encased in sod. All around their boots, the ground had been stripped bare of topsoil. Twenty-five miniature golems, made of dirt and grass, had sprouted from the ground.

As his team set off, Rrummblinss dropped to his stomach with his troops mimicking his every move. In the eerie light, these small mounds of earth glided across the open grassland and disappeared into the darkness. If they moved slowly enough, the camouflage would make them almost undetectable to the Remulan sentries manning the ramparts.

Each golem carried two cantaloupe-size containers filled with black powder and a modified Enfield revolver. Each little soldier's gun had a small rifle stock added to the handle and a wooden forestock surrounding the five-inch barrel. Some troops would tunnel into the ramparts and set their charges below the siege engines. Others would move up the earthen walls like spiders to lob their bombs into the unsuspecting camp.

His arm tiring, Ben switched hands on the log. He kept swimming and kicking upstream, waiting.

Any minute now.

The strum of the Remulan siege engines again drowned out the constant rumble of the giant falls far downstream. Once the two log squads had rounded the bend that concealed their initial landing, they had heard, then seen, massive rocks being launched from the twin forts.

Like clockwork, a trebuchet's giant wooden arm uncoiled before its huge pouch snapped and released its heavy payload. A few seconds later, there would be a loud thump, splash, or crack as the missiles struck in the distance.

Ben looked to the sky, trying to see the giant boulders as they flew away from the fort on the left bank. The flash of orange, reds, and yellows blinded him, and the shock waves punched his chest.

"To the bridge!" Ben yelled in Greek and then in English.

Ben's team turned their log parallel to the river. He took his place at the end while the Lochem and the Lancers moved to positions on either side. Together, they each swam with one arm while Ben kicked his numb legs as hard and fast as he could. The current helped them pick up speed.

Torch lights on the bridge grew brighter. They could make out the shadowy outlines of the bridge's defenders. Thankfully, only a few guards were picketed near their targeted landing spot. A cluster of Remulans stood along the shoreline, nearer the forts on either side of the bridge, which spanned the seventy yards of the Tefnut River. The other team's log floated a little behind and thirty feet to Ben's right.

They had plenty of momentum as they hit the thirty-yard mark from their destination. A wooden pontoon bridge spanned the water. Ben yelled in both languages, "Turn and take positions!"

Though they hadn't practiced these maneuvers, Ben hoped they could execute them as if their lives depended on it. He joined the Lancers on their side of the log while Esther and the other Lochem moved to opposite ends. Together, they turned the giant tree trunk parallel to the bridge while they stayed on the far side.

Lining up with his holster on top of the log, Ben tried to launch himself up. Luckily, they had added smaller logs to the sides as stabilizers earlier so the trunk didn't rotate.

The platform tipped backward as Ben scrambled up the rough bark. The Lochem on the ends grabbed the small trunks on the other side, counterbalancing the log. It rocked back and forth. Water sloshed onto his face, and Ben gritted his teeth, fearing the worst.

With his torso draped over the tree, the makeshift raft settled enough for Ben to look to his left. Both Lancers were in similar positions as he reached for his holster. He got a firm grip on the handle of his Pocket Army before releasing the slip knot that held the revolver in place. He pulled the gun free.

A javelin sunk into the trunk only inches from Ben's left shoulder. Several others splashed in front of and behind their makeshift boat. Ben shook off the close call. On the bridge stood four ancient Roman legionaries a short ten yards away. Costumed in feathered helmets, green capes, and large rectangular shields, they looked menacing.

With his off hand, Ben grabbed the shaft of the javelin to keep secure. He tried to use it to compensate for the swaying motion of the log and his frozen, waterlogged fingers while he aimed. Instinct told him to wait. He needed to be closer. With the distance between them disappearing, the legionary Ben aimed at pulled out a short sword.

It's a gladius, Ben corrected himself.

He was close enough now to see the man's eyes in the moonlight and torch flames. The soldier wore a sneer. Ben's anger took hold. These Remulan bastards tried to kidnap Abu and were behind the kidnapping of Louisa. Also, Ben had almost died at the hands of Remulans on multiple occasions.

Ben aimed for center mass and squeezed the trigger. The man's eyes bulged, and he dropped his sword, reaching for his midsection. More shots rang out, but Ben ignored them. He fought the recoil and pulled the trigger once more. The legionary fell forward and splashed into the river. Ben looked for another target and found none of the original four.

Their raft struck the bridge with a jolt. Ben moved up the log until he straddled it, facing toward the fort on the left bank. His bare toes dug into the rough bark. One Lancer had done the same, but Acting Lance Duffadar Ghadge couldn't quite make it. His arms flailing, he cursed in Dogri, fell backward, and splashed into the water. Esther and her Yoke worked to secure the log to the bridge as fast as possible.

The outlines of several Remulans appeared against the backdrop of smaller explosions near the fort.

Sowar Jadav, riding on the log, fired his Enfield revolver toward the clump of soldiers near the shore. Ben aimed and squeezed out one shot at a time until only one bullet remained. Three legionaries with their long rectangular shields locked appeared to solidify from the murky blackness.

"Need to reload," said Sowar Jadav.

"Captain Ben, toss me my rifle."

To Ben's right, Acting Lance Duffadar Ghadge stood on the bridge, dripping wet. In front of him, Esther and her Yoke had locked their headstone-shaped shields and braced to meet the Remulans.

"Jadav, get to the bridge!" Ben shouted.

He untied his holster and threw it over his neck and shoulder like a bandolier. He shoved his revolver into the holster, hoping it would stay in place. Ben yanked his saber-handled long knife from its attached scabbard, then stretched forward until he lay flat on top of the log.

With a hand on Ghadge's carbine and ammo belt, Ben sliced the leather tie. Off balance, he pushed himself back to a sitting position. He tossed the rifle across the gap between the log and the bridge to the Acting Lance Duffadar. The Lancer snatched the carbine out of the air and turned just in time to catch the ammo belt that followed.

Sounds of distant explosions, gunfire, and shields banging together were followed by steel on steel. As Ben took hold of his Winchester, he sliced it free before shoving his knife into his belt. Agnes felt good in his hands and calmed him. He swung his leg over so that he faced the bridge. With his feet on the stabilizing log, Ben launched himself across the last yard. His frozen legs buckled on hitting the logs, which sent him stumbling forward.

As Ben found his footing, Ghadge shot over Esther's shoulder. She jerked her head away from the shot. It struck the face of a legionary who had swung his gladius toward her. The man's face imploded. The Remulan fell backward, and his arm went slack. His sword bounced harmlessly off Esther's shield.

Esther blocked a low thrust with her shield. As if they were one being, her Yoke threw his spear over her shoulder to skewer the last opponent. The man made a feeble grab at the shaft protruding from his neck until the Lochem pulled it free. A fountain of blood erupted before the dead man crumpled to the logs.

Ben stepped around Esther to form a three-man firing line with the two Lancers. Near the shore, a solid formation of legionaries marched out. Ben's small group was lucky the gate and the drawbridge nearest the bridge were closed tight, or more soldiers might have overwhelmed them.

With Jeevan's drill instructions in his head, Ben called out, "Get as close to shore as possible! Fire at the slow march!"

Almost as one, they fired into the wall of darkened shields marching toward them. Together, Ben and the Lancers took a step and pulled the levers on their rifles, ejecting the used cartridges. Ben loaded and fired twice for each of the Lancers' breach-loaded volleys.

By the fifth step, half the legionaries had fallen. On the seventh step, Ben kneeled to reload. He grabbed a bullet from the belt of his holster and shoved it past the loading gate on the side of his Winchester. All the while, the Lancers kept firing and moving. As he rammed home the twelfth cartridge, he evaluated the situation.

The remaining legionaries on the bridge marched toward certain death. Their discipline and resolve made Ben shake his head at the useless deaths. The Lancers took down two more, and yet the remaining three closed ranks and jogged forward. Ben aimed and squeezed. As if choreographed, the three soldiers fell in unison.

Stubborn bastards.

Ben glanced behind him. The other squad had cleared the right side of the bridge as well. Esther and Ki were standing near their respective logs in the center of the bridge, each holding a torch. They nodded to each other and bent to touch their torches to a fuse.

Esther dropped her torch and sprinted toward Ben with her Yoke beside her. They had about thirty seconds. Ben turned and ran to catch up to the Lancers.

"Go! It's going to blow!"

Now came the second and third most dangerous parts of the plan. To get to safety, away from the explosions at the center of the bridge, they would put themselves within easy bow range of any archers on top of the earthworks. The fort itself stood about fifty yards from the shoreline with a wide ditch surrounding the ramparts. Ben prayed that the continued bombardment from the stirithy shock troops would occupy the attention of all the soldiers in the fort. Then he prayed they wouldn't get themselves killed by the bridge explosion itself.

Esther screamed in Greek, "Get down!"

Ben and the men in front of him threw themselves onto the logs. He covered his head with one hand as the logs beneath him buckled and threw him into the air. Ben crashed with a thud. Pain shot through the arm and shoulder that had taken the brunt of the fall. Through it all, he'd somehow held onto Agnes.

The bridge continued to undulate from the massive waves the explosion had caused. Ben tried to get to his feet when a shower of cold water drenched them all. The bridge moved. Shattered by the black powder explosions, it had broken in two. The halves floated free, wobbling in the current like a severed ribbon in a gentle breeze.

Ben felt death's chill warning when several arrows hit the wood a few feet away. He knelt and looked back toward the fort. The explosion on the bridge must have gotten some Remulan officer's attention. There was a lot of movement along the ramparts, but from fifty yards away, in the middle of the night, the archers were difficult to locate.

Ben aimed at the shadows and fired as he yelled, "Get back!"

The Lancers jumped to their feet and turned to flee when Esther and her Yoke ran past them to form a small shield wall. Several arrows smacked into their wooden shields.

Ghadge patted the Dimaerites on the shoulder. "Thanks."

The Lancers fired over the Alexandrian soldiers' heads at the snipers on the ramparts. Ben stepped close behind Esther, who kept her shield raised above her head. As a group, they backed away from the fort, one step at a time.

This is bad.

Pushed by the current, the broken end of the bridge swung closer to the bank. They couldn't get out of the bowmen's range. Without warning, the ropes connecting the wooden span to shore snapped. Unmoored, the thirty-yard span of logs became a giant, out-of-control raft. More arrows fell as the five of them clung to one another, trying to stay upright.

Ben snapped his head around at the sound of concentrated gunfire. To his relief, he saw the outline of one of their boats, angling to intercept them. Muzzle flashes of several rifles erupted from the vessel. A line of Lancers kneeled in the boat, firing at the ramparts.

The group's slow movement away from the fort was excruciating. Yet the suppressive fire of the Lancers, the darkness, and the growing distance caused the arrows to fall more and more errant. The stirithy steering the boat tried to pull up close to their location, but Ben's group would need to move to reach it.

Ben tapped each Lancer on the shoulder and said, "Our ship is here." He pointed at the part of their raft where they could meet the boat. The men stumbled away.

Ben put his hand on Esther's shoulder and yelled in Greek, "We need to move!"

She jerked her head in acknowledgment. "Coming."

The group moved with caution down the swaying wooden float. With the boat just a few feet away, two Lancers threw ropes from the bow and another from the stern. Together, they tugged the boat next to the raft, and everyone hopped on board. Ben found a seat as they pushed free of the broken bridge. The small boatmen pulled hard on their oars to let the bridge float past them. Just before it cleared, the pontoon segment began to spin in the current.

Urged to a frantic pace, the oarsmen pulled as fast and as hard as they could to increase the distance. Ben continued praying as he watched the exploded end of the bridge continue its slow spin. He could have sworn they were about to get hammered when the skipper jerked the tiller, turning at the last moment. The bridge missed them by a foot, if not less. It slammed into the bank and broke apart.

Behind Ben, a small flotilla of boats carried the rest of his group between the smoldering forts and the jumble of wood from the wrecked bridge. As Ben's boat rounded the next bend, Rrummblinss and his men waved from the shoreline. Several boats went to meet the victorious teams.

Used to putting herself in danger, Louisa didn't know whether she should be insulted or relieved to be left once again with Abu and Masako. She'd rather be out there with the others. Of course, her rational, calculating personality knew it made sense from a practical standpoint.

All of them were trained soldiers. Even if Ben was almost twenty years out of uniform, he had commanded men in combat. Louisa hoped they wouldn't stand in her way when it was her turn to contribute to the group.

She had spent the night trying to stay calm and be a strong positive presence for Masako, who fed off Abu's nervous energy. While they waited for the attack to begin, Abu fidgeted but never vocalized his worry.

The oarsmen rowed faster to match the captain's pace. Explosions and gunshots sounded in the distance. As her vessel rounded the bend, the hazy outlines of two massive forts appeared, bookending the river. Fires glowing within the fortress walls illuminated tendrils of smoke wafting into the night sky.

In the midst of the flat-bottomed boat flotilla, which reminded Louisa of Seine river barges, she saw the first boats enter bow range. Along each boat's gunwale, the foxlike sailors had taken the lids from crates and turned them into angled shields. Enough of the Remulan soldiers had survived the sneak attack to send dozens of arrows flying from the ramparts toward the first boat.

Like porcupine needles shooting into the air, then slowing at the top of their trajectory before falling and picking up speed, Remulan arrows raced toward impact.

A handful of quills slammed into the lids.

The violence echoed across the water like hammers on a roof.

Louisa squeezed her eyes shut. A sudden flash of fire belched from the pin-cushioned boat as the Lancers' rifles roared vengeance.

Masako nestled closer, and Louisa hugged her tighter. Their boat had a rower to the front of their bolt hole and another to the rear. The three of them hunched beside a big crate with a thick wooden lid over their heads. The oars slapped hard at the water, and the stirithy boatmen encouraged one another with loud jokes to cut the tension. At least, Louisa imagined they were jokes because of all the purr-hissing laughter that ensued.

She swayed with the rocking waves and peeked through the gaps in their armor. The keelboat in front of them heaved and rolled as a tremendous splash showered its bow. Another catapulted boulder flew a few feet over the boat and whopped into the river, which shot a geyser of spray. The small vessel rocked in its wake.

"What's going on?" Abu asked.

Louisa crossed herself. "Stay down."

She shrieked as a giant harpoon struck their stirithy rower and pinned him to the side of the boat. The wooden deck shuddered at the impact, and the boat lifted out of the water. The impaled fox's eyes grew wide before his head fell, his limp arms hanging.

Dear God. Louisa dug her fingers into a screaming Masako's arm.

Louisa's world flipped. Her head banged against something hard, and her vision blurred.

So cold.

Freezing water filled her mouth. She tried to keep her head above the surface.

Masako! Abu!

Anguished, Louisa spun around in a circle, treading against the current. The glow of the nearby fort reflected a little light across the murky river. The weight of her soaked clothes pulled her down as the draft moved her past the fortress. She spit out more water and worked her leaden arms back and forth, yelling, "Abu! Masako!"

"Miss Louisa!" Abu's cry came from far behind her.

Louisa twisted her torso against the current, treading water in a circle. Her ship was moving farther downriver with a considerable chunk of the starboard railing missing. Abu stood at the stern of the boat, pointing toward her. She waved her hand, and he waved back.

Masako? Louisa weakly echoed the young girl's name. "Masako."

Something warm ran down Louisa's cold face. Her sight narrowed. A wave of dizziness made her turn onto her back to float in the choppy river. A haze of gray obscured the normally brilliant stars. A sliver of white streaked past her shaky vision. Nauseous, she turned her head and spewed the contents of her stomach into the water.

Wiping a hand across her mouth, Louisa swished her other hand back and forth to stay afloat. *Need to find her. I'm so tired.*

Something hard banged into her side, and Louisa tried to reach for it. She lifted, floating higher. She tried to blink to stay awake, but her eyelids wouldn't cooperate.

———————————————

The boots were so heavy, Masako wasn't sure she could keep treading water against the strong current. She swam a few strokes, the boots dragging her down. She took a deep breath, then doubled over and unlaced one boot. Then she popped her head out of the water to take another deep breath and plunged under to pull off the other boot.

Its shoelace had a knot she couldn't untangle. The laurel wreath tiara made from her slave collar had caught in her hair, a painful distraction. Her breath was running out. She panicked and poked her head above the surface.

Think before you move.

The tiara could wait. The boot could not. With another gulp of air, Masako reached for the knife on her belt. She got a solid grip on the handle before pulling it out of its sheath. Her head went under again, and she reached toward her boot.

270

With one hand, she pulled the tangled leather laces while sawing with the other hand. The string separated, and she kicked her foot free. Her lungs burning, Masako scissored her legs and reached toward the only hint of light in the liquid blackness.

As her head cleared the surface, she sucked in a life-giving breath.

"Masako." Miss Louisa's voice was faint.

Masako sought the source of the voice and looked for any of their boats. From the back of a ship, Abu waved and pointed to Miss Louisa floating on her back about twenty yards distant.

Masako carefully returned her knife to its sheath and swam toward her mentor. Only ten feet away, another head popped to the surface. The man's eyes bulged with fright as he sputtered and slapped at the water with one arm. Masako tried to change direction.

Who? she thought.

"Ahura Jupiter, serva me," croaked the man as he saw Masako.

Remulan!

Masako swam through the water as fast as she could, but a rough, calloused hand grabbed her ankle. She snapped her lips closed and went under. Kicking out, she tried to dislodge the man's grip. Her heel slammed into hard muscle. Another kick, and the man still hung on.

The burning in her chest came back, along with the panic. Masako remembered the knife and, with her lungs screaming, found the sheath on her hip. After two tries, she got the knife loose. The urge to take a breath was overwhelming, but she doubled over and sliced across the arm that held her ankle. She was free.

Masako reached upward, pushed, and kicked until her head surfaced. She gasped. Water and air filled her mouth, choking her. She took a deep breath through her nose.

The Remulan's calloused fingers ran along her calf as he tried to find purchase. Masako bent her knee and kicked again. This time, her heel met the soft bones of the man's nose. His feeble grip came loose.

Masako swam the way Abu had taught her. Both arms moved in front and out to the side while her legs bunched up and pushed apart like a frog. As she crossed the last ten yards, time slowed. When she reached Miss Louisa's side, someone yelled behind her, "There she is!"

Masako didn't look back because Miss Louisa's eyes had closed, and she'd begun to sink. Masako grabbed Miss Louisa's shoulder and pulled her up while trying to tread water and hold a knife in her other hand. A shadow blocked out part of the eerie light reflecting on the river, and a wooden hull bumped into the other side of Miss Louisa. Strong hands reached down and pulled the unconscious woman out of the water.

Another arm flashed down. "Masako! Grab my hand!"

Masako tightened her grip on the knife, afraid to let it go. She reached for the man's arm and was plucked out of the water, then hauled over the side of the boat. She saw Miss Louisa lying on the deck, her face covered in blood.

She's going to be okay. She has to be.

Her tears ran free, but Masako was too wet for anyone to notice. Exhausted, she closed her eyes and slumped next to the warm body of someone who wrapped a blanket around her.

Chapter 27

Kerma City, Choru, An 5660, Day 26

A loud rumble prodded Louisa's unconscious mind.

"How is she?"

"She'll be fine."

Wrapped in a toasty cocoon, Louisa did not want to wake up.

Just a little longer.

Muffled sobs seeped into her consciousness. A familiar voice, wracked with pain, said, "Thank Allah, she's okay. It happened so fast. I should have jumped in when they fell in the water."

Ben said, "It's not your fault, Abu."

A large hand smoothed Louisa's hair. She opened her eyes, and Khepri stared down at her. Louisa's throat was dry, and she croaked a scratchy, "Masako?"

Big amber eyes flecked with brown sparkled back at her as Khepri nodded. Louisa pushed herself up on her elbows. She lay in a grassy field a hundred yards from a gigantic wall. The roar of falling water crashing in the distance threatened to block out all other noise.

Umrao stood next to Ben and Abu. The tall Lancer held a sobbing Masako over his shoulder and said something to the girl. When Masako saw Louisa, her heaves came to a haltering stop. She squirmed free of Umrao's hold and ran to kneel at Louisa's side, then threw her arms around her mentor's neck.

Ben squatted on the other side, his eyes shot red with worry. "I'm so grateful you're okay. We're lucky we didn't lose either of you." He grasped Louisa's hand, rubbing his thumb in nervous circles over the top. "Do you think you can stand?"

With a nod, Louisa patted Masako's back. The girl pulled away with a sniffle and a big grin. Louisa grabbed Ben's hand and held Khepri's soft, padded, hand-shaped paw. Together, they stood.

"Thirsty," Louisa squeaked.

Ben handed her his canteen, and Louisa took several small sips. She remembered the blow to her head and patted where the wound should be. No pain and no damage.

She caught Khepri's eyes and smiled. "Thank you. Again."

The giant wolf winked.

Louisa turned to address Ben. "I'm happy you're safe."

Ben brought her into a hug. "Me, too."

Awkward in his embrace, she thought, *Ironic*.

If he noticed, it didn't show. The warmth of his emotions made her ignore the chilly dampness of their clothes as they squished together. Slow and timid, she encircled his waist and hugged him back. Eyes closed, she pressed her cheek into his chest, listening to the rhythm of his beating heart. His chin rested on her head, and she dropped her defensive walls. She sighed, safe and content.

"Not everyone was lucky. Rrummblinss lost six men," Ben whispered.

Louisa flinched to remember the stirithy oarsman as his eyes faded to nothing. She mouthed a quiet Hail Mary for the fallen. She didn't know whether these aliens had souls, but she hoped God would show them the same grace he did all his creatures. She pulled away and crossed herself as Ben whispered, "Amen."

The Good Doctor looked from her to Abu to Masako as he quirked a lopsided grin. "That had to be one of the dumbest things I've ever done. Next time that crazy stirithy makes a plan that includes me, please knock some sense into me."

Louisa smiled. "What if it's my plan next time?"

Ben turned to Abu. "In that case, Abu." He paused to smile at Masako. "And Masako. The two of you knock some sense into both of us."

Masako grabbed Ben's and Louisa's hands and said with confidence, "I'll help." Confused, she tilted her head. "What does knock and sense mean?"

"I'll tell you later." Abu laughed and patted Masako's head. "Dr. Ben, you can count on me as well. Though it's much easier to keep you in line than Miss Sophia."

Louisa pursed her lips. "I thought we were a team."

Ben muttered under his breath, "Trouble in Abusa."

Abu and Louisa said, "Huh?" "What?"

With a shake of his head, Ben said, "Nothing. Let's go."

As she turned to follow, Louisa realized what he'd said. *Abusa?*

They approached a small gate set into the massive wall. There, Ssherrss, Rrummblinss, and several of their group were conferring with a contingent of Egyptian-clad soldiers who appeared to be of Nubian descent. With An poking his head over the mountain peaks at their backs, long shadows preceded them.

Louisa had good instincts regarding heights, and the wall dominated the landscape, thrusting at least a hundred feet into the air. It began at the mountains on both sides of the small plains at the top of the plateau, and the two halves met over the Tefnut River. Huge metal grates allowed the mighty river to rush under the fortification toward the falls somewhere close behind. The falls had to be close because the roar was so loud that Louisa had to shout to be heard.

Off to the side of the conference participants, Khepri cupped Esther's head in her hands.

Ben leaned in and half-yelled, "She's fixin' Esther's hearing. Rifle went off next to her ear."

The Good Doctor's endearing accent and strange phrases made Louisa smile.

Ssherrss led them through the small gate into a narrow corridor with several switchbacks and countless murder holes. They emerged to see a few dozen Kerman spearmen, wearing short, blue-and-white-striped tunics and carrying church window–shaped shields. The men steered them to a building next to the never-ending water flow, roaring over a precipice.

Spray from the falls filled the area, and its mist soaked into Louisa's still-damp clothes. Irritated, she picked at the silk of her Greek-style blouse, which clung to her body.

Visible beyond the falls from this eagle's perch were two unique landscapes. The river wound through a dense jungle stretching straight ahead to the skyline. To the south, the jungle gave way to the white sands of a desert leading to the southern horizon.

Around the building on the cliff's edge, dozens of giant bats soared, drifted, and dove through the air. Some creatures carried cargo or even people underneath their long-outstretched wings. As the bats neared the building, it became obvious that they were babiakhom with their arms stretched wide, drifting on the winds.

Abu yelled, "They're flying us down to the city! Ssherrss just said!"

Ben slowly shook his head. The news made Louisa's day. As a child, she'd always wanted to fly like the birds nesting on the cliffs she had loved to climb. Jealous of their freedom, she'd settled for climbing as high as she could as often as possible.

Inside the building, the walls had to be several feet thick because the noise of rushing water became a distant rumble. Their escorts used their normal speaking voices and a wind singer's translation to explain that the song dampened the sounds outside. They described what would happen next.

In the next room, each of the group's leaders and children would buckle into a harness hanging from a six-inch gap in the ceiling. The straps were part of similar gear worn by a babiakhom on the floor above. The wind singer and his or her cargo would move as a single unit toward the edge. Passenger and wind singer would jump off the double balconies extending well past the massive cliff's lip. With some magic, the babiakhom would glide them down to the palace, where they were to meet with Kerma's leadership.

The Lancers and the Lochem were to escort the others to the palace the old-fashioned way, walking down a road carved into the cliff. Their trip could take as long as four hours, but the council, as Louisa thought of them, would reach their destination in minutes.

Masako was icy calm while Abu fidgeted. Louisa bounced from foot to foot, waiting for her turn in line. She was anxious to experience something she thought she would never do. The only thing close on Earth would be riding in a hot-air balloon, which never excited her as much. She always thought that experience would be more similar to climbing than soaring on the wind.

Pale and wan, Ben looked sick, but he insisted on going first. He mumbled something about making sure it was safe. When his turn came, Ben walked through the opening stiff as a board. From the doorway, he waddled toward the takeoff point. Ten feet from the cliff, he paused for several seconds and appeared to be speaking to himself. He placed one hand on top of his hat and held his rifle in the other, then jogged toward the edge.

As he leaped into the nothingness, Louisa could have sworn she heard the screech of a scared little girl. Ben and his tethered partner disappeared below the edge. Several seconds later, the babiakhom and long-legged Ben, his eyes clenched tight, swooped into view above the ledge before they dove out of sight.

Next up, Abu laughed as he raced toward the edge. He almost pulled his flyer off the cliff. A whoop of pure joy floated upward after he disappeared.

Louisa helped Masako get into the tackle. Since their first climbing lesson, the eight-year-old had come to relish the thrill of heights almost as much as Louisa did. When she was secure, Louisa gave her a thumbs-up, which Masako mirrored. At the edge, the little girl jumped with her arms held wide.

Louisa buckled into the harness, glad she had chosen to wear the Persian-style riding pants. It would be awkward to wear that contraption with a dress. Urged forward by a soldier, she grew more excited as she stepped onto the bone-dry balcony.

On her first inspection, the dry surface was confusing, but a barrier of air kept the spray from the waterfall at bay. To the side, several babiakhom sat around a table, playing a game that used wooden sticks. Louisa assumed the wind singers were the source of the impressive feat.

Can they strategize while creating the invisible umbrella?

As she scooted toward the ledge, she got her first glimpse of the city of Kerma. A thousand feet below, the metropolis stretched out for several miles. She estimated it to be as big as Florence. Before she could take in more, she reached the point of no return.

From above, her female flyer addressed her in the way wind singers do. "Don't worry. Try to enjoy the flight."

Through the overhead gap for the harness in the ceiling, Louisa gave the flyer an okay sign. The babiakhom's baboon lips curved into a smile. "On three." With her fingers, the flyer counted. At three, the attached pair jogged the last bit and jumped.

Louisa's stomach catapulted to her throat as they plummeted, the wind whipping her braided hair. The straps of the harness snapped taut, and her body jerked upward. She glanced above as the pair gained altitude. The flyer's wings stretched wider. Louisa closed her eyes for a few seconds, tuning all her senses to the swoosh of the wind and the breeze against her face.

Eyes open again, she gazed down. Shadows of the conjoined pair slid over the urban landscape below. Most of the city resembled a hodgepodge of postcards from Earth's most famous ancient cities. Entire neighborhoods contained Egyptian architecture lifted from a postcard about Aswan, while other sections contained buildings that appeared to be temples in the Greek and Roman styles.

As Louisa peered beyond the city's massive walls, her concern about the Remulans grew. She counted nine massive Remulan forts. The flaming pitch and the stones hurled at the city were unmistakable even miles away.

Inside the city walls, many buildings had been built by the Ancients. Unlike the Tomb of Mortals, these buildings had been constructed in all shapes and sizes with numerous types of material. Regardless of their composition, each of them danced. It was the only description Louisa could think of.

Veins of reds, blacks, grays, blues, yellows, and greens moved on the surface of the buildings. The streaks of color came alive, whirling and swirling into one another. They formed geometric and non-geometric shapes before dissolving and seeking new dance partners.

Louisa ignored the hypnotic display and leaned into the breeze, enjoying the experience. Soon they began losing height, and their destination became apparent. Enormous green spaces lay ahead, resembling Versailles's lush gardens and manmade pools.

Gardens surrounded a large complex of the Ancients' buildings that danced with their living art. At the center of the complex stood another glass pyramid, but unlike the mirrored surface of the one at the Tomb of Mortals, this chameleon rotated through all the colors on the other buildings. The glass turned solid gold, then moments later blue, then gray, and so on. Her flyer's wings beat against the onrushing current, slowing their speed.

A babiakhom's feminine voice whispered in Louisa's ear, "When you reach the ground, I will release the harness."

Louisa held her thumb above her head. Fifty feet, twenty feet, five feet. Her guide's wings beat faster, and with a jerk, Louisa's momentum stopped. She swung back and forth as she glided over a grassy field, going lower until her feet were mere inches from the lush grass. The tension on her shoulders and legs disappeared as she dropped free to the ground. Her flyer floated to the ground a few feet away. They had landed in a large grassy area near the pyramid.

Louisa managed to get herself out of the leather harness. She handed her gear to the babiakhom who had flown her there. "Thanks for the ride," she said with a grin.

"You are welcome. Until next time. Have a pleasant stay. Don't mind the Remulans." The wind singer chuckled and jogged away. Her arms went wide, extending her bat-like wings. In seconds, her feet rose above the ground. Soon she was horizontal and flew higher.

"How awesome was that!"

She turned with a smile to Abu. "One of my most amazing experiences ever."

"Can't wait to tell Umrao about it. He'll be so jealous," Abu said.

The teen turned away, gloating. Then he glanced toward the edge of the clearing and doubled over in laughter.

Masako looked in that direction and said, "Not nice, Abu."

Louisa didn't understand until Abu waved toward Ben leaning over a large marble urn, dry heaving. She rolled her eyes at the teen. Flying disagreed with the man who, a few hours earlier, had faced death by blowing up a bridge.

Few of us can be perfect.

Ben wiped his mouth on his sleeve. He joined them as the last of the council landed in the clearing. "I was wrong. This is now the stupidest thing I've ever done."

"Don't like heights?" Louisa nudged Ben.

"I don't have trouble with heights. I have trouble with falling from heights."

Louisa smirked. "Next time, open your eyes and stop screaming like a mikró korítsi long enough to enjoy the experience."

"God willing, there won't be a next time. And my scream is quite manly."

Abu laughed. "Masako's scream is more manly."

Masako punched Abu's shoulder. "I didn't scream."

"Ouch." Abu turned to the girl who glared up at him, hands on her hips. He chuckled. "No, no, you didn't."

When everyone had arrived, the council got themselves sorted. Louisa held Masako's hand as they followed a squad of Kerman heavy infantry through the gardens. That is to say, they followed dark men, sculpted like statues of Greek gods, carrying spears, and wearing Egyptian banded armor, each with a crucial piece of linen hanging low to cover the groin. Distracted by the bulging biceps and strong jawlines, Louisa gave in to a few salacious thoughts. And she didn't need to speak Eblan to get the gist of the twins' conversation, based on their crude comments and gestures.

As they rounded a long, high hedge, the group came to a terraced landing over-looking a pool shaped like a giant X. Dignitaries of human and alien races stood behind tables where the high vantage point provided views over the gardens.

At the central table, everyone stood except for a lone exception sitting in the center, a middle-aged Nubian woman with piercing brown eyes and a perpetual frown. The woman to whom everyone deferred wore a gold headband across her forehead, and two large scarab earrings jutted out from her puffy afro. A rearing cobra extended from the front of the headband, as fierce as the woman's eyes and ready to strike.

Rrummblinss stepped forward and made a sweeping bow. He spoke in Aaruan, but they all heard it in their native tongue. "Queen Nabra, it is an honor to see you once again."

One corner of the queen's frown threatened to turn up. "Sekhrey Rrumm-blinss, I suppose you were to blame for our Remulan friends' trouble last night."

"Guilty as charged, Your Grace, but I had a little help from my new friends."

The queen scanned their diverse crowd, pausing on Ben and Louisa for a moment before settling on the twins and their constant companion, Thoresten. "Lil and Ki, I was still a princess when you last visited. How fares Inanna?" Her lips twisted into a half smile.

Lil frowned. "As you undoubtedly know, Your Highness, our mother is fighting several other welven factions to stay in control of her city. She will prevail. She always does." A mirthful smile lit up silver-haired welf's face. "You've hardly changed since we saw you last."

The queen harrumphed. "Liar. The world's worries come at a price to us mortals, and I know it's written on my face." She turned from the twins back to Louisa and Ben. "And you must be the infamous Earthlings of whom the rumors spoke."

The still-ashen Ben struggled to say something, and Louisa stepped forward. She dispensed with formality. "Your Majesty, it's a pleasure to meet you. You are correct. We are from Earth. I am Louisa, and this is Ben; his son, Abu; and our friend Masako." Then Louisa gestured toward the group. "And that is our companion, Duffadar Nahal, who leads the soldiers we brought." She noticed Ali hurrying forward, and she pointed to him. "And this is Professor Mousa."

Ali gave a slight bow of his head. "Your Majesty, I am from the Temple on Earth led by the Keepers of the Seba. I represent them among this group."

A hysakas, taller than any Louisa had ever seen and wearing an Egyptian priest's short tunic, broad necklace, and headdress, spoke up, "Keeper Mousa, are the rumors true? Did the Seba get—?"

The queen raised a hand and glared at the priest. "Louisa, I would like to welcome you and your fellows to the Kingdom of Kerma and her capital city by the same name. I would hear your story, and what is so important that you fought through the Remulan siege to reach us?" She turned in her seat as if she had just remembered those behind her. "For the goddess's sake, sit down."

Everyone standing around the tables obeyed. Louisa tilted her head and took one step forward. "I'll try to be brief. Our group was searching for a temple thought to have been abandoned thousands of years ago. We stumbled upon Ali's people, who still lived at the site. Without understanding the ramifications, we took the Seba, and when Ali's men tried to retrieve it, we accidentally activated it." There were a few gasps from the crowd and one loud growl. "Our small group of about twenty, along with Ali and several hundred of his people, appeared on Aaru."

Louisa paused for questions. The queen jutted out her chin, a sign to continue.

"We woke in the Fields of Eisodos and realized something incredible had happened. Ali informed us about the Lamentations and how were stranded on Aaru because the Seba takes five hundred years to gather enough power to return to Earth. We believe there must be a quicker way to charge the device, and we set out to find a way home."

The priest started to speak again, but the queen cut off his words with a scowl. She looked back to Louisa.

"Later, we had our first experience with the Remulans. Ben, Jeevan, and his soldiers helped stop the Remulans from overrunning the Alexandrians. With our help, they turned back the Remulan invasion." Louisa flashed a smile at Ben and Jeevan. "We met with Polemarchos Alexandria ben Zev i Hurasu after the battle. In return for our help, the polemarchos directed us to an Ancient site in the mountains and provided an escort." Louisa nodded to Esther, Khepri, and Ssherrss.

A gray-haired, clean-shaven man in a blue linen toga at one of the farthest tables stood up. All eyes flashed to him. "Pardon my interruption, Your Majesty." The queen's dour expression deepened, but she gave a flick of her fingers in assent. The older man's green eyes sparkled with youthful intelligence. "I would ask that after Your Majesty's esteemed visitors settle, I be able to meet with their Alexandrian escorts." The man turned to the Earthlings. "I am Prínkipas Archimedes ben Solan i Draco, the ambassador of Alexandria to Kerma. All of you are welcome to visit me at the embassy anytime."

Abu coughed and shared a surreptitious nod with Thoresten.

What is that about? Louisa wondered.

Queen Nabra cast a corkscrew eye at the ambassador. "Fine, Archimedes. Now sit and let the young woman continue." She turned her hardened gaze back to Louisa.

"We explored the Tomb of Mortals," Louisa said, "and learned amazing information about the Ancients and their magic artifacts."

She turned to point toward the magnificent waterfall. "Based on our findings, we determined that there might be a way to power the Seba inside an Ancient facility located behind those falls. That is why we fought our way here."

Silence reigned for about a minute. The queen's expression appeared unfocused as if she were trying to solve a mental puzzle. She nodded to herself and addressed Louisa. "This is most intriguing and troubling at the same time. There is a door halfway up the cliff directly behind the falls. No one has ever unlocked the door, so we do not know what lies behind it. It may be as you say."

Queen Nabra motioned to the handsome man of about thirty sitting to her right. "Tomorrow, Prince Tambal will take you to the door. I wish you luck."

With piercing eyes that locked onto Louisa's, the prince said, "I look forward to our time together." He leaned back, and his eyes roved from Louisa's face down to her feet.

As if, Louisa thought, giving him a curt nod. Turning toward the queen, she dismissed his flirtatious stare.

The queen plucked a small ripe banana from a large bowl of assorted fruits. "From your story, your small group of soldiers made a difference in the battle you mentioned. How were you able to do that?" Her eyes never wavered as she peeled the banana.

Someone tapped Louisa's forearm, and she turned.

Ben gave her an almost imperceptible nod before saying, "Your Majesty, as Louisa mentioned, I'm Ben. Our soldiers have weapons called guns that are much more powerful than any bow on Aaru. Our guns shoot a projectile up to five hundred yards and are able to penetrate both a shield and armor."

A collective gasp rippled through the gathering.

Ali spoke before Ben could continue. "It's true." The professor pinned the giant hysakas priest with a stare. "**Hem-netjer** . . . " He paused.

"Rashida," rumbled the priest.

"**Hem-netjer** Rashida and Your Majesty, we were unable to bring many troops or even the most advanced weapons from Earth, but we have been able to duplicate what we have with us. We built most of the components for two thousand guns. With more life singers and the metal singers we brought, we will finish assembling them."

"If the Reapers come, would this be enough?" asked the queen.

Ali shook his head. "I do not believe so, but if we have time, we will build more."

Ben interjected, "There is one rather large limitation to our weapons. They require a special projectile we call a bullet. We've brought several thousand bullets for each gun, but only our people can make more."

The queen's eyes narrowed. "Do you mean to hold this monopoly while the entire planet is at risk?" She placed both hands on the table and leaned forward as her voice turned hot with anger. "Do you intend to let the damned Remulans slaughter and enslave my people?"

Ben stood straighter. "Yes and no, your Majesty. Until we can give the secrets behind guns to everyone on Aaru, we will control the production of bullets."

The queen's eyebrows shot up in surprise.

Ben held both hands out to his sides, palms up. "The Remulans are the very reason we will keep our secrets. With guns, they are as dangerous as the ripvor."

The queen's frown became a scowl. "Point taken. Ben, was it?"

"Yes, ma'am."

A man wearing a banded breastplate sitting beside the prince said, "Your Majesty, I would like to witness the power of these *guns*."

"An excellent suggestion, General Kinya. Please set it up." The queen took a bite of her peeled fruit.

The general stood, walked to an attendee, and gave him instructions that no one else could hear.

Queen Nabra swallowed. "Bring our guests refreshments and breakfast. I'm sure you are all famished."

"Thank you, Majesty. We are. Some more than others." Louisa smirked at Ben.

The council took two tables and enjoyed cider with a breakfast of eggs, skewers of grilled goat, and many tropical fruits, both familiar and unknown. While everyone ate, servants placed large pottery vases at distances of twenty-five, fifty, one hundred, and two hundred yards on the grass field below the terrace. In addition, they placed two sets of armor at fifty and then one hundred yards. Each had a shield in front of the breastplate tied to long spears thrust into the ground.

"My Queen, we're ready to begin," stated the general.

Ben and Jeevan walked away from the tables with their rifles. Louisa hesitated a moment and moved to stand next to the two men. They gave her a quizzical look until she held up her small revolver.

Ben handed Louisa his Winchester. He held his revolver up for the queen. "We have brought two different types of guns. The first is called a pistol or revolver. We use these for short distances."

With his legs spread shoulder width apart, Ben aimed at one of the five clay pots twenty-five yards away. People at the tables jumped in their chairs as the Pocket Army went off, and the target shattered. Exclamations came from the audience. Ben fired four more rounds without pausing, exploding the clay pots, one, two, three. After the fourth shot, though, his last target remained.

"I've got this one." Louisa raised her bulldog using a two-handed grip. She exhaled a slow, controlled breath and squeezed the trigger. The last pot collapsed in upon itself as the bullet struck true.

Applause roared from the tables. When it died down, Ben took back his rifle, held it up, and addressed the queen. "Queen Nabra, this is a rifle. Jeevan and I have different rifles. Both strike targets at greater distances. Jeevan will shoot at the farthest targets while I shoot at those in between."

He motioned to Jeevan, who put his carbine to his shoulder. Ben did the same, saying, "Fire at will."

The rifles discharged a second apart. One of the farthest jars exploded a moment before one of the mid-range targets. Ben fired two shots for every one of Jeevan's. A pottery target shattered every few seconds until only the two sets of armor remained. The two men shared a look and fired at the same time. Ben emptied his last three rounds, making a fist-size hole in his target's shield. Jeevan kept firing until his targeted shield fell to the ground, exposing the damage to the breastplate behind.

Stunned silence met Ben and Jeevan when they turned to the observers.

The general whispered to the queen and then spoke to a servant, who raced away. Louisa thought she saw the queen smiling.

The queen said, "Impressive. The general would have you do one more test, but from what I've seen, a Remulan legion would be no match for a thousand men with these weapons."

Ben nodded. "And if the Remulans were to gain these weapons before the rest of Aaru, nothing could stand in their way."

The queen grimaced and nodded. "With enough guns, we would have a similar advantage on the Reapers."

A servant ran past the tables, holding a large silver platter. He ran out to the post holding armor at the fifty-yard mark. He replaced the wooden shield with the silver disk.

The queen waved to the target. "Please try to shoot through this shield."

Ben nodded to Jeevan, who reloaded and took aim. The shot rang out, followed by a loud clang as the bullet ricocheted off the silver metal.

"It would appear your bullets are no match for star steel."

"So it seems," came Ben's reply.

The queen's stare bored into the three of them. "I understand your reluctance to share the secret, but I must insist that you use the weapons you brought with you against the army at our gates."

Ben started to reply, but Louisa tapped his arm and spoke first. She had seen this play before and had run through all the scenarios while they waited for the shooting demonstration to begin. They needed to help the queen if they wanted to get the help they needed. She knew where Ben would draw the line. She would try to stay true to his wishes as she forged ahead. "Your Majesty, we have no love for the Remulans. As it stands, they are as much our enemy as yours. We will help, but under a few conditions."

The queen's forehead wrinkled.

"We'll help you finish the two thousand rifles while we will control the manufacture of the bullets. Ben and Jeevan will also train your soldiers to use the weapons effectively."

The queen's frown deepened.

Here goes nothing.

Louisa put as much steel into her voice as possible. "Our conditions are that Ben, Jeevan, and his men will command this new military unit. And it will only fight to keep the Remulans from taking the city or fight the ripvor. *If* they are instructed to do anything other than that, we will stop making bullets. When you run out, the guns will be useless."

The queen's demeanor turned icy. In a low, menacing voice, she said, "You will not dictate to me in my city. My people and our entire way of life are at risk. What keeps me from forcing you to do what we need?"

Louisa didn't flinch at her glare. "Because I don't think you are like them. You're not like the Remulans. As for forcing us, Earth has been using these weapons for centuries. We know how much devastation they will bring to your world, and we hope to delay it. We won't be forced to help anyone slaughter their enemies. We would rather die." She crossed her arms. "But we will help you defend yourselves from being slaughtered."

The queen conferred with the general before regarding Louisa once again. "If we agree, what do you need to make this work?"

Louisa noted that the queen had used the "royal we" in addressing her, adding subtle weight to her position. She looked at Ben, who nodded. "Ben, Jeevan, and Professor Mousa will work with the general on the details."

Ben whispered to her, "Thanks. Thanks a lot." Then he said louder, "We'll need life singers to shape wooden parts for the guns. The life singers and Rrummblinss's metal singers can assemble the guns." He nodded to the general. "We will need two thousand men who are good at ranged weapons. Archers or slingers. We will use our current rifles to test the men until we find enough." He waved toward Jeevan. "I would command the regiment with Duffadar Nahal as my second. His men will be our junior officers. It will take time to assemble everything and time to train the men properly. I cannot yet give you a timetable."

The queen and the general had been nodding along to Ben's plan. She said, "As you saw on your way here, time is not something I have in surplus to give." She sighed in resignation. "Very well, General Kinya, make it happen as quickly as possible."

Then to Louisa and Ben, "Please enjoy your accommodations here at the palace. I trust you will start your preparations this afternoon." Queen Nabra appeared to dismiss them without giving her formal agreement to their conditions. Once again, they were at the mercy of others.

"Yes, ma'am," Ben replied.

Chapter 28

Their chiseled escorts led them from the terrace toward an Ancients' building connected to one side of the large glass pyramid. Colors danced across the surface of the long, stark white rectangular building as the pyramid's glass changed from blue to green, with similar technicolor variations taking place on each face of the monument. The images forming across both buildings seemed to be choreographed, with one ephemeral design completing the next before transforming again.

As Louisa neared the building, she noted that the Kermans had altered the structure to suit them better. In front of the Ancients' original entrance of automatically opening glass doors, the Kermans had built a second entrance. Several of the Nubian demi-gods stood motionless beside large steel double doors that locked from the inside.

The glass doors slid open as the group approached and stayed open until each person had passed. Inside the building, the utilitarian style and scale of the architecture resembled those of the Tomb of Mortals.

A giant foyer led to a grand staircase that curled up and around an open rotunda reaching at least five stories high. Large hallways shot off to the left and the right. As the group neared the staircase, a third passage extended away behind the stairs.

The first soldiers stepped onto the initial oversize step and stopped. The platform and all those in front of the men moved upward. Another step grew from the floor to replace the one floating up. The next group of men stepped forward and ascended.

Ben muttered, "Would you look at that?"

As the previous group moved up, another group of three or four climbed onto the new stair step. Louisa's turn came. Given the full dimensions of each step, she didn't wait for the new one to reach its full height. Instead, she held hands with Masako, and the pair hopped on as it rose.

Ben and Abu paused a second before getting onto the step as it flowed up the magical banister.

Masako exclaimed, "That's some pumpkins!"

Louisa chuckled at how the young girl, with her limited but growing vocabulary of English and Greek, had somehow picked up Abu's favorite saying.

They rode their step past the first and second landings up to the third floor before stepping onto the banister-less floor to follow the troops into one of the three corridors.

They passed many doors, including a dining room and a communal privy. The Kermans had hung signs written in Aaruan hieroglyphics to the side of each entry. Down a side hall, their hosts had converted extensive suites into bedrooms. Ben insisted Louisa and Masako take the one next to his and Abu's.

The young girl dashed into the room, with Louisa following. Then Masako closed and locked the extra door installed behind the sliding one. The room had a huge down-filled bed, a comfortable sitting area, and two other doors.

Behind the first was an Ancients' privy with a sizeable sunken bowl. At the bottom of the depression, the Kermans had installed a marble chair with an open seat. Instructions hanging by the door explained how the floor used magic to absorb the waste. As Louisa opened the next door, a splash gave way to a giggle. Masako grinned at her from inside a sunken tub that had filled with water up to the girl's knees and was still rising.

The Kermans' augmentations of the Ancients' facility were both practical and elegant. They had turned the sterile, yet miraculous, inventions of the Ancients into the most luxurious room Louisa had ever inhabited.

After Louisa gave Masako a proper scrubbing, the girl fell asleep, exhausted. Their luggage arrived, and Louisa spent the next hour luxuriating in the bath before taking a long nap.

———————————————

Most of the group's inner circle sat around a large dining room table in the shared cantina. Waiting for Louisa to join them, Ben tapped his fingers on the table in agitation. He wanted to have a little meeting before the others joined them for supper.

He thought about the Kermans' use of the Ancients' buildings. They had been very successful in adapting the living quarters as their own. For example, human-size chairs ringed the dining table. The Ancients' table adjusted to arrive at a middle height as each person sat down.

Before Ben delved deeper into this engineering distraction, Louisa swept in like an emerald-clad Helen of Troy. In a silk Grecian dress, she flashed him a smile.

Ben's breath caught at the sight of her. He opened his mouth, but nothing came out. Like a love-struck schoolboy, he raised his hand in greeting. Louisa had stepped behind the chair next to him and stopped. She tilted her head and raised an eyebrow.

Her look was as effective as a cuff to the head, similar to those Ben's mother had given him. He jumped to his feet, and his chair tilted back so far that it almost fell over. It dropped down with a loud thud. His face grew hot as he pulled Louisa's chair out.

As she sat, Louisa said in a low voice, "Thank you." Then she smiled at the rest of the table. "Hello, everyone. Sorry I'm late."

Ben held up a piece of paper with a handwritten note: *Watch your words. People are listening.*

Before the meeting, Ben had reviewed Louisa's discussion with the queen and the promises made. In the end, he admitted she had come up with a novel solution that had been better than any he had considered. Thus, he could only agree by nodding when Ali said, "Louisa, you did a good job negotiating with the queen. If the ripvor are coming soon, we need to build an army to be ready. Practicing against the Remulans won't hurt."

Ben grimaced at the possibility of more fighting but also at the professor's nonchalance. He leaned over the table. "Easy for you to say. Are you volunteering to lead men into battle?"

Ali's face reddened.

Ben said to Louisa, "It's good you suggested training the troops and got to set the conditions, or we might have been on the hook for more."

Louisa sighed. "I tried. Did anyone else notice that she didn't explicitly agree with our conditions?"

Ben reviewed the end of the conversation until he understood what she meant. "Well, nothing we can do about it now. We just have to hold up our end of the bargain and refuse to go against our conditions. Once we train the regiment, we're not really in control of them. They'll all be the queen's men."

With added enthusiasm, Ben said, "I spoke with the general, one of his life singers, and Rrummblinss. It'll take two weeks to grow the first batch of wooden stocks and a few days to assemble all the rifles. While they grow the stocks, we'll make the pistols. Depending on their abilities, we'll arm some men with revolvers and others with rifles. Jeevan, how long will it take you to get them ready to fight?"

The duffadar rubbed the silky black hair under his lip. "At least eight weeks."

"Despite what Louisa said, I did open my eyes on the way down here. Given what I saw from the Remulans, plan for six weeks, tops."

Jeevan grimaced. "That's not enough, but we'll do what we can. It'll take a few days to find a thousand recruits. Then we'll start working on basic formations and firing drills. We'll use our rifles for practice, to get them used to shooting guns."

"Good. Push your men and the recruits as hard as possible. If the Remulans break through before we're ready, I don't think the Kermans can hold the city. Also, train the Lochem on the pistols. They can help in a pinch. Even though they aren't loyal to us, they aren't loyal to the queen either."

The duffadar now rubbed the entirety of his beard between his fingers. "Do you want the twins, Thoresten, Ssherrss, and Khepri to train on the revolvers?"

Ben thought about it for a few moments. "If the welves or the dwarf ask, then yes. Train Ssherrss, Khepri, and their new wife because I want everyone in our party able to defend themselves."

"Speak of the devil," Louisa hissed under her breath.

Ki, Lil, and Thoresten strolled into the dining room.

Lil sauntered up next to Ben's chair. The welf smiled down at him, her chocolate eyes filled with glee as she put a carefree hand on his shoulder. She winked at Louisa and said in Greek. "Did we miss anything?"

Not this shit again.

Ben stiffened. "Nothing. Have a seat."

The temptress did a sultry walk around the table to an empty chair.

With everyone present except the Alexandrian members of their council, Ben said in English so the newcomers would not understand, "If that's everything, then Jeevan, start the training while the rest of us go to the waterfall tomorrow."

As dinner wrapped up, Abu pulled on Thoresten's arm, holding him back. The two stepped toward the corner, allowing everyone to leave the room. As Louisa exited, she gave Abu a troubled frown, and he replied with an innocent smile.

Abu sighed in relief when Louisa was gone. Alone with the dwarf, he whispered in Greek, "When I was in Grrommerrk, someone told me the Alexandrian ambassador, that prince guy, is related to Masako. Is he?"

"He is," rumbled Thoresten.

Abu frowned at the dwarf's lack of conspiratorial tone, so he abandoned his own and said in his normal voice, "Can he be trusted?"

Thoresten shrugged. "Don't know."

"What should I do?"

The dwarf put a massive hand on Abu's shoulder. "Are you not an orphan? Who would you have chosen to be with when your parents died? The man who took you in, or the family you had never known?"

A flood of emotions shook Abu into silence.

As he recalled those first months with Dr. Ben, Thoresten patted his upper arms with both hands and said, "I will leave you to your decision." The barrel-size man walked out.

Abu stared at the floor, unseeing, as he tried to rein in the grief that threatened to run wild. To master himself again, he mulled over what Thoresten had said, trying to put his advice into action.

Our circumstances are similar but different as well.

Abu's parents were Mahdi and Yara, and he knew he had no other family. What would he have preferred if he had had a grandfather and a granduncle he had never met? Within a month of being with Dr. Ben, Abu knew he would have chosen to stay with the archaeologist because of his own insatiable need to learn.

But when Abu put himself into Masako's situation, he knew his choice would be the opposite. The need to know where he came from and who his people were would have gnawed at him. Masako's circumstances would have left a hole in her soul, and he knew that he, Dr. Ben, and Miss Louisa could never fill that void in the same way.

As much as Abu wanted to keep Masako close, he had to let her go.

Chapter 29

Tefnut Falls, Choru, An 5660, Day 27

Flush with excitement, Louisa skipped up the road leading to the plateau overlooking the city. On her way to explore another complex built by the mysterious Ancients, her imagination had gone wild.

A tug of sorrow came when she thought of reaching their goal. She tried to focus on enjoying the present but kept wondering what would happen if they could power the Seba. She didn't want to go back to Earth, but would she stay on Aaru if the rest of her tribe opted to return? She had no doubt that if they were successful, Ali and his hysakas priesthood masters would take control of the device. If that happened, the ability to go home would be a onetime offer with no chance to return to this incredible world.

No bridge to cross yet. Do what you do best.

A new presence nearby caused Louisa to turn. The prince was fast-walking next to her. He smiled, and she caught herself smiling back at his handsome face. As if pulled by a magnet, she stopped skipping and kept pace with him.

Louisa adjusted the haversack she'd sewn from some of the Ancients' vests and asked in Greek, "Can I help you, Prince Tambal?"

The prince replied in the same language. "Your excitement is contagious. May I ask what has given you the spring in your step?"

Louisa laughed. "Don't you get excited at the prospect of adventure? Exploring the unknown?"

The prince's forehead knotted up and then relaxed. "A little, but I have a feeling you'll be disappointed. People have tried to open the waterfall door for thousands of An. There's little chance you'll succeed."

"Are you always a pessimist?"

"Just a realist. On other topics, I'm very optimistic."

His mischievous smile gave Louisa pause. "Such as?"

"Romance, for example." He blinked in slow motion.

"Prince, are you in love?"

He laughed. "Not yet." Then he stared at her with an intensity that should have made her uncomfortable.

Louisa glanced around and caught Ben listening in on their conversation. He averted his eyes as soon as she tried to make eye contact. Knowing about Ben's jealous streak, she decided to have a little fun at his expense. "Well, Prince, I hope you're able to find someone to share your amorous feelings with."

"I think I have."

"What's she like?"

His gaze started at her feet and worked upward at an unhurried pace. He stopped at her face. "Intelligent, beautiful, adventurous."

Louisa bit her lip to stifle a chuckle lest he mistake her humor for rejection. "This woman sounds interesting. I'm sure she would like to get to know you more." She fell silent and watched the path forward as she considered the sense of humor of Klotho, the Greek goddess of fate.

When they had first arrived on Aaru, Louisa had imagined this exact scenario. Would she choose to become a queen or stay the heroine of her own story? Presented with this opportunity after picking another path was funny. She gave her chosen *sidekick*, Ben, a surreptitious glance. Her heart beat faster at his frown. Why did his jealousy bring her joy?

With his frown twisting into a slight grin, Ben eased his way to the opposite side of the prince. "Good morning, Prince Tambal. Sorry, I couldn't help but overhear. I was wondering, what will your wife think of this new love?"

Louisa stumbled forward. The prince reached out and steadied her. His eyes never left hers, and without missing a beat, he said, "She'll welcome a second wife with open arms because she wants me to be happy."

Sure-footed once again, Louisa tugged her arm, trying to free herself from the prince's grasp. Her sense of fun disappeared. With a sour taste in her mouth, she said, "Well, I wish you luck finding someone who's willing to be a second wife." She tilted her nose upward. "It's not something I could ever do."

"I'll take it." The prince chuckled. "Your luck, I mean. I'll need all I can get to find such an incredible woman." He released her arm. "Excuse me, I should check on my men." He picked up his pace, moving to the front of the column.

As he took long, athletic strides away, Louisa sighed. She turned on her meddling *savior*.

With the prince out of earshot, Ben laughed and slapped his knee. "Smooth as a porcupine's backside."

Louisa growled, "I had it under control."

"Really? That's twice that I've saved you from ending up in someone's harem." The right side of his mouth turned up in that damn lopsided grin.

Louisa glared at him. "Whatever, McGehee. Worry about getting past that door."

Ben's chest heaved with suppressed laughter. He walked beside Louisa with a smugness that made her want to punch that stupid grin off his face. After several minutes, he said, "I'm curious. Why'd you wear your workout clothes?"

At least, befuddlement had replaced his smugness. "I'm ready for what we might run into." She poked a finger at him. "Remember our agreement?"

"Made under duress," he mumbled before nodding. "I won't hold you back."

"Good." They went quiet.

Under the cliff's shadow, they walked along the road with its many switchbacks as it rose upward. Sometimes they headed toward the cascading water, and other times they marched with their backs to the falls. About two-thirds of the way up the cliff, they neared the latest switchback, but there were two roads this time. One ran away from the falls, and the other led them along the cliff wall behind the rushing water. One of their escorts handed them each a water-resistant poncho and earplugs.

Thankful for the added protection and to be walking on a flat road, Louisa was soon covered head to toe by the mist from the falls. She paid careful attention to each step on the now slick cobblestones. The roar of the falls had grown so loud, it was almost impossible to communicate unless she screamed into the ear of the person she wanted to speak with. At the front of the procession, two wind singers walked with the prince.

Why don't they do something about the water and the noise?

An had moved above the moon named Son, marking mid-morning, and they walked in the sun for the first time that day. The short-lived daylight dimmed as they trod behind the enormous sheet of water. Prism displays lit up the cliff walls as the light refracted through the rushing water. A thick, chilled mist made Louisa's lungs ache from the cold. The column marched twenty minutes to reach the center of the falls and the giant metal doors, which showed no sign of rust or weathering after thousands of An.

As their group gathered near the entrance, the roar of the falls ceased in an instant. Two babiakhom had taken up positions on either side of the doorway, and they were responsible for the mist disappearing as well.

The prince turned to their group. "It's all yours. Good luck." He stepped to the side and conferred with several of his soldiers.

Louisa inspected the door from about ten feet away. It appeared to have a cut-out on the right side. Similar to the lock on the pyramid door at the Tomb of Mortals, she didn't have much hope that they'd figure out the mechanism.

Ben addressed the council, plus Ki, Lil, and Thoresten, in Greek. "Ssherrss, please evaluate the doors and the surrounding rock to see if you can work with it?"

The foxlike metal singer placed a four-thumbed hand on the door and one on the rock next to it.

"The rest of us will work on the lock." Ben pulled out the Ancients' magical hat from under his rain gear. Abu held his pork pie while Ben tied the bonnet on his head.

Lil asked, "What is that?"

Ben readjusted the glass object and then plopped his hat over it. "It's an artifact we found at the Tomb of Mortals. If you ask it questions in your head, this will show you a vision of the answer."

Ki grabbed Jeevan's special bonnet from his hand and said in Greek, "I want to try it."

Thoresten grabbed her wrist. "Be careful. It stung me."

The tall dragon's-breath redhead tsked at the dwarf and flicked her fingers. She removed her white helmet with one hand and placed the device on her head with the other. Nothing happened. She scrunched up her face and narrowed her eyes. Everyone stared at her for several seconds.

Ki frowned. "Doesn't do anything."

Ben smirked. "You must imagine pictures that represent your question for it to work. Or speak Ancient."

Lil elbowed Abu, who had begun to tie on his headwear. "Let me try."

Louisa held hers out. "Here, try mine."

Lil took off her strange red Nipponese-designed war helmet and put it at her feet. She set the cloth that held the glass bowl on her silver hair. The welf closed her eyes. Across the small circle they had formed, Ki closed her eyes as well.

Lil's eyes popped open, and she tilted her head toward her sister. "How'd you do that?"

Ki opened one eye. "Do what? You said, '*This is stupid.*' And then asked why it hurt Thoresten. How should I know?"

Ali interjected, "Miss Ki, no one spoke."

"But I heard her," Ki replied, troubled.

Louisa said, "Ki, why don't you try to think something without talking?"

The sly grin Louisa detested spread across Lil's face. "Sister, stop teasing me. We're supposed to share everything." She turned toward Jeevan and smacked her lips. "Why are you being so greedy?"

Disgusting harlot, Louisa thought as the duffadar's eyes grew wide.

"Amazing, it's like their minds are tethered together," quipped Ali.

Louisa had an idea and presented her theory. "We know it stings anyone who uses the former slave races' magic. We also know that regular humans cannot hear each other's thoughts. Ben and I tried it. What if the artifact believes Ki and Lil are Ancients because of whatever gives them their long life?" She pointed to the cutout. "One of you put should put your hand in there."

Ki walked to the side of the door and thrust her hand into the cubbyhole. A blue light flashed over her hand, and she jerked it away. After a quick inspection, Ki moved her hand back into the cutout. The light flashed back and forth across the top of her hand for a few seconds. Nothing else happened. She tried it palm up, and nothing again.

That's disappointing, Louisa thought.

"Too bad. It was a good idea." Ben intertwined his fingers at waist level and closed his eyes. "Maybe the artifact will tell us the combination if we ask the right question."

Ssherrss continued his inspection while all the others tried asking the glass bowls their imagined questions. After about ten minutes of frustration and having no ideas to add, Louisa pulled out a small pair of binoculars from her haversack. She walked away from the door. The sudden roar of the water made her wince when she stepped out of the magical bubble created by the wind singers.

With the binoculars, Louisa inspected the cliff walls around and above the doors. Every half minute, she stopped to wipe the lenses. At the edge of the falling water, the mist had thickened. Back and forth, she moved up the wall.

There.

A hundred feet above the door, she saw a roughhewn channel cut into the cliff. The thrill of the discovery and knowing she might soon scale the cliff face gave her a jolt of adrenaline.

Louisa rushed back to the group in time to hear Ssherrss say, "Therre iss nothing I can do. The Ancientss rreinforrcced the rrock facce and doorr so only they could worrk eitherr. Even if we could dig through the rrock by hand, I assssumme whateverr wallss they have insside would be unworrkable."

"Thanks. Had to try." Ben addressed everyone else. "Any ideas? I hate to give up so soon, but it's like we are trying to break into a bank vault with a wooden spoon."

"I found something." Everyone turned to Louisa. She pointed straight overhead. "It's about a hundred feet up." Some of the group spun around to wrench their heads back as far as possible.

Ben shook his head. "I don't see it."

"Here, go over there, and use these." Louisa held out her binoculars.

"Thanks." Ben took them and walked into the mist. A few minutes later, he returned to their bubble. "She's right. There's a tunnel carved into the rock." He turned to the prince. "Prince Tambal, can one of the wind singers go inspect the rock cut-out"?" He pointed to the spot.

"I think so." The prince had a quick conversation with one of the babiakhom. The wind singer walked away from the crowd. The bubble of mist-free silence grew smaller, and everyone stood closer to the remaining wind singer.

The first wind singer jogged toward the edge of the air dome, raised his arms, and extended his wings. His feet lifted off the ground, and he glided forward and up. He turned back at the end of the protective area, doing a switchback process as they had done on the road, always moving higher. When he reached the top of the air bubble, he popped through. A smaller sphere encased his body, pushing the water away. When the wind singer came to the location, he hovered in place.

Everyone's head tilted back to watch him. The flying babiakhom reached inside the channel. He tugged on something several times, but nothing happened. Soon he floated down to land next to the prince.

Louisa heard his words in that strange way that happened when wind singers were involved. "There is a small steel grate. Even if we cut it open, it's too small for me or Xaxon with our wings."

Louisa stepped in front of Ben. "Am I small enough?"

The babiakhom looked her up and down and then appraised the rest of the entourage. "You and the metal singer are the only ones small enough."

She grinned. "Can you fly me up there?"

He shook his baboon-like head. "No. You are too heavy to lift. Even the two of us would struggle."

"That's not a problem. I will climb. Does anyone have an idea about how to open the grate?"

Thoresten said, "Star steel might cut the metal."

Ki pulled a gleaming knife from the scabbard tucked into her belt. She brought the sheath out as well. With stern eyes, she held both out to Louisa. "Don't lose these. Do you understand?"

"Yes." Louisa took both and replaced the blade in its protective covering. She moved the pouch containing the Seba objects out of the way and dug into her haversack. After removing a ball of leather string, she cut two strands long enough to make a makeshift belt. With the sheathed knife tied to her waist, she retrieved her Ancient headgear bonnet from Lil.

As she tied it on, Ben tugged at her elbow. "The cliff is too wet. It's dangerous."

"I'll be fine. It won't be a problem." Ben's concern sparked warmth inside Louisa as she patted his hand. "I have an idea for extra safety."

She beckoned the wind singer toward her. "Can you fly up and hold a rope? I'll tie it to my waist. If I fall, could you glide me down?"

"Yes." The lips of the babiakhom's yellow and pink snout curled into a smile. "Take off the rain gear. You won't need it."

"Great." Louisa gazed around the circle. "Anyone bring a rope?"

With one end tied to herself and the other connected to the babiakhom, Louisa approached the rough cliff rock. With a wave over her shoulder, she said, "Wish me luck."

A strong breeze blew against her clothes, and a blast of air flowed up the wall ahead of her. Although damp, the rock under her fingers no longer dripped with moisture. Laughing at the fantastic abilities of the wind singer, she stepped into her first toe hold.

Slow at first, she soon slithered up the wall as if her hands and toes were suction cups. The rest of the world disappeared, and there was nothing but her beating heart and the next hand or toe hold. Too soon, Louisa reached the cutout. With only a foot between the cliff's edge and the grate, she needed to get the square cover out of the way. Then she could move into the tunnel behind it. Finding the best purchase for her feet and her left hand, she pulled the star-steel knife from its sheath.

Looking over her shoulder, Louisa said to her backup, "Get ready. I'm going to cut the grate."

Not knowing how much effort it would take, she pressed her left fingers on the rock like a vice as she raised the knife. She swung toward a small piece of metal attached to the top of the grate. Sparks flew as the blade bounced back, and the shock traveled up the steel into her arm.

The recoil almost caused Louisa to lose her grip on the wall.

"Whoa!"

With pursed lips, Louisa blew out a nervous breath. She found a significant piece of metal carved out of the bar she had struck. She put the blade into the groove and sawed back and forth. Within a few strokes, the metal parted, leaving a precise cut. Instead of trying to hack at the metal, Louisa used the sharp side to saw through the next bar. It took some effort, but the hardened metal gave way to the star steel.

With her three-point hold on the cliff, Louisa sliced through the bars, one after another, switching hands when she grew tired. When she made the last straight-line cut, the metal grate fell with a bang against the rock.

Louisa replaced the knife in the sheath and used one arm to drag the grate to the edge. With every tug, she winced as the metal screeched against the rock. The wind singer moved closer, and Louisa lifted the grate until the babiakhom had a grip on it. He floated a few feet behind her as she inched into the rock tunnel toward the opening.

Louisa carefully took off her haversack and pushed it over the threshold of the cut grate, then into the tunnel beyond. She crawled across the rough rock and lifted herself to avoid the cut pieces of metal. On the other side, rock had given way to smooth metal. She untied the safety rope from her waist and let it drop as she moved forward.

Louisa next removed a tiny lantern from the haversack. She took a match from a small drawer in the lantern and lit the wick. She turned her shoulders at an angle and squirmed forward with her bag and light source leading the way. The claustrophobia took her back to the much smaller flue she'd squeezed through to rob a wealthy merchant's house in Cambridge. She ignored her irrational fear.

Fifty feet into the cliff wall, the vent branched in three directions. Louisa squirmed her way forward until the flame of her lantern flickered but stayed lit. The outline of another grate appeared on the tunnel floor a few feet ahead.

Scooching around her haversack, Louisa moved forward to peer through the latticework of metal into the gloom. Her meager lamplight illuminated nothing but empty space. She placed the lantern on the other side of the grate. Like a contortionist, she twisted until the star-steel blade came free. With a similar cutting technique as earlier, she sawed around the grate and left one row of metal squares attached. It fell and landed with a loud, terror-inducing bang.

If anyone or anything is here, it had to hear that.

She blew out a big breath and settled her mind. *It didn't drop far—ten to twenty feet tops.*

From a side pouch on the haversack, she pulled a twenty-foot-long strand of thin rope she had fashioned from scraps of the Ancients' vests. She tied the rope to the part of the grate she had left in place and let the cord drop. From a quick pull, she could tell that little, if any, of the rope lay on the floor. With her lantern in hand, she crawled over the hole until her feet were over empty space.

Louisa inched backward, and her feet dropped free until she held herself up with elbows on each side of the opening. With a pointed toe, she kicked her leg in a wide circle to catch and wrap the cord around her leg several times. Still holding the lantern, she looped the haversack over her neck before grabbing the silky strand.

Her heart was pounding at twice its normal speed as she let the rope take all her weight. To calm herself, she cycled through the breathing technique that enabled her to become a shadow. Inch by inch, she slid down the rope until her entire body cleared the ventilation shaft. The lantern spotlighted a hallway with the same muted gray walls and flooring as the little vent.

Eyes shut, Louisa poured all her sensory receptors into her hearing and listened for a full minute. She slid to the rope's end, a foot off the floor.

Here goes nothing.

She dropped the rest of the way and had to shut her eyes again because the hallway walls put out enough light to simulate the noonday sun. As she blinked to clear her vision, she listened for anything moving. The lantern winked out with a turn of a small dial, and she returned it to the haversack.

Louisa pulled her revolver and scurried mouse quiet down the hallway in the direction she estimated the entrance must be. Double doors blocked the path but slid open as she neared them. Bright light burst forth, showing a large square room. She popped her head into the opening and was reminded of the elevator in the welven palace. It had no visible controls either, and she wanted to explore more before risking being trapped in the small room.

Louisa backtracked past the hanging rope until the corridor ended in a T-section going to her left or right. She chose the path to the right and passed several doors that opened as she neared. First, there was a privy, followed by what she assumed was a dining hall. The hallway took a turn to the left. As she rounded the corner, the door at the far end of the passage slid open.

Louisa fought down sudden panic. She took a quick step backward and another to the side, then hugged the wall out of sight. She closed her eyes and ran through the scene. Made of a gleaming white porcelain surface, a headless egg-shaped body with two metal arms and two metal legs walked out of the open door.

It's like a hatchling couldn't get its head out of its shell.

Afraid to get caught while in a trance, Louisa refrained from using the special headgear to find out the purpose of the automaton. She found it curious that the walking machine looked nothing like one of the hybrid bird-reptile Ancients.

It's shaped like one of their eggs, though.

Another swoosh came from around the corner, causing Louisa to peek. The back of the creature disappeared inside the room on the right, and the door closed. With one eye on the portal, she took slow, shallow breaths. The door opened, and the thing walked out, carrying a barrel in its three-pincered hands. It disappeared behind the door at the end of the hall.

Unsure whether the creature would come her way, Louisa abandoned that section of the facility. After returning to the last intersection, she took the left junction. The path wound around several turns before the angle of the floor became a steep incline. Almost imperceptible at first, a hissing sound grew louder with each step she took upward until it became the unmistakable sound of rushing water combined with a strange whooshing noise.

At the top of the incline, Louisa stepped onto a landing with a single arched opening encased by star steel set to her left. She tip-toed to the side of the archway and listened.

Hearing nothing else, she glanced into the chamber behind the arch, memorizing the layout. A picture window ran the length of the room above a floating counter. Beyond the glass, a giant paddle—bigger than the biggest paddle boat—turned, powered by water flowing under the bottom of the wheel. The torrent pushed it to spin so fast that it blurred. Most remarkable, the blades and the rest of the turbine were made of bright, shiny star steel. The only other feature in the room was a floating table in the back corner.

Taking a deep breath, Louisa walked into the room. The scene in the window mesmerized her. Without thought, she moved forward until her hands rested on the counter connected to the wall under the window. Images popped up above the black glass surface.

She stumbled backward, and her heart rate soared.

What the hell?

Line, bar, and pie charts moved and adjusted as if alive. Now that she could count to a hundred in Ancient, many of the numbers were understandable. Yet she still found most of the text incomprehensible. Familiar with pressure gauges on steam engines, Louisa speculated that these charts measured vital information about the giant turbine.

The city's power source.

Unable to estimate how many millennia this facility would continue working to power the buildings below, Louisa pondered how long it would take her race to equal the abilities of the Ancients. With a shake of her head, she tore herself away from the hypnotic view of the turbine and inspected the back corner.

Several curved crystal headgear devices and a collapsible scroll lay on the table, along with two unknown items. One was a two-foot-long bar of star steel; the other, an oversize handle of a sledgehammer or a small spear. In place of a large metal head, it had a small, upside-down black cone.

The handle was made of a pliable grippy material instead of wrapped wood. Louisa picked it up and used pictures and words to ask her bonnet a question. A squawking word echoed in her head. She experienced a dream showing her a stream of light emerging from the cone end of the handle. A small bolt of lightning extended about a foot and a half from the handle. The squawk rang out again, and the light disappeared.

When the artificial memory stopped, Louisa blinked out of the trancelike state that came with it.

What technology can contain lightning?

Louisa stretched her arm as far away as possible and pointed the cone toward empty space.

She imitated the sound. "Squawk."

Lightning popped from the cone, emanating constant crackling. Louisa moved to the back wall made up of the same gray metal as most of the facility. As the tip of the lightning touched the wall, the metal hissed, and the area around the light turned bright red. She kept pushing until the handle was an inch from the red ring. As she pulled her arm back, the hallway and the incline were visible through a glowing cauterized hole in the wall.

Wow!

Out of the corner of her eye, she caught the glint of star steel from the entrance casing.

I wonder.

With a smile, Louisa performed the same experiment. She pushed a little faster this time, and the gleaming metal parted like warm butter. Instead of pulling straight back, she cut toward the entrance of the arch. The entire light blade popped free, leaving a deep, white-hot cut in the metal casing.

"Squawk." The light disappeared.

Louisa started to put the handle into her kit and saw something glowing within the haversack. Light pulsed from the crack in the pouch holding the Seba objects. With a quick tug, she untied the bag and held up the first spherical object. The text and the borders glowed bright and then ebbed before repeating.

Puzzled, Louisa pulled out a second sphere, and it did the same. Without thinking, she placed the two parts of the Seba on the table to retrieve the others. As soon as the artifacts rested on the table, the light became brighter as it continued to pulse.

Is this it?

After she put all the objects on the table, Louisa untied her bonnet. The glass glowed inside the sleeve. Getting excited, Louisa placed the bonnet, hole down, on the table and pulled out the Ancients' scroll from her haversack. Soon everything pulsed.

What about the automaton?

With a glance at the open entrance and then back at the objects on the table, Louisa settled on her glowing hat. It had provided some protection against the flying ghosts back at the Tomb of Mortals. She grabbed one of the other curved glass bowls and replaced it with the one in her bonnet. She tied the hat back on her head and asked whether the headgear was activated. The two symbols and the squawk for "Yes" appeared.

It took Louisa a minute to form the following question. After trying different combinations, she asked how much power the glass bowl had. A chart appeared with a blue bar stretching to the top, next to the number 100. She had to assume this meant the device held a full charge.

Satisfied, Louisa picked up the lightning-cutting handle and sat with her back to the wall to watch the opening. Now armed with a weapon that could stop the metal creature, she focused her thoughts on the bigger picture.

What should I do?

The phrase kept running through Louisa's mind. She didn't know how long the charging process would take, which might settle the issue for her. If it took more than a few hours, she would need to go out and tell everyone she had succeeded. If it took less time, she could hide her success.

Louisa didn't want to go home, but she wanted the option of going home if she changed her mind. If Ali never discovered that the Seba was charged, her choices were wide open. He would have no reason to take the Seba from her until they gave up on the quest to power it.

Louisa rubbed her arms, trying to warm herself. Her outfit was still damp despite the babiakhom's blow-drying. Did she need to tell Ben right away? She thought about the ramifications and came to one significant conclusion.

We can't abandon the Kermans to the Remulans. I'll keep it a secret until after that threat is over. But what about Ali?

The professor didn't need to know anything unless there was a little invasion from an army of giant reptiles. That might make her play her hand sooner than later. Any guilt she had soon went away because they were already helping prepare for the possible Lamentations by making more guns.

There's no reason to tell anyone but Ben and Jeevan when the fight is over.

Satisfied with the plan and needing a distraction, Louisa picked up the star-steel bar and asked how it worked. When she finished the vision, she shook her head to make her thoughts her own again. The ability of the tool amazed her. One simply had to picture a tool or an instrument, and the bar would reshape itself.

With a few of her guided thoughts, the bar became a hammer, a wrench, and a wood plane. The metal kept morphing in her hands. It stayed cool but moved like a molten flow before solidifying each time.

While Louisa had worked with the *reshaper* tool—what she named it—her headgear and the scroll stopped pulsing on the table. She had been inside the facility for an hour and a half, and the others would need an update soon. With only the Seba objects still glowing, she gave herself another half hour before she would abandon her plan. Her frustration mounted with each passing minute.

Fidgeting with anxious energy, Louisa stared at the objects as if willing them to stop blinking. She remembered her mother telling her that watching water come to a boil would make time crawl. Still, she couldn't pull her eyes away.

The Seba artifacts winked out, one by one, with five minutes to spare.

Yes.

Elated, Louisa had the urge to scream a victory cry but resisted. Her hands shaking, she repacked her haversack with her new finds and the fully charged old ones.

She ran through all her mental exercises to force herself back to calmness. There was a story to tell, and she needed everyone to believe it.

Ben paced back and forth, his mind a cage of worry. After each circuit, he looked up the cliff, praying to find Louisa emerging from the cliff tunnel. What would they do if she didn't come out soon?

Idiot! Never should have let her go.

They could send Ssherrss or Rrummblinss in to find her, but both stirithy had already said they couldn't climb the cliff. The Ancients had altered the rock not to allow them to use their magic to grip the stone. With a couple more babiakhom, they could fly someone up. They might need to get the smallest Lancer, Lance Duffadar Ram, to go inside to find her.

Ben had begun his next turn when Abu yelled, "She's there!"

An arm sticking out from the cliff waved a piece of cloth. The tenseness left Ben's body, and the rest of the group relaxed with a collective exhalation.

A few minutes later, Louisa floated to the ground, tied to the wind singer who had retrieved her. Ben tried to speak but found his jaw clenched. He fought tears of relieved anger. She gave him a small sheepish smile. He released his emotions with a long deep breath.

"Were you successful?" Ali almost shouted.

Louisa shook her head. "No luck. Much of the facility was too dangerous to search. At one point, I almost ran into a strange headless creature with an egg-shaped body. It had metal arms and legs." She held up a bar of star steel. "There is a room that looks over a giant waterwheel turned by the river. I believe it powers the city. I found this reshaping tool there. Watch." She grinned at them. "It's amazing."

As Louisa displayed the bar's abilities, the crowd *oohed and ahhed*. Ssherrss waved his hand over the bar and confirmed that he could not duplicate it. The prince told Louisa to keep it until they showed it to the queen. Queen Nabra would decide what to do with it.

With a sigh, Louisa said, "I was afraid of getting trapped or being attacked by the strange creature." Her eyes drifted down, and she kicked the ground with her foot. "Maybe we could come back."

During Louisa's retelling, something kept bugging Ben. Her reaction to the failure wasn't very Louisa Sophia–like. Obstacles fueled her fire, and she never gave up when the reward was great. Ben's disappointment in not charging the Seba mingled with his relief at Louisa's safe return. Everyone looked to him for leadership despite this setback, meaning he had to stay focused.

Ben gave Louisa's shoulder a few reassuring pats as he tried to sound optimistic. "Once we get the troops trained, we'll come back. But even if it's a dead end, one of the other locations on the other continents will have what we need. Don't lose hope."

With tight lips, Louisa nodded.

Ali added, "Once we adequately prepare for the Lamentations, I'll go with you."

At Ali's words, a glint of mischief sparked in Louisa's eyes. Without being able to put his finger on it, Ben's relief and optimism soured into suspicion.

Chapter 30

Kerma City, Choru, An 5660, Day 28

Abu kicked a rock out of frustration. His eyes didn't even follow its path. He stared at his feet as he trudged along. Grumpy, he could only describe the day as disappointing. The trip to the waterfall facility had been a total waste of time.

Forced out of bed before the cock's crow, Abu had eaten a rushed breakfast of dried meat and cheese. Then they'd wandered along dark, deserted streets and hiked for hours up the side of a cliff. What little hope he had from Dr. Ben's promise of adventure disappeared up the rock wall. Miss Louisa got to explore, leaving the rest of them to twiddle their thumbs. For all that, what did he have to show? Wet underclothes chafing his crotch. That's what.

Rrummblinss slapped him square in the back. "Cheerr up, mmy frriend," he said in Greek.

Abu snarled, "Why?"

The blond stirithy purred a chuckle. "Do you ssmmell it?"

Abu turned to the flamboyant soldier. "Smell what?"

Jutting his snout upward, Rrummblinss sniffed twice. "Frressh baked brread and kussharri. I'mm fammisshed."

At the mention of bread, Abu's stomach grumbled.

More purring laughter. "Ssoundss like yourr sstommach agrreess. Let'ss find that pot of kussharri and then explorre the ccity."

Abu resisted an urge to snap at the short creature he thought of as his friend and mentor. He was hungry, and getting to tour Kerma might salvage the day.

Probably make me tutor Masako when we get back. Sometimes Abu hated being fourteen. Today was one of those days. Why couldn't he do what he wanted to do? Why did he need to ask permission? *Well, don't.*

Over his shoulder, Abu locked eyes with Dr. Ben, who was walking a little ahead of Miss Louisa and Khepri. Abu yelled, "Dr. Ben, I'm going to go eat lunch with Rrummblinss! Then we're going to explore the city!"

Dr. Ben's brow furrowed. "Was that a question?"

Abu swallowed. *Don't mess this up.* "Uh, sorry, may I go?"

"If you promise to be back by Triplets!" his—Guardian? Adopted father?—yelled back.

"I promise." His mood lifting, Abu turned around.

"And absolutely no drinking. Don't think I didn't know about the other night."

Abu didn't dare look back. *I didn't even see him that night.* "Yes, sir!" he called out like a Lancer responding to Jeevan's duffadar voice.

"Do you hear me, Rrummblinss? No trouble."

The stirithy snickered, became serious, and turned around to walk backward. "On mmy honorr, I will keep himm ssafe." He placed his hand on his stomach. "Sstitch it on mmy hearrt."

Abu shook his head. *Funny saying. Is that where his heart is?*

Miss Louisa chimed in with a stern voice. "You should promise on something less questionable than your honor, Captain. Abu, keep him out of trouble."

Abu chuckled as the irrepressible Rrummblinss spun around. His bandit's face showed what Abu could only imagine was contrition. The prospect of several hours of freedom swung Abu's mood from grumpy to happy like a pendulum.

Over his shoulder, Abu smiled. "Yes, ma'am."

He nudged Rrummblinss and picked up his pace. "After lunch, we need to find the Alexandrian Embassy."

Their procession had just turned the last switchback before reaching ground level. The pair fast-walked past the prince and his retainers to the front. Setting a brisk pace, Abu gazed in earnest over the city for the first time that day.

By his estimation, they were about level with the top of the palace pyramid. His first view of Kerma had been while swooping in like a bird. His second experience had been nothing but hints and shadows of the slumbering metropolis. Spread out before him now, the city's heartbeat throbbed as throngs of Kermans clad in earth-toned linens hustled about their daily lives.

At the city's limits, half a dozen flaming balls of pitch and many solid boulders crashed into the massive wall. A few fell inside the city, but none carried over the buffer area kept clear of buildings next to the city walls. Without these signs of violence, there would be no visible evidence the city was under siege.

Abu pushed those troubles aside and went back to his inspection. Along the major avenues, the shops and the houses were two- and three-story limestone affairs with flat roofs and bright red doors. Set farther along narrow, haphazard streets were thousands of smaller flat-top homes made of whitewashed brick.

Intermingled among the human-built portions of the city, with no apparent pattern, were the Ancients' buildings and the unceasing light shows on their walls. It took effort for Abu to block out the incredible displays and focus on the rest of the city.

In the area surrounding the pyramid-shaped palace stood countless villas with open courtyards. On the far side of the city, laid out in a perfect grid pattern, were temple complexes with mixtures of Greek, Roman, and Egyptian buildings. All roads in that neighborhood led to a giant sunken amphitheater at the area's center.

Abu soaked it in, trying to capture this view in detail for the journaling he had begun a few days after arriving in Aaru. Since putting pen to paper, he'd imagined the name Abu Saqr coming to rival Homer's when people thought of legendary epics.

Ben's suspicions had grown by the time they were down the cliff. Louisa spent most of the descent hanging out with her friends. At first, he did not pick up on it, but now, he was sure she was avoiding him on purpose.

Despite his misgivings, he enjoyed the walk back to the palace, entranced by the city and its residents. The people of Kerma, in many ways, lived like the ancient Egyptians. Well, not really. The ancient Egyptians didn't have aliens running around, performing magic.

Or did they? Is that where the legends of the gods came from?

Still, from a cultural standpoint, the Kermans would have been comfortable in eleventh-dynasty Egypt.

An hour after reaching street level, they turned onto a vast, tree-lined avenue leading up to the palace pyramid's main entrance. A series of massive stairs rose from ground level up a hundred feet to the entrance. The Kermans had augmented the stairs and added two human-size steps between the each giant Ancient-size step, making the ascent a little easier.

A little winded by the time he reached the top, Ben walked through an opening big enough for a steamship. Inside, He stood gaping at the sight within. Hollowed out, the pyramid had an outer layer of rooms with doors set into a slanted glass wall. It ran from the floor to the squared-off ceiling with a hole at its center. The rooms at the top had to have a view fit for a pharaoh.

At least ten level walkways crisscrossed the empty space above Ben's head. In the middle of the building, cables extended from a hole in the ceiling to a raised platform at the pyramid's base. Halfway to the top, a circular platform floated upward at a steady pace between the four thin lines. Ben could find no connection to the wires.

How does that work?

Several men stood on the levitating elevator. At each stop, the walkways extended in four directions, going to the rooms along the walls. The now-empty lift stopped at the pyramidion, closing off the hole at the top.

Their procession came to a halt. A few minutes later, the platform lowered and sped up. As it neared the ground floor, Ben saw the queen, the general, and two of her bodyguards riding the large disk.

The prince approached them, and Louisa grabbed Ben's elbow. "Let's go."

After reaching the raised platform, the queen and her entourage moved to meet them halfway.

The prince bowed. "Your Majesty."

The regal woman with the perpetual frown asked, "Were you successful?"

The prince's eyes darted to Louisa, and his face lit up. "More than we had hoped, Mother."

The queen jutted her chin at him.

The prince said, "Louisa found a small air vent, and she was able to enter. I will let her tell you what she found."

With a quick head bow, Louisa said, "Your Majesty. We were successful in entering the complex. As we suspected, it is a power station that uses the river to generate power for the buildings in the city. Inside, I saw a creature made of porcelain and metal that appeared to be a worker. Due to that, I could not fully explore the complex, but I obtained this." Louisa pulled the reshaper tool from her haversack and held it up. "A tool of the Ancients."

The rod morphed into different tools as Louisa repeated her earlier demonstration, using her headgear.

"Very impressive." The queen's expression never changed.

General Kinya shifted his weight. "You should keep this wondrous tool, Your Majesty."

The queen pursed her lips and stared at the general. "No, I need weapons, General, not metal rods that change shapes. The Earthlings may keep it. Maybe they can use it to help build the weapons we will use to defend our homes. We will send explorers to the facility." The queen turned back to Louisa. "And the Seba?"

Louisa's gaze drifted down. "I'm afraid not, Your Majesty."

"Very well." The queen turned to Ben, boring a hole through him with her intense gaze. "I have kept up my end of our bargain. I expect you to redouble your efforts to create the weapons and train my troops."

Ben nodded. "We will work as fast as possible." He remembered and added, "Your Majesty."

Her frown disappeared in what Ben thought might be her version of a smile. "Good. Send updates through Prince Tambal."

The general's eyes narrowed, and he scowled for the briefest moment before his face became stoic again.

The queen turned without another word and walked toward the platform. As she moved upward, the prince said, "I will show you the way to your quarters."

From the opposite side of the big entrance to the pyramid, they walked down a carpeted corridor that entered one of the rectangular buildings. The path continued down the middle of a large indoor atrium and play area. Dozens of dark-skinned Kerman women and girls sat around tables, sipping drinks, eating, and immersed in discussions. Bird chirps echoed around the room, with hundreds of giant ferns and other tropical plants growing in hieroglyphic-decorated pots.

Ben dodged several children who raced between Ssherrss and him. Oblivious to who they were, the kids yelled and laughed, playing a version of tag. As the children crossed the carpeted path, a handsome woman of about thirty yanked the arm of one boy.

She lowered her long, angular face to the child's level. Still clutching his arm, she shook her finger at the boy and lectured him in an angry, hushed tone. With Ben's limited Aaruan, he made out some words.

. . . playing with the . . . children

All conversations stopped, and every head turned to regard their procession.

Another beautiful young woman about twenty years old walked toward the prince. She had long, tight braids that hung to her waist and wore a white linen dress so thin, it was no more than a film of gauze. Ben's face grew warm at the unhidden features of the woman's body.

The prince held out his hands in greeting, then scanned the crowd. Ben noticed that the young man had captured Louisa's attention. With a big grin, the prince turned back to the woman, pulled her to him, and kissed her. She returned the kiss with passion. Ben looked back to Louisa.

She rolled her eyes and gave a derisive, "Pfft."

A few feet away, the scolding mother stood up straight. Pure hatred shot from her gaze toward the prince and the woman. The couple still embraced, but now they had their heads together in conversation.

The scowling woman's lips were moving, and Ben scooted closer to listen to her whispers.

Tonight . . . his wife . . . seized . . . in front . . . him . . . his soul will be destroyed forever.

What the hell is that about? Ben wondered.

The woman's eyes flashed at Ben, and her whispers stopped. She snarled and, bending her head, spat.

What? Why?

She spun with a flourish and stormed away.

"Ben!" Louisa called.

Ben stared at the woman's back for a few seconds, trying to make sense of her venom. With a shrug, he focused on Louisa.

She beckoned Ben over to the prince. In a few long strides, Ben stood with Louisa before the beautiful young couple. One of the prince's babiakhom attendants joined them.

The prince pulled the woman closer with his arm still around her waist. "Ben, Louisa, this is my wife. Princess Tiye."

They once again heard his Aaruan words as background to the translation in their native tongues.

Princess Tiye gave Ben a brief nod before she stared at Louisa, assessing every detail intensely. "I hear you rebuffed my husband's proposal. You should reconsider." Her commanding voice in the background had a musical lilt.

Louisa sighed. "Princess, I am flattered, but the prince does not understand my situation." She smiled up at Ben and grabbed his arm. "Dr. McGehee and I are courting."

The princess gave Ben a dismissive glance. "You are not promised, and he will not become pharaoh. No. You should reconsider."

"Ben may not become a king, but I *would be* his *queen*. It appears the role of the queen is filled for Prince Tambal." Louisa smirked. "Unless you plan on stepping aside and becoming a second wife."

The princess threw her head back and laughed. "I see what drew him to you. Your loss."

As her stomach settled from the evening's meal, Louisa leaned back and let her mind drift away from the current conversation. Abu was still regaling her with his afternoon adventures when Masako entered the dining room.

The young girl raced up to the table and punched Abu's arm. "You left me."

Louisa and Ben chuckled as Abu rubbed his injury and said, "Life's not fair. Get over it." Then he smiled and ruffled Masako's hair under her tiara. "Next time, kid."

Masako glared at him while readjusting her hair. Louisa pointed Masako to the open seat on the other side of the table, and the girl nodded.

Abu turned his attention back to Louisa. "And that's why the temple district is so incredible. You need to see it, Miss Louisa." Abu tore off a hunk of chicken from his drumstick and chewed.

Louisa took the reprieve to lean toward Ben and whisper, "Like father, like son."

Ben raised an eyebrow.

To Louisa's relief, Abu turned to the dwarf and began bending Thoresten's ear, comparing rituals for the goddess Ishtar versus those for Odin. Louisa gave

Ben a wry smile. "Abu is beginning to prattle on about obscure facts as much as you do."

Ben chuckled. "Am I that excitable?"

"More."

"Is it such a bad thing?"

She grew serious. "Not at all. I find it endearing." Then she grinned. "For about ten minutes."

"Okay, you win. I'll keep future lectures to five minutes." Ben leaned over and, in a conspiratorial tone, said, "I wanted to ask you a couple of questions."

Louisa gave a sheepish smile. Would he finally ask her for a kiss? No. Not with so many people around. Maybe he would ask for some time alone. Her face reddened as she leaned closer and lowered her voice, making it as husky as her soprano would go. "I'm listening."

"When we met the princess, did you sense anything . . . ," Ben paused, ". . . wrong?"

Louisa heaved a sigh. *At least, he didn't ask about the Falls.* She whispered, "You're referring to the bitch spewing curses toward the prince and princess."

"Yes. I wondered if anyone else saw that."

"I heard her but didn't know what she was saying." Louisa popped an olive into her mouth.

"It was disturbing. The woman said something about the princess getting seized in front of the prince and that he would cease to exist." Ben shook his head. "That is the worst curse an Ancient Egyptian could give someone. Oh, and she said the word *tonight*. But I don't know if that was part of the curse."

With a napkin covering her mouth, Louisa spit out the pit. "I asked Khepri to explain palace politics. Did you notice the two cliques dividing the entire room?"

Ben tilted his head. "Really?"

Louisa said, "A woman would have picked up on it right away."

"So." Ben arched an eyebrow. "And?"

Still inches from his ear, Louisa said, "Khepri spilled the beans, as you like to say. General Kinya is the prince's *older* brother by one of the late pharaoh's consorts." She let this sink in. When she saw recognition on Ben's face, she continued. "They don't get along, and, by extension, neither do their households."

"Hmm."

Louisa added, "Do you think we need to worry?"

"Not sure."

The two fell silent. Something about the general did not sit right with Louisa. The familiar premonition of danger she sometimes had during a job kept tugging at her. She had learned the hard way never to ignore her intuition, but with no inspiration about what to do, she did just that. She ignored it. To keep Ben from venturing into what happened at the waterfall, she stood. "I'm exhausted. I'm going to turn in early."

"Uh. Well, goodnight." Ben's forehead wrinkled.

Louisa walked away and pretended not to hear his next words.

"Oh, I forgot to ask . . ."

Chapter 31

Kerma City, Choru, An 5660, Day 29

Louisa made another circuit around her living area. Guilt wasn't part of her agenda in life. In the past, she'd only lost sleep over questions like: *Which rich person's goods would pay next month's rent?* Wracked by guilt since the trip to the falls and her decision to deceive the others, she struggled with this new emotion.

An urge to climb, to get another shot of adrenaline, and to get free from her thoughts prompted Louisa to stop in front of the armoire. Decision made, she double-checked all the equipment she had lugged across the universe before changing into her work outfit.

With a glance in the mirror, Louisa thought, *Too suspicious.*

Louisa rolled up her pant legs and sleeves before slipping on a chiton dress to cover her black clothes. She thought of waking Masako to tell the girl where she was going but dismissed the idea before it finished forming.

Will Khepri come?

Louisa would need to abort if the wolfwoman wouldn't join her on this adventure. She had never stressed this special climbing equipment as much as she planned on doing tonight. Since the risk wasn't zero, she couldn't stomach living through the embarrassment if, on the slim chance, she fell and broke a leg.

Outside, Louisa and Khepri stood near the corner at the base of the Ancients' pyramid-turned-Kerman-palace. Hours after sundown, the always-changing backlit colors of the glass building illuminated the two friends in a soft glow.

Khepri growled in Greek, "How long is this going to take? I am not your maidservant."

"Not long. Are we up past your bedtime?" Louisa chuckled.

"Humph." Khepri gave a canine yawn. "Yes. I'm usually cuddled up with my Ssherrss by now."

As Louisa pulled her chiton over her head, she asked, "Speaking of cuddling, how is it going with Hemmetrre?"

Khepri shook her head. "Slow." The wolf woman added, "Should you be doing this?"

Louisa did not press her friend further about her complicated marriage arrangement. "I need this. I need to release some energy." Louisa gave the wolf her most sincere smile. "I appreciate your help."

Khepri chuckled. "If you and Ben would give in to your instincts, you could use your energy on what you really need."

Louisa's face grew flush at the thought of Ben's lips close to hers. "Stop it."

"Fine. Do what you need to, and don't you dare fall." The hysakas took the chiton and crammed it into Louisa's haversack.

After unrolling her sleeves and pant legs, Louisa checked the knot around each shoe and slipped the special devices over her gloves. She cinched the ties with a tug of her teeth and tested her hand movements.

"Are you sure those things work?" Khepri's snout pointed toward her gloves.

"I've used them before, but never to go so high."

Louisa turned toward the angled glass of the pyramid and reached up. With a slap, the suction cup on her hand stuck to the glass. Pulling her arm, she lifted herself off the ground and toe-kicked the cup on her foot to the glass. She reached higher with her free hand and slapped.

"How do they work?" Khepri asked.

"Hard to explain." Louisa used a fingernail to break the seal on the first hand-cup before moving her hand higher. "It's made of a substance called rubber. A photographer created them twenty years ago." More of a challenge, the toe cups required Louisa to rock her foot, heel to toe, and then side to side.

"Rubber? Photo giraffe? Never mind," Khepri said, growling in frustration.

Louisa focused on the intricate process and was ten feet off the ground when Khepri said, "I'm not waiting here all night. If you go to the top, you're on your own."

When Louisa had climbed halfway to the apex of the building, she detached the cups on her right hand and foot from the glass. With a twist, she flipped her body to face away from the pyramid. She put her right-hand palm down onto the now blue glass to give herself three points of attachment.

From several hundred feet up, the eerie gardens, lit by gas-fed lamps, stretched to the small defensive wall surrounding the palace complex. Beyond, the lights of the city sparkled, spilling out of windows and balconies, taking Louisa back to her time at St. Denis. She had spent many nights at the top of the basilica, admiring the lights of Paris and dreaming about her future adventures there.

She closed her eyes and took a deep breath, thrilled at the slight breeze on her face. She tried to clear her mind of all recent worries. As the self-recrimination melted away, her sense of freedom swelled. But her bubble of joy burst when a pair of reproachful blue eyes appeared in her mind. She dispelled imaginary Ben's look of disappointment.

A movement caught her eye. A man exited from the entrance set into the middle of the pyramid. He stopped in the light near the door and looked both ways.

General Kinya?

The general kept moving his head from side to side as he walked deeper into the gardens.

What are you up to? Nothing good happens this late at night. I should know.

Beyond Louisa's suspicion, she felt jittery with energy from the jolt she always got when adventure was afoot. She locked the general's last position in her mind, determined to discover his secret.

To pursue her quarry, Louisa needed to get down the fast way. At the base of the pyramid, Khepri tapped her giant foot with impatience. Louisa hoped she wouldn't need Khepri for what came next. During one of the two times she'd used the suction cups in a heist, she had to try a quick escape technique. It worked that time, but the technique stretched her skills to the brink.

Louisa's right hand popped free, and she flipped over to face the glass.

This is not smart.

Using the heel-toe wiggle, Louisa released her other foot. With only one suction cup still attached, her body weight pulled her down. She slid with an irritating squeak. Spreading her feet wide, she kept the cups out of the way. Then she extended her free hand at an angle and popped that last cup free.

The faster she slid, the higher Louisa's fear rose. She kept her hands and feet off the glass while estimating the distance to the fast-approaching ground. When she was halfway to the bottom, she slapped the cups on her hands to the glass. She was unable to establish a total vacuum, so the rubber screeched and squealed. It slowed down her plunge, but she would still come down hard.

Ten feet off the ground, Louisa pulled her hands off the glass and twirled her body to face outward. With a kick of her heels, she launched herself parallel to the ground. When her toes touched the grass, she tucked into a roll and came to her feet a few yards away from Khepri.

"Woah," the wolf howled. "That was incredible." Khepri panted as she stepped beside Louisa. "Now, we go back."

"Not yet." Louisa grabbed her bag. "I just saw the general skulking around the garden." Out of the haversack, she pulled her now-modified balaclava mask. With one of the curved Ancients' devices fitted into the top pouch, she pulled it down over her head and face. Finally, she took out the reshaping tool. "I'm going to find out what he's up to." Louisa ran toward the general's last location.

"Really? Now, you're making me traipse all over the gardens?" The hysakas hurried after Louisa.

"Stop complaining."

When she reached the path where she had last spotted him, Louisa couldn't find her target. With a sad expression, she turned to her friend.

Khepri sniffed the wind and moved toward a large hedge. Louisa jogged to keep up. A large sign written in Aaruan hieroglyphics stood at the edge of the tall bush.

Louisa pointed. "What does it say?"

"The Ta-Seti Maze."

Louisa took a step into the hedge-rowed path.

Khepri whispered, "What are you planning?"

"I'm going to find the general. Alone. You will give us away."

"Why? He's gone for a walk in the garden. People do that. Besides," Khepri looked down at her short, sleeveless, white Grecian dress, "you should have warned me to wear my *sneaking around clothes*."

"Maybe he's meeting a lover, but my instincts tell me he is up to no good. Now, stay out of sight. If I'm not out in an hour, go get help."

"How are you going to find him without me?" The wolf tapped her snout.

"Luck." Louisa patted her friend on the arm and entered the maze.

Several minutes in, she backtracked to the third set of turns. Old memories came flooding back.

Ten-year-old Louisa had stopped her raised foot, trying somehow to see through the utter blackness surrounding her. She inched her big toe along the ground and sighed.

Her uncle's voice reverberated through the darkness. "You have one minute left to reach the exit."

She forced down her panic. How many times had she failed this test? Each time, it began with him rearranging the obstacles in the room. Her uncle would give her fifteen minutes to grope around in the dark, seeking and memorizing a safe path. For the test, she had two minutes to traverse from one end to the other. Failure came from running out of time or touching an obstacle. Somehow, her uncle knew if she even brushed one.

Snapping back to the here and now, she maneuvered around another hedge. She kept close to the shadiest part of the bush without getting snagged and tried to blend into the darkness. Ahead, the maze opened into an area with a fountain in the middle. Female Egyptian goddesses formed the fountain's central pillar. Water, lit by a mysterious source, shot up before falling back into the surrounding pool.

Mata's moon rays sent long shadows away from the two men who stood with heads together in front of the fountain.

What are you up to?

The two broke apart, and the one she didn't recognize stepped over the fountain's retaining wall and waded to the center. Getting drenched, the breast-plated soldier stood before a lioness-headed statue. He pulled down on her sword-wielding arm, and the lioness figure swung outward. Then he stepped into the opening and pulled the statue closed.

That's not suspicious. Not at all.

After the man's exit, General Kinya turned toward Louisa. Her training kicked in, and she lowered her eyes. Frozen in place, inside the last shadows of the maze hedge, she watched him approach with her peripheral vision. Her breathing slowed until she became the darkness. With the general a few yards away, she opened her senses, ready to act if he moved her way.

As he rushed past, a mere foot from her, a musky scent filled the air. She remained a shadow until the sounds of his sandaled feet, rustling through the thick grass, became muffled in the maze. After a quick peek over her shoulder to ensure he'd gone, she raced toward the fountain.

I should probably get help.

Louisa hurtled over the low wall of the pond.

The water came over her knees, and she almost fell face-first. Then, bending like a yogi, she high-stepped, sloshing toward the goddess statue. She pulled on the arm with all her strength until she heard a click. Using the stone elbow as a handle, she swung the door open. The lip of the doorway stood six inches above the waterline. A set of water-splattered stairs dropped into the darkness.

Huge drops of fountain water rained down, drenching Louisa. With a foot on the threshold, she grabbed the doorframe and pulled herself onto the top step. Her foot flew out from under her, and she gripped the stone casing to keep from falling back into the water. Still holding the reshaping tool in one hand, she didn't dare let go even as the skin on her free fingers scraped on the stone.

Heart hammering, Louisa pulled herself upright and tested the way forward. The velvety moss-covered landing was as slippery as her uncle on rent day. Using the walls for support, she moved down the stairs one cautious step at a time. By the time she reached the bottom of a corkscrew turn, she had counted forty-two of the narrow steps. A glow of light illuminated a stone floor one more flight down. Twenty-three made it sixty-five steps as she poked her head out of the stairwell into a lit stone tunnel.

The three-foot-wide and seven-foot-tall passage had gas-burning sconces set about a foot from the ceiling. With the lights spaced twenty feet apart, there were no shadows where Louisa could hide. There were also no people.

Where did you go?

A long way down the corridor, the tunnel curved. After placing the reshaping tool in her left hand, she pulled her bulldog revolver from its pocket. She hugged the inner wall as she came into the curve. Voices and running boots bounced off the walls. Louisa recognized some of the words. After lowering her torso down the wall, she moved in a crouch around the curve until the man she hunted came into view. He stood on her side of a steel-barred gate.

His Latin words echoed back to her. "Hurry! We don't have much time."

Past the bars, a green-feathered helmet bounced up and down as the slap of sandals led the way.

Remulans. Merde!

With his biceps wrapped in a green armband, the Kerman soldier walked toward the gate with a key, and the threat solidified in that instance. The general and his men had switched sides.

Run, damn it, Louisa thought, but her feet refused to move.

It wasn't a snap decision. Louisa ran through the cold, meticulous calculation in less than a second. Her tribe—no, they were so much more. Her family was in danger. If she didn't slow them down, it would be too late for the cavalry to save the day. Against every instinct and all her training, she thought, *I am willing,* as she stood tall.

Her mouth went dry as she stepped into the center of the tunnel. With her feet shoulder-length apart, she aimed with one arm. She pulled the trigger and realigned her wrist from the recoil, then squeezed again. The big Kerman soldier slumped forward, his face slamming into the iron bars. He slid down on Louisa's side of the gate with a groan. She sprinted ahead, her gun leading the way.

Get the key. Get the key. What if they have a metal singer?

The nearest Remulan legionary whipped his short sword free. Countless unadorned metal helmets bobbed behind the first two Remulans. The first two wore helmets with sideways plumes of green feathers. A few feet from the gate, Louisa stopped and raised her arm. The soldier's eyes flashed from her revolver to the key still held in the dead man's hand. He lurched forward and thrust his sword through the bars, trying to reach her.

As she stared into his murderous eyes, all remorse disappeared. Louisa side-stepped his thrust, gritted her teeth, and fired into the legionary's face.

She jerked her head away from the horror she had wrought. The soldier's shield bounced off the steel bars, arresting his momentum. His body went limp. He slumped to his knees with his arm hanging through the gate. Five yards behind the body, the second man with a plumed helmet screamed and barreled forward, sword arm raised high.

Have to keep them on the other side.

With two quick steps, Louisa leaned over the men, who, in death, embraced each other from opposite sides of the locked gate. She squeezed her hand past the bars. With the legionary only feet away, she aimed an inch above his shield and pulled the trigger. The soldier took another step and fell to his knees.

A steel-helmeted soldier without the adornments appeared behind the dying man. This new legionary pushed the kneeling man aside and tried to step past his fallen comrade. Louisa fired again. Blood sprayed from the back of the legionary's neck, and his sword clanged to the ground. With shock in his eyes, he brought his free hand to his throat and staggered backward.

Louisa put her empty revolver away and snatched the key from the dead Kerman's cool hand. She shook the door to make sure it remained locked.

Run! Louisa screamed inside as she spun and raced the way she had come. She was almost to the curve when a searing pain exploded in her left shoulder. Her arm limp, she tumbled to the ground and lost her grip on the reshaping tool. It rolled around the curve. Another arrow smashed into the wall next to her.

Get up, damn it! Get up! Go!

Louisa pulled herself up with her one good arm. She crawled around the curve until she thought they couldn't get a decent shot at her. Arrows broke against the far wall as Latin curses bounced down the corridor.

The silver tool lay a foot from Louisa's knees. She grabbed it, thought of a walking stick, and pulled herself to her feet. The entirety of her upper body screamed in pain. She swooned when she glanced down. A wicked arrowhead stuck out from her chest an inch from her armpit. She forced her eyes forward, away from the wound. Blood flowed down her side, warming her water-chilled skin.

She took a deep breath and jogged toward the stairs. Pain lanced through her shoulder with every step as she repeated the phrase.

Get to Khepri. Get to Khepri.

At the stairwell landing, Louisa scrambled up, using the tool to keep her from planting her face on the hard stone stairs. Fear kept her going as she counted off each step.

Can't rest.

She had lost too much blood and couldn't start again if she stopped. Twice she slipped, and her knee took the brunt of the blow. It was insignificant compared to the fire in her shoulder. She pulled herself up and pushed on.

Sixty-four.

Her foot sought the next step and missed. She tumbled out of the opening into the pond surrounding the fountain. Water rushed into her mouth and nose. She gagged, and her body spasmed with panic as water flowed into her lungs. The rough stone surface at the bottom of the pool penetrated her pain and fear. She pushed off and exploded into the open air. Choking, she coughed. She gasped for air, and the thought of drowning fled, replaced by *Remulans!*

Louisa still held the Ancients' tool-turned-walking stick in her clenched fist. At thigh level, the water resisted her every step. She turned back to the lioness-headed stone woman and leaned into the statue with her uninjured shoulder. Gritting her teeth, she swung the door to the tunnel until it clicked closed.

The fountain spray ran down her hooded mask into her eyes. It took all Louisa's will to picture the reshaping tool in its original shape. She shook her head.

Concentrate.

Her eyes getting heavy, Louisa bit her lower lip to force herself awake. She wanted to trap the Remulans in the tunnel but knew she couldn't lock the door from the outside. Suddenly, she realized, *Why not clamp it shut from the inside?*

She held the bar at an angle next to the breast of the goddess. An imagined four-foot-long, pointed spear appeared in her mind. The tool morphed in her hand. Her image had become a reality as the pole extended. The star steel carved through the rock of the statue to impale itself several feet into the stone wall of the staircase.

Next she imagined both pointed ends of the spear spread out like grappling hooks. The metal next to her fingers flowed into a hook and locked into the flesh of the rock door, doing the same inside the tunnel wall.

Get to Khepri.

Empty-handed, Louisa pushed her way through the water in the pool. She couldn't remember getting out, but somehow she stumbled through the maze, her drenched, slippered feet squishing in the soft grass. With a shake of her head, she cleared her vision and stumbled onward.

What's the next turn?

"Louisa!"

Who's that?

Powerful arms cradled her. Louisa stared into sad canine eyes. She reached up to scratch the dog's ears. "Always wanted a dog."

"Louisa. Louisa. What happened?" Faint Greek words whispered in her ear.

Pain wracked Louisa's shoulder as she bounced along with the hysaka's long strides. Then, with the suddenness of a wasp's sting, fire filled her body. "Argh!"

Louisa's vision sharpened, and the mind fog cleared as the pain drained away. Only weariness remained. Concern filled Khepri's eyes. With the fear of eminent death gone, Louisa struggled against her friend's powerful arms.

"Stop moving," Khepri growled.

Louisa went limp, letting herself enjoy the feeling of safety. After a big breath, she stuttered, "Remulans. General is a traitor. In the maze. Tunnel. Get Lancers."

Khepri changed course, and the hedges receded behind her.

"Sleep, Louisa. You're safe."

Sleep. Can't sleep. Louisa closed her eyes.

The bed rattled from urgent concussive blows of someone pounding on a door. Ben lurched from his first dreamless sleep in a long while to being wide awake.

What the hell?

"Ben, open the door!" Khepri yelled in Greek. The door shook again with another boom.

Must be the middle of the night.

Ben scrambled out of the covers, grabbed his revolver from the bedstand, and raced barefoot to the door. He threw it open. Khepri stood before him, holding a person wearing a familiar black costume. Bloody water pooled on the ground, dripping from the limp body.

"Is she—?" Ben stuttered.

The hysakas pushed past him. "She'll live." Khepri lowered Louisa onto the bed to lay her on her side.

Abu ran out of the other bedroom. "What's happening?"

A barbed arrow point stuck out of Louisa's chest while its broken shaft protruded from her back. Ben swallowed, his gut clenching. In a trembling voice, he asked, "What happened?"

Khepri tugged the mask over Louisa's head. Water ran down her ashen cheeks. Khepri said. "We followed the general. He's a traitor. Louisa went into a garden maze after him. She said there's a hidden tunnel, and Remulans are coming."

Ben couldn't form words as he stared at Louisa's face. A hurricane of emotions threatened to capsize what control he had. He couldn't move.

"I'll take care of her. You must stop them." Khepri gripped Ben's arm and shook him. "Ben! Go!"

Ben tore his gaze from the women he loved and unlatched the gate to his anger. He yelled, "Abu, wake everyone! Tell Jeevan the Remulans are coming!"

"Yes, sir!" The teen hurried to the door.

"Then get your gun and come straight back. I need you here to protect Louisa and Masako."

From down the hallway, Abu yelled, "Yes, sir!"

Ben ran to the side of his bed, sat, and tugged on his boots. He threw open the top dresser drawer and pulled out his holster, knife still attached. With it buckled, he slid his revolver in place and grabbed Agnes, leaning against the chest of drawers. He took a step toward the door, then turned and snatched his hat.

"Khepri, where's the tunnel?"

The hysakas shook her head. "Northeast of the pyramid."

Ben knew he must look ridiculous, outfitted in his smallclothes and weapons, but he didn't have time to worry about it.[1] As he ran toward the rest of their party's rooms, others staggered out in similar states of dress.

Abu ran past him, going in the other direction to Louisa's room.

Shirtless Jeevan and topless Ki hurried toward him. The larger of the two welven warriors had her bow and quiver slung over one bare shoulder and her big metal club over the other. Jeevan had his carbine in one hand and his holster around his waist. The barrel-chested dwarf, every muscle rippling, rushed after them. He carried his two hand axes and wore only a loincloth and a Nipponese helmet.

Ben came to a stop with the pair. Others crowded around them.

Ben said, "Remulans are sneaking into the palace using a secret tunnel in the garden." He took a breath and switched to Greek. "Ki, I need you, Lil, and

---

1. Smallclothes is a Victorian term referring to men's undergarments, usually of silk, linen, or cotton, but also sometimes shirts and breeches.

Thoresten to warn the prince and queen. General Kinya let the Remulans inside the city. They must rally their troops fast to stop this from becoming a disaster."

Ki nodded to Lil, who wore most of her armor and had all her weapons. "Let's move." Ki grabbed Jeevan and gave him a quick kiss. "Play rough. You know how much I like that."

With her sister and the dwarf in tow, Ki pushed through the crowd.

Ben focused on the duffadar, whose complexion had turned ruddy brown. "Rally your men by the entrance to the garden. We will retake the tunnel."

With a big grin, Jeevan said, "Let's have some fun."

"What do you want us to do?" Esther asked.

"Get your Lochem and stand guard here. Louisa's injured." Ben turned to each one. "Ali, Ssherrss, Rrummblinss, and Abu will help you secure both exits so there is an escape route if the Remulans make it this far." He turned to Ssherrss. "Khepri's taking care of Louisa in my room."

Ben headed toward the back stairwell when Abu said, "Dr. Ben, Masako is with Miss Louisa. Let me go with you."

"Son, I need you here." Ben put a hand on Abu's shoulder. "Even one gun can make the difference." The boy's face grew solemn as Ben continued, "Understand?"

"Yes, sir. I've got this."

"I know. I wouldn't trust anyone else."

Ben ran to the stairs and took the giant steps two at a time. At the bottom, he poked his head out to find an empty hall. His boots slapped the stone as he raced down the corridor. At the intersection leading to the gardens, he stopped. Peeking through Agnes's sights, he looked right and left. A motley crew of Lancers pointed their carbines in his direction.

Ben moved his barrel to the ceiling. "It's me, boys."

"Cap'n Ben." Acting Lance Duffadar Bhagat, his uniform coat unbuttoned, gave him a half-salute as he jogged toward the garden exit.

Ben and four Lancers took positions on the path outside the doors. In less than a minute, the rest of the 13th Bengal Lancers had formed up on the garden path. The gas-lit torches cast a murky glow over the garden.

Jeevan positioned himself on the left of the two ranks—one of eight and one of seven. Ben took the rightmost spot while two Lancers monitored their rear.

Jeevan bellowed, "Follow Captain Ben! At the ready and on the double!"

They jogged forward together. Ben angled them to the right toward the rectangular building north of the pyramid and at the center of the palace complex. Ben zigged and zagged them around hedges, flowerbeds, and short walls but kept the formation headed in the same general direction.

As they moved around a stand of tall, thin cypress trees, Ben saw the Remulans before anyone else did.

"Halt," he hissed. "Remulans."

Fifty paces ahead, several archers and a group of legionaries were trotting out from behind a tall hedge toward the building. Ben knew Jeevan couldn't see the Remulans, and they wouldn't have enough time if the enemy charged, so he called out the order. "Second rank, fire on the infantry as soon as you are clear. First rank, kill the archers. Double time to me and fire at will."

With Agnes ready, Ben jogged out from the trees into the clearing. He stopped when he knew the Lancers had enough room. He located his first target.

Several Remulans yelled a warning, and the disorganized legionaries charged toward them or stopped and aimed their bows.

Ben pulled the trigger with his sights on a man drawing back on his bow. Ben stepped forward, cocking his rifle, and located another threat. Rifles popped off as each Lancer had a clear view of his target. An arrow whistled past Ben's head, and a loud cry rang out to his left.

By Ben's third shot, the rate of gunfire had picked up. A unified Latin war cry carried over the blasts from the rifles as he scanned for more archers. Unable to find any, he focused on the infantry charging across the well-manicured lawn. More legionaries appeared from behind the hedge and joined the charge.

Like a clarion call, Jeevan's voice broke through the din. "Together, lads! Rank one, fire!"

Five or six rifles let loose in unison. The middle four legionaries crumpled to the ground.

"Fire!"

Ben added his shot to the subsequent reports, and six more enemy soldiers fell. He stepped forward as he cocked.

"Fire!" The Lancers' carbines barked. The last ten screaming, sword-wielding soldiers were ten yards out.

"Fire!" Like antelope shot at full speed, seven legionaries tumbled. Momentum carried their lifeless bodies cartwheeling over their shields.

Ben cocked and blasted another from the side. The dead soldier came to rest at the feet of a Lancer. One Remulan sliced down with his gladius, attempting to remove a sowar's head. The soldier used his carbine to turn aside the strike. With practiced calm, another Lancer shot the Remulan in the head.

One last legionary attempted to bull-rush Lance Duffadar Ram. The Kalari master stepped forward, past the thrust of the man's gladius, and stuck the butt of his carbine into the dirt below the man's rectangular shield. Rolling with the legionary's momentum, Ram used his rifle like a fulcrum and pancake-griddle-lifted the startled soldier above his head. With a flourish, Ram slapped the legionary to the ground. Two more Lancers finished the stunned man.

Several Remulans ran from behind the passageway created by two tall hedges. The Lancers gunned them down in short order.

"Forward!" Their rifles ready, the Lancers moved in loose ranks. Ben found Sowar Chib on the ground, clutching at the green-feathered shaft in his leg.

Ben stepped over to the wounded man. "How bad?"

The Lancer grinned through a grimace. "I've had worse."

A fusillade of rifle fire exploded behind Ben. The Lancers aimed down the opening in the hedges. Ben focused on the injured man and the rear guards. "Singh, take Chib back to my room. Khepri's there."

"Yes, sir!"

With a jerk of his head, Ben caught the attention of the other Lancer. "Let's go."

They followed the reports of the Lancers' carbines and the trail of dead Remulans into and through the maze of fifteen-foot-tall hedgerows. The pace of each volley increased as the two hurried around another turn into a middle garden with a fountain. Dozens of dead legionaries littered the grass outside a pool surrounding four water-spouting statues.

Two green-cloaked soldiers burst from an opening in a broken statue that was the fountain's centerpiece. The two fell before taking three sloshing steps. They added their bodies to the score of dead Remulans in the shallow pool, its waters now red. Several Lancers ran to the retaining wall, kneeled, and aimed at the opening.

For a moment, Ben puzzled over the star-steel pole poking out from the doorway of the tunnel.

Louisa.

Ben found Jeevan. "Thoughts?"

The duffadar's eyes were on fire. "We have them trapped."

"But how do we close the tunnel?" Ben asked.

"Damfino. But I'm not sending the lads in there." Jeevan's eyes widened. "Hey, beautiful."

Ki and her blood-splashed breasts bounced toward them.

The redheaded amazon grinned at her beau. "The prince is coming with what's left of the royal guards."

Ben asked, "That bad?"

Ki shrugged. "Could have been worse." She inched closer to Jeevan. "We got there just in time. General Kinya was about to slaughter the prince's family."

Ben shuddered. "Did you get him?

"He got away." Ki scowled.

"The queen?" Ben asked.

Ki acted as if she didn't know and wasn't interested in learning.

Jeevan saw the Kermans first. "Lancers, stand aside."

Ben stepped back to the hedge as a stream of powerful Kerman heavy foot soldiers carrying shields and spears jogged by. An officer at the front ordered his men into the fountain. They formed a wall of spears around the opening.

Prince Tambal stopped beside Ben and said in Greek, "I cannot thank you enough. We owe your people everything."

Ben filed the prince's words away. Maybe they could use the situation to get some concessions later. His scar tightened as he smiled. "You'll need to thank Louisa. She discovered the plot."

The prince's eyes lit up, and he cracked a wry smile. "Where is she? I would love to thank her."

Ben frowned. "I bet you would. She was wounded." The prince's smile disappeared.

"But she should be okay."

"I'm glad," said the prince.

Ben asked, "How will you take the tunnel back?"

"Don't have to. The tunnels are flooding as we speak. The traitor emptied them without us knowing. That bastard Kinya will pay."

Several desperate Remulans rushed out of the opening. Impaling spears cut their war cries short.

Ben turned away from the slaughter. "Jeevan, we're done here."

This is shit.

Checking his revolver for the umpteenth time, Abu waited. He leaned back against the corner wall and peered over the shoulders of the two Lochem. They and two more Alexandrian soldiers had taken up positions at the intersection of the two hallways. The smaller corridor was the main entrance to their third-story sleeping quarters.

Abu peered down the long central passageway toward one set of stairs. Behind him would be another staircase. The back stairs were past their rooms at the other end of the shorter corridor. Esther and two more Lochem guarded that stairwell.

Irritated at being left behind, Abu let out a loud sigh that sounded more like a whine.

"Apple?" Rrummblinss asked in Greek. He held the half-bitten fruit inches from Abu's nose.

Abu shoved it away. "No."

The stirithy shrugged and took another bite.

"I don't know how you can eat right now."

The stirithy chewed the apple like the fox creature he was. Rrummblinss said between bites, "Trrusst mme, I mmuch prreferr to bbe in the commpany of a womman bbeforre a fight, but when I can't, I drrink, and when I can't, I eat."

Abu shook his head. "Do you ever stop obsessing over women?"

"Nope." Rrummblinss crunched away. "Betterr than acting like an immpatient child waiting to get hiss nammeday gift."

Abu peeked around the corner toward the other stairwell off the main hallway.

"Bessidess, I'mm not jusst a loverr, I'mm alsso a fighterr."

Abu turned back. "Well, I sure hope so, Don Juan Rrummblinss. Here they come."

The Captain of the Troop stepped past Abu and peered around the corner. Abu poked his head out over the stirithy's. A crowd of Remulans barreled down the hall toward them.

One of the Lochem called to his companions guarding the other direction. All four soldiers backed around the corner into the shorter and more narrow hallway. Abu and Rrummblinss scrambled out of the way as the Alexandrians moved into what Abu now knew to be their yoke positions.

The two holding swords touched shields in the center of the hallway. Two spearmen were a little behind and to the side of their partners. The Spears' shields connected at an angle with the Sword half of their Yokes. One held his spear in his left hand while the other used his right. After watching them drill, Abu knew each warrior to be proficient with either hand.

Abu hadn't counted how many legionaries were coming—more than five and less than ten. A sword left its sheath with a hiss. Rrummblinss winked at him and took another bite.

Two Remulans turned the corner, and a Lochem spear on the left snaked out, catching a legionary in his exposed sword arm. As the soldier screamed in agony, blood squirted up, arching over the combatants. The Remulan on the right blocked a spear thrust and bashed his rectangular shield into the Lochem's oval one. As the wounded man stumbled backward, several more legionaries came around the corner. They collided with the waiting Alexandrians.

Shocked by the closeup brutality, Abu took two steps back and shivered.

Get a grip. These Italian bastards are just like the thugs in Aleppo.

Abu clenched his jaws as he tried to find a shot. The Lochem's formation had an advantage in blocking the corridor with four, while the legionaries could only get three into the passage. The Spears in the Yokes inflicted several wounds. Despite this, the Remulans remained disciplined. When one legionary was wounded, another filled the space with practiced precision. If they fell, their comrades stepped on or over them to take their place in the fight.

The Remulans disengaged, taking a collective step back, and three javelins flew over their heads from the main corridor. Rrummblinss pushed Abu forward. One four-foot dart landed where he had been standing a second earlier. Another shiver shot through the teenager, but a bolt of energy came with it.

No one was injured, but one javelin had done its job. It embedded into the shield of the Sword half of the Yoke, making the protection useless. The man stepped back, and his partner moved into the gap. The Remulans were ready. They rushed forward, bashing into the Lochem as they made the exchange.

At that instant, an opening appeared in front of Abu.

God's able, and I'm willing.

Abu squeezed his trigger, and the head of the man before him snapped back. The Remulan fell into the man behind him. Abu pointed the barrel at the next man's center mass and pulled the trigger again. Folding in on himself, the legionary toppled forward. With the next enemy soldier in line, Abu started to squeeze his finger, but a blur of blond fur shot into the gap.

Apple in one hand, and a slender two-and-a-half-foot length of pointed star steel in the other, Rrummblinss hopped next to the fallen man. As graceful as Abu imagined D'Artagnan to be, the stirithy lunged. The point of his sword disappeared behind another legionary's shield. Never slowing, Rrummblinss spun and parried the blow coming from the next Remulan over. The first man yelled and stumbled to one knee.

Rrummblinss tossed his apple at his second target's face and riposted. The low lunge brought the point of his rapier below the man's shield and through the Remulan's sandaled foot. With lightning-quick hands, the stirithy pulled back and stabbed the kneeling legionary through the throat. The soldier with the foot wound hopped on his one good leg, screaming.

Crazy-ass fox.

Another Remulan shoved the legionary with the fatal neck wound to the side and let out a savage yell. He thrust toward Rrummblinss, who skipped out of the gladius's reach. Abu raised his revolver, and his bullet took the man in the chest. Rrummblinss laughed and retreated between the legs of two Lochem, who closed the wall. More Remulans stepped over their dead and dying comrades.

"Push!" screamed one of the Lochem in Greek.

The four moved as one, shields bashing and spears flashing into the less organized Remulans. The man with the injured foot took an Alexandrian sword to the side. Another Remulan caught a spear in the eye. Together, the Lochem shoved the Remulan force out of the corridor and around the corner.

From the opposite side of the intersection, a javelin plunged into the side of a spear-wielding Lochem. The legionary tried to free the weapon, but it had bent while penetrating his breastplate. The dying Lochem shrieked in agony as the point twisted.

Rrummblinss ran and, using the bent javelin's shaft for added support, jumped toward the Remulan killer who still grasped the javelin. From high above the legionary's shield, Rrummblinss's sword slammed through the man's head. The shiny point emerged from the back of the soldier's helmet. The stirithy yanked his sword free and landed next to the fallen legionary.

Abu stepped behind his friend and scanned the empty hallway as the dead man's body bounced off the marble flooring at Rrummblinss's feet. Abu refocused on the melee behind him and saw another Lochem thrust his khopesh into the throat of a wounded Remulan lying on the ground. The savagery made Abu turn away.

Ali must have been monitoring the fight because he kneeled beside the wounded Alexandrian. Abu said a prayer asking Allah to help the professor heal the man.

I'm supposed to be doing something.

But what it was escaped him as he stared at the carnage all around.

Reload! Every chance you get, reload.

The reek of urine and emptied bowels made bile rise in Abu's throat. The teenager backed toward his room, trying to escape the stench. On his way, he concentrated on reloading the gun to block out the memory of the blood and gore. His hands trembled so much, he couldn't get the first bullet into the reloading chamber of his Pocket Army.

Like a cool breeze on a sweltering day, the scent of lemons and lavender rolled over him, and loving arms brought him into a hug. Abu dropped his arms to his sides, still holding a bullet in one hand and a gun in the other. Miss Louisa gave him a sad smile as she put his head on her shoulder. With a tear falling down his cheek, Abu closed his eyes and listened to the sweet soft French lullaby as two small hands took hold of his.

Ben's energy levels were falling fast. The rush brought on by a battle always came with an inevitable crash. A few minutes earlier, he had never felt so alive. Having spent four years at war, he knew the dangers that came with his intense feelings of euphoria.

He remembered his first wound. By the second week of convalescence, he'd become antsy to the point that his doctors threatened to strap him to his bed. He didn't understand what was wrong with himself until a nurse called him a battle addict. She said she saw it all the time, men who lived for the rush. The nurse also said he would never make it home if he didn't learn to rein it in.

When Ben returned to the regiment, he observed the ones who couldn't turn it off. Like berserkers of old, they would throw themselves into the worst of the fighting. One good man after another threw his life away. Their need to reach new fear-driven heights outweighed their instincts for self-preservation. It made Ben seek ways to control his demons.

He had journaled after every dangerous situation for the rest of the war. He hated that fate had brought him full circle. He couldn't afford self-pity and didn't dare sleep. Not until he'd written down everything going on in his head. It didn't stop the urge, but the process utilized his intellect, which had always been his best weapon. With this technique, he learned to restrain, harness, and let loose the beast within when necessary.

Ben organized his thoughts for the coming journaling while he followed the Lancers back to their quarters through the dark gardens. Not until they came upon the first dead servant in the building did he worry about Abu and Louisa. As they dodged more and more bodies, his worry built, and his fatigue dissipated.

His heart racing, Ben jogged forward and bounded up the giant moving staircase. From the landing, he saw bodies piled around the intersection leading to their rooms. He panicked until he saw a Lochem soldier wave.

Ben waved back but ran past the man and headed to his room. As he rounded the corner, he almost ran into a kneeling Khepri. She was placing a shield on the chest of a dead Alexandrian soldier.

Ben skipped to the side to avoid her and regretted that he had never learned the man's name. Rrummblinss raised his hand as Ben brushed past the golden fox and raced into his room.

Louisa was leaning on a big-cushioned lounge chair with her legs pulled up. Her face was pale, but she managed an exhausted smile. Masako sat with Abu in an adjacent chair. She rubbed the teen's back as he leaned forward, elbows on knees, his head hung low.

"You okay?" Ben asked.

"We're good." A pained expression came across Abu's face. "Except for Leto."

Ben turned to Louisa, his eyes seeking validation.

With a weak nod, Louisa said, "We're fine." She mouthed a silent, "It was bad."

His son's hollowed look reminded Ben of many shell-shocked soldiers, but he gave a relieved sigh. "We stopped them. The tunnel's closed."

Then his fear and worry turned to anger. He squatted down to Louisa's eye level and put both hands on the armrest. "What the hell were you thinking?"

Louisa closed her eyes. When she opened them, she whispered, "Sorry." She reached for his hand and gave him a weak smile and a weaker squeeze.

The memory of Louisa's limp, bloody body and the thought of losing her silenced Ben. His chest tightened, and he choked back a sob. Rubbing the top of her hand with his thumb, he brought his other hand to her cheek and neck. She nuzzled into his caress.

He stared into her brown eyes, delving into her soul, as his voice cracked. "We can't lose you." A tear dropped to his cheek. "I can't lose you."

Louisa gave a slight nod and closed her eyes. The weight of her head increased on his hand, and her breathing turned into soft, ragged snoring.

Chapter 32

It had been two days since the Remulan attack, and Masako had just started to feel safe. As she entered the dining room for breakfast, she found a small crowd waiting for her. A chill ran down her spine at the serious faces of Abu, Miss Louisa, and Dr. Ben. The massive dwarf was the only one who smiled at her.

Did I do something wrong?

Dr. Ben motioned for her to sit beside Abu and across from the other three.

"Masako, may we see your coin?" Abu asked.

With a raised eyebrow, Masako pulled the coin from her pocket and said with a trembling voice, "Why?"

"We found your family." Abu wore a tight-lipped grin.

Fear and hope swirled in the pit of her stomach. Abu, Dr. Ben, and Miss Louisa were the closest thing to family she'd had since her caregiver had died. The thought of losing them conflicted with her dream of having a proper home—a place where she belonged.

At a loss for words, Masako handed the coin to Abu. He passed it to the dwarf and said, "Thoresten will explain."

The coin looked tiny in the dwarf's meaty hands. He extended his open palm over the table toward her and said in Nipponese, "Only members of the shogun's family may carry this coin. Your mother was Hojo Yoshitoki, the third daughter of the shogun. Your father was Prince Dorieus ben Leonidas i Draco, the second son of the king of Alexandria."

Masako stared at her hands and rubbed them together with nervous energy. She blinked for several seconds, trying to comprehend what she had just been told.

Thoresten slammed the coin on the table. Masako looked at the dwarf.

"That's right. You are a princess of both nations."

"A . . . ," Masako's voice trailed off. Then she asked in English, "What is the word for ohimesama?"

"Princess," Miss Louisa said, her face still pale from losing so much blood two nights ago.

Abu put his arm around Masako and hugged her. "That's right. And your father's uncle was at our meeting with the queen. I spoke with him yesterday. He would like to meet you."

Not understanding most of what he said, Masako scrunched up her face. Abu repeated what he had said in Greek to Thoresten and finished with, "Please translate."

As the dwarf explained in Nipponese, Masako stared into Abu's eyes and chewed her lower lip.

This can't be real. What will happen to me?

Voice trembling, Masako asked, "When?"

Abu squeezed her arm. "Today. If all goes well, you will stay at the Alexandrian Embassy until they take you to your grandfather, the king."

Masako whispered, "I don't know." Tears threatened to flow as she thought about starting over again. Being alone with strangers, even if they were family, was frightening.

Stop it. This is what I wanted. I'm not a baby.

In a halting manner, Abu searched for words they shared as he said in a mix of Greek, Nipponese, and English, "It's for the best. If you stay with us, you will always be in danger." His three dimples flashed at her as he smiled. "Princess. You will have the best of everything." He ruffled the hair under her tiara. "Deep down, you always knew."

I don't care.

Masako turned to him and wrapped her arms around his waist. She buried her head in his chest, never wanting to let go, and cried.

"You look like your mother," said Ambassador Archimedes ben Solan i Draco in Nipponese. He put his hands on Masako's upper arms as he kneeled in front of her. The man's long face, gray hair, and brown eyes under bushy gray eyebrows reminded her of Bahram, the slave who had died helping her escape the welven assassins.

The ambassador's eyes became unfocused, and his voice cracked. "I wish Cora, my sweet wife, was still alive to meet you. She so adored your father. At least, she got to see your parents get married." He blinked, and a tear rolled down the side of his face.

The stranger's emotion tugged at Masako's heart, taking her by surprise. Not sure why, she placed her hand on his cheek and wiped away the tear. In Nipponese, she said, "Don't cry, mister."

The ambassador's sad eyes sparkled as he chuckled. "Uncle." He laughed harder and shook his head. "Grand Uncle is more precise, but you may call me Uncle, and I will call you Princess Masako. Is this okay with you?"

She nodded.

"Good. At dinner tonight, I will tell you all about your parents. Would you like that?"

With no memory of her parents, Masako had only the stories her caregiver had shared. They were her greatest treasures, and she couldn't wait to add more. "I would like that very much." She bowed her head. "Thank you, Uncle."

He patted her arms and stood. "Very good." To the assistant female babiakhom behind him, her uncle said in Greek, "Please translate." He then looked at the group standing behind her.

Miss Louisa and Abu had helped her pack that morning. Dr. Ben had joined them as they rode in a wagon to the Alexandrian embassy.

Masako's uncle spoke in Greek, but she heard his words in the welven tongue of Eblan. "It will take some time, but I will ensure the princess gets back safely to Neos Hierosolyma."

The words of the evil white elves echoed into Masako's ears, and she ground her teeth. She promised to learn Greek and Nipponese so well that one of the languages would become her native tongue.

Ben replied, "How will you accomplish that with the siege?"

Her uncle smiled as if he had a secret. "Princess Masako is not only an Alexandrian princess. The Yuhi ambassador has diplomatic immunity with the Remulans. Once a week, our enemy allows diplomats they are not at war with to come and go. Once she is out, I will have someone take her to Neos Hieroslyma."

"Will the Nipponese ambassador cooperate?" Ben asked.

Her uncle nodded. "I believe so. I know him pretty well, and he will want to keep the princess safe."

Miss Louisa said, "Make sure she gets out before the actual battle begins, and please let us know when you arrange the trip so we may say a proper goodbye."

The sweet smell of lemons and lavender gave Masako a sense of calm when Miss Louisa stepped close behind her. Masako turned toward her smiling mentor, who said, "Until you leave, we will visit you often."

Miss Louisa reached above her head and pulled a long pin from her white felt hat with the pink ribbon hatband. She bent to place the pin, topped by a small pearl, in Masako's palm. She curled Masako's fingers around it and cradled Masako's fist in her hands. "If you ever need help, send me a message that mentions this pin. Understand?"

"Yes, ma'am."

Concern filled Miss Louisa's eyes. "What is your job?"

Masako told herself to be confident like Miss Louisa and raised her chin. "To learn and to take advantage of opportunities I'm given."

"Right. Well." Miss Louisa let go of Masako's closed hand. She cleared her throat as she stood and stepped aside. "I will see you soon."

Abu took her place and painted his best attempt at a cheerful smile on his tear-streaked face.

Chapter 33

Kerma City, Chor, An 5660, Day 32

"Queen Nabra, it is always a pleasure," Ben said with a slight bow.

The queen had sunken eyes, and her ceaseless frown twitched at the corners. A wind singer translated as she spoke. "I'm sorry it has taken three days to meet with you. I wanted to thank you personally. The people of Kerma owe you an immeasurable debt." She looked at each of them and stopped at Louisa. "We owe you not only for my life, but for the lives of my son and my grandchildren. I promise to repay you when the threat to our nation is over. I'll start by returning the magic tool I believe you used to help delay the attack."

Louisa took the silver pole, still shaped like a staff with two grappling hooks on the ends. With a smile and a bow of her head, Louisa said, "You're welcome, Your Majesty, and thank you." She raised the pole off the ground. "Khepri and I were at the right place at the right time."

Queen Nabra sighed. "Someday, I wish to hear exactly how you came to be in that place at the right time. Your soldiers' ability to repel the assault emphasizes our need to redouble our efforts to arm our soldiers with your weapons."

"We are prepared to turn our full attention to that task." Ben gestured between Jeevan and himself. "I have one question about the attack. What happened to the general?"

The queen's frown deepened, and sadness filled her eyes. "His family escaped, and we assume he did as well. At the beginning of the night, he smuggled his wives and children out through one of the main gates disguised as part of a diplomatic caravan. How he escaped, we are not sure. For all we know, he might have perished when we flooded the tunnel. Why do you ask?"

"I wanted to know whether we have anything to fear from him. I suspect he harbors resentment for our part in stopping him. He might still have people loyal to him inside the city."

The queen nodded. "I'm sure you are correct on both counts. He is a very stubborn man, but he is also a brilliant strategist and never rash. I believe he will leave you alone." Her eyes grew distant. "I fear the Remulan emperor will give him command of his forces. That would make his loss a double blow to Kerma. Again, thank you, and please hurry with the training. The fate of Kerma rests on your collective shoulders."

"We will do our best," Ben said.

Ben, Jeevan, and Louisa turned toward the exit leading to the incredible floating elevator. Ben stopped as Louisa peeled away and approached a legless counter in the corner of the room. Some of the table's glass material was missing in the middle and had been patched with a bronze material. On it rested a large crystal vase filled with enormous red flowers. She leaned forward to smell them. "Lovely."

Turning back to the queen, Louisa asked, "Your Majesty, are there other tables like this in the palace?"

Queen Nabra tilted her head. "Yes, there are a few. Why do you ask?"

Louisa shrugged. "Oh, no reason. I noticed that it had been damaged and then repaired by a metal singer. This is the third facility created by the Ancients that I've been inside. I've never seen their work damaged before."

"You have a good eye. We have occupied this city for thousands of An, and now that you mention it, every table like that has similar damage."

Louisa smiled and lowered her head. "We won't keep you."

Ben stared at Louisa as she turned toward the door. He said nothing until they were floating back toward the pyramid's base. "What was that about?"

With a sideways glance in Ben's direction, Louisa gave a dismissive wave of her hand. "Nothing. I just thought it was odd."

The small hairs on his neck stood erect.

She's up to something, Ben thought as he replied, "Humph."

Chapter 34

"Goodbye, Uncle," whispered Masako as the wagon moved away from the Alexandrian Embassy. Hours before sunrise, her uncle's flame-lit shadow soon winked out of existence. That she hadn't yet cried was a point of pride for Masako, and she swore she would not cry in front of the thin, stern Yuhi ambassador.

The last six khonsu had been the best twelve days of Masako's life. Her uncle showered her with love. He doted on her daily, sharing stories about her parents and her Alexandrian ancestors while he helped her improve her Greek. Every other day, Abu or Miss Louisa, and sometimes both, visited her. Too fast, the days flew by.

When the time came to leave, Masako begged to stay, but her uncle insisted she flee before the Remulans took the city. After saying goodbye to Dr. Ben, Miss Louisa, and Abu, she spent one last evening with her uncle. Masako knew she would never see him again, and her heart broke.

Her uncle's plan was simple. The Yuhi ambassador would sneak Masako out of the city using his diplomatic immunity with the Remulans. When they reached the first river port, she would be transferred to the care of some Alexandrians who worked for her grandfather, the king. They would take her to Alexandria.

Masako saw the Yuhi ambassador walking a few yards in front of her wagon's team of horses. The man's clothes—a simple gray kimono—matched his drab disposition. When her uncle had introduced him, the Yuhi ambassador had welcomed her in a scratchy voice with five short words: "I will take you home." He had not spoken to her since.

Masako wrinkled her nose. *He's not nice.*

By the time they approached the main gates, An's light had brushed the sky with pink, cranberry, and orange. They took a narrow tunnel off to the side of the road and the city's main gates to exit the city. The tunnel was lit with small sconces that cast creepy shadows. Masako's skin crawled with each clip-clop of the horses' hooves. At the end of the passage, they reached a series of grates and doors.

When the last door swung open, Masako's stomach lurched. Lined up in several long rows were Remulan soldiers standing at attention on either side of the road. With green cloaks tied around their necks, each grim-faced man wore a helmet and held a large, rectangular shield painted the same shade of green. The soldiers varied in age, but all the older men had an intense stare that screamed danger. The Remulans' commander stood next to another soldier who held a long pole with a large all-white flag.

As Masako's wagon merged back onto the eons-old highway, the lines of soldiers lifted their shields and turned as one to march beside them. The bumpy ride smoothed as the wagon rolled onto the road's short grass with its slight spongy give.

The Yuhi ambassador took long strides to reach the Remulan commander. Masako couldn't understand anything, but the man from Yuhi became animated as he spoke. The soldier wearing the helmet with the sideways feathered plume said something in return. The ambassador began shouting at the commander.

Spittle shot from the ambassador's mouth, and his face turned dark red the more he yelled.

The Remulan commander marched onward, enduring the tantrum with stoic dismissal. After several minutes, the Yuhi ambassador had shouted himself hoarse. His face flushed, he stomped back to the wagon. He fell in beside the wheel on Masako's side and, without looking at her, said in Nipponese, "Do not speak. You are a lowly servant girl." He kicked at a pebble that had fallen on the pristine grass highway. "Understand?"

Scared, Masako bowed her head as she stared at the ears of the horse in front of her. Her uncle had made sure she looked the part and dressed her in a cotton dress with a simple rope tie. All her belongings were in a little bag at her feet, except for the knife she had tucked inside a pocket.

"Your life depends on it," the Yuhi ambassador hissed. He returned to his original position in the small column.

Masako rode in silence, her stomach twisting into a tangle. She wanted to lean over the side and get rid of the now-sour breakfast. Everyone in the small column walked between the dirt walls of two large forts before turning off the smooth highway. The legionaries escorted them through wooden gates into another giant earthen fortress.

A loud murmur was heard among the countless soldiers busy inside the fort. Rows and rows of tents, laid out in straight lines, filled much of the space. Large open lanes crisscrossed the field of canvas. Masako's column walked straight up the center avenue toward a massive tent in the middle of the fort.

The wagon stopped in front of the tent. Another conversation took place between the commander of the soldiers and the now sullen ambassador. The Yuhi ambassador nodded and turned to his group. "Everyone inside." He put his hand on the elbow of one of his bodyguards and shook his head. "Not you."

"Hurry. Get down," the wagon driver demanded in Nipponese.

Masako scrambled to the ground. She tried to hide behind the driver as he and the other servants followed the Yuhi ambassador into the tent. The scent of jasmine tickled her nose as she stepped between two gold-cloaked soldiers. Rich tapestries hung on the sides of the tent, and plush rugs hid all traces of the earth beneath.

Soldiers, slaves, and servants moved all about the space, but nothing held Masako's attention except the man wearing a purple toga and sitting on a tall folding chair in the middle of the tent. An aura of pre-eminence radiated from him. He waved the Yuhi ambassador forward. The legionary soldier in the shiny, filigreed armor standing beside the emperor's chair seemed familiar to Masako.

General Kinya.

With a green-plumed helmet under his arm, the traitorous general had a sour face as he tapped his toe in agitation.

The once-arrogant Yuhi ambassador bowed at the waist and shuffled with slumped shoulders toward the sitting man. As Masako focused on the scene in front of her, a soft, age-spotted hand grabbed her elbow and dragged her forward. Startled, she stared at the silver-haired man wearing a long teal tunic.

Why do they want me?

While Masako stood beside the Yuhi ambassador, the older man wearing teal pushed her to her knees and hissed, "Kneel before the emperor." She heard his words translated into Eblan while echoing in the language of the Remulans.

The Yuhi ambassador crossed his arms and didn't look at Masako. "Emperor Octavius, what is the meaning of this?"

The emperor ignored the Yuhi ambassador and frowned at the old man holding her. "Aquila, be gentle."

The Remulan emperor smiled and turned toward her. "Princess Masako, it is a pleasure to meet you." His smile twisted into a sneer when he looked at the Yuhi ambassador. "Did you think I would not have spies within all the embassies?"

"Your Majesty, I—" The ambassador choked back his next word as the emperor raised his hand.

The emperor peered down at Masako again. "Did this man tell you he was actually taking you to Yuhi instead of Alexandria? I think not."

What? Masako's eyes widened at the Yuhi ambassador, who frowned and moved his head from side to side.

The ambassador straightened his shoulders. "Your Majesty, you do not wish to make an enemy of Yuhi."

The emperor chuckled. "You are just concerned about your own skin." He leaned back in the chair and brought his fingertips together. "The shogun will have your head for losing his precious granddaughter." He bounced his bridged fingers back and forth. "But there may be hope for you yet."

The ambassador's raspy voice trembled. "What do you want?"

"The princess's friends, the Earthlings, have become a festering wound that I would excise." The emperor leaned forward. "Bring your famous Yuhi assassins to kill the soldiers from Earth and capture their leaders."

"No!" Masako shouted and tried to jump to her feet, but Aquila shoved her back down. *Abu, Miss Louisa.*

Her fear turned to anger, and Masako's face flushed red. Miss Louisa's voice echoed in her mind: *Think before you move.*

Even if it cost her life, she had to do something. *The pin.*

Masako scratched her head and surreptitiously removed the hairpin with the pearl. She glared at the emperor and shouted a Nipponese insult. For good measure, she added another one she'd heard Abu call Umrao but did not understand: "Kutabare wanker!"

From his seat in the center of the room, the emperor turned his gaze on Masako. "Have them kill all the Earthlings if they cannot capture the leaders."

Masako visualized each step as he spoke and then kicked out her leg. She spun around, twisting in the older man's grasp, and whipped his leg out from under him with another kick.

Aquila let go of her as he fell. "Ahh."

Masako hopped off the ground and rushed to the Yuhi ambassador, who drew back. She grabbed his wrist and pulled herself close.

Wide-eyed, the ambassador said, "What are you doing?"

"Take a message to my uncle," Masako hissed and thrust the pin into his hand.

The ambassador closed his hand on the pin and gave her a slow blink, but he shook his head. "No."

"You little brat!" Anger laced his voice as Aquila pulled himself up on one knee and reached for her.

As she turned toward his voice, Masako found the handle of her small knife in her pocket. She freed the blade from its sheath as her mind raced through the next steps.

She darted around the old man's grasp and ran toward the emperor. General Kinya stepped forward and blocked her path before she could lunge.

General Kinya chopped his hand across her wrist, and Masako's arm went numb. The knife fell to the carpet. The general used his other hand to spin her shoulder, then wrapped his arm around her waist, pinning her arms at her side.

"Let me go!" Masako squirmed and bent her head, trying to reach his forearm with her teeth.

Still lounging in his chair, the emperor ordered his bodyguards back as if nothing had happened. "Very good, Princess." His body shook as he laughed.

"I hate you," Masako growled.

The shaking stopped, and the emperor said, "Bring me the Earthlings' leaders, and I might give you the princess."

"It will take some time to summon the shinobi," answered the Yuhi ambassador.

With a wave, the emperor said, "If I take the city before you bring me what I want, you will be out of luck, so stop wasting time."

Masako stared at the Yuhi ambassador, trying to search his face for a hint of confirmation. She caught a slight nod of his chin as he bowed.

Whoever you are. Thank you. It was the best prayer that Masako could give.

The ambassador turned and ushered the rest of his followers out of the tent.

General Kinya shoved Masako and sent her stumbling. She fell to the blue carpet, burning her knees. He picked up the knife and helped the old man to a chair before he returned to his place next to the emperor. As Masako came to her feet, strong, calloused hands took hold of her arms and pulled her to a standstill. The garlic smell of the legionary's breath made Masako blink.

"Now, Princess. It's time for you to tell me everything you know about these Earthlings." The emperor straightened his toga.

Masako was so angry, she thought she would explode. "No," she hissed.

With a sigh, the emperor gestured to someone behind her. "You will."

A shadow fell over Masako as a giant presence stepped next to her. She looked up and to the right at a furred arm and a snarling hysakas.

"This is Shemush." The emperor chuckled. "You will never forget his name."

Chapter 35

Kerma City, Taru, An 5660, Day 45

More tasks than time, Ben thought as he reread the letter's contents.

The day after meeting with the queen, they left the palace and moved into their new quarters. Because the need for a rifle range limited their options, General Maa, the new general in charge of the Kerman army, didn't have an existing military barracks for them to use for training.

After much discussion, General Maa commandeered a small college. Located in the corner of the city next to the outer wall and the cliff leading to the plateau above, the facility had several open spaces. They set up their targets in a lush park next to the stone escarpment at the rear of the campus. On the plus side, the campus was close enough to the falls that there was a low, never-ending rumble to muffle the crack of the rifles at practice. On the negative side of the ledger, the noise guaranteed the campus was never quiet, even in the middle of the night.

Converted classrooms became barracks for the two thousand archers being trained as riflemen. Ben's group took over the faculty quarters. To meet their needs, Kerman army cooks and quartermasters supplemented the college kitchen and cleaning staff. Still, they needed more.

Outside Ben's window, the constant staccato shots of dozens of Henri-Martini carbines and the pops of Enfield revolvers had become commonplace. The

Lancers had their recruits up an hour before dawn each day and drilling at first light. The noise subsided an hour after sunset only when the British soldiers put the recruits to bed, exhausted.

After signing his name and rank, Ben rolled up a letter into a travel tube.In the letter, he requested that General Maa add eight life-singer medics to the regiment. The letter, written in Ben's best Greek, was one of many such scrolls on his over-size desk. When he'd first moved into the headmaster's rooms, Ben had marveled at the incredible life-sung workmanship of the desk in the well-appointed office. Yet such frivolous thoughts were a luxury he could no longer afford.

Reports about the siege pointed to time running out. The Remulans had focused all their artillery on a section of the city wall close to the main gates. It was a matter of weeks, if not days, before the Remulans breached the defenses. Even with a platoon of stirithy metal singers repairing the masonry, the constant barrage of giant boulders had the wall on the verge of collapse.

Ben picked up the latest missive from Rrummblinss. His stirithy metal singers, working with Kerman life singers, would deliver the final five hundred carbines by the end of the week.

Thank God, we have all the revolvers.

With only a few weeks of training, the men needed every hour of preparation. The new rifles would help speed up drills and target practice.

At the top of the hour, a bell rang out above the din of the guns.

Time to go.

Ben scooped up all his completed letters and rushed out the door. He dropped the tubes with his Kerman secretary. The man had been a professor at the college and volunteered to help until they could resume teaching.

Scheduled to meet with Jeevan, Ben picked up his pace. Together, they would tour the area behind the damaged section of the city wall and lay out their strategy for when the inevitable happened. Ben pondered his adopted son's actions. Since Masako had left, Abu had not been himself.

Louisa might know how to bring him out of the doldrums.

The thought of Louisa brought mixed emotions. Ben's heart rate jumped, but he again suspected the beautiful young woman was keeping secrets. Even as busy as he was, he sensed she was avoiding him.

But why?

The answer kept eluding Ben because whenever he ran into her, he usually had so much on his mind that he forgot to ask her.

After waiting five minutes outside the Languages building, Ben flagged down a passing Lancer. "Sowar, have you seen the duffadar?"

The man stopped in his tracks. "No, sir. He wasn't at muster this morning."

"Did anyone check on him?"

"I believe Lance Duffadar Ram went to find him."

Ben nodded. "Thanks."

He marched toward the small cottage that Jeevan and Khepri had claimed. About to knock on the door, he noticed Thoresten sitting cross-legged on the ground under a nearby tree. The dwarf's armor lay on the grass beside him while his short sword leaned against the same tree. Buried in the trunk above his head were two hand axes. Thoresten appeared to be asleep.

Ben stopped short when the dwarf's eyes popped open.

The broad-faced man was grim. "Jeevan's busy," he said in Greek.

Ben's voice grew stern. "We have too much to do for him to be *busy*."

As Ben turned away, Thoresten said, "Ki left him."

Ben froze and turned back to the dwarf. "When?"

"Last night."

"Why?"

Thoresten's voice had a melancholy tone. "The poor fool fell in love."

"I'll check on him."

"Just did. It's not pretty."

Ben ignored the Norse Samurai and strode to the cottage. He opened the door without knocking. Sobbing came from inside.

As Ben turned the corner of a small bar, he spied two legs ending in woolen socks spread out on the floor. Jeevan sat with his back against the cabinets under the sink. Tears streamed from his disconsolate, bloodshot eyes. The duffadar reached for a mug lying sideways on the floor. Its contents flowed down the mortar grooves of the cobblestone.

Good Lord, Ben thought.

Jeevan tilted the wooden cup back upright, and he chuckled. He brought the mug to his lips, tilted his head back, and slapped the bottom. He slurped the last drops before letting the cup fall back onto his lap.

A silly grin that never reached the heartbroken eyes flashed Ben's way. "Cap Ben. I'm sso gla' you're." Jeevan belched and laughed. "Glad you're here. Wanna drink? I wanna drink."

Ben shook his head. "You've had enough."

Jeevan slurred, "Nnoo! Sshhee's had enuf o' me." He swayed back and forth. "Ssoo haf a . . . a taste wif me."

Resigned to help his buddy forget his problems for a day, Ben found another mug in a half-opened cabinet. A fancy, blue-glass bottle fashioned by a stirithy's songs sat on the counter half empty.

Or half full.

A sniff of the bottle brought tears to Ben's eyes. The strong alcohol reminded him of bourbon. He poured himself four fingers of the amber liquid and reached for the handle of the mug Jeevan held high.

As Ben poured three fingers for the plastered duffadar, Thoresten rumbled, "I'll take one if you're pouring."

The dwarf filled all the spare space in the small kitchen.

"Sure. Help me get him to the table." Ben bent to grab Jeevan.

The stoic dwarf nodded and leaned over to help. He pulled the wobbly Lancer to a chair at the table. With one hand on Jeevan's shoulder, the dwarf used it to keep the drunk upright. Ben placed three mugs and the bottle in the center of the table. He sat on the other side of the duffadar, who stared at nothing with a dazed expression. Ben shoved a mug into Jeevan's hand, and the Lancer's eyes snapped back to reality.

For several blinks, Jeevan smiled at Ben before turning to Thoresten. A sorrowful cry passed Jeevan's lips. "Why?"

Thoresten slapped Jeevan's back. "Because you told her."

The duffadar wobbled. In slow motion, he refocused on the dwarf, his eyes bleary. "Tol' her what?"

"You love her. You told her you loved her. That's when she runs."

Was I this pathetic? Ben wondered.

Ben had gone on a month-long bender and didn't remember most of that time after he caught Armistead and Nannie together. His only clear memory was waking up in a brothel, half sober. For the first time in decades, he remembered the words that changed the course of his life. "Move, hansome. Me arm's asleep."

Ben laughed. *So that's why I went to London. Amazing. God's words from a prostitute's lips.*

The other two men at the table were so different, yet united in the source of their pain. One reeled from fresh, jagged wounds while the other's healed-over scars throbbed from a chronic ache.

Ben raised his cup and said in Greek. "To God's sense of humor."

Jeevan raised his mug, his voice dripping with sarcasm. "Har! Fuck'in Har!" He threw back the entire contents of his cup and slammed it onto the table.

Thoresten gave a knowing, rueful smile. "To Odin's sense of humor." He took a sip.

Ben took a small swig. The duffadar thrust his chin up once, then again until Ben swallowed all four fingers and slammed his mug on the table next to Jeevan's. "Ahh!"

He poured another round.

Raising his mug, the dwarf shouted, "To a life of loving, fighting, and dying a glorious death!"

Ben mumbled, "Amen." He swallowed the burning liquid in two gulps.

Jeevan shouted the dwarf's Greek back in English, his eyes ablaze. When his cup hit the table, he said, "Morrow, I ready ta kill Remlans."

The pleasant poison seeped into his body, and Ben poured another round before he toasted.

"To killing Remulans!"

Chapter 36

Kerma City, Taru, An 5660, Day 46

"Kill Remulans. Kill Remulans."

Jeevan's slow, raspy whisper reached Ben's ears. He turned a sly grin toward the frowning duffadar, who was rubbing his temple.

His voice just short of a yell, Ben said, "What was that about Remulans? I didn't hear you."

"Ow!" Jeevan threw both hands over his ears. "Karma, Captain Ben. Remember karma."

Ben slapped his friend hard on the back. The duffadar's face went from milk chocolate to cream. He gulped back whatever had threatened to come up.

Ben laughed. "You'll thank me later. I need you to focus on this pain to block out the other. That's why I told Khepri not to cure your hangover."

Jeevan narrowed his eyes.

Ben made to slap his back again, and the duffadar backed up a step. He sucked in several quick breaths until his color turned to coffee with milk. "You made your point. I won't drink another drop. Ever."

Ben's switched to his officer voice. "You won't drink until this situation is over. You cannot dwell on Ki."

Jeevan's bloodshot eyes watered.

Ben ordered, "That is what I'm talking about. Stop crying."

Jeevan turned away from Ben's stare.

"I need you. No, your men need you," Ben demanded.

Jeevan looked back at Ben.

"You need to be the Duffadar Nahal who loves being a soldier and would die for his men." Ben leaned forward and glared at Jeevan. "The little things we do over the next few weeks will determine whether this city lives or dies."

The Lancer wiped his eyes on his sleeve and squared his shoulders to attention.

"Do not let your troubles cause you to miss something that costs us everything." Ben jabbed his finger at the duffadar. "Do you understand me?"

Jeevan took a deep breath and gave a slight nod. His voice stayed quiet but firm. "I understand."

"Good. Now assess the situation." Ben waved his arm toward the seventy-foot-tall wall.

On either side of the at-risk wall section, the Remulans had pulverized the closest bastions. Enemy artillery had the two fortifications so zeroed in that the Remulans struck them two to three times an hour with burning pitch to ensure the Kermans couldn't reclaim them.

A battered walkway at the top of the curtain wall was almost unusable, but most of the Remulans' artillery focused on one long patch between the two bastions. Fifteen feet of the wall had already crumbled under the barrage.

There was a series of covered scaffolds erected under the damaged stone. Some brave, or plain crazy, metal singers were busy trying to strengthen the mortar and add rock back to the wall wherever possible.

A trebuchet-launched boulder struck the merlon on the city side of the wall. Broken stone crashed onto the angled, reinforced roofs built over the scaffolding. The debris skipped and slid down the metal to fall to the ground. The original round rock landed in the large clearing that separated the wall and the city's buildings.

"We need to build shielding like that for the defensive wall and something up top to deflect those stones. I'll work on it." Ben pointed at the scaffolding's protective coverings.

To the Kerman rifleman he'd chosen as an aid, Ben said in Greek, "Corporal, send your best archer up the scaffold to the second platform in the center." He pointed at the wall. "Have him shoot five arrows for us to understand the farthest range of the Remulans in all directions from the wall."

The soldier smiled. "Yes, sir. I am the best." He ordered five more men to clear out the target areas before he jogged away.

"What else, *General* Nahal?"

Jeevan frowned, and his voice took on a sardonic tone. "I wish you hadn't told them duffadar was equal to a major."

Ben chuckled. "It made it easier. That way, your lance duffadars became captains, and your sowars became lieutenants."

Jeevan grimaced and rubbed the back of his neck. "I know. Good call on taking the range from higher up. They will have to crawl over the rubble to get in, and they will set up archers on top of the debris." Ben nodded, and Jeevan continued, "We need to create a killing field in front of the breach. We'll build a semi-circle palisade made of sandbags."

"Why sandbags?"

Jeevan pointed at the ground. "It's the best use for all the dirt. We'll dig two trenches—one at the foot of our wall and another halfway from the city wall. Maybe the two obstacles will force them to bunch up when they try to cross. Also, the sandbags will absorb most of their artillery shot with minimal damage. For the firing wall, we'll cover it with slanted metal roofs, like you mentioned, to protect from archers."

"Good. And?"

The duffadar rubbed his beard. "If I were the Remulan general, I would build some thick wooden walls. Light enough to carry over the rubble, but thick enough to stop a bullet. General Kinya saw our shooting exhibition and will have some idea how thick to make the shields."

"I agree. Maybe they will bring some individual shields covered in star steel. The thinnest layer would probably do it. What's our counter?"

The first arrow flew straight toward them, falling a hundred yards short. It had carried four hundred yards.

Ben followed Jeevan as he walked to within fifty yards of the shaft.

Jeevan said, "It went a lot farther than I'd hoped." The duffadar mimed pointing his rifle before putting his hands down. "At five hundred yards, we are at our effective range." His gaze moved along the curve of his imaginary wall. "The Kermans need to level those buildings." He jutted his chin at the cluster of buildings, first on the left and then on the right.

Ben took his hat off and wiped his forehead with his sleeve. "I'll tell them. Now, how do we counter portable walls?"

Jeevan shrugged. "Fire? Grenades?"

Ben shook his head. "We don't have time to perfect Ketchum's or Adam's designs.

The Lancer raised his finger. "What about the improvised ones used in Crimea?"

"I'm not familiar with those."

Jeevan smiled for the first time since he and Ben had left the campus. "They filled thick bottles with black powder and nails, then added a soaked rag for a fuse. They rolled them into the trenches where they would explode."

"How do we keep the bottles from breaking and the enemy from pulling the fuse out or dowsing it with water?"

"Don't know, but I bet you and Ssherrss will come up with something. By the way, why don't the Remulans' metal singers dig under the wall?"

"I read some histories of Kerma, especially the battles. During the first Lamentations, the ripvor did just that. Reapers devastated the city, and the Kermans were almost wiped out." Ben pointed at the wall and the horizontal slits that ran like two long lines across the surface. "To counter the metal singers' magic, they harnessed the river to build several water-based defenses. Water disrupts singing to some extent. Those slits pour water down the wall, and underground there is a giant trench that becomes a waterfall. When the city is under attack, the water defends against metal singers."

"Interesting. Does it affect other types of singers?" Jeevan asked.

"Wind singers must generate a wind bubble to fly in the rain. It limits how far they can fly or how much they can carry. Also, they can't send messages very far. Life singers must touch the subject. They may heal an individual, but in the rain, they can't train a field of melons."

"Good to know. What about you? Any ideas about our defenses?"

Ben adjusted his hat just right. "We must hold the high ground."

Nodding, Jeevan said, "If the Remulans take the walkway near the breach, they can drop burning oil on our fortifications closest to the wall. Also, we must keep the Kerman artillery on the next-closest bastions active. If not, the Remulans will move their artillery to fire through the hole and wipe out our secondary defensive line." Jeevan closed his eyes and winced in obvious pain. "To do that, we'll have to secure the top of the wall up to the breach, making anyone on top a target for their siege engines."

"You're right. That's why it's important to build some extra protection for the defenders at the top of the wall. That won't fully protect you from fire attacks. But fire attacks would risk their troops as well. I doubt they'll use them."

Pointing his finger at his chest, Jeevan said, "Protect me?"

"When the wall falls, you'll take two companies up the left side of the wall. Have Bhagat take two companies up the right side. Secure the walkway, and rain hell down on the Remulans from above and behind them. That is how we counter the shield-walls."

Jeevan rubbed at his temples. "As if my headache wasn't bad enough."

"Starting today, we'll rotate the regiment. Every day, two companies will come here for twelve-hour shifts." Ben hesitated. Was it a mistake? "They're too raw. We can't station all the men here. They need more training."

Decision made, Ben nodded and continued. "Half the men will build the fortifications to your specifications while the others rest. When the wall falls, those two companies will force the Remulans to bring up their shield-walls, then the Kermans will plug the hole until the regiment arrives." Ben pointed to the broken part of the city wall.

"What about you?"

Ben frowned. "Ram and I will fill the center with A Company, and then four companies will man the sandbag wall, with one company in reserve. The Remulans are sure to keep their artillery attacking those sections of the city wall until they risk hitting their men. You and Bhagat will only take the high ground when the enemy fully commits. It won't keep them from targeting you, but it will make them cautious."

Jeevan nodded. "If you build the metal roof things and create some sort of grenade, then we should be able to turn them back."

Ben smiled. "We'll be ready, and we will win because God is always able, and we are willing."

"To kill Remulans." Jeevan laughed, then groaned and closed his eyes.

Chapter 37

Louisa rechecked her list. She had accounted for everyone on it except for Ben. What should she get the man who dominated her thoughts? When he wasn't around, she wanted to be near him, to smell him, to touch him, to hear him speak. But when he was present, she could think of nothing but her deceit.

Am I doing the right thing?

And each time she asked herself that question, she answered it the same way. If Ben and the Lancers left now, Kerma and all her citizens would suffer. The Remulans would prevail in the coming battle. Could they have gone to Earth and brought back more help? Maybe. Every time she saw Ben, Louisa excused herself at the first chance to assuage her guilt.

Can't avoid him tonight.

It would be their first Christmas on Aaru, and when the truth came out, it would be their last as a group. Even though she and Ben were the only Christians, Abu, the Lancers, and even Ali agreed to celebrate with them by exchanging gifts. Ben had also invited all the Aaruans who were traveling with them. There would be enough going on that she could keep her distance.

Louisa glanced back over the list and chuckled when she got to Ali. She had a metal singer create a copy of her binoculars to reinforce that she was still watching him. Khepri and Ssherrss would receive a basket of baby stirithy items such as teething chews and tracking bells. Abu would love the Aaruan adventure book she had picked up at the local market. The trader said the plot had a lot of action and a little romance—an excellent distraction for the boy who had become distant after Masako left.

But what to get Ben?

A puppy would be ideal. Louisa remembered Ben once mentioning his fond memories of his childhood dog, Rufus. That gift would wait. Ben had too much responsibility at the moment.

I bet he'd look dashing in a new hat.

Chapter 38

Kerma City, Taru, An 5660, Day 66

For Abu, these last five weeks had been strange. Not because the teenager was on another planet or friends with aliens. It wasn't even the more normal weirdness in his life: girls. No, his sense of unease came from all the people he cared for the most.

Until Masako left the city, Abu had visited with her every other day. Now that she was gone, he did nothing but worry about her and the long journey she had to endure. Every morning and every night, he added her to his prayers.

Dr. Ben had become obsessed with getting the regiment ready for the coming battle, but he also acted strange each time he and Miss Louisa were in the same room. The happy-go-lucky duffadar, who was more uncle than military leader, hadn't smiled for weeks. Miss Louisa appeared to be avoiding Dr. Ben, and Abu couldn't tell why. He was almost sure it wasn't Dr. Ben's unusual behavior, so what could it be?

Abu's best friend and his former crush were both obsessed with training. Umrao would lead a section of one hundred men, while Esther took charge of every spare Alexandrian troop stationed at the Alexandrian embassy. Now with fifty Greek soldiers, she drilled her small company with determined proficiency. When the two lovers weren't training, they wanted to be alone.

The only constants had been Rrummblinss, Khepri, Ssherrss, and Ali. Rrummblinss had often been absent, working with his men on different metal-singing efforts. The stirithy leadership had voted to provide only passive support and no more.

Abu filled his days trying to stay busy. Every morning, he worked with Ali to catch up with his studies, Earth-based, Aaruan, and Ancient. Each afternoon, he practiced shooting, riding, and Kalari with the Lancers.

For the last month, Miss Louisa had spent all her free time at several of the city's libraries. Khepri had gone with her most days to help translate Aaruan hieroglyphics. When Abu asked about the research, she said she was learning everything about the Seba to help with the quest to power it.

Today, after he cleaned up, Miss Louisa had asked him to work on transcribing the Seba scroll. She wanted to know the exact steps for returning to Earth.

"Well, that's everything." Abu pointed to his notepad, where he had written the English translation of the steps needed to activate the device and send whoever was near it back to Earth.

"Thanks, Abu." Louisa leaned over the table and patted his forearm.

"Sure. Do you want to run through the steps except for the last one? I'm sure it will do the floating thing like you saw at the temple without activating. That way, we can make sure everything works."

Miss Louisa shook her head. "We don't want to waste any energy it has left."

"Okay. Well, I guess I'll find out if Dr. Ben needs some help." Once more, Abu noticed the noise of the range and tried to block out the near-incessant rifle fire.

"Before you go, do you think there's any more information on the scroll that we haven't seen?" Louisa raised her eyebrows at Abu.

He picked up the Ancient-made scroll. He pressed his finger on the surface, and the alien words that had faded away a minute ago popped back up on the flexible glass. "I don't think so."

Louisa came around the table. She placed her hands on Abu's chair and peered over his shoulder. The act of moving his finger along the glass pushed the symbols upward. He did so until they disappeared over the edge. He kept going for several seconds, but nothing happened.

Abu reversed direction and pulled the words back down until they went off the bottom. The original section of instructions came into view and then raced off below. Again, he kept trying to push down, but nothing happened.

Louisa gave a disappointed sigh. "Oh, well. I was hoping."

"Hoping what?" Abu looked over his shoulder at her.

With a flat grin, Louisa said, "Some books hinted at being able to control more attributes. Like where you land on the destination planet, how big of an area gets scooped up. I believe these have already been set up."

Abu turned back to the scroll. "Have you asked the headgear?"

She nodded. "Every question I could ask."

The scroll sat in Abu's hand, silent. It did not divulge any other information.

Maybe there is nothing else to it. Could just be a list of steps. If I were an Ancient, how would I find out how to work the device?

"I'd probably ask someone," Abu whispered to himself.

"What?"

With a shrug, Abu said, "Oh, nothing. I asked myself how an Ancient would figure out what it does."

"Are you sure you're just fourteen?" Miss Louisa laughed.

Abu gave her a questioning look.

A bright smile flashed back at him. "You're so smart, Abu." Miss Louisa patted him on the shoulder. "Why don't you ask it for help?"

Of course. It might work.

Turning red, Abu gave her a sheepish grin. He faced the scroll and spoke the Ancient word for help: "Squawk, squawk."

Nothing happened, and Abu's shoulders slumped.

"Hold on." Louisa went to her bag and placed each piece of the Seba on the table in the proper position. "Try again."

Certain it was a lost cause, Abu shrugged. "Squawk, squawk."

A floating representation of Ancient symbols appeared a foot above the diamond-shaped artifact lying on one side.

"Fantastic!" Abu pressed the first of four phrases on the list with a finger. It translated to *Work*. The scene morphed and got taller. He hadn't understood the second or fourth words, but the third meant *Destination* or *Destinations*. The instructions from the scroll for going from Earth to Aaru and Aaru to Earth appeared in midair.

"It looks the same," Miss Louisa exclaimed.

After trying to get it to return to the previous list, Abu said, "Squawk." The Ancient word for "back" and the floating image showed the first list. He pressed the second phrase on the list. Another list of what appeared to be instructions came up, but some symbols seemed to be optional. The options translated to *Small* or *Little*, *Normal*, and *Large* or *Big*. The first two were highlighted in white and the last in blue. "What do you think?"

Louisa pursed her lips. "Appears to be how big of an area gets transported."

Abu reached out and tapped the word for "Normal." It turned blue, and the last one turned white. "We don't know how big the small area is, but if we ever get this to full power, then I doubt we want to take half the city with us."

"Before we go back, we could follow the ceremony's instructions. Find out if the Seba lights up the area in question."

Abu thought that might work, and it gave him another idea. "What if the smaller area takes less power?"

"See? So smart." Miss Louisa frowned when she said it.

"Is there a problem? We might be able to go back home."

With a sigh, Miss Louisa said, "Do you want to go home?"

Abu hadn't given it any thought. Until they powered the device, it wasn't possible. Now, faced with the potential, he felt a pang of sorrow in his gut. His eyes darted away from Miss Louisa's questioning look, and he replied ruefully, "Not yet."

"Neither do I."

"But we still need to tell Dr. Ben."

Miss Louisa averted her eyes. "Let's see what else we can discover."

"Squawk," said Abu, then he poked the word "Destinations." A globe of Earth appeared above the table. Abu imagined looking down upon his home from the surface of the moon. It would be the only way to describe how realistic this miniature planet was.

Near the top of the brown of Africa glowed a blue circle. Like random sparks, small white dots sparkled around the globe. Abu narrowed his eyes, seeking a pattern. Miss Louisa pressed on the other side of the planet, and the blue circle in front of Abu shrank into a white blip, with two other white sparkles nearby. When she moved her finger away, the miniature planet rotated an inch.

"Interesting." Abu touched Madagascar and moved his finger in the air. The globe spun toward his finger. He continued the motion until he saw the blue circle on a long island off the edge of Asia.

Pretty sure that's Japan, Abu thought as he spun the miniature Earth around, examining every white dot.

"Conclusions?" Miss Louisa said, as if she already knew the answer.

"These are all the locations where the device was activated on Earth." Abu turned the ball and pointed. "Here, near Sweden and Denmark. That would be the Norsemen. The blue one is when they brought the Nipponese." He turned the globe to the Ottoman Empire, a finger's width from Aleppo. "This is probably where they grabbed the Romans and Sasanians." His finger went to another white dot close to his hometown. "And this is probably the location of Mari."

Louisa spun the globe and pressed the spark in Africa closest to the Nile River Delta. "Might as well get closer to Cairo *if* we go home."

"I guess. Let's find out what else this does." Abu used his hand to spin the miniature planet as fast as he could make it go. "Squawk." The spinning orb disappeared, to be replaced by the original four choices. Abu tapped the last one.

Some unknown words were at the top, but the number one hundred was next to them. Below those words was a row of well-known words, and below them were numbers. The translatable words read *Small*, *Normal*, and *Large* and had corresponding numbers of *eight*, *six*, and *four*.

Abu squinted as he comprehended what he saw. He turned to stare at Miss Louisa. He shot her a look powered by hot anger. Scolded children appeared less guilty than her.

"Let me explain." Crestfallen, Miss Louisa shook her hands in front of her body.

Abu snarled, "I'm going to . . ."

Clang! Clang! Clang! Clang! Clang!

Concern replaced guilt on Louisa's face, and Abu's anger soured to worried dread.

The city's warning system, made up of giant bells aided by wind singers amplifying their ring, signaled the event they never wanted to occur. The Remulans had breached the wall.

Clang! Clang! Clang! Clang! Clang!

The echoes of bells drifted away, and oppressive silence settled over the city, seeping into the classroom where Abu glared at a red-faced Miss Louisa.

After turning away from Abu, Miss Louisa stuffed the Seba objects into her bag. As soon as she touched the diamond, the evidence of her lies blinked to nothing. "When this is over, I'll explain everything. Please don't tell Ben until then."

"But we don't have to fight. We can go home."

Miss Louisa shook her head. "Is that what you want, Abu? Are you willing to let the city fall to the Remulans?"

Abu's stomach turned at the thought of the horrors those bastards would unleash on these poor people. How many would they kill? How many would they enslave? His doused anger began to glow. A new ember sparked in his gut, settling his uneasiness and stoking his resolve. "No. But after this is over, you are going to tell everyone the truth."

"Promise," she said.

Chapter 39

Kerma City, Taru, An 5660, Day 66

Aquila slithered up to Octavius's lounge area. The first councilor of the Imperial Court loved being the bearer of good news and could not hide the sparkle in his otherwise deadened gaze from Octavius.

Ahura Jupiter knows we need some good news, Octavius thought. *We haven't had much since those damned Earthlings showed up with their guns.*

With his warmest smile, Aquila bowed to Octavius. "Your Majesty, the wall has fallen."

Caesar Octavius Remus the Second's lips twitched but never became a full smile. "And the legions?"

"The Fourth is storming the breach. General Kinya has the Ninth and Sixth ready to follow. Ahura Jupiter willing, the city will be ours by morning." The first councilor showed all his teeth.

With a snap of his fingers, Octavius summoned a servant to retrieve his still-full glass. He eschewed alcohol on the day of any battle. Even with little to do, he needed a clear head. The excitement of the news even caused him to lose his appetite for the fresh-squeezed fruit juice he had chosen to replace his usual wine.

Octavius stood and walked to the exit of his tent. As the two Pretorian Guards opened the flaps, he paused and turned toward the little princess. She sat on the carpets near the edge of the tent, drawing on a piece of parchment. A legionary watched over her while two women, some of the camp's followers, tried to entertain her.

The girl hadn't said more than *yes* or *no* since Shemush had extracted everything she knew about the Earthlings. A brave little thing. She had not given up the Earthlings' leaders' names until the life-singing torturer had upped the pain quotient higher than Octavius had wanted. His conscience dismissed any guilt. An emperor must attend to many unlikable duties, and the torture of a little girl was less egregious than many.

He gestured to one of the women, and she patted the girl's arm to get her attention. A princess of two nations, the girl took more after her Nipponese mother. Masako looked at the emperor with a brief spark of rebellion in her almond-shaped eyes.

"It would appear that the Yuhi ambassador has failed you again, Princess. Come with me. You should watch the beginning of the end for your friends." Octavius walked out of the tent without waiting. He knew the servant would have the girl racing to follow.

Octavius was showered with accolades as he marched down the Via Praetoria of the 5th Legion's temporary castrum.[1] His legionaries came to attention and saluted their god's representative on Aaru. They called out, "All hail the Emperor," or "Praise Ahura Jupiter, may His Light shine upon you, Emperor."

With a nod, a smile, a wave, or even a tiny touch, Octavius lifted the morale of the men who would risk their lives for him.

---

1. Romans named all types of fortifications a castrum. Ideally, each fortress would have four main roads intersecting in the middle of the fortress's grounds.

At the end of the avenue, he veered to his right. With hands clasped behind his back, the emperor ascended a small staircase cut into the earthen wall and walked to the corner. When the princess stood beside him, he put his hands on the palisade and stared out over the section of ground known as "no man's land." During the last few months, constant warfare had stripped bare the half-mile that led up to the imposing walls guarding Kerma.

Giant stones and burning pitch rained down from the city's defenders, targeting his soldiers in front of the jagged gap in the crumbled wall. A living cloud of black floated toward the walls, taking a sinuous path. The swarm of bata reached the top of the wall, and the Kerman artillery stopped firing, one by one.

Octavius pointed at the mound of rubble crawling with his legionaries. "I'm sure your friends, Abu, Miss Louisa, and Dr. Ben, are somewhere on the other side of that hole in the wall." He grinned down at the princess. "They will die trying to stop my legions."

"Kill me, too." The words tumbled out of the girl as her face twisted with rage.

Octavius chuckled. "Now, why would I do that? You still have a great deal of value."

She balled her hands into fists and leaned toward him. Spittle shot out of her mouth as she shouted, "I will kill you!"

Her guard grabbed the princess's arms and raised her an inch off the ground.

The princess's antics had grown tiresome, but Octavius wanted to leave her with no hope. He squatted down to stare into her eyes. Tears streamed down her flushed face as her mouth contorted in a snarl.

"Your friends have cost me too much. I will not stop until they are dead. That is my solemn promise." Octavius shook his head. "Forget the dead, and live for yourself." He jerked his chin, and the legionary holding the princess tucked her under his arm. The soldier trotted down the stairs with the girl kicking, screaming, and hitting his armored chest.

When Octavius could no longer hear the girl's tantrum, he turned to Aquila, who stood out of the way like a statue. "And our surprise for the Earthlings?"

"He is ready, Your Majesty."

"Will it work?"

Aquila stepped over to the wall beside Octavius. "If General Kinya told us the truth about star steel stopping the Earthlings' guns, it might be enough."

Octavius raised his eyebrow and looked askance at Aquila.

The first councilor gave a slight bow. "Do not worry, Your Majesty. Your legions are prepared to die to the man to overwhelm the defenders."

From the corner of his eye, the emperor tracked a pair of wind singers in their blue imperial messenger uniforms. He followed their descent from the southern horizon toward the castrum for a few seconds.

Turning back to the battle, Octavius, the most powerful man on Aaru, nodded as he said, "Ahura Jupiter willing."

Chapter 40

Kerma City, Taru, An 5660, Day 66

At the first ring of the bells, the former college campus erupted in choreographed chaos. As in each of the last five days, the soldiers of the 1st Kerman Rifles mustered for action. Ben had just finished working with his first battalion's Pistoleros—a name that stuck once Ben had thrown it out in jest—on their shield formation.

The regiment's two battalions consisted of support personnel, five hundred riflemen, and five hundred men armed with pistols, swords, and shields. Each battalion's five companies comprised a hundred riflemen and pistoleros. The ten most senior Lancers each commanded a company, while the seven youngest Lancers and the thirteen most capable Kerman riflemen each led half of a company.

Ben's men rushed into formation alongside Jeevan's second battalion in the college's sizeable open quad. Today's order of battle had been predetermined the day after Jeevan's broken-hearted breakdown. The first part of the plan required half of their supplies to be pre-positioned, along with a fifth of their men. These two companies manned the fortification built within a small city square off the damaged section of the city wall. The advance guard would assist the ten thousand Kerman infantrymen who waited to stop any immediate incursion.

Ben inspected himself, checking his supplies one last time. He carried Agnes, loaded, while his double holster held a Pocket Army revolver on each hip. From his belt hung his shortened saber and a large leather kit holding seventy more rounds. As ready as he could be, he surveyed his men. The battalion's NCOs counted heads and passed their totals to company commanders, who reported to him.

The last to report, Lance Duffadar Ram, ran over and saluted. "A Company is ready." He smiled. "The battalion is ready."

In the leadup to previous battles, Ben might have said something to his troops, but the 1st Kerman Rifles didn't need a speech. Hardened veterans, each man and woman under his command had someone they loved living within these walls. These soldiers had been chomping at the bit to bring hell to those threatening their way of life. Instead of words, Ben said a quick prayer.

God, protect these men and give them the will to prevail over the evil they face today.

Ben returned the lance duffadar's salute. "Ram, you know the drill. On the double."

"Yes, sir." The first battalion's second in command turned to the men and spoke in Aaruan, "Column, right turn! Double march!"

As one, the men in the column jogged out of a college gate. Across the quad, Jeevan's second battalion moved in the direction of a different exit. Ben turned toward the rear of the column. He would catch up after ensuring their supply wagons were ready. He jogged to the rear, and a familiar trio marched toward him.

Outfitted in their full Nipponese Samurai armor, Ki, Lil, and Thoresten made quite a sight. Every bit an Asian Valkyrie of death, Lil stepped forward. Her platinum hair reflected like a star against the polished, liquid dragon–red, banded armor. She stopped him with a hand to his chest and spoke in Greek. "Do you mind if we accompany you?"

Ben shook his head. "By all means, but I'm not sure accompanying riflemen will be the best place for you."

Ki grinned under the pearl-white, horned helmet that covered her striking red hair. "Thoresten told us the plan. We believe your men will see the most action."

"I guess." Ben's voice became stern. "Follow Ram, and don't get in the way."

"Yes, sir, General Handsome." Lil snapped a mock salute. "Have I ever told you how sexy scars are on a planet with so few?"

Not wanting to feed Lil's perverted mind, Ben rolled his eyes and jogged around them. The last company started moving when he saw Louisa and Abu climb into one of the ammunition wagons. As he paused at the first wagon, Ben addressed the battalion's quartermaster in choppy Aaruan. "All ready?"

The grim-faced man nodded. "Yes, sir. Supply wagons are loaded, and runners are ready. Life singers and stretcher-bearers are ready."

"Good, set up aid stations first." Ben hoped that would get his idea across. He should have asked for a wind singer to help interpret, but he had to be able to operate without one. After they stopped the Remulans, he promised to spend more time working on the Aaruan language.

"I understand, Captain." The man gave a salute.

Ben returned it. "Go."

The wagon rolled after the last of the soldiers, and Ben waited to walk next to Louisa's wagon as it moved up the line. Abu gulped and averted his eyes.

What is that about?

"Are we ready?" Louisa tilted her head toward him.

"We'll know soon enough. Do you have everything you need?" He darted his eyes toward the teenager, trying to get Louisa's take.

With a shrug, Louisa patted the large bag hanging over her shoulder. "I've got everything, and Abu's ready." She nudged him. "Right?"

In subdued tones, Abu said, "Yes. I'm ready." Then his voice grew firm, and he stared at Ben with intensity. "Remember the Prophet's words. Four things support the world: the learning of the wise, the justice of the great, the prayers of the good, and the valor of the brave. I will pray for you to be brave." Abu lowered his eyes and chewed on his lower lip with nervous energy that Ben couldn't quite chalk up to the coming battle.

"Wise words. Thank you." Ben pointed his finger and scolded, "Stay together, and stay with the supplies. I don't want either of you within an arrow shot of the fighting. Understood?"

"Yes, sir." The young man turned away and avoided eye contact.

"Okay," Louisa said with resignation.

As Ben's gaze swung back and forth between the two, he tried to understand why they were acting out of sorts, but he had more pressing worries. "See you when this is over." Ben picked up his pace to get back to A Company.

———————————————

It took them thirty minutes to reach the battle, but Ben heard the occasional report of a rifle or a pistol after the first ten minutes. At the twenty-minute mark of the march, the first sounds of a medieval battle were obvious. The thunking twang of ballistas releasing bolts, cries of rage, and the wails of the dying soon joined in. As they neared their destination, the noise rose from a gurgle to just under a roar.

The entire time, Ben pondered possible hiccups in their plans. He understood that few of the best plans survived contact with the enemy. The long march made him anxious, and he questioned his decision to continue training instead of pre-positioning all his forces at the breach. He would know soon enough. If the sandbag wall still held, it was a gamble that had already paid off because each extra day of training increased the effectiveness of his troops.

Ben had been taken by tactical surprise when the Kermans warned them about the swarms of bata. These were flocks of giant bats, which wind singers trained and commanded in battle. There were other animals that the beast-speaking wind singers could bring to bear. Ben doubted any of the ones described would pose as much of a threat as the bats in this battle.

The most significant direct threats to their success came from archers or catapults if the Remulans didn't care about the lives of their men. Ben hoped the Remulans, the Ancient Roman doppelgangers that they were, didn't have anything up their sleeves.

The road the regiment followed had been curving, but then they rounded a bend. With a sudden jolt, he saw the entire macabre scene. From a distance, it appeared as if a titan-size claw had ripped a gash in the Kerman wall, which had withstood more than one of the legendary Lamentations. Wide at the top, the grievous wound tapered down to a narrow passage swarming with a mass of humanity. The visual spectacle turned the dream-like sounds of the clang of steel on steel, the echoes from each carbine shot, and the cries of the wounded into a reality.

Ben's mind flew back twenty years and a world away to Vicksburg. He had watched wave after wave of Union soldiers break upon the doomed city's fortifications. Grateful then to have seen the carnage from a distance, Ben trembled in the present as battle-induced fear filled his whole being.

As they marched nearer to the cacophony of war, the thrill Ben dreaded shot through him. His hellish vision transformed from the long-ago ghosts of blue and gray to the present-day writhing mass of green and red. As his senses became hyper-alert, the paintings of the *Siege of Acre* and the *Conquest of Constantinople* flashed before him.

How will artists paint this day?

Those random thoughts halted with the column. Company A had stopped behind Jeevan's great sandbag wall. Lance Duffadar Ram shouted his commands, directing the men into their positions.

Sowar Singh snapped to attention and saluted. "Captain, Reporting for E Company of the Second Battalion and C Company of the First."

Ben stood straighter and whipped out a textbook salute. "Singh, give me the quick rundown."

The sowar lowered his hand. "Yes, sir. The wall collapsed about an hour ago, but the Remulans continued to fire their artillery through the gap for the first twenty minutes. The Kermans began using the siege engines behind our wall to return fire."

Sowar Singh gestured at the four nearby catapults flinging rocks. One boulder flew over the gap out of sight while another crushed several legionaries at the top of the rubble. "Despite their losses, when the bombardment ended, the Remulans were topping the rubble. They would have overwhelmed the Kermans except for the constant fire from the First Rifles."

Ben nodded.

"With our help, the Kermans met the Remulans only a few feet below the summit and have been slowly losing ground. Our snipers were initially taking a huge toll, along with the catapults here. The Kermans somehow brought ballista to the top of city walls on both sides of the gap and catapults onto the nearest bastions." He pointed at the fortifications to the left and right of the hole. "The

Remulan artillery dropped off, but soon after, they attacked with thousands of bats." The Lancer waved to a brown furry lump on the ground about ten yards away.

Ben hadn't noticed. There were dozens of small dog-size bodies scattered behind the 1st Rifles' wall. "Go on."

"The bats neutralized the Kerman artillery and wiped out the soldiers along the top. But when they came for us, the beasts had taken enough losses that we downed them with minimal damage. Other than that, the men have been taking shots of opportunity. Right before you showed up, the Remulans brought up large wooden shields to protect their troops as they descended the pile of rubble."

Ben thought about the information and hoped the Remulans were out of bats. "Anything else?"

Singh smiled. "The Remulans are scaling the walls on either side of the breach."

With a long look at the city walls around the breach, Ben could not find any climbers. They were sure to be on the other side to keep from being picked off by his riflemen.

Jeevan, Bhagat, it's up to you.

"Very well. Great job. For the moment, C Company will be our reserve unit. Pull E Company back to the resupply stations. Get them fed and watered, then relieve C Company as the reserve. Give C a quick break before they take their place on the wall."

"Yes, sir." Sowar Singh snapped to attention, saluted, and trotted back to the sandbag wall.

Ben said, "As soon as all the men are in position, notify the Kermans to fall back behind our lines."

The short, wiry man bounced up and down excitedly before saluting and jogging away. Ram bellowed at one of his subordinates who hadn't been moving fast enough. Ben inspected the section of the palisade assigned to A Company.

They'd built their firing line wall with hundreds of thousands of sandbags. At fourteen feet tall in front of a deep trench, it would be a formidable obstacle to the Remulan legions. Jeevan had built the wall with two ledges on the back side of the rampart. The lower ledge used sandbags and was two feet tall, with firing holes at seven feet.

A foot above the first set of holes ran a wooden platform. Riflemen reached the higher shooting positions using ladders. From there, they could fire down over the top of the wall. Metal shields, overhanging the entire rampart, protected the soldiers from arrows. The steel awning angled upward to provide a little protection behind the wall.

As Ben walked to the end of the center section, he inspected the gaps in the wall and the ten-foot-wide, fifteen-foot-deep trench. He had insisted Jeevan build the missing areas to allow the Kermans to retreat and his men to attack if necessary. At present, a giant wooden bridge spanned the hole. As Ben turned to go back to his designated command post, he found the trio of Samurai.

A shiny round black beetle in his armor, Thoresten sighed and asked in Greek. "When does this party get started?"

Ben shook his head. "My men are about to be extremely busy. With luck, you'll grow bored."

Ki smirked. "Don't underestimate those fanatics."

With his voice turning somber, Ben said, "I won't, but I can only deal with the surprises when they come." He pointed to the bridges. "If you want to be helpful, assist my men in pulling up the bridge as soon as the Kermans are across."

Lil gave him a wink. "Aye! Aye!" Then she stepped closer and whispered in his ear, "I don't see your firefly around. If you need a little pre-battle stress relief, let me know." She reached around and squeezed his butt.

Ben slapped her hand away. "You're incorrigible."

"But very encourage-able and even more flexible." Her eyes twinkled with mischief.

"I don't have time for this."

Ben stomped away, leaving the welven strumpet laughing in his wake. As he reached the center of the wall, he nodded to the squad of Pistoleros, who would act as his runners. Then he climbed the ladder to the upper walkway. After leaning Agnes against the wall, he took out his binoculars and sighted them through the gap between the awning and the sandbags. An hour of shooting had left a cloud of spent black powder hanging in front of the sandbag wall. Beyond the haze, he zeroed in on the action halfway down the rubble debris.

Locked in close combat, rows of red-clad Kerman infantry pushed upward against the shields of the much larger formation of Remulans. Wearing cloaks of green, the legionaries shoved and thrust down the pile. The thought of being in front of either shield-wall made Ben shiver.

As Singh had described, the Remulans had brought wooden walls thick enough to stop a carbine-fired bullet. Lines of shield-walls stood on either side of the Remulan block to protect them from riflemen shooting from the far ends of the sandbag wall. The angle allowed Ben's troops to fire at the Remulans on the back rows, but they couldn't do more than that or risk hitting the Kerman infantry.

Crumpled shield-walls lay scattered around the summit, proving that the portable walls were not impervious to a catapult ball. Each ten- to twelve-foot-wide barrier had a base that allowed the legionaries to stand it on the ground, and it was wide enough for six men to hide on the other side.

They had made the screens short enough to shoot arrows from behind them. Every few seconds, an archer popped over the top. The man aimed and let a shot fly at the Kermans locked in battle with the Remulan shield-wall before ducking back. Focused on one pair of walls, Ben saw a Remulan who wasn't fast enough. A mist of pink lingered in the air as he dropped from a sniper's bullet.

Behind the primary Remulan formation, waves of shield-walls inched over the crest of the breach. On Ben's left, one of the man-powered walls moved toward the first defensive trench dug at the halfway point of the battlefield.

Damn, Ben thought as the breakaway shield-wall reached the ditch. It tilted upward until it stood on one of the smaller ends. The legionaries pushed, and the shield-wall fell over the gap. After a bounce, it settled in place. During the maneuver, five of the six Remulans propelling the wall fell from the withering fire of the 1st Kerman Rifles. The last legionary zigzagged his way up the scree to the line of shield-walls. For a single bridge, the enemy had sacrificed all those men.

The clarion call of several horns cut through the din, and the Kerman heavy infantry began their practiced retreat. A secondary reserve formation waited behind the engaged units.

The columns of men in the reserve units turned sideways, allowing a small gap. A second set of horns blew. The back ranks of men turned one row at a time and raced through the narrow alleys until the last two rows bracing against the legionaries were all that remained.

Those two ranks began taking measured steps back, but the Remulans were ready and pushed hard. The Kerman cohesiveness collapsed in several places as men lost their footing in the rubble or died by Remulan swords. There were no replacements to fill the gaps, and the numbers of enemy troops were too great. Many died when the last men tried to turn and flee. Ben pivoted away from the slaughter, disgusted and seething at the same time. Half or less made it to safety a mere ten yards away.

The roar of coordinated carbine shots brought Ben back to the fight. The Remulans scrambled through debris, charging downhill toward the fresh formation of Kerman infantry. Another volley of fire roared from the top of the

1st Rifles' wall when a gap appeared between the two enemy units. The rifle fire decimated rows of Remulans, and their charge faltered.

With disciplined practice, the Kermans marched backward. They put distance between themselves and the Remulans, giving the riflemen enough time to instigate a second round of devastation. The legionaries responded by rushing portable shield-walls to their front. With the pause, the Kermans moved faster over the bridges stretched over the first defensive trench.

A body fell through the viewport of Ben's binoculars, and he moved his focus up the giant wall. At the ragged edges of the walkway, Kermans and Remulans were in a desperate fight. Moving the binoculars away from the gap, he saw a group of 1st Rifles racing across the walkway toward the action.

Ben swept his view in the opposite direction, searching for his troops. A giant boulder tore through one of the fortification's merlons, throwing several men like rag dolls off the wall and crushing several more.

More trebuchet- and catapult-hurled projectiles struck the wall.

Ben's jaws tightened, and his blood boiled. *Where are the metal shields?* He spit venom. "God damn it."

A dark cloud streaked into his vision as the curse left his lips. The flock, or whatever the hell a group of bats was called, raced high over his defensive position. Thousands of flying mammals dipped and swirled over the city wall to disappear. Behind the bats flew a squadron of human wind singers wearing manufactured wings. Each held something familiar in his outstretched hands.

About time.

As Ben heard the distant rumble of exploding grenades, the Remulan barrage slowed on the damaged section of the wall. He and Ssherrss had spent three days perfecting the design. The little hand bombs had to not burst open on hitting the ground and be hard to disable. After numerous tests, they settled on a double hourglass design.

Like an hourglass inside another hourglass, the bottom chamber held the black powder, while the top inner orb held the cloth fuse. The flammable liquid-soaked fuse had enough oxygen in the container that the fuse burned inside, making it difficult to pull out or douse.

With a half-inch-thick glass outer bubble, the grenade could be hurled thirty to fifty feet and bounced off cobblestones, and it wouldn't break. The nasty part of the little bombs consisted of tiny spikes jammed in the space between the outer and the inner glass.

Thank you, Lord. Please forgive my blasphemy.

After a demonstration of the grenades, someone within the Kerman general staff had enough imagination to use the new weapon in a novel way. The innovator had armed the limited number of wind singers Ben had seen. If the little bombs detonated close enough to the enemies' siege engines, many would be out of commission.

Ben lamented that he and Ssherrss had not had time to perfect the timing of the fuses. With the weapon's current limitations, the flying bombers had to drop into arrow range to release their grenades. Ben prayed it had not been a suicide mission.

With fewer boulders to contend with, the riflemen on the walkway above pushed the Remulans back. Behind them, men hauled the metal roofs Ben had designed into place atop the wall. The metal roofs should protect them from Remulan artillery. On the left side of the gap, a random trebuchet-flung stone struck the *u*-shaped covering.

The rock slammed into the metal wing, stretched ten feet over the outside of the wall. Braced from below by another metal grate wedged into the wall itself, the wing held firm. After an initial loud bang, the boulder rolled down what was essentially a slide and up the other wing to bang into rock-catcher spikes at the end. The ball, having lost most of its momentum, rolled back and forth on the slide before coming to rest in the middle of the contraption.

Ben relaxed. His creation worked under live fire conditions. It wouldn't stop a direct hit coming down in the center of the walkway, but it would neutralize projectiles on less severe trajectories. With Ben's worry about the artillery on hold, he set his binoculars aside and scanned the field before him.

The remaining Kerman infantry had kept a steady backward cadence. They had crossed the first trench and had bunched up in front of the wooden bridges over the last defensive ditch, moving as fast as possible.

While Ben focused on the action up top, the legionaries in the breach had reorganized themselves. The enemy now inched forward from inside protective wooden cocoons. With four shield-walls forming a square perimeter, the Remulans raised two more overhead to protect the men inside from any gunfire overhead.

What the hell?

Every minute, more of these improvised turtle shell–like forts flowed over the summit. The sheer number of protective barriers worried Ben. Was this the Remulans' ace in the hole? He had not accounted for the Remulans' ability to defend against rifles from above.

Unaimed arrows arched away from the walking wooden forts. Many arrows snapped against the metal awning above Ben's head. Cries of anguish followed others as they landed among the last Kerman infantry crossing the bridges.

A Kerman catapult boulder slammed into the roof of a Remulan moving fort. Broken boards, blood, and splinters shot into the air. The surviving legionaries maintained discipline. They dropped the fractured wall before stepping over their fallen comrades. In a futile attempt to survive, they tried to hide under the one remaining shield-roof while the Kerman Rifles rained death from above. Soon, the wounded turtle stopped moving altogether, its walls collapsing on top of the dead.

With the 1st Rifles now controlling the top of the walls on either side of the breach, they should be able to decimate any unprotected Remulans. But only if Ben could neutralize those wooden turtles. Many of the Remulans' mobile forts were now too close for the catapults to be effective. Ballista bolts blew holes into wooden shells but did little more than slow the enemy tortoises' progress.

If the Remulans reached the trench at the foot of the sandbag palisade, they would use their shield-walls to cross the gulley and scale the defenses. Given enough legionaries, they could overwhelm Ben's riflemen.

Need to change the game, Ben thought. The beast within cackled with glee at what was to come. Ben shoved the monster back. He had to control his emotions if he hoped to lead them to victory.

He scampered down the ladder and yelled, "Ram! To me!"

The Lance duffadar hopped down from the bottom ledge a few yards away. "Here."

"We can't let those shields get to the wall. I'm going out with the Pistoleros."

"Let me, Captain."

Ben shook his head. "No. I need you to get word to all the other companies. Have their Pistoleros attack when we do. They need to capture the closest of the enemy's big shields. Then throw grenades at the next group of Remulan walking forts." Hands moving, he drew a line in front of himself. "I want to create a new firing line using the Remulan shield-walls fifty yards out."

Ram nodded. "Got it. What do you want me to do after that?"

Ben thought for a second. "Send the men on the bottom firing line to the new wall. Keep the men at the top where they are. We'll keep leapfrogging to take back the gap."

"What about their artillery?"

Ben looked over to where Jeevan and his men were fighting. "Good point. Now that we have the high ground, we'll hold at the first barrier and use the grenades to draw them out while Jeevan and Bhagat pick them off." Ben peered through the closest firing hole. The wooden tortoises had crept to within sixty yards. They would be much closer by the time Ben's men could attack.

Ben pointed to one of his runners and said in Aaruan, "You. Come here." He relayed his message through the Lancer, who spoke much better Aaruan. "Ram, tell him to take half the Pistoleros and attack from the right bridge. I'll take the left. Make sure he understands. The Grenadiers should blow up only the second row of Remulan formations. Capture the first ones and spin them around."

Ram raised his eyebrows. "I'll do my best."

Idiot. Should have gotten those interpreters.

Ram raised his voice and relayed the message in the Ancient Egyptian dialect. All the runners leaned in to listen. Finished, he asked, "You understand?"

As a group, they answered. "Yes, sir!"

The Lance duffadar pointed to the first man. "Go." Then he singled out five more runners. "B Company. D Company." He swung his head to the right, and two men raced away. "C Company. And E Company." He waved his arm to the left, and the other two jogged in that direction. "Move it!" The men picked up their pace.

Ben pointed to the rest of his runners. "Bring Pistoleros. Meet bridge."

He glanced to his rear. Supply runners moved to replace depleted boxes of ammunition. Stretcher runners hauled the wounded back to the aid stations. The rest of the Kerman infantry had moved to their designated rally points. He could draw on them if he needed to.

By the time Ben reached the gap in the sandbag palisade, a hundred men waited behind the raised drawbridge. Each man carried a shield, and every third one carried two brown-glass grenades in his free hand. Each Grenadier had a small kerosene lantern tied to his hip. He simply had to lift a small lid, light a fuse, count the appropriate seconds, and throw.

Ben yelled in Aaruan, "By squads! Pick a target!" He motioned toward one of the Remulan mobile forts until his men nodded. "Kill! Grenadiers throw at targets behind!" Again, he made hand motions of throwing and showing the grenade going over until he read comprehension on the men's faces.

The men shuffled into squad formations. Five men formed a shield wall. Five more, including three Grenadiers, made up the second row. After inspecting his men, Ben nodded to the soldiers holding up the drawbridge.

The prospect of imminent death brought a shot of adrenaline, and Ben's body vibrated as he restrained the creature of death that tried to possess him.

He drew a revolver. "Lower the bridge."

The men holding the ropes let the bridge drop toward the other side. When wood slapped on dirt, Ben screamed, "Charge!"

He jogged over the wooden planks behind the first squad and directed them to the Remulan turtle at the center. As the Pistoleros yelled out war cries, several legionaries poked their heads around their shield-walls—only to lose their lives as Riflemen on the palisade took shots of opportunity.

Just thirty yards from the trench in front of the sandbag fortifications, Ben's squad closed on their target in seconds. Battle noise faded into the background as his vision sharpened, and he fought to control his emotions. A Remulan stepped away from his protection to meet the charge and caught three revolver-fired bullets in his chest.

The tortoise configuration of the Remulan shield-walls saved the legionaries within from Ben's Riflemen, but it limited the men inside from engaging Ben's soldiers with swords, bows, or javelins. Armed with six-shooters, the Pistoleros ran to the corners and aimed through the small gaps in the walls.

The pistols belched fire, and legionaries screamed. Ben's men overwhelmed their target and took no casualties, like shooting fish in a barrel. For his Grenadiers, Ben pointed at targets in the next row of Remulan moving forts. A brown hourglass arched high and landed on a wooden roof that formed a turtle's back. The explosion sent wood flying in the air and thousands of splinters into the Remulans below.

Time's up. An evil cackle escaped his lips.

Enemy soldiers ran from behind their shield-walls where Riflemen on the sandbag wall picked them off.

Some of the Pistoleros formed up to charge the next row of wooden turtles. Ben grabbed one man's shoulder.

"No, damn it!" he screamed over the gunfire. "Turn this! Make a wall!"

The soldier yelled to his fellows, and together they grabbed a Remulan shield-wall and spun it around. They did the same with the next one and placed them side by side. Ben ran to the next squad and got them to do the same. Riflemen ran to take up positions behind the screens.

Bone dry, Ben tried to spit but had no saliva left to dislodge the burnt, acrid taste in his mouth. Spent black powder had turned the battlefield's hazy cloud into a thick black fog, limiting everyone's vision to thirty yards.

Shouts drew Ben's attention. One of his squads had not comprehended their orders, and instead of building a wall, they attacked another Remulan turtle. This tortoise wasn't having it and spit out legionaries, each welding a gladius and carrying a star steel–covered shield. To Ben's horror, they cut down two of the Pistoleros. The others backed away.

Oh, shit! Ben had miscalculated, and it might cost them everything. Desperate, he spun around, seeking a runner to bring the Kermans, when a red-and-silver blur ran past him.

"That's more like it!" Lil yelled. She sprinted toward the Remulans chasing after the fleeing Pistoleros.

Thoresten, grinning, ran after her with a small ax in each hand. Ki stepped next to Ben, leaned her big club against the portable wall, and removed her bow. With practiced calm, she drew the string taut and released. Her arrow jammed into the eye socket of a legionary about to stab an injured Pistolero.

Ben turned to the closest men, screaming for them to form a shield-wall and draw swords. Across the field, more groups of silver-shielded Remulans raced from behind shield-walls. They closed with his revolver- and rifle-armed soldiers. Useless bullets sparked off the enemy's star-steel shields as the legionaries hacked and stabbed more of his men to death.

With his squad formed into two rows, Ben directed them toward the star-steel legionaries near Lil and Thoresten.

The red-armored welf moved with lethal efficiency. On the run, Lil flicked her wrist, and the ball chained to the end of her scythe shot out. It wrapped the leg of the closest Remulan. She yanked, and the legionary's leg kicked up, sending him tumbling. Several Remulans behind him slowed to step around the prone man.

With another flick, the ball flew back as two legionaries reached Lil. She shot the steel sphere at one man's face, forcing him to block with his shield. Then she spun around the lunging gladius of the other legionary. The point of her scythe slammed into the back of the man's neck.

Ben's formation crashed into the shield-wall of a growing line of Remulans. His men struggled in the medieval sense while he stepped close behind the first row of Pistoleros, raised his arm, and fired his revolver at an angle, down over a Remulan's silver shield. Dead, the man went limp, but, wedged between the Kerman shields and the legionaries behind him, he hung in place.

Ben fired again and again as the angles permitted. The revolver clicked empty, and Ben stepped back to swap guns.

Two men at the end of his squad's shield-wall fell. Desperate, Ben surrendered to the lethal rage inside him. He fired at an exposed arm as a legionary swung toward a Pistolero's exposed back. A chunk of the man's arm disappeared, and the Remulan howled as he spun away.

Ben took that moment to yell in Aaruan, "Pull back!"

From the corner of his eye, Ben saw blurred streaks of white and black crash into the rear of the Remulan shield-wall. With a great scream of terror, one legionary fell to his knees, blood spurting from his gaping neck.

An ax slammed into the helmet of the man behind the squirter, cleaving half the man's face away. Blood-covered, Thoresten spun around and sent a shower of blood off his polished armor while his axes slashed in every direction. In a matter of seconds, instead of ten Remulans, there was now an unmoving mass grave.

Using the reprieve the dwarf gave them, Ben took stock of the battle. His men were holding their own, but the black smoke had obscured many Remulans advancing toward his Riflemen. He needed to coordinate the fire of the 1st Rifles to quell the most significant threats.

Fear driving him, Ben ran to the commandeered wooden wall and yelled at the Riflemen to target the smoky areas with volley fire. Racing along the wall, he instructed squad leaders about the threat. As he reached the sixth squad, he left instructions with a sowar there. The man took his order along the left side of the wooden wall to pull the Pistoleros back to guard the flanks.

With his back low against a wooden wall, Ben tried to catch his breath as he reloaded his empty revolver. Then he swapped guns and filled the half-empty one. He jogged back to the center of their defenses and his original squad.

Panicked cries cut through the discord.

Ben stopped in his tracks and sought the source. It seemed to be where the dwarf and the welves were fighting.

A thin strand of patience kept Louisa from rushing to the front lines. She and Abu hadn't had a second to rest since they'd jumped from their wagon near the aid station. An endless stream of stretcher-bearers carried wounded Kerman soldiers into the aid station to its one life singer. With at least a modicum of battlefield first-aid training from Ben, she and Abu helped to triage the patients. They stanched the bleeding wounds of the most injured and tried to keep them alive long enough to reach the life singers.

Surrounded by endless pain and suffering, Louisa let fear creep into her imagination. When Sowar Jadav appeared with an arrow in his arm, she saw visions of a wounded Ben lying on the field. Louisa squatted over the sowar's stretcher and tried to refocus as she stuffed linen cloth around the shaft to stop the bleeding. What began as her imagination running wild soon became an intense premonition in her gut.

"Louisa!"

She snapped her head around. A big hysakas jogged her way. The wolfwoman wore a regulation Alexandrian uniform, including a breastplate, bracers, grieves, and a helmet. Louisa didn't recognize her friend dressed that way for several seconds.

"I'm okay, Miss Louisa," Jadav said as he replaced her hand on the bandage.

Louisa stood. "Khepri, why are you here?"

The giant wolf gave her a toothy grin. "Esther brought us. Lance Duffadar Ram called the Kermans back into the front. We're going to the defensive wall as another reserve force."

Her brown linen blouse smeared with blood, Louisa shivered at the prospect of more of her friends in danger. With the premonition rattling around inside her head, she decided. "I'm coming with you."

Khepri tilted her head. "You sure?"

"I'll be safe at the wall. I need to see." She picked up a bloody towel and tried to wipe the blood off her hands.

Her friend nodded. "Okay. Stay close to me. Let's go."

Louisa spun around, seeking Abu. The teenager was wrapping a man's thigh on the far side of the aid tent. She yelled over her shoulder at Khepri, "I'll catch up!"

Louisa carefully stepped over and around the wounded on the floor to reach the young man who had become so important to her. Masako's determined face flashed through her thoughts for a moment, and an ache filled her heart.

Thank God, she's nowhere near this nightmare.

Louisa's thoughts turned to her relationship with Abu. At times, she played the role of a concerned aunt and sometimes his older friend. She knew he needed more and hoped they could reach that point someday.

Louisa tapped him on the shoulder and said, "Abu, I'm going to go to the wall with Khepri. Will you be okay here?"

He never stopped winding the long linen cloth around the padded bandage he had used to stanch the wound's bleeding. "Yes. Promise me—"

"Yes?"

"Stay safe, and watch out for Dr. Ben."

"I will."

Louisa ran to where she had stashed her bag and raced after Khepri as she pulled on the strap. She caught up to Esther's group of fifty Alexandrians a hundred yards from the sandbag wall. They had stopped well back from where any random arrows fell. Although the battle thundered its ugliness, she couldn't see a thing.

She found Esther, Khepri, and Ssherrss in a deep discussion. In Greek, she said, "Esther. Ssherrss." She gave a slight bow of her head. "I need to get to the wall."

The Alexandrian teenager's green eyes narrowed. "You may come with us. Stay in the middle."

Louisa nodded.

Esther pointed to three men. "With me. Miss Louisa will be in the middle."

The three men and Esther formed up around Louisa and lifted their shields. Between two shields in front and the ones angled over her head, she was as safe as she could be. With Khepri crouched under raised shields, the other Alexandrians formed a protective arrow formation.

"On the double."

The soldiers surrounding her jogged in place, and Louisa matched their pace as they moved forward. Because of the loud racket of the ongoing fight, the feet of the Greek soldiers pounding the cobblestones were mere taps. They ran across the hundred yards, and no arrows came close. Safe under the protective awning, Louisa looked for Ben on the wall without success.

She and Esther stepped up on the sandbags, and each one stared through the closest firing hole. Thirty yards ahead, Riflemen behind wooden walls were shooting into the hazy black fog. Men with shields guarded either end of the wooden barrier. There were dozens of Remulan bodies and a few men wearing the uniform of the 1st Kerman Rifles within her view. Try as she might, she couldn't see much farther than fifty yards ahead and to the sides.

Frustrated, she stepped back off the ledge. "I'm going up."

"Miss Louisa. Dimaerites Esther."

Esther nodded at the sound of her name.

Louisa turned to find Lance Duffadar Ram with a severe expression. She asked, "Where's Ben?"

He tilted his head toward the sandbags. "Out there."

"Show me," she ordered.

"Follow me." The Lancer stepped over to a ladder and climbed.

Louisa stayed on his heels. Once on the wooden platform, she moved over to make room for Esther. The shortest Lancer had pulled a few sandbags off the top and put them on the wooden walkway in strategic locations to help him peer over the ledge. He moved more sandbags so that the even shorter Esther and Louisa could peer over the top.

Higher up, with almost no obstructions, Louisa saw much of the sandbagged wall as it curved to either side, going toward the giant city wall. She also had a clear view over the shield-walls held by the Riflemen directly in front of her. Limited visibility allowed her to see thirty yards beyond those positions. The black powder cloud blew on a Remulan-favoring breeze toward the gap in the massive wall. It hid the enemy troops from the defenders at the wooden wall and from Jeevan's men above and behind the enemy.

Ram pointed a little to his right.

Louisa followed, searching for that distinctive hat. She found it about forty yards out on the good guys' side of one of the shield-walls.

Ben was giving orders that sent several men running. He leaned against the wall and reloaded his revolver. As he stood and jogged to the right, the noise of the battle changed. Ben stopped, and his head snapped toward the sound before he sprinted in that direction.

In front of the shield-walls held by the 1st Kerman Regiment, Louisa saw the unmistakable red, white, and black of the twins and Thoresten. They battled at least a dozen Remulans, who carried star steel–covered shields. No other 1st Kerman soldiers were near that melee in the larger battle. Ben and the threesome were on their own.

Even outnumbered four to one, the fearsome trio overmatched the legionaries.

Ki spun her entire body around with her giant club extended. A legionary staggered backward from the blow. Ki continued the motion, bringing the club over her head on the next pirouette to slam down over the man's shield, whacking his helmeted head like a nail.

With movements like a lithe white cat, Ki rotated the opposite direction. She back-handed the giant rod into the side of a Remulan who had tried to take advantage of an opening that existed only in his mind.

During that time, Lil and Thoresten had downed a legionary apiece.

"By the Gods!" Ram pointed to the black fog behind the fight.

Out of the smoke marched a solid wall of at least fifty of the star steel–shielded Remulan soldiers, heading straight for the trio. A man in a pork pie hat streaked out from behind the wooden walls toward the welves.

"Stop!" came unbidden from Louisa's throat.

Halfway to the fight, Ben paused and squatted over the body of a Rifleman. He jumped to his feet, a brown grenade in each hand, and ran toward the dwarf. Seeing Ben, the mound of a man changed from offense to defense, staying between the two Remulans he faced and Ben.

Ben dropped one of the glass containers at his feet and held the other overhead. He seemed to stand there forever.

"Throw it," Louisa whispered.

As if he'd heard her, Ben reared back and flung the hourglass high above the Remulans closing on the welves. The bottle arched through the air, and the grenade exploded. Louisa staggered back, almost losing her balance, but grabbed the canvas bag and righted herself.

Instead of three rows of tight-knit Remulans, about half of the formation had fallen. The legionaries tried to reform, but another explosion ripped through them like a scythe cutting wheat.

Louisa swung her haversack onto the ledge and pulled out a pair of opera binoculars. In moments, the scene came closer. Smoke from the explosions obscured more of the field. Just as she became confident that Ki, Lil, and Thoresten could handle the rest of the legionaries, something glinted out of the haze.

A chill ran down Louisa's spine as she pressed her eyes harder into the eyepieces. Smoke swirled around a sparkling man who stepped from the fog. Covered head to toe in star steel–coated plate armor, a stocky Lancelot held a giant double-bladed star-steel battle ax in each hand.

The closest Rifleman's voice filled with awe and dread. "Seba Bomani."

Louisa didn't need to know the Aaruan word to interpret what he said.

Star Knight. An evil dwarf version of Sir Lancelot.

Ben recognized the new threat first and fired several shots. Each bullet ricocheted away with a spark but didn't slow the man. Ben drew his second revolver and maneuvered around the remaining Remulan combatants who engaged the welves and Thoresten. Ben shot the Remulans in the side or the back, one after the other.

Lil dispatched the man in front of her. She ripped the scythe away from the side of his neck and stepped toward the Star Knight. She spun the chained ball of her weapon by her side. The ball and chain shot out and wrapped around a silver-plated forearm. She pulled hard to lock the Star Knight's arm in place.

As short and wide as Thoresten, the dwarf swiped with his other ax and parted the chain. Lil stumbled backward but sent the scythe flying, end over end, to hit the man near the tiny slit in his helmet. Armed with her star-steel longsword, Lil charged as the harvesting tool fell useless to the ground.

The Evil Little Lancelot's axes moved in concert, one blocking, one striking. It was all Lil could do to keep from being rendered in two. She kept blocking and skipping away. For the first time since the sisters' duel with their father, Louisa rooted for the woman who irritated her the most.

As if telepathically connected to Lil, Ki joined the ballet of death by slamming her iron club into the back of the Star Knight's head. Lil timed her block and slashed in concert with her sister's blow.

The dwarf staggered a step forward, his next block too low. Lil's long sword slammed across his wrist and would have severed the arm of any man not wearing star-steel armor.

Halfway through the arc of Ki's next strike, the Knight spun, his ax cleaving Ki's club in two. His other ax came around flat, slamming into Lil's face.

"No!" Louisa screamed as the welf flew backward.

"Get up!" Esther yelled in Greek.

The Star Knight turned toward Ki and threw one of his battle axes as if it weighed nothing. With her star-steel short sword already drawn, Ki turned the spinning ax from her head, but she couldn't keep the blade from slicing through her right shoulder. Ki staggered back, her sword slipping from her fingers, as the Knight stepped in to finish her.

Louisa sucked in her breath.

They're all going to die. Ben's going to die, and it's my fault.

At the last possible moment, the ax met star steel. Thoresten carried Lil's longsword and a star-steel short sword. He drove the Star Knight back from the love of his life. As the fight moved away from her, Ki dropped to one knee, trying to stop the blood with her other hand.

Ben ran to Ki and began tending to her wound.

Louisa turned to Esther, dropping her binoculars into her bag. "Get Khepri to Ki. I'll meet you there." She pulled the silver reshaping tool and the soft handle from the pack, then tucked the handle into her belt. With a tap on her head, she checked the security of the Ancients' crystal bowl bonnet under her postillion hat.

Wide-eyed, Esther asked, "What are you going to do?"

"Help them." Louisa pulled herself onto the top sandbags. She jumped, then dove through the gap between the wall and the awning.

She tucked her head and somersaulted over the sandbags as she visualized a long pole. Fall-running down the bags, Louisa stabbed the now fifteen-foot-long bar into the last sandbag with both hands on one end. She kicked out, and the thin fulcrum carried her over the defensive trench. When her weight had taken the pole over the summit of its arc, she used every bit of strength in her upper body to push against the star steel and shoved away.

With her heels pointed toward the cobblestones on the other side of the trench and her head turned back toward the sandbags, she bent her legs. Her knees compacted as her heels touched the ground, and she rolled backward, taking out the jolt as her uncle had taught her. Her momentum carried her back toward her feet, and she jumped high. With a 180-degree pirouette, Louisa landed and sprinted toward the battlefield as she pulled the handle from her belt.

Stay alive. I'm coming.

Nothing else mattered. The terror of losing Ben shot so much adrenaline into her bloodstream that her vision narrowed, and she floated forward in slow motion. The gunfire, the metal hammering against metal, and the cries of the dying faded to a murmur. Unable to see over the wooden walls, she raced through the murky haze based on instinct, willing Ben's heart to draw her to him.

As Louisa reached the wooden barrier where she had last seen Ben, she flew through a gap and saw the outline of the Star Knight thirty yards ahead. He towered over a kneeling Thoresten, whose back was to her. The Knight brought a battle ax over his head and swung toward the Samurai, who used both swords to block it. Thoresten also turned away a second ax, but he was weakening with each blow.

From behind the head of the stocky Star Knight rose a pork pie hat with the number seven over crossed sabers, followed by Ben's blue eyes.

What the hell is he doing?

Ben hopped on the back of the Star Knight and wrapped his long legs around the man's midsection. With one of the silver star shields on his left arm, Ben had his long knife in his right hand.

Like a wild horse with an unwanted rider, the shining dwarf spun and twisted. The Knight swept an ax over his head, trying to scratch his back, but only banged on Ben's shield. The crazy Texan kept stabbing his blade at the Knight's helmet, desperate to find the slit and the eyes behind it.

With a new visualization, she summoned the rod of contained lightning from the handle. To her horror, the Star Knight jumped and fell on his back, sandwiching Ben between the armored dwarf and the cobblestones below.

No!

Fifteen yards away, Louisa heard a crunch and Ben's moan. The Star Knight rolled to the side and pushed himself up to stand over Ben with his back to Louisa.

With Thoresten still kneeling between her and the star steel–armored demon, Louisa timed her next steps. As the Knight brought his ax over his head, Louisa kicked off with one foot, jumping toward the unmoving Thoresten. When her foot landed on the dwarf's shoulder, she launched through the air and brought her blade of light across the shaft of the battle ax.

The Star Knight swung his arm toward Ben's prone body but pulled up short to stare at the bladeless handle.

Louisa landed with light feet and took two quick hops, then stopped. Her terror turned to rage, and she snarled.

"What?" the Star Knight rumbled in Aaruan.

His armor sparkling, even in the haze, the Knight turned as Louisa stepped forward. The crackling lightning jammed through the man's shiny plate armor, through his chest, and out his back until the handle slammed to a stop.

Behind the helmet's slit, the warrior's eyes widened in shock. Louisa stood in place until his eyes grew dim, and his weight threatened to fall on her. She stepped back and to the side while visualizing the blade of lightning away.

Like a felled tree, the warrior crashed in slow motion to the cobblestones with a loud clang.

From under a flattened hat squashed over his face, Ben groaned. Louisa kneeled and flipped the pork pie away. Blood ran from a cut over his brow, pooling on his neck.

Louisa pulled the shield off his arm and tossed it to the side. She grabbed Ben's shoulders and dragged him to her bosom. She put her hand behind his head and found it slick with blood. Her voice cracked. "Ben. Ben. Wake up." She held his head away to see his face, and his eyes fluttered.

Unfocused, he stared at her with a blank expression.

"It's me. Louisa."

Light dawned. Ben slurred, "Louisa." The corner of his mouth turned up in his silly, oh-so-handsome, crooked smile. He brought his hand up and caressed her cheek.

Louisa dove into one blue pool, then the other, finding only certainty, longing, and love. The thought of never experiencing the fullness of his love made her choke up. Not only had she almost lost him because of her lies, but she had let the fear of heartache stop her from surrendering to her undeniable feelings.

No more fear.

Ben's face grew solemn, his finger tracing her jawline. With a clear, firm voice that sliced through the cacophony of madness surrounding them, he said, "I love you."

Her breath on hold, a tear slid down her cheek.

"I love you, Louisa Sophia, and I will die loving you."

I love you, too.

Louisa leaned in, filled with a need to merge into him. At the first feathery touch, she crushed her lips to his. His arms enveloped her, his hands communicating his desire.

Time stopped. She drifted in a dizzying blend of love and belonging.

Somewhere trumpets blew, fading away along with the battle noise. The silence was so startling, Louisa pulled away. The moment their lips parted, a sense of longing filled her. The intensity of her need, her craving to return to that place, almost made her ignore the rest of the world.

As Louisa held Ben's face, she whispered. "I'm going to hold you to your word, Benjamin Moore McGehee." She sighed, returning to the bleakness of their reality.

A group of Alexandrian soldiers, looking outward, encircled them in a protective ring. Nearby, Esther grinned at her like a fool. The sensation of warm blood on her hand made Louisa remember Ben's wound, and she sought Khepri.

Kneeling next to Thoresten, the hysakas tended his injuries. The dwarf's breastplate lay to the side, revealing the perfect butcher's slice across the Samurai's stomach. Thoresten used his hands to push part of his intestines back inside. Khepri's hand rested on his chest, and the gap in his skin diminished with each passing second.

The life singer's wolf eyes flicked to Louisa before returning to the dwarf's wound. "It's about time. Sometimes, you two smelled almost indecent."

Blood rushed up to Louisa's face. "What's happening?" She hurried to add, "Is everyone okay?"

"The Remulans retreated, and yes, they'll live. Ki was in bad shape. I did enough to keep her alive. Sent her back to the aid station to get more treatment. Thor here will recover, and I'll take care of Ben in a moment."

"And Lil?" Her concern took Louisa by surprise.

"Knocked silly."

Ben struggled against her, attempting to get up. Louisa hopped to her feet and helped him to his feet.

"I'm fine. Khepri, help the men who need it." Ben swayed on his feet.

Louisa glared at him. "You need it. You've got a badly bleeding head wound."

Ben touched the back of his head with a sheepish frown and winced.

A murmur went up from the troops, and everyone looked toward the gap in the city wall. A fresh breeze had scattered much of the smoke, exposing the silhouettes of two men. A Remulan legionary waved a white flag from the top of the rubble mound. He walked next to General Kinya, wearing the polished armor of a legionary officer.

Ben put his arm over Louisa's shoulder. "We better go find out what they want."

Louisa helped him shuffle forward, and Esther's troops provided an escort. Several times they had to take a wide circuitous route, picking their way through the hundreds if not thousands of dead. Bile rose in Louisa's throat at the carnage, but she found solace in that most of the bodies wore green.

General Kinya and his escort came to a stop ten paces away. Esther and her men stepped close behind Louisa.

The general said in Latin, "The emperor would like to set up a parlay with you Earthlings." He scowled as he said, "And the queen."

Louisa injected venom into her Latin reply, "Why?"

The man's face was grave. "We have just received word. The Lamentations have begun."

The End of *Echoes of Ancients*

Thank You for Reading

If you enjoyed Echoes of Ancients, Book 2 of Lamentations and Magic please consider leaving a review. As an Indie Author, every review is important.

Echoes of Ancients -
Amazon

The Louisa Sophia prequel, *Louisa Sophia and a Legion of Sisters*, is available now on Amazon. Step into a world of daring heists, fierce friendships, and high-stakes adventure! Follow Louisa Sophia as she fights to protect her friends and outwit danger on a treacherous journey across 1870s Europe. Learn more about what made Louisa the woman she is in Ancient Civilizations.

Louisa Sophia and a
Legion of Sisters -
Amazon

To signup for one of my newsletters, go to RussellCowdrey.com.

Please follow me on Amazon, Facebook, Instagram, TikTok.

Thank you again for joining me on this journey, and remember; God's able, if we are willing.

History is Magic,
Russell Cowdrey

www.ingramcontent.com/pod-product-compliance
Lightning Source LLC
Chambersburg PA
CBHW061334310726
48974CB00001B/40